THE PRIVATE ISLAND

Ali Lowe is the author of three acclaimed novels: *The Trivia Night, The Running Club* and, most recently, *The School Run*, which was a WHSmith Book of the Month in Australia.

Ali is a journalist by profession: she was Features Editor at *OK*! in London and has written for bridal magazines, parenting titles, websites and newspapers. She has dual Australian and British citizenship and lives on Sydney's northern beaches with her husband and three children.

Also by Ali Lowe

The Trivia Night
The Running Club
The School Run

THE PRIVATE ISLAND

ALI LOWE

HODDER &
STOUGHTON

First published in Great Britain in 2025 by Hodder & Stoughton Limited
An Hachette UK company

This paperback edition published in 2025

The authorised representative in the EEA is Hachette Ireland,
8 Castlecourt Centre, Dublin 15, D15 XTP3, Ireland
(email: info@hbgi.ie)

1

A CIP catalogue record for this title is available from the British Library

Paperback ISBN 978 1 399 71787 8
ebook ISBN 978 1 399 71788 5

Typeset in Plantin Light by Manipal Technologies Limited

Printed and bound in Great Britain by Clays Ltd, Elcograf S.p.A.

Hodder & Stoughton policy is to use papers that are natural, renewable and recyclable products and made from wood grown in sustainable forests. The logging and manufacturing processes are expected to conform to the environmental regulations of the country of origin.

Hodder & Stoughton Limited
Carmelite House
50 Victoria Embankment
London EC4Y 0DZ

www.hodder.co.uk

For Mum and Dad, with love.

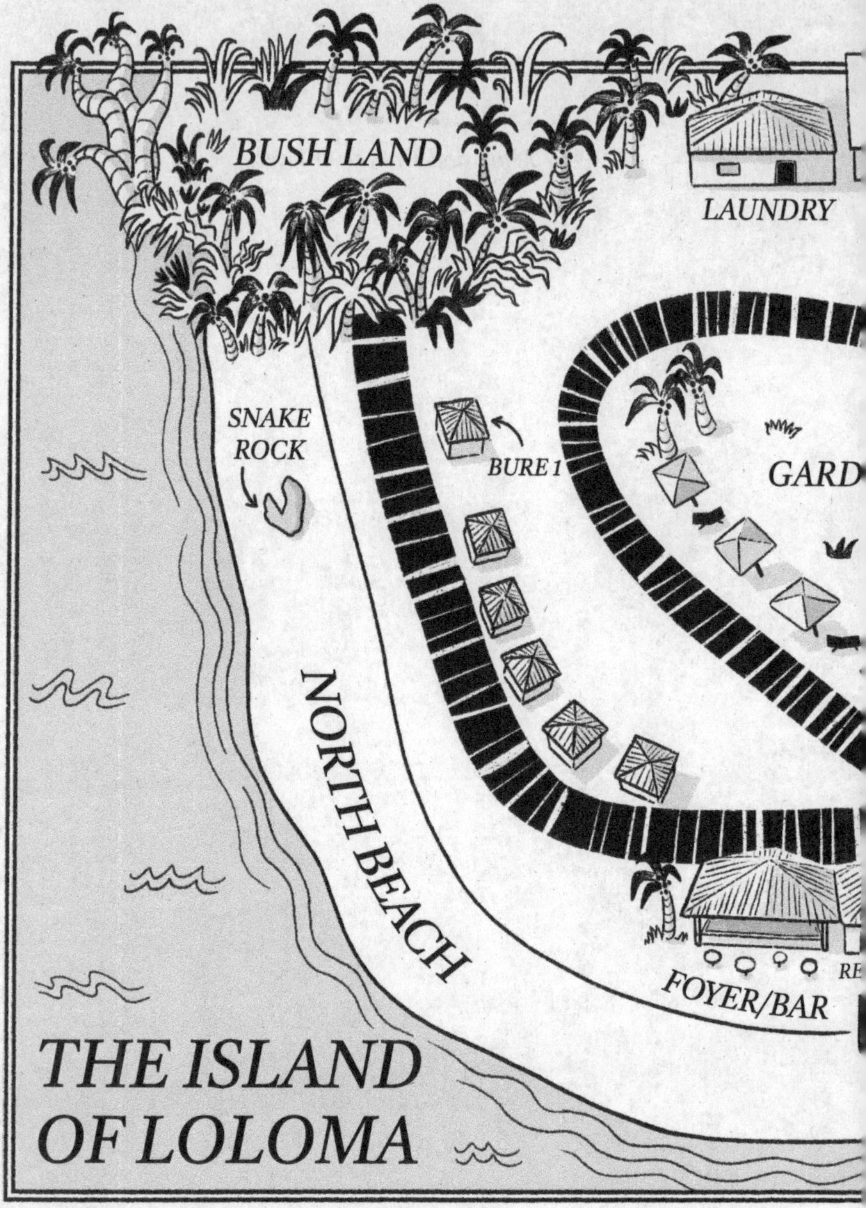
BUSH LAND
LAUNDRY
SNAKE ROCK
BURE 1
GARD
NORTH BEACH
FOYER/BAR
THE ISLAND OF LOLOMA

VILLAGE
TO BUSH WALK
BAR
POOL
SPA
DOCTOR
MAIN BAR
RESTAURANT
DANCE FLOOR/ FROG RACE
SOUTH BEACH
MAIN ENTRANCE

The imprints of her footsteps in the wet, glutinous sand fill as the tide rolls in. She tests the water inside the foot-shaped puddle with the tip of her toe and feels the lure of its warmth. But she will not immerse herself.

She takes a deep breath and stares out at a horizon that's white with the lip of a wave, denoting the outer reef. She is safe here at the edge of the water, where the South Pacific is gin-clear and tepid like a child's bedtime bath, but she understands the hazards even of these shallows. A place where venomous yellow and black sea snakes stalk their territory between the rocks underfoot. Where octopuses with stunning, iridescent blue rings, which can inject a human with enough poison to kill twenty-six men, float listlessly between strands of knotted seaweed on the ocean floor. After the agony comes the convulsing, followed by paralysis, then a stopped heart.

Even the most beautiful things, she thinks, can be deadly.

She takes a step back and wraps her arms around herself against the onshore breeze. She wonders if the goose bumps that cover her flesh are a sign of foreboding, because how can she be cold here, on this sun-kissed Fijian island?

She closes her eyes and breathes in the salty air of the ocean. When her eyelids open again, she catches, in her peripheral vision, the movement of something on the fringe of the wave as it kisses the shore. It moves in a rhythmic motion, a sort of caress against the wet sand, like a human making love. Squinting to get a better look, she steps into the water instinctively, forgetting the tropical oyster shells clamped to the rocks underfoot, which could slash the tender, unhardened flesh on the arch of her feet.

She gasps as the torso comes into focus, the flesh a shade of bluish grey. It is the waist and hips she makes out first, the naked pubis.

Her eyes dart further down to the thighs and calves, almost completely eaten away. Flesh hangs off bone, and flaps of skin dance on the surface of the water, ebbing and flowing like flotsam on the moving tide.

She does not want to see the face, but like a voyeur passing a car crash on the road, she cannot stop herself. Her left hand flies to her mouth. Part of the cheek is gone, where hungry sea creatures have nibbled away at the soft flesh. The forehead is scored with abrasions from where it has been dragged cruelly across the shoal on the tide. Hair floats like seaweed about the face.

She steps back, a hand to her beating heart. She looks from left to right, for someone – anyone. She cannot cry out for help, cannot raise the alarm because she is winded, her breath stolen clean away. All she thinks of as she stands, frozen and useless, her lacquered toes just inches away from the mangled body of someone who was once living and breathing just like her, is the Tennyson poem her father read her as a girl: 'She has a lovely face; God in his mercy lend her grace, The Lady of Shalott.'

PART ONE

FRIDAY 29 DECEMBER

Cocktail of the Day:
Heart of the Ocean

(Cointreau, lemon juice, syrup, bitters, cognac, prosecco)

I

Una

Una plucks four red hibiscus flowers from their stems and steps inside the bure – or bungalow, as some of the guests like to call it. Bure One sits on a cobbled pathway that runs parallel to the main beachfront, the first to link the most expensive rooms at Loloma Island Resort together like the chain of a necklace.

Bure One, like all the exclusive rooms along the path, opens out almost directly onto the seafront, requiring just a single hop to reach the silken sands of the South Pacific from the front door. The most luxurious of them all, Bure One enjoys uninterrupted ocean views, without so much as a palm tree, a bush or even a fallen coconut to block its cerulean vista. A super king bed sits regal in the centre of the room, its sheets pulled so tightly across the mattress that they shine like the glossy coat of a meringue. Two bedside tables, fashioned from native beach mahogany, gleam with polish, their reading lights pointed down at exactly thirty degrees. On the hand-carved coffee table sits a fresh fruit basket and a large hessian beach-bag that reads *LOLOMA RESORT & SPA, FIJI*. Loloma means 'love' in Una's native tongue.

Una scoops up a handful of bottle-green hibiscus leaves to accompany the inviting tropical pink flowers and begins to spell out *Welcome Home* on the bed. It's a nice touch, Mr Roko says, a gesture that makes guests feel like Loloma is a home away from home, their own spot in paradise – a simple courtesy that guarantees the drop of guests' shoulders, the slowing of their racing city heartbeats. It is for this reason that the bed, more than any other feature of the room – more than the marble-set bathroom sinks or the built-in wardrobes with their sliding doors – must be pristine. Not just because Una has been instructed it should be so, but because she herself believes it should.

It is deeply ingrained in Una Simpson, this need for perfection. Her mother had been like that, too. Una does not have children of her own, because she never found a man who quite *challenged* her enough, and at forty-three, it is too late now. But if she had become a mother, she is sure her offspring would have been just as fastidious as she is. These days, she babies her nephew, Sailasa, instead. Her late sister's son is now a man and working alongside her at Loloma. He, like the rest of Una's colleagues, both loves and hates her attention to detail. They all enjoy her cleaning up after everyone in the vicinity yet roll their eyes in the cramped staff village when their mugs are swept away and washed before they are finished with. 'Una found my coffee!' It is a familiar lament. '*Every time!*'

But the fact is, Una sees everything: the faint purple ring of a wine glass on the gleaming surface of the coffee table, the slightest smudge of a fingerprint on the vanity mirror, a cobweb in the highest corner of the hand-painted tapa cloth roof, a strand of blonde hair on a bathroom tile, a speck of blood on a pillow slip. And she *notices* everything: snatched conversations, a covert glance, the almost-wink of an eye, a husband who casts a lusty glance at another woman across the crowded bar . . .

Happy that her work is done, Una closes the door of Bure One with a click and sweeps the sand from the patio with a traditional Fijian broom made of dried reeds. As she listens to the scratch and swish of the bristles, she thinks of Christmas Day and Boxing Day just gone, of bins overflowing with luxury wrapping paper and boxes balanced on top of waste-paper baskets labelled *Cartier* and *YSL* and *Chanel*, of the sound of Christmas carols carried around the resort on tuneful acapella voices.

Those guests have gone now, and soon the New Year's Eve revellers will arrive, bringing with them their sequinned gowns and their lavish Venetian masks for the biggest event on the resort's calendar, the New Year's Eve 'Love' Ball. Una is fascinated by it: the frocks, the glamour, the drunkenness, the drama. There is never a dull moment on the New Year's Eve shift – or afterwards for that matter. When their shifts are over, the staff will celebrate in their live-in quarters, ringing in the New Year with cups of kava and leftovers from the guests' lavish celebratory dinner.

Una clicks off the brake on the trolley with her foot. The large grey cart is laden with fresh white towels, bed linen and miniature Bvlgari shampoos, conditioners and shower gels for the bathrooms in each of her allotted bures, and she is forced to give it a hard push to gain momentum on the cobbles. The mini bottles shake as the trolley rattles along. The guests tend to pocket them on the first day to take on future holidays (because even the wealthy like to get things for free), which means she has to refresh them on a daily basis.

She puts the brake on outside Bure Two, the second of her four designated suites, three of which look out on the northern tip of the Mamanuca Islands. The last, Bure Four, is set back from the seafront in the resort's lush garden and is Una's favourite of all ten guest rooms due to its surrounding frangipani trees, with their pretty white-yellow flowers and strong jasmine fragrance. The three beachfront bures – with glass-panelled doors to afford a generous view of the ocean – share Bure Four's beautiful floral aroma only when the wind is blowing just right, catching the scent and carrying it off on the breeze.

Today isn't one of those lucky days. Instead, outside Bure Two, Una smells something rancid – the distinctive aroma of decay. She turns her head and sniffs tentatively again, but the pungent smell has gone. Much like the scent of the frangipani, it has been whisked away to some other spot on the island by the breeze.

'Una!'

Una's hand flies to her chest. It is only Nunia.

'You scared me.' She scowls. 'Why are you creeping up on people like that?'

Nunia looks down at her feet, her toes painted blood red. Una's eyes follow and note the chips in the polish. Una's own toes, painted peach, are perfect, of course. She gets the spa manager, Ema, to do them for her in quiet moments. Una has always taken pride in her appearance: neat hair, a little coral lipstick, a dab or two of rouge . . .

'I wasn't creeping,' Nunia insists. 'Do you want your transfer list before the first boat arrives or not?' She holds up a clipboard in her left hand and taps on it with fingernails that are as chipped as her toes.

'Your nails,' says Una. 'Get Ema to see to them before Mr Roko notices. You work on reception, Nunia. You're the face of the resort!'

'Pah,' says Nunia and waves a dismissive hand in Una's direction.

Una picks up a stack of beach towels and rests them on her belly, which she would like to protrude slightly less than it does. 'Well, who have I got?'

Most of today's arrivals will make their way to the island on Loloma's own private speed-boat from Port Denarau Marina on the main island of Viti Levu; others will come on the passenger ferry that leaves from the same place. However, some guests do not like the public ferry because it resort-hops, from the six-star Turtle Cove Resort & Spa that sits on stilts twenty metres out to sea, along to Sunshine Island, the family-friendly Totoka Resort, and then, finally, to the most exclusive of them all, Loloma.

Nunia, in the regulation white 'bula' shirt that denotes she's administration staff (considerably more modern than Una's avocado-green maid's dress with its stiff white collar) shoves the plywood clipboard under her arm and secures one of Una's hibiscus flowers into the side of her hair with a bobby pin. 'Benedict and Luella St John-Gray in Bure One. First visit to Loloma,' she says. 'I heard Roko say she's an heiress of some kind. *Verrry* rich.'

Una shrugs, unimpressed. All of the guests are wealthy. They have to be in order to pay the prices they do; a week's stay at Loloma is more than Una earns in a whole year. The resort is marketed as 'six-star plus', the ultimate adults-only destination where children under the age of fifteen are kindly uninvited. Guests always arrive around lunchtime, only a couple of hours after the previous guests have checked out, because the Los Angeles and Sydney flights land at Viti Levu's Nadi International Airport late morning. As their boats appear on the horizon, resort staff assemble ready to perform the Loloma welcome song, and however fuggy guests are from travel or jet lag or an early wake-up call, the upbeat choral greeting ensures the general vibe on arrival is happiness. It's the opposite a week or so later, as they depart the island to the same staff voices singing a mournful goodbye. Una wishes it wasn't such a miserable send-off – she's heard more upbeat tunes at funerals.

'An *heiress.*' Nunia rubs her thumb with her index and middle fingers to denote wealth. 'Maybe she'll leave a big tip.'

It's a nice thought. Like most of the staff at Loloma, Una relies on tips to supplement her income. Most guests are generous: a note or two handed to her with a flourish, so that the benefactor can receive gratitude for their generosity, or tucked discreetly under the fruit bowl. However, on more occasions than she cares to remember, Una has been left nothing but foul stains on the toilet basin and dried spheres of minty toothpaste in the bathroom sink. She knows not to expect gratuities or indeed to rely on them. What she desires most is kindness and respect from her guests, and in return, she will do her best for them – after all, she wants holidaymakers to return to her beautiful island again. It is in everyone's interests, isn't it?

Nunia peruses her list. 'In Bure Three, you've got Fergus and Kitty Miller. They're coming in on the speed-boat with Luella and Benedict St John-Gray.'

Una makes a mental note. She hasn't had anyone named Fergus before, but she thinks she had a Kitty a couple of years back. 'And in Bure Two?'

'Dr Sofie Barthélemy. French. Lists her place of work as the Pitié-Salpêtrière Hospital in Paris.'

Una is impressed. She has heard of that hospital – it is where Princess Diana died, and Una considers herself somewhat of a royalist. She was pivotal in decorating the resort for King Charles's coronation. She even persuaded Roko to allow the chefs to bake a cake.

'Dr Barthélemy is travelling alone,' says Nunia. 'So is your last one, Thomasina Delana.'

'Delana. That's a South Pacific name,' says Una.

Nunia nods. 'She's in Bure Four.' She studies her fingernails as if to ascertain if she can get away with the chips for another day. 'Two single women this time. Unusual, no?'

'Perhaps.'

It is unusual for lone female travellers to visit Loloma – with a name that translates as 'love', their island home naturally attracts couples. However, it's not unheard of. Sometimes they come for the spa and the dawn yoga, or to escape their young children or husbands. They say things to Una like: *I just wanted a week without having to cook any meals!* Una prefers these guests by a golden mile – they're tidier than men, for one, and then there's the basic fact that a single person in a bure makes for one less name to remember. Roko is militant about remembering names. If guests feel cared for, they will re-book, he says, which in turn pleases the big bosses. *Make them feel like they're the only guest that matters! Do* not *forget their names, for pity's sake!*

Una repeats under her breath, 'Luella and Benedict St John-Gray, Kitty and Fergus Miller, Dr Sofie Barthélemy, Ms Thomasina Delana.' She will remember those easily. A little unusual, all of them – none of them easy to forget.

Nunia fans her face with her clipboard. 'Ugh, what is that *smell*?'

'You notice it, too?'

'Yes! It's *awful!* Must be a sewer issue.' She grimaces and turns to leave. 'You should call maintenance before the boat comes in.'

'I will.' Una clicks open the bure with the key card she wears around her neck. 'See you later.'

In the bathroom, the smell comes to her again through the slatted wooden window at the very back of the bure, with its outer layer of mosquito netting. She winces and pulls the blinds shut. Did the newlyweds who left early this morning notice it? She empties the bathroom bin, ties a tight knot in the top of the rubbish bag and turns to the bed. On the bedside table is a bottle of

Fiji water with a fifty dollar note under it, a pair of used sponge earplugs and a well-thumbed book, face down.

Una puts the tip in her pocket and picks up the book. The blurb on the back says it is about serial killers, and on the front is a photo of a man with close-set eyes and thick-rimmed spectacles. His face makes Una shiver, and she places it on the coffee table next to the rubbish bag. Creepy or not, she will take it with her to the staff village for Sailasa. He loves a good crime book. The gorier the better for her inquisitive nephew.

Una cleans the rest of the room methodically and arranges the leaves and petals on the bed. When she is satisfied that her work is done and everything is pristine, she backs out of the villa, mopping as she goes so as not to leave footprints behind her. Outside, she takes the foot-washing bucket – filled with sandy water from the previous guests' repeated trips to and from the beach – around the side of the bure to rinse out and refill from the outdoor tap.

That's when she locates the source of the smell – a rancid stench that fills her nostrils like a rotten egg. Her hand flies to her mouth, and she stumbles over herself to step back. A mongoose, its stomach torn open, stares up at her, eyes wide, from the sand. Maggots, hundreds of them, feast greedily on its entrails, shaded in their labour from the sun by the imposing awning of the bure's bamboo thatch.

2

Luella

Luella St John-Gray clutches her handbag to her chest at Nadi airport as she passes three traditional Fijian warriors in grass skirts. Tall, handsome men with bare chests clutching wooden axes. So young, so rugged, so *vital*. They'd probably have her handbag in a flash. Nowhere to stash it, though. Not much room in a grass skirt.

Luella rolls her neck on her shoulders and looks away.

'Darling?' Benedict ushers her forward to the glass-fronted cubicle, where a border security officer in a blue suit and with a stern expression holds out a hand for their passports. The woman looks Luella up and down with disdain.

'Hair behind your ears, please,' the officer says.

'Ears?' snaps Luella. 'In Britain, we look at someone's face.'

The security officer regards her, expressionless, and hands back the passport. Benedict keeps nagging her to change it into her married name, but Luella cannot abide pointless admin, even if it is a legal requirement. She stuffs the document in her bag and sweeps through the gangway separating the passport control cubicles and the baggage carousels from the outside world.

Benedict leans in. 'Almost in paradise, darling,' he says. 'Just remember, downtown Nadi is not indicative of where we are going.'

Luella bites the inside of her cheek. Why does Benedict address her this way, as if she is stupid and not an intelligent and well-travelled thirty-nine-year-old woman? She *knows* this airport town is bustling and industrial, that it is the antithesis of the turquoise and golden palette of the island destination to which they are heading. Still, she will let this indignity slide. It is too humid to argue.

A baggage handler attempts to lift the smaller of her bags. 'I'll take that,' Luella says and passes it across to Benedict to put on the luggage trolley instead.

The journey to Loloma Island Resort is expected to take an hour and a half. A twenty-minute cab from Nadi Airport to Port Denarau Marina and then an hour by speed-boat to the island. Benedict has informed her umpteen times that he has done the route before, only to a different island with a different woman – a long-term ex about whom Luella does not care a single jot, because what could *she* have possibly offered Benedict that Luella cannot? Luella has visited the South Pacific, too, also with a former lover, who, as it turned out, was only after one thing – and it wasn't her svelte size eight body.

'It's not too late to get a chopper,' Benedict says as he pulls her larger Louis Vuitton suitcase off the conveyer belt and deposits it on the luggage trolley.

'No!' Luella holds up a palm. She will not do it, because helicopters are simply not safe. Flying death-traps! She, for one, does not want to go down somewhere over the South Pacific and end up the subject of newspaper fodder on account of her sizeable wealth. She would much rather expire somewhere more upper class: perhaps Monaco or St Tropez, right outside Le Club 55, for example, or even the Paris Ritz. Besides, she shudders to think what the maintenance would be like on a helicopter in a place like this: blades falling off and everything. Pilots drunk on the job! It doesn't bear thinking about.

Luella applies some ludicrously expensive factor 50 sun cream to her face (because what would be the point of paying for acid peels like paint-stripper if she is going to cultivate more age spots in the space of a week?) and conveys as much to Benedict.

'It's not the third world,' Benedict tells her. 'It's *Fiji*, darling. It's heaven on earth! The people, the hospitality . . . it's all exquisite. We are going to have the most wonderful holiday, Luella. What's not to love about seeing in the New Year in paradise?'

Luella smiles sweetly. One must endure what one cannot cure, after all – and in this case, she must tolerate Benedict's wanderlust for developing nations.

'Of course, my darling.' She cups his cheek with her palm and plants a light kiss on his lips.

They walk through the baggage hall, through the dodgy X-ray machines at customs and into the arrivals hall, where the sticky air appears to be being merely churned around by giant plastic fans. Air-conditioning appears strictly sanctioned for the customs area and Luella feels her nostrils flare at the combined smell of hot chips and sweat and duty-free perfume, and . . . *is that coconut oil?*

Men and women with dots of perspiration on their foreheads and upper lips, dressed in printed shirts and sarongs and dresses, are positioned all over the place, holding shell necklaces and placing them round the necks of weary travellers. Luella pulls her handbag in close. Ugh, she's barely out of the airport, and they're trying to sell her things!

'No, thank you.' She ducks her head out of the way as a woman attempts to lift a circle of shells to her head.

'*Bula!*' The woman smiles, hand still hovering in front of Luella's forehead. 'Welcome to Fiji!'

Maybe she hasn't heard Luella correctly! 'I *said* no, thank you,' she snaps.

The woman's smile falters, and she turns towards Benedict as if for an explanation. Benedict leans his six-foot frame forward to accept a shell necklace and thanks the woman, who casts an anxious glance back at Luella.

'Come on, darling,' he says, a hand on the small of Luella's back. 'It's a custom, a welcome gift. Just take one.'

Luella stares pointedly ahead at the row of drivers holding up hotel placards with travellers' names on and pretends not to hear. Benedict takes a shell necklace for her anyway, muttering his thanks, and hurries behind her towards a smiling limousine driver, who is holding up a whiteboard with the words: *ST JOHN-GRAY / LOLOMA RESORT* written in thick black ink.

At Port Denarau Marina, the heat is even more stifling. Luella pulls on her sun hat, flicks open the lavish Japanese uchiwa fan she bought at an upmarket boutique in Kyoto and pulls it up to her face. In front of her, a young Fijian woman in a tight cobalt-blue dress drags two young boys wearing Manchester United shirts along by the hands. On her back is a baby in a fabric sling drinking water from a Fanta bottle. Just ahead, a porter in a lime-green T-shirt and shorts shouts to his colleague loudly in their native tongue; behind a tourist information desk, a lady laughs loudly, and at a desk selling diving tours, a woman braids a giggling child's hair. The café inside the marina, named the Dolphin Café, blasts out nineties hits and a pungent smell of garlic. It is sensory overload, and Luella feels slightly affronted that everyone needs to be so . . . loud.

'Can we go straight to the boat?' she calls impatiently across to Benedict, who is over by the water, taking photographs and in no apparent hurry to make this cultural melting pot a mere pit stop. He puts his phone in the pocket of his linen shorts and beckons her over with his hand. 'There's just a little delay while the boat chaps sort out the luggage,' he tells her. 'Come and look at the view with me, darling.'

Luella pouts and points towards a white speed-boat at the very end of the jetty. 'That boat says "Loloma Island & Resort", does it not? Are they going to invite us on board, or do I have to row to the island myself?'

Benedict digs his hand into the pocket of his shorts. 'I'll investigate, my darling,' he says. 'Sit tight.' He opens his wallet and marches with purpose to the information desk for Loloma Island Resort, where he waves a large wad of Fijian dollars at the perplexed desk clerk. But the woman waves Benedict's hand away in a simple movement that requires no translation. *Thank you,* it says, *but however much you pay me, the boat is simply not ready.*

Luella sighs. She snaps her fan shut and shoves it in her Chloé bag, pulling out a bottle of water instead. She unscrews the lid and glugs the icy liquid, irritably snapping her gaze away from a small child who sits on the floor of the marina, watching her.

'It's just so hot, isn't it?' says a soft, barely audible voice behind her.

Luella turns to see a woman in last season's Stella McCartney resort wear with wildly frizzy hair fanning herself with a dog-eared paperback. She leans against the wall of the boat terminal as if she is about to expire.

Luella makes a mental note to book herself in for an iron infusion and a B12 shot when she returns to London.

'I didn't realise it would be *this* stifling,' the woman continues. 'It's playing havoc with my hair. Talk about frizz!'

Luella isn't in the mood for tedious small talk – she does not consider it a bare necessity of life as so many others do – so she simply nods and turns towards the water, where the faint waft of fish from the fishing vessels jostling for space against the wall hits her like a sudden slap to the face. She takes out her Aesop rose petal and bergamot facial hydrator spray and leans into the fragrant mist.

The woman edges forward, undeterred. 'I see from your luggage tags you're also off to Loloma Island,' she enthuses. She must detect the raise of Luella's right eyebrow because her hand flies to her chest. 'Gosh, I so apologise. It is rather presumptuous of me to look at your luggage tags,' she says.

Luella offers a curt nod, and the woman looks confused, as if she can't work out if Luella is confirming their mutual destination, or whether she agrees that the studying of someone else's personal luggage is, in fact, wholly intrusive. Luella does nothing to clarify the situation either way.

The woman presses on regardless. 'We're going to Loloma, too! I'm Kitty – Kitty Miller, and that's my husband, Fergus.' She gestures over to an overweight man with a ruddy, booze-bloated face and red hair, standing at the water's edge. 'Fergus loves the water, unlike me. I'm an awful bore, but I'd much rather be perched on a sun lounger with a book.' She holds up her battered paperback with a peeling library sticker on the spine. 'I hope you don't mind me asking, but are you on your honeymoon? You have a rather newlywed glow!'

Luella smiles stiffly and glances up at Benedict as he strolls back from the information desk. 'Just a holiday,' she says and hopes it invites no more questions.

Just a holiday. One of many: the Maldives, Malaysia, Whistler, Zanzibar – all this year alone. She and Benedict enjoy frequent vacations, and this one is no more special than the rest – except, of course, that it straddles two calendar years: a sojourn that will take them out of one year and deposit them head first into the next before almost anywhere else in the world, twelve hours before their native London and a whole seventeen before the glitter ball drops in New York's Times Square.

'How divine,' muses the woman named Kitty. 'And do I detect an English accent?'

Luella sighs. 'Yes.'

'Oh, how wonderful. Were you on the Fiji Airways flight from Heathrow via LAX?'

Luella nods.

'Us too! Right at the back near the loos, unfortunately!' Kitty wrinkles her nose.

Luella is tired and does not have the energy to muster a response. These are not like-minded people. They will not be friends. They will not exchange phone numbers and arrange to meet up over champagne at the Sloane Club in a month's time.

'Loloma Island is meant to be incredible,' Kitty waffles. 'According to the resort website, the views from the mountain at the top of the bush-trek are phenomenal. It's definitely on my holiday to-do list. How about you?'

Luella does not respond. She takes a step back and turns to look out over the marina.

'Do you have your mask for the New Year's Eve "Love" Ball?' Kitty persists. 'I mean, of *course* you do – we were asked to bring them, after all. I presume you got the email? Rather bossy, wasn't it? "You must have a mask!" I'm really rather impressed, if I'm honest. It must take an awful lot of work to co-ordinate such an affair!'

Luella studies the woman's face. Kitty Miller isn't unattractive. In fact, she is rather striking in a horsey kind of way – vibrant eyes and a full mouth. There is a sort of aristocratic air about her – a little Camilla Parker-Bowles, perhaps. But they flew *economy*, which is puzzling.

'I was feeling inspired, so I actually made my own mask,' Kitty continues in lieu of a response to her questions. 'Out came the feather box and the craft glue, and I went hell for leather!'

Luella grimaces. 'How creative.'

'Where did you get yours?' asks Kitty.

'Philip Treacy.'

Kitty Miller's smile falters, and she takes a sip from her plastic water bottle, which has a chewed nozzle and says *London Marathon* 2017 on it.

Fergus Miller appears beside his wife and looks Luella up and down. 'Fergus Miller,' he says, in a voice reserved for perverts and voice-over men. 'Delighted.'

Luella sees how the man's mousy wife seems to shrink in his presence. She stands a step behind him with her hands clasped at the navel and wears a pasted smile. When he has finished studying Luella's form, the man squints across at Benedict, before retracting his neck and leaning forward to squint again.

'Benedict *Gray*?' His eyebrows are a knot. 'What the absolute *devil* . . . ?'

Benedict looks confused for a second or two, before recognition seems to register and he breaks into a wide smile, and Luella gets that overwhelming feeling of dread. *Oh please, no*. This is the problem with having a husband you have only known for two years – all sorts of irritating people come out of the woodwork.

'As I live and breathe!' Benedict laughs. 'Fergus *Miller*! What on earth are you doing here, old chap?'

'Seeing the New Year in in style!' Fergus guffaws. 'Same as you, I presume! I didn't see you on the flight. What row were you in?'

'One,' says Benedict. 'You?'

'Only the best, eh?' The man does not mention his position beside the lavatories but extends a pudgy hand instead.

The two men shake vigorously. *Oh for, pity's sake,* Luella thinks, *if I have to spend New Year with these two drips, I'm going to charter a chopper and fly it back to London myself, death-trap or not*. She takes out her fan once again and wafts herself frenziedly.

'Oh, darling, you'll never believe this,' Benedict cries (and Luella almost *actually* cries), 'Fergus and I worked in Whitechapel together for a year or two. Must be, what, a decade or so ago now? We went on the lash a few too many times, didn't we, Miller?'

Fergus mimics swigging back a pint of beer and says, 'Paaarr-tay!'

Luella's lower left eyelid twitches.

Little Mrs Mouse, who wishes her God-awful hair wouldn't frizz, looks between the two men and shakes her head in utter wonderment, as if she's just seen the Taj Mahal for the first time, or, say, stepped onto the surface of the moon. Luella would like to tell them all, *Come on, now, it's not really that big of a coincidence, is it? Two monied couples picking the most exclusive resort in the same country?* There are only 195 nations in the world, half of which most sane people wouldn't visit on holiday, but anyway.

The woman speaks up. 'Well, it's lovely to meet you! I'm afraid my name is rather more bland sounding than yours.' She glances at the tag on Luella's hand luggage once again. '*Luella St John-Gray!* How *wonderful!* It's a pleasure to meet you both, and what a crazy coincidence!' She shakes her head some more.

'*St John*-Gray?' asks Fergus. 'You kept the double-barrelled bit on the down-low back in the City of London days, didn't you, you dark horse!' He jabs Benedict on the bicep. 'Eh? *Eh?* You were just plain old Ben Gray back then, weren't you?'

Benedict laughs. 'Well, those were the days when it was way cooler to be an East End barrow boy, so just "Gray" it was!'

'Well, quite,' enthuses Fergus. 'And what are you doing now, Benny, my man? Still in finance?'

'Of sorts,' Benedict tells him. 'I fund start-ups. You know, find things that are going to fly, inject a bit of cash and make a mint for all involved. I mean, I pick and choose. Work when I want to, you know.' He glances at Luella and smiles.

'Bloody hell, old chap, you don't say?' Fergus guffaws. 'I'm looking for top-notch backers for my own start-up. Potential with a capital P. We should talk.'

Kitty smiles and holds up a finger. '"In a gentle way, you can shake the world",' she says, then adds, 'Gandhi.'

Luella sighs. How tedious this work talk is, and now the mousy woman is spouting irrelevant quotes from Gandhi. *Benedict had better not . . .*

'Fantastic,' says Benedict. 'I'd love to hear about it. You were always good at turning the sums, Miller.' He turns to Kitty. 'My apologies. Kitty, did you say? I'm Benedict.' He holds out his hand and clasps Kitty's right hand in both of his. 'Delighted to meet you.'

'Likewise!' The woman's skin flushes pink, and she retracts her hand. 'Gosh, it's hot, isn't it?' she says again.

Luella looks at her husband and then at Kitty Miller with an amused glint in her eye. She can't blame the woman for wanting to join Benedict's fan club. He *is* devastatingly handsome, after all. Devastatingly handsome and all hers . . .

'So,' Fergus says to Luella, in the manner of a smarmy game show host, 'what do *you* do?'

Luella blinks. 'Excuse me? What do I *do*?'

Benedict squeezes her hand. He knows she will not like this line of questioning.

'For work?' Fergus clarifies. 'What do you *do*? Are you a lady who lunches like Kitty here? Eh? *Eh?*'

The mouse looks *mortified.*

'Benny here was raking in the cash when we were back in the big smoke, weren't you, Gray?' He turns back to Luella. 'I imagine he's keeping you well?'

Benedict looks decidedly uncomfortable but breaks out into a grin when Fergus offers him a congratulatory pat on the back and says, 'Well done, my boy!'

Luella feels the blood rise up through her neck. Who is this man, who actually believes it is 1960 and women are 'kept'? Luella is all for men holding open doors and pulling out chairs for her when she sits down, but to assume she is the little wife at home with the sewing machine is frankly enraging.

She offers Fergus Miller an icy smile. 'Actually, I don't work a jot, because I am *filthy* rich,' she says, her gaze boring into his yellow-tinged eyeballs. 'I have more money than I know what to do with. I could *swim* in the stuff if I wanted to – in an Olympic-sized pool, you understand. I could certainly buy the island we are all about to stay on if I felt so inclined, along with every single boat in this marina. So no, I am most certainly not a kept woman, as you seem to be suggesting. Rather the opposite, in fact.'

Everyone falls silent for a moment, and Luella feels an almost *sexual* pang of satisfaction. Benedict looks at his feet, and Kitty's stare is so wide it is as if her eye sockets are about to force her eyeballs out like a silicon ice cube tray and pop them onto the ceramic-tiled floor. She goes to speak – a protest of some kind? – but thinks better of it, shrinking under her husband's steely gaze.

There follows a long moment of silence, until Fergus suddenly guffaws with laughter and his wife, evidently relieved, joins in with a snort.

'A lady with a sense of humour! I like it.' Fergus points at Luella with a fat index finger that she would quite like to shove in the rotating blade of the boat they will imminently board. 'Good for you, Benny, my man! Let's have a cocktail at the bar tonight for old times' sake. You know, seeing as we're all going to be holidaying together in paradise and all.'

'Be rude not to,' says Benedict, making the decision for both himself *and* Luella, like he always seems to do whenever the subject of who-supports-whom comes up.

Luella has come to realise it is Benedict's way of establishing some kind of control over their domestic arrangements – those arrangements being that she is her husband's keeper, and it is the very sizeable inheritance she received from her late father's estate that pays for everything. Benedict's 'job' is little more than a hobby. Some ventures win; others fail. She lets him have his little toys, lets him play.

'Count us in.' Benedict smiles. 'We'll be there, *won't* we, darling?'

'Yes,' mutters Luella through gritted teeth, because she isn't rude. They don't know she's going to fucking kill him when they get to the island.

'But, Fergus,' urges Kitty, her hands a steeple, 'we wouldn't want to intrude on a romantic holiday. Perhaps Luella and Benedict would like to be left alone tonight – there's nothing worse than feeling pressure to socialise.'

Fergus looks at her quizzically.

'I quite agree . . .' begins Luella, who has suddenly warmed up to Kitty Miller. She is about to echo the woman's sentiment when Benedict chimes in.

'Nonsense!' he says. 'The more the merrier!' He takes Luella's hand and lifts it up, as if to display some kind of ownership, and grins. 'We'll try to explore a little outside the room on this trip, won't we, darling?'

It is not the kind of comment this wife is used to from her husband, but she will let it slide. She understands the words have been uttered because Benedict and Fergus are part of an old boys' network of some kind and that this kind of blood, unfortunately, runs deep. She sniffs her annoyance away.

'Well, if the villa's rocking . . .' snorts Fergus.

Luella closes her eyes and mutters 'idiot' a fraction of a decibel too loudly.

3

Kitty

'It's "bure",' Kitty tells them. 'It's actually "if the *bure* is rocking". That's what they're called here in Fiji, the hotel rooms. The word "bure" actually means "traditional Fijian cottage or bungalow". It says so in my guidebook.' Kitty rummages in her basket bag and pulls out a book entitled *Lonely Planet Fiji*. 'They're traditionally made of straw and thatched with bamboo, and you pronounce it *boor-ray*. There are ten *boor-rays* at Loloma, and . . .'

Fergus holds up his hand. 'Thank you, Kitty,' he says, and Kitty feels the smart of embarrassment. She was going to tell everyone about the custom of making floor mats from pandanus leaves! She closes her guidebook discreetly and slides it back inside her bag.

Fergus turns to Benedict. 'A drink, then! We'll hold you to it. You can hardly stand us up – the place is only a few hundred square feet.' He winks at his old friend. 'We'll find you! *Eh?*'

Kitty smiles politely. She has a brain full of facts about Fiji to share, but she will save them for over drinks later. She loves nothing more than a hearty chinwag – you can find out so much about other people through a good natter. She is sure Luella has some exciting stories to tell, too – she certainly *looks* well-travelled.

'I hear the resort makes a great cocktail,' says Benedict.

Fergus grins. 'Are you a Sex on the Beach man, or do you prefer a Slow Comfortable Screw?'

Kitty glances over at Luella and notices that the woman is at the tail end of an eye-roll, which Kitty considers to be rather rude. Fergus was only making a joke. And it was actually a rather good one, Kitty thinks, the way he played with the names of the cocktails.

'Neither.' Benedict laughs. 'Luella likes to mix it up. Try them all.'

'Kitty likes an Old Fashioned,' says Fergus, nudging her so hard she has to move her right foot to steady herself. 'Just a couple though, or she's anyone's! She's a delightfully cheap date, aren't you, darling? Not like some of the women Benedict here used to . . .'

Kitty sees Luella's eyes snap up, and she casts a nervous glance at Benedict.

'Now, now, Miller, none of that chatter,' Benedict says. He turns to his wife. 'I'm a one-woman man these days, and this woman right here' – he reaches out and pulls Luella in close – 'is the only one in the world for me. She's perfection.'

'Damn right she is!' Fergus looks Luella up and down again, only this time he is biting his lip and nodding, like he wants to warm apple pie her.

Kitty looks down at her sandals. Fergus never treats *her* like that, enthusing about her beauty or looking at her like he could devour her whole. Unfortunately, Kitty married a man's man, one with a hairy chest and a deep voice, a tad more testosterone than others – a man who is rather more neanderthal than he is metrosexual, which Kitty supposes she must prefer. She can't really remember.

She watches as Luella folds her arms across her chest and hisses, 'Shall we go?' at Benedict through pursed lips.

Kitty understands this is a rhetorical question, because Luella is already leading the charge down the jetty at a million miles an hour, towards a man who holds a wooden sign that reads *Loloma Island Resort transfer*. Benedict scoops up his and Luella's matching hand luggage – dotted with Ls and Vs and gold monogrammed initials – and Fergus follows close behind.

Kitty notices that her own husband does not offer to wheel her John Lewis carry-on case but instead uses his spare hand to pat Benedict's shoulder, so that Kitty is forced to yank up the handle and pull it along the bumpy, slatted jetty herself. The wheels keep getting stuck in the space between the slats. She uses her other hand to stop her sunglasses sliding down her nose, which is shiny with oil after twenty-six hours in the air.

'Isn't this utter class?' Fergus grins as they reach the boat. 'Look at the size of it!'

'The size of it?' Luella guffaws. 'It's a bee's dick wider than the dinghies you see on the news bobbing towards Dover.'

Kitty thinks the comment is rather inappropriate, given the large number of displaced men, women and children seeking asylum on UK shores, but Fergus laughs and says, 'She's a live wire, eh, Benny?'

Kitty fakes a smile and swallows down her own unease about the boat. Luella is right about one thing: it doesn't look too sturdy. Kitty is not worried about it falling apart, per se, but rather the way it will dance on the waves as they enter the open sea – a tiny vessel in a vast ocean. She suddenly regrets eating that vegetarian frittata on the plane. The thought of it makes her nose sweat even more. But the fact is, she *had* to eat it. Fergus used the only entrance ticket to the business class lounge at LAX on their layover from the UK, so by the time they boarded the plane, he'd already had breakfast and Kitty had not. It was a case of vegetarian frittata or bust. So yes, the waves may be problematic (Oh Lord, did the frittata have *carrot*?) but nonetheless, they all climb on board: Luella, Benedict, Fergus and lastly Kitty, and Kitty feels an unholy lurch of her stomach as the boat sways underfoot.

Fergus looks at her and sighs. He produces a duty-free carrier bag from his leather bum bag – which also contains their passports and credit cards – and shakes it out.

'Apologies, but my wife is a puker,' he announces, as if it isn't already obvious by the Nadi Airport plastic bag he is waving about in front of her face. Kitty would like to disappear over the side of the boat right about now. 'Ironically, her middle name is Marina, which means "in the sea" in Latin,' he quips.

'It's "*of* the sea".' Kitty grimaces as the boat pulls away from the mooring. 'Anyway, don't worry about me. I'll be absolutely fine!'

Thirty seconds later, she leans forward in a dramatic heave and empties her stomach, its surprisingly sizeable contents missing the bag entirely and splashing keenly across the open section of Luella's Hermès sandals, which Kitty assumes to be the genuine article and not the Primark rip-offs she has in her own wardrobe. She watches, mortified, as Benedict twists the pink cap of a chilled Evian bottle and empty the contents over his wife's frittata-splattered toes.

Kitty stammers an apology and turns away.

She sits with her head pretty much inside the bag for the best part of an hour and feels utterly wretched. It smells of the sickly floral perfume she sprayed on one of those pointless blotting sticks at LAX. They're not even at the resort yet, and she has already messed up in a rather gargantuan fashion. She promised Fergus she would get it right, for both their sakes, and now she has gone and vomited, of all things. In fact, she messed up right from the get-go, blurting out that they'd been sitting on the plane right by the loos and laughing like a lunatic when Luella told them she could buy the whole of Port Denarau Marina!

Kitty gives herself a mental kick. She *assured* Fergus she would not put a foot wrong; she *swore* she could be relied on. Because the fact is: they have both vowed to be *very* different people on this holiday, to come out of themselves, to become actors. And now Kitty needs to step up and play her part.

4
Luella

Luella uses the boat trip as a chance to practise her breathwork. Make no mistake, she is not woo-woo. She does not wear hemp, God forbid, or wave placards at anti-vax rallies. But she does enjoy the practice of controlling her breath – and not just because it has become trendy. Holding one's breath for short periods is proven to boost immunity *and* help promote age-reversal. Plus, it's a wonderful thing to do when you want everyone around you to shut the fuck up.

In the first five minutes of this boat journey alone, she has already had to endure the contents of Kitty Miller's stomach slotting neatly between all five of her left toes – on Hermès sandals no less – as well as listening to Fergus Miller refer to Benedict as 'Benny, my man' countless times. So yes, holding her breath with her eyes shut is just the tonic Luella needs right now in lieu of consuming something that comprises forty per cent alcohol.

When she has finished her ten minutes of deep, steady breathing, Luella stands up and moves to the bow of the boat, holding onto her hat with the palm of her right hand. She sees islands on both sides of the boat, hears the skipper point out the tiny rocky island of Monuriki, where the film *Cast Away* was apparently filmed over twenty years ago. Not that she gives a monkey's. A grown man talking to a *volleyball*? What complete toss.

The captain leans into her with a smile and shouts, 'Loloma, straight ahead!'

Luella squints and sees nothing but a dot at this stage. Still, something happens to her pulse. A quickening of sorts, a missed beat. She is not a catastrophist by any stretch, nor is she the slightest bit spooked by spiders or heights or natural disasters. She does not fear much at all, aside from helicopters – and that is hardly a fear, merely a realistic assessment that they are fraught with potential jeopardy. Yet the dot on the horizon ahead of her seems somehow to jolt her, to instil a feeling she is not used to – an unease, an *anxiety* of some kind.

She takes in her immediate surroundings and suddenly sees danger in all of it: the depth of the water below her, the single charcoal cloud on the horizon pouring with slatted rain, the excessive speed of the boat as the prow slices through the water like a knife through butter, its bow hitting the waves with a repeated *thwack*. Luella stares ahead, her eyes set, takes in the colours: the green, the gold, the blue – and, despite the heat, she feels a sudden chill.

I won't leave this island, she thinks. *This is the place I will die.*

She blinks, tuts. *Oh, for God's sake,* she tells herself. *Dramatic, much?* She shakes her head at her own stupidity and focuses on the view ahead. As they get closer, the speck of the island becomes a golden circle dotted with palm trees and surrounded by glassy cyan sea: Loloma Island, the island of love.

5

Una

Una leans up against the shiny mahogany reception desk, a broom in her hand. She notices the unbecoming slump of her body and pulls herself up, reminds herself of Roko's favourite saying: *If there's time to lean, there's time to clean!*

'Boo!' She feels someone grab her shoulder, and her hand flies dramatically to her chest. Sailasa. His jokes will be the death of her.

She hits him with the broom. 'Shoo, Sailasa!'

'Ow.' He jumps back, laughs at her. 'Don't hurt me!'

Una smiles and shoos him away further, a futile endeavour since Sailasa is almost six feet tall – but he's a gentle giant. His face has thinned in these last few months, and he has lost the look of his mother, Una's late sister, Adelina. It is seven months since Adelina was taken by cancer, and Una finally no longer feels a pang of grief when she looks at Sailasa, because she knows her beloved sister is in a better place.

Sailasa pulls her into a tight hug before letting her go. 'The boat just radioed. ETA is five minutes.'

'Just five? Come on then.' She places the broom inside the door of the office attached to reception and beckons him towards the beach, looking up as she passes the coconut tree with the pendulous fruit. 'One of those coconuts is going to fall soon,' she warns.

Sailasa smiles and shakes his head. 'You're more likely to be struck by lightning.'

'Rubbish!' She scowls. 'But can you imagine how Roko would react if I caused a scene four minutes before the guests arrived. My brain splashed all over the path?'

'He wouldn't mind if *you* did it.' Sailasa grins. 'But for anyone else, it would mean immediate dismissal for sure.'

Una has seen it before. Poor Christina Cole, the young maid at Loloma's sister resort, Sunshine Island, who was fired three years back for knocking a diamond earring worth over one million US dollars into the sink. The way the story filtered back to Una was that the gem hung perilously in the tiny, millimetre-wide gap between the plug hole and the stainless-steel plug itself, like fingers gripping to a cliff edge. Then, when Christina attempted to retrieve it with the long nail of her little finger, it dislodged and went right down. And despite the unlucky maid admitting it to management straight away as opposed to pretending she knew nothing about an earring and a sink (*What earring? What sink?*), the guest made such a fuss that Christina was told to pack her bags immediately. The worse part was that she'd been heavily pregnant and delivered a dead infant soon after, the stress of the incident and the threat of unemployment too much for her to bear.

The unfortunate episode and the guest's response filtered through management circles and reinforced the idea that the guest is always right and the worker dispensable. And as much as Una admires her manager, Mr Roko, she knows that if it came to the crunch, he'd save the ship before the sailors. He would have to.

Roko is waiting for them as they step onto the beach. He is dressed in his trademark cream linen suit, flanked by the usual welcome committee: restaurant and sports staff in baby blue 'bula' shirts with geometric white printing, reception staff in white, as well as the old-timers in the resort's band in their trademark purple shirts of the same style.

Roko pushes his hand through his hair and smiles. 'Rooms all shipshape, Una?'

'Of course,' says Una.

'Good job. We'd be lost without you.'

Sailasa pokes her in the rib with a finger, and she smiles. It's common knowledge amongst the staff that Jose Roko, a widower of several years now, would like to take Una as his second wife. But Una does not feel the same way about Jose, even though she doesn't feel he is a *bad* man.

'Another day, another group of guests,' Roko says, and Una nods.

Together they watch the white prow of Loloma's own speedboat cut a triangle through the blue-grey ocean, towards the milky turquoise lagoon surrounding the resort, the inner reef. The coral reef, just thirty metres out to sea, provides a natural safety enclosure around the island, with waist-deep water almost as far as the eye can see. Tropical fish dance in this perennially warm shoal, and the waves only gently lick the shore – a drawcard for even the most trepidatious swimmers and kayakers. But outside of this natural seawall, the waters of the archipelago are treacherous, the drop from the reef like plunging from a rooftop car park after dark. Water that's warm and welcoming close to the shore becomes perilously cold, and the pretty turquoise-green palate turns a sinister blue-grey. The seabed, misleadingly accessible just a metre before, can no longer be seen, let alone reached easily by the point of an arched toe.

Una gets ready to offer up the smile she gifts every single guest as they arrive before she opens her mouth to sing. It is the biggest smile she has, the loudest and most tuneful voice, because at Loloma Island Resort, perfection is not just expected but demanded, and much like the secrets of the ocean, the intricacies and sometimes sinister complexities that lie beneath the surface of this island home must always be kept tightly hidden.

6

Una

Mr Roko counts the group in as the boat slows down its approach to the shoreline. *Dua, rua, tolu . . . one, two, three.* The band boys strum the opening bars of 'Bula Maleya' on their guitars and ukuleles, and the staff choir joins in. Una closes her eyes briefly as the sound covers her like a warm blanket and the goose bumps spread up her arms as they always do when the music reaches her ears. Sometimes, she feels there are no words to describe how beautiful it is, the sound of this rich harmony.

'*Bula Maleya kei Viti telega. Cauravou era yalo qaqa.*'

Greetings Malaya and Fiji also. All the young men are very strong.

Filipe, one of the resort's dive masters and Sailasa's close friend, runs down the beach towards the crowd of welcomers, clutching a wooden Lali drum. He wears an anxious expression, and his shirt buttons are done up unevenly. Una is not used to seeing Filipe either late or in a flap as he is right now – like all the divers she's known during her decade at the resort, he is incredibly calm, never frantic. It must be a hangover, she decides. She *knows* for a fact he was drinking kava until late last night, because she heard him stumble back to his room in the staff quarters at two in the morning.

'In line, Filipe,' Roko hisses from behind a tight smile.

Filipe inserts himself between Sailasa and Una.

'Can anyone smell kava?' Sailasa whispers.

Filipe sniggers, and Una grins, despite her rumblings of moral outrage.

'Your shirt, Filipe,' she warns, and Filipe hurriedly rebuttons himself as Una lifts her arm to wave at the boat as it bounces towards them.

Up on her tiptoes Una goes, trying to get a glimpse. And then they appear, the first of the New Year's Eve guests: a man, overweight with red hair, waving with a still arm and a frantic hand. Another, tall and muscular, his arm making the broadest of arches as he smiles widely at the staffers with their instruments and song greeting them from the shore.

And then they are closer, and Una sees a woman in a wide-brimmed hat, her head upright and her chin pointed. Una takes in the high arch of her cheekbones and way she holds herself, her chin high, knees together and to the side, her hair fashioned into a low, neat bun. She wears a nautical T-shirt and linen shorts. She does not smile at the music or gasp or clap like most guests do; she just stares ahead as if she is unable to be hypnotised by the music, as if there is nothing moving or magical about this isolated slice of paradise and the harmonies that call to her from across the waves.

Una feels affronted by it and realises she has already made an assumption, whether right or wrong (although she is almost always right in her instincts), that she will not like this woman, that perhaps this wealthy guest has, as Nunia might call it, an 'off' look about her. Bad energy.

As the boat slows and Filipe runs forward with a block of metal steps on the very edge of the water, Una notices the final guest in the boat: a small woman who is sickly pale, doubled over and clutching a plastic bag to her mouth. Una puffs out her cheeks and turns to Sailasa, who grins back: there's always one with seasickness.

The boat comes to a stop, and Filipe and Sailasa reach for the rope that's been tossed to them. Together, they pull the speed-boat to shore, where it slides easily onto the wet sand, making a sound like feet crunching on gravel.

'*Bula!*' Mr Roko steps forward. 'Welcome to Loloma Island Resort!'

The pale woman stands up and attempts a smile.

The taller man jumps out of the boat first and bypasses the steps.

Mr Roko holds out his hand. 'Jose Roko, General Manager,' he says, and the two men shake. 'Welcome!'

'Benedict St John-Gray. It's a pleasure.' The man turns back towards the boat and holds out a hand. 'If you'll excuse me a moment . . .'

The glamorous woman, who, Una assumes, is Luella St John-Gray, takes the offered hand thanklessly and lifts a shiny calf over the side of the boat. She descends the steps one at a time, the straps of her leather sandals hanging over the index finger of her right hand.

Mr Roko leads the guests to the bar area, which backs onto the main restaurant, and invites them to take a seat. Nunia collects the guests' passports to begin the check-in procedure, and the bar manager, Joji, hands out refrigerated hand towels infused in frangipani essential oil, followed by a fruit cocktail. Kitty Miller's shoulders drop as she places the white towel over her face, and Una smiles. It is a common reaction – a physical and mental shift from everyday life and air travel to complete relaxation. Luella St John-Gray's shoulders remain upright. She takes a cold towel from Joji's tray and clicks her fingers for another. Joji blinks twice, panic-stricken, not certain what she wants.

'Oh, for pity's sake,' snaps Luella St John-Gray, clicking her fingers four or five times in succession. 'Another hand towel, please?'

Joji glances at Mr Roko, and Mr Roko nods sharply towards Luella with eyes that scream, *Give the woman another damn towel if that's what she wants!* Joji obliges and looks away discreetly as the woman begins to wipe her *feet*, of all things!

At the head of the table, Mr Roko offers an upbeat '*Bula* everyone!' before beginning his customary welcome speech, the first of two he'll do today.

He talks the four assembled guests patiently through the resort's services, including opening times for the spa and boutique and the laundry facilities. 'We are at your service.' He gives a bow. 'You're on "Fiji Time" now, and we want you to relax and enjoy yourselves, stress free. On that note, we encourage you to separate yourselves from your mobile phones as much as possible. We are also fans of good old-fashioned writing here at Loloma – there is a notepaper and pen in each room, and we encourage you to leave a note for your housekeeper if there is something non-urgent you would like to request.

'And just a little housekeeping of our own,' he continues. 'I am duty bound to inform you, for your safety, that Snake Rock, which is the large U-shaped rock you can see at the far end of our northern beach, is strictly out of bounds after dark. The surface of the rock contains oyster shells that can cut very deeply. We discourage you from climbing on it in the daytime without rock shoes, and you should certainly not do so at night when your foothold may not be visible.

'We are a small island, only 172 acres, but we are also high. If you intend to climb the bush-track to the mountain on the eastern side of the island, we encourage you to wear trainers as the terrain is rough underfoot. The peak is 275 metres high with sheer cliff drops, so please do watch your footing.'

Una sees the man called Fergus raise his eyebrows in a manner that suggests he doesn't like being told what footwear he should be wearing.

'To access the bush-track, you will need to head to the far side of the island, past the laundry and maintenance area and over towards the staff village, where you will see signposts. This route will also take you to our award-winning spa. Our friendly reception staff have access to the booking system, and they can make you an appointment, so please feel free to book at reception or at the spa itself. If a treatment is in progress, just leave Ema a note.'

Roko claps his hands. 'And now, without further ado,' he says, 'let us meet the staff!'

Roko gestures towards Ema, the spa manager, who steps forward and offers a few tasters from the spa menu, including the Loloma Aromatherapy Couples' Massage.

Kitty Miller sits up in her chair; she seems to have recovered from her sea sickness now she is back on solid ground. 'Ooh, that sounds *amazing*.' She beams, and Una nods approvingly. Guests like these are a pleasure to look after – the excited, positive ones.

Ema steps back, and Roko gestures towards Sailasa, who steps forward with an enthusiastic smile. Una watches Luella St John-Gray give him the once-over like she might a diamond bracelet in a jewel cabinet. She feels a stab of annoyance.

'Sailasa runs the water-sports team alongside our environment manager Filipe.'

Filipe raises a hand in greeting and Sailasa offers a warm '*Bula!*'

'Filipe and Sailasa will be able to book you in for scuba-diving, surfing trips and so on at the water sports shed on the beach, right in front of reception. If anything is not on our daily schedule, please ask – for example, we have taken guests to dive at the Salamander Shipwreck near Nadi on request, and we regularly do trips to famous local surfing spots such as Cloudbreak and Restaurants. Do not be afraid to ask!'

'One's called *Restaurants*?' asks Kitty.

'Indeed it is,' says Mr Roko with a smile.

'We have a dive with some available spots at three o'clock this afternoon,' says Sailasa. 'If you want to start your holiday underwater. If that is the case, please leave your passport at reception as we will need the details to complete your dive waiver.'

Roko now gestures towards Una. 'Our wonderful Una is the head of housekeeping,' he tells them. 'She looks after four of our luxury bures, and Kelera and Letitia, two of the other housekeepers on the island, take care of the other six. Please see Una for any issues related to your rooms or if you require additional cleaning or an earlier or later turn-down service in the evening.'

Una smiles amenably. 'Please ask me for anything you need.'

Next, Mika steps forward. 'Good afternoon,' he says. 'I am your entertainment manager, and it is a pleasure to welcome you to Loloma Island Resort & Spa! Tomorrow night, we would like to welcome you to a traditional Fijian evening here in the bar. We invite you to sample our traditional drink, kava, which is made from the ground roots of the yaqona tree. We also welcome you to take part in an authentic Fijian cane toad race.'

'Toads, you say?' The red-headed man, called Fergus Miller, turns to his wife. 'Didn't you study them at university?'

'Oh hardly!' Kitty Miller says, dismissing Fergus's comment with the bat of a hand. 'Just one module a thousand years ago.'

The woman looks up and catches Una's eye. She offers a small smile and an embarrassed shrug. Una offers her an enthusiastic grin.

'I'm glad you're looking forward to it, Mr Miller,' Roko says. 'Our toad race is legendary. It is always a hit with the guests.'

'Please come prepared with plenty of Fijian dollars if you'd like to place a bet on a specific toad,' Mika tells the guests. 'We do not allow you to charge betting money to your rooms unfortunately, but if you would like to bet on a toad, you may request a cash advance from reception. It is one of our most popular activities and is always a lot of fun.'

Filipe steps forward again. 'We also donate a portion of the winnings to the Loloma Conservation Fund,' he says. 'Forty-two per cent of the world's coral species can be found right here in Fiji and one of the greatest threats to our coral reefs in Fiji is climate change.

'One of the things we do here at Loloma to protect our reef is grow coral under the sea bed. Later in the week I will do a talk about our regeneration project for anyone who is interested.'

Kitty Miller nods enthusiastically.

'Thank you, Mika and Filipe,' says Mr Roko. He opens up his palms to the guests like a preacher. 'Finally, I would like to say a few words about New Year's Eve. Fiji is one of the first countries in the world to see in the New Year. We'll be celebrating in style. New Year's Eve dinner will be a degustation menu, which includes pork cooked in a traditional Fijian underground oven called a lovo. The meat is covered in banana leaves and potato sacks and cooked over a period of several hours. It's a true Fijian experience!'

'Sounds delightful,' says Luella St John-Gray, her mouth twisted into a grimace.

Una chews the inside of her cheek as she regards the woman, who evidently feels nothing but disdain for this island and its staff. She hopes it is merely jetlag that is making her so irritable. In fairness, she has heard the flight from the UK is particularly gruelling.

'Sunday's New Year's Eve party will begin at eight o'clock sharp,' Mr Roko continues. 'The only thing we ask is that you remember your mask – it's a *masquerade* ball, after all. Nunia and the reception staff have spares at the desk if you have forgotten to bring one. And with that, please enjoy yourselves. Your bags should already be in your rooms. Thank you, or as we say here in Fiji, *vinaka*!'

Kitty Miller claps her hands, but no one follows suit, so she stops. 'Thank you so much,' she enthuses.

At least someone's polite, thinks Una.

As the guests take their leave, Una casts a final glance at Luella St John-Gray to see if the talk of New Year's Eve high jinx has thawed her any. But it seems it hasn't. The woman remains seated, her head tilted up and to the right and her mouth set in a pout as she gazes sulkily out to sea.

7

Kitty

'Oh Fergus!' The blast of cool air inside the bure grabs Kitty in a tight embrace. 'Isn't it incredible?'

'Not bad, old girl. Not bad at all.'

The bure is small but utterly charming. Kitty takes in her surroundings. Each side of the entranceway is flanked by a large window with a wooden shutter, although Kitty feels the shutters may not be needed, because the roof of the thatch outside hangs low to provide natural shade, like a giant beach hat that's become slightly unravelled. Kitty feels that just this touch alone will serve as a reminder from inside the room that she is on a secluded island in the South Pacific, thousands of miles away from traffic and pollution and the muggy, metallic smell of the London Underground.

She looks up. The vaulted ceiling, held up by natural timber beams, is painted intricately in geometric shapes of white and brown. She has read about it in her guidebook and knows it to be hand-painted tapa cloth, a traditional fabric made by beating the fibrous inner bark of the Moraceae family of trees, namely the mulberry and fig. The paint used is traditionally made from plant and vegetable dyes in red, brown and black. Kitty stares upwards in awe. For her, it is this ceiling that makes the room. It is a work of art.

'Marvellous,' she muses to herself. 'Truly stunning.'

Her gaze drops to the bed in front of her, a super king with crisp white sheets, covered in flowers.

'Oh!' Kitty coos. She smiles as she reads the words: *Welcome Home*. She feels she's having some kind of inner burst of happiness with all this Fijian *authenticity*. She could almost *cry* (although in fairness, this could be perimenopause). 'Look, Fergie,' she cries. 'They're hibiscus flowers. Oh, Fergus, it's paradise here. *Paradise!*

So many flowers to look at. There's a nature trail you can do through the island. We must do it – we must. Say you'll do it with me?'

Fergus ignores her. 'Bloody hell,' he says, fanning his T-shirt in and out. 'I'm sweating like a bitch.'

Kitty flinches. She wishes he wouldn't speak like that, using such derogatory words – they make him sound like a misogynist! But, she muses with a quiet sigh, she's hardly going to change him now, is she? Not now he's in middle age. You can't teach an old dog new tricks, can you? *Or can you?* Kitty muses on it as she twirls a hibiscus stem in between her thumb and forefinger. This is an opportunity for a reset, for their fortunes to irrevocably change – as long as Kitty gets everything right.

'Move, darling!' Fergus swings his suitcase onto the bed, on top of the flowers. The pink petals are squished, and Kitty almost feels she can hear them squealing in agony underneath the weight of thirty kilos of XL-sized Thomas Pink shirts, khaki shorts and docksiders. She feels her shoulders slump. She hadn't even taken a picture of the pretty arrangement yet.

Fergus unzips his case, rummages around, and pulls out a fresh polo shirt. He takes off the one he has travelled in, drags it crudely across his wet forehead and between his rather sizeable bosoms, and drops it to the floor.

Kitty bends down and picks it up. She'd better start a laundry bag.

Fergus turns towards the bathroom.

'Wait, Fergus, could you . . . ?' She nods towards her own suitcase on the floor beside the coffee table. 'Could you just help me lift this up onto the bed?'

Fergus burps loudly. 'Better out than in,' he announces.

'Um, Fergie?' Kitty says again. 'My suitcase?'

'Oh, do come on,' he says. 'Use your muscles, old girl.' He picks up his Sudoku book and disappears into the bathroom. 'If you need me,' he says, 'I'll be taking a dump.'

Kitty sighs and opens the wardrobe on Fergus's side of the bed. She lifts out his shirts and places them neatly inside the drawers, his trousers on hangers and his shoes, in their pairs, on the rack at the bottom of the closet. Then she zips up his empty case and lifts it down onto the floor, taking a passing glance at the bed.

All that remains of the proud pink flowers are dark maroon balls, each one reminding Kitty of the curled-up body of a dying spider.

8

Luella

'Well, this is the life!' says Benedict as he flops back on the sofa under the window.

'I suppose not – as far as mud huts go.'

Luella looks up at the ceiling, which looks as if it's been made from papier mâché. The geometric shapes are making her eyes hurt. *Note to self,* she thinks. *Don't look up!*

It's a little dark inside the room for Luella's tastes, and she pulls back the shutters a little further, only to see the thatch of the roof hanging down so low it blocks out the light. She'll talk to Jose Roko about that. Perhaps they can pin it up or something. She will not pay the exorbitant cost of this room if she's going to have to sit in the dark.

She takes a slice of pineapple from the welcome basket on the coffee table and finds it to be slightly under-ripe. She places the remainder on one of the side plates beside the basket and kicks off her shoes.

Benedict is studying the guest relations information. 'You'll like the cocktail list, darling,' he says.

'Uh-huh?' Luella peers inside the fridge and finds a bottle of champagne. She pulls it out and hands it to Benedict to open.

'And the dive team seem to have a lot to offer,' he announces. 'How about we save this bottle for later and go out this afternoon?'

Luella rolls her shoulders. 'Go out where?'

'On a dive, *ma chérie*. To the reef. There's a three o'clocker on offer – I think that's what the dive man said.'

'Simon,' observes Luella.

'Sailasa, I think it was,' says Benedict.

Luella yawns and sits on the end of the bed. 'Not today.'

'Oh, come on, darling! Why not?'

Luella sighs. 'We've only just set foot on the island – that's why. We've got days to go diving. Why do we have to do it the moment we get off the boat?'

Luella does not meet Benedict's eye. She knows how much he loves to dive and how much he's been looking forward to getting in the water, but she is simply not in the mood.

'Go on. It'll be a wonderful way to shake off the jet lag.'

'I said no!' Luella does not understand why her husband always feels the need to be *doing* something. Can they not just enjoy the beach for a couple of hours?

Benedict's shoulders slump. He gets down on his knees in front of her on the bed and rests his head on her thighs like a child. *Oh, for God's sake!* Now he's going to make her feel guilty.

'Come on, darling,' he says. 'Pretty please?'

'Oh, do get up,' she snaps, and Benedict smiles because he knows she is wavering.

'How long is it? The dive?'

'An hour,' he says hopefully. 'And then we can lie on the beach and fry like bacon, I promise.'

Luella sniffs and looks up to the nauseating, patterned ceiling. She feels all-powerful in this moment. She pouts and inspects her nails. 'Fine,' she says. 'Whatever.'

Benedict fist-pumps. 'You little beauty,' he says, lifting her hand to kiss it.

Luella offers a reluctant smile.

'You know how much I love you, don't you?' he asks.

'Yes,' she says, a little like a parent who has allowed her child to take a biscuit from the off-limits glass jar.

'I'll book us in now.' He wriggles out of his shorts and pulls on a pair of trunks.

Luella watches him as he throws open the door and steps onto the pathway towards the dive shed. He turns and blows her a kiss. 'You won't regret it!'

9

Sailasa

It is the very first day of Sailasa's shift on the island: twelve days on, three days off.

This morning, after his break in the city, he breathed a sigh of relief when the ferry stopped at Loloma.

When he headed back to Nadi three days ago, it was the first time he had ever not wanted to go home for his days off, the first time he truly wanted to stay on the island – away from danger, where they couldn't get to him. He had even toyed with sleeping in the dive shed. But it was a ridiculous thought – Roko would have found him. Or Una. It's hard enough already pretending to her that nothing's wrong.

He opens the door of the shed now and does a quick inventory of the equipment. He counts twenty life jackets and twenty snorkels, nineteen masks bobbing up and down in three large buckets of disinfectant by the door (one has gone AWOL), twelve kayak paddles, four beach volleyballs, six shiny metal oxygen tanks and twenty neoprene wetsuits in varying sizes. Everything is present and correct, except the snorkel mask and a missing fishing rod. It must be in the fishing boat somewhere, under a seat perhaps, or even on the glass flooring that affords guests close-up views of the tropical fish below – for a price: six hundred Fijian dollars per adult for a day's deep-sea fishing in the open ocean. Sailasa shakes his head at the idea of spending that much money on a single boat trip.

Ten paying adults on a private trip could change his life – get him out of trouble, even.

He's been offered money by guests before. *Come to Australia and work for us, Si!* they say. And more than once he's had an offer from a woman, sometimes a couple. *Come to our bure for the night, no strings attached, and we'll give you the cash straight.*

He's heard it all, and yet he's never been tempted – until now.

Sailasa checks the levels on the oxygen tanks. He anticipates taking two groups of scuba-divers out this afternoon, one at three o'clock and one at five, the usual schedule. He never tires of it, taking these trips, because at least under the water he can forget about the complexities of his life above it, about the weight of his responsibilities. Underwater, he is with his other family: the fish and the coral. Beneath the sea, all he needs to do is remember to breathe – although that's how he feels on the land, sometimes, too.

He checks tank two again, because he knows he is distracted today and he is doing important things on autopilot without even registering. He gets this sometimes when he's on his pushbike: he has been daydreaming, and at the end of a journey, he cannot even remember how he got to the place he's arrived at, like he's been in some kind of trance.

He checks it again, aware his mind is wandering. A tank must be fully open before a dive. If it is not, air will struggle to get through to the diver as they get deeper in the water. Sailasa understands a lack of concentration like this could prove fatal twenty metres below sea level.

But what will he do about the money? There was the American woman last year with the dark eyes and the dark skin who asked him to join her for a drink back in her room, said she would give him money. He said no, of course, but what he wouldn't do to have her back here now. She was beautiful, too. It wouldn't have been a hardship.

He wonders if he *should* talk to Una about it. She'd find a solution; his aunt always does. But he's thought about it before, telling her, and, like it did last time, his brain comes to the exact same conclusion: he just does not want her to know. It's a pride thing. She is his blood relative, and she will feel compelled to help him, share his problem (*A problem shared is a problem halved, Sailasa!*), and he doesn't want to put this on her. It is his mess to clean up. And besides, he doesn't want her to think that he can't manage his own affairs. He loves Una as any nephew should love their aunt, and he wants her to think he is a success and not that he is sinking like a boat with a punctured hull.

'Hello there!'

Sailasa is snapped out of his trance by the man from the welcome talk, the one with the wife who snapped at Joji.

He holds out a hand. 'Benedict St John-Gray. Sailasa, right?'

'Yes. Well remembered, Mr St John-Gray. So you want to book a dive?'

'Yes, indeed. My wife and I would like to go this afternoon if you have room for both of us. Did you say you have a spot at three o'clock?'

Sailasa scales the afternoon lists with his finger, even though he knows there is plenty of room. It's force of habit. 'Three o'clock . . . yes. Remind me of your room number?'

'Wonderful. Bure One. My wife is Luella St John-Gray. We did our PADIs in Mauritius on our honeymoon a year ago, but we're both a little rusty, so this will be a fun refresher.'

'Great.' Sailasa nods and scribbles 2 *x Bure* 1 on the booking sheet. Then he adds *Cyl* 1 *&* 2 to denote which tanks the couple will take.

'Do you need wetsuits?'

'We have our own, but we'll need masks. Oh, and flippers. I'm a UK size ten and my wife's a UK size six.'

Sailasa nods and pulls the metal tanks forward. Then he grabs two masks and two sets of flippers from the shelving unit behind him.

'OK, Mr St John-Gray, all set. Make sure you are here at the dive shed at 2.50 p.m. so both you and your wife can sign the waiver before our three o'clock departure. Filipe will have it prepared for you.'

'Wonderful, thank you so much.'

'*Vinaka*, Mr St John-Gray.'

'*Vin* . . . ? I'm sorry, I didn't catch that . . .'

'*Vinaka*. It's *thank you* in Fijian.'

'*Vinaka*, Sailasa. Much obliged.'

Sailasa smiles, and the two men observe one another for a moment – or at least that's what Sailasa thinks is happening, until he realises Benedict St John-Gray is staring over his shoulder at the row of fishing rods on the side wall.

'I say, that rod . . . is it a new Shimano?'

Sailasa follows his gaze. 'Yes, it is. Mr Roko loves to fish, so he has the Shimano rods brought in from a supplier in Australia.'

Sailasa doesn't know what's so special about Shimano rods and why fishermen seem to go so nuts over them – a fishing rod is a fishing rod is a fishing rod, as far as he's concerned. He's been fishing in these waters all his life, and he doesn't think you need designer gear to get lucky. But like everything, it's the prestige of having something with a name attached, isn't it?

'May I take a look?' Mr St John-Gray asks.

'Of course, sir – please.' Sailasa stands aside to let the other man pass, then carries a kayak paddle out of the shed and places it down beside one of the long yellow boats on the beach. When he gets back from his third trip setting equipment out, Mr St John-Gray is still studying the rods.

Sailasa feels a quick flush of excitement. 'Would you like to book a fishing trip as well?' he asks. He and Filipe get a small commission on fishing trips, so they try to sell them when they can. Sailasa will give it a red-hot go this week; he needs that commission. Without being too pushy, though. Guests don't like pushy (who does?), and Roko would get mad if he thought Sailasa was pushing anything onto anyone. *It's about reputation,* he always tells them. *We don't want people going home saying they were pressured into things.*

'Would I ever!' says the Englishman. 'I'm a *huge* fisherman. I won't book now because I'll need to run it past the boss, and she's having forty winks at the moment.' He laughs. 'Remind me later in the week, would you?'

'Of course, sir,' Sailasa responds graciously, careful to keep any panic out of his voice. It is not a no. It's a later. Sailasa can work with a later.

Benedict fingers the shiny black shaft of the rod before turning towards the door of the shed. 'I'll see you soon, then,' he says. '*Vinaka!*'

The shed is empty again, and Sailasa spends a good fifteen minutes cleaning equipment and another fifteen singing the welcome song to a new group of guests as they arrive on the resort tug-boat from the ferry. This group are cheerier than the last as they disembark, full of smiles and shell necklaces and cheers. Guests from the Sydney and Melbourne flights are always merrier because they're less jet-lagged than the international cohort.

First to get off the tug is a middle-aged woman in a bright sundress, clapping rhythmically to the music, accompanied by a sulky-looking teenager in a crop top and denim shorts. They're followed by a couple who look like zookeepers, in matching khaki shorts and shirts, and then a striking, dark-skinned woman of around forty who Sailasa suspects has been enjoying a little too much of Fiji Airways' hospitality on the flight over. She wobbles up the beach towards the group of singing staffers in a typically Australian uniform of denim shorts, a white T-shirt and a large straw hat, and when she reaches them, she twirls around to the sound of the upbeat song and throws her hair back with a loud *whoop!*, her straw hat dropping in the sand at her feet. She laughs and bends down to retrieve it, and Sailasa smiles as he sings.

When the welcome song is done, Sailasa and the other staffers follow the new guests from the sand to the brick pathway of the reception area to listen to Roko's second welcome speech of the day. Overhead, the chopper whirls and whips the sea into a frenzy on the south side of the island as it comes into land with the last of today's arrivals: a French doctor, he has heard. It's the quickest available transfer – fifteen minutes compared to fifty from Port Denarau to Loloma, but it is not for the faint-hearted. Sailasa travelled in it once, with an unwell guest. It had made him feel sick as a dog up there, bobbing about under the clouds. He'll stick to the ocean, his preferred domain, snorkelling and boating and diving, crawling along the ocean bed, planting coral for Filipe as part of the hotel's reef regeneration programme. Below sea, not high above it.

When Sailasa returns to the shed, Filipe is inside, adding a name in pencil to the scuba list on the clipboard.

'What do you think of them?' he asks. 'This week's guests?'

Sailasa shrugs. 'Nothing to say yet.'

'The woman was rude.'

'To Joji? Yeah. Hopefully she's cheered up after a rest – otherwise, this will be an unpleasant dive.' Sailasa rolls his neck around. His shoulders are tight. 'You checked their passports?'

'Yes,' says Filipe, drawing in a puddle of water on the floor with his left big toe. 'I wrote their passport numbers on the waivers. All they need to do now is sign.' He nods towards the clipboard. 'I've just added Fergus Miller, Bure Three. He caught me at reception and signed up.'

'He's on his own?'

'Yeah.' Filipe springs into action decisively. 'I'll carry the tanks down to the boat.'

Sailasa nods and taps his pen on the clipboard. Either he or Filipe will have to buddy up with one of the guests under the water. It always happens with an odd number. '*Vinaka*,' he says. 'OK, so tank two for Benedict St John-Gray, tank one for his wife and three for Mr Miller. I'll take four.'

Filipe gives a thumbs up, picks up two of the tanks and makes off down the beach towards the boat.

Sailasa is halfway into his wetsuit when he sees Benedict St John-Gray and his wife walking hand in hand down the path and onto the sand. The husband is already in his wetsuit, and the wife wears a white bikini with a sort of long, knitted crochet jacket over the top. Her hair bounces on her shoulders and her cat-like eyes stare ahead. Sailasa feels them on his chest as she gets closer, and he pulls his abs taut until he has hiked up the neoprene across the upper half of his torso. He doesn't know why he does this; it's not his usual style to act like a peacock. He is not showy – maybe when he was a kid, but not now. But then again, he never thought he'd get into debt, either, so things can change. People can.

'*Bula!*' he calls.

'*Bula!*' Mr St John-Gray waves.

His wife does not reply.

Sailasa hands a pen to Benedict St John-Gray and then one to his wife and directs them to sign and date the hotel water sports waiver. Then he passes the flippers and masks over the desk. 'If I could please ask you to put your wetsuit on now, Mrs St John-Gray, we can do the rest on the boat,' he tells them.

Luella St John-Gray does not put on her suit. Instead, she walks down the sand towards the boat with her husband, without her mask and flippers. 'Your equipment, Mrs St John-Gray . . .' Sailasa calls after her as he gathers up his own oxygen tank.

'Bring it to the boat, would you?' she calls over her shoulder.

Sailasa's arms are already full, so he will need to do another trip. He follows the husband and wife up the sand, places the tanks in the boat and turns back to the shed, where another woman stands waiting. Sailasa sees a man he presumes to be Fergus Miller emerge from the door of the shed behind her.

'*Buuu-laaaaa!*' the woman sings.

Sailasa smiles and returns the greeting.

'Ah, there you are,' says the man. 'Miller, Bure Three. I'm the three o'clock tag-along with Benedict and Luella St John-Gray.'

'Welcome,' Sailasa says. 'And you, madam? I don't seem to have you on the list, but we do have room on the boat if you'd like to join us?'

He hands Fergus Miller a pen and watches him sign the waiver.

'Madam? Oh gosh, just call me Kitty, please! And no, thank you. I *hate* the water – everything about it. No, no. I'm just going to sit on that sun lounger right over there and read my book until the boat comes back. Can't think of anything better. But I can certainly help with the equipment. What can I carry?'

Sailasa smiles. 'Thank you, that is very kind, but I can manage. You go and relax. Mr Miller, I will carry the last oxygen tank to the boat, so would you please collect some flippers from the bucket and follow me?'

The ride out over the reef is only ten minutes long, and as they head into the depths, clouds that were non-existent over

Loloma loom pendulously over the murky water. The boat moves a little more buoyantly than it would normally do on the waves. Sailasa looks up at the sky and calls to Filipe, 'Let's stop here.'

Filipe nods and brings the boat to a halt and, as they bob on the water, he begins his detailed safety briefing. 'Sailasa will be in the water with you, and I will stay on board the boat,' he says. 'Sailasa will buddy with Mrs St John-Gray, and Mr Miller will buddy with Mr St John-Gray.'

Luella St John-Gray frowns. 'Well, what's the point of doing this if I can't go with my husband?'

'We will all be together,' says Sailasa. 'I promise it won't make a difference. Your buddy is really only there if you get into trouble.'

Benedict St-John Gray puts his hand on his wife's knee, and she gives a *whatever* shrug and takes her mobile phone out of her beach-bag, which she has tucked under the seat behind her calves.

'These are the signs you must use to communicate under the water . . .' Filipe demonstrates them all: the *OK*, *down*, *low on air* . . . All the while, Luella St John-Gray taps away on her mobile phone.

Sailasa cuts in pointedly over Filipe. 'I know you have all dived before,' he says, 'but if I could have your attention for a moment, it is important you listen to this safety briefing. What I am telling you now could save your life if you get into trouble.'

He gives the assembled crew a detailed yet brisk reminder of the risks of doing the wrong thing: the bends, an arterial gas embolism, a lung over-expansion injury. All the while, the snooty woman taps away at her phone handset.

'Finally,' Sailasa tells them, 'it is essential you stay close to your buddy at all times.' He glances at Luella St John-Gray, fearful she might arc up about the buddy situation again, but she is still not listening. 'Alert them using the *help* sign if you are in distress. Do not swim off alone.'

Luella St John-Gray looks up from her handset and sighs audibly now. 'I think we know all of this,' she says. 'Can we just get in?'

Filipe looks at Sailasa. 'Of course,' he says. 'I have double checked the equipment so I think we're all good to go.'

They all mask up except for Filipe, who stands fully clothed in the boat, and one by one, they silently drop backwards off the side. The cool is a relief for Sailasa. Under the waves, he turns to the guests and gives the *OK* sign with his fingers and waits for each one to offer the same gesture in return.

They turn in a group to head north, and after only a few seconds, he realises he cannot see Mrs St John-Gray anywhere. She has swum away from the group, at least forty metres, and is motionless, her arms floating, unanchored, out wide.

Shit! He feels a pang of panic. Why is she floating like that? Has she passed out? Why is she so far away from the group?

He controls his breath as he approaches her at speed. Her hair is the only part of her body moving. It sways gracefully about her body like ocean kelp. He makes a grab for her shoulder and gives it a sharp tug.

Luella St John-Gray's body contracts, turns rigid. Her face spins around, whip fast, like she's been stung.

He lifts up his hand: *OK?* he asks with his fingers and blinks at her wide-eyed.

She stares back at him; her eyes are fire. She lifts up her hand, scratching Sailasa's forearm as she brings in the scarlet fingernails of her thumb and forefinger together to form the *OK* sign and shoves the claw-like shape right in his face.

10

Luella

Luella feels the man grab her under the armpit and gets the fright of her life. She rounds her fingers into an angry *OK* sign and twists her body briskly away using her palms as paddles. How dare he touch her!

Directly above her, the hull of the boat casts a dark shadow on the cloud-dappled waves. She is annoyed. The hotel manager obviously wants them all to stay exactly underneath the boat so they can't get lost. For God's sake, they're not children. And Luella draws the line at being *groped.* She is an experienced diver – she did her PADI only last year for pity's sake – and she is certainly not paying through the nose to go on a diving trip where she cannot explore more than a metre from the boat.

She kicks her flippers away from the group, further from the reef, further from the compact figure of Simon or Silas or whatever his name is, and further from Fergus Miller, who keeps jabbing at her with his fat index finger and pointing out every single clownfish he sees, like they're in *Finding Nemo*.

Luella's body moves effortlessly, and her breathing is rhythmic. She hears the swish of it: in and out, in and out, as if she is on a hospital ventilator. She bites down on the regulator and kicks her flippers some more until she is a satisfactory distance from the rest of the group. Some kind of black fish with vivid yellow stripes fights her for right of way, and she shoos it away with her hand.

In front of her, Fergus appears again, his body fleshy and pale, like some kind of gelatinous sea creature. Irritated to high heaven now, Luella tries to get past him (can't she escape anyone in this place? Are they all insistent on getting right up into her face with their jabby sign language?) and feels a slight tug to her back, as if they are momentarily tangled. She pulls away, and she thinks she sees Fergus tap his temple in her peripheral vision. She smiles. Now, now, there's no need to be grumpy, is there?

Luella continues on, and the water seems to take on more of a chill as she proceeds deeper – she feels it despite the thick neoprene of her wetsuit. In her stomach, a flicker of fear. She hears it more keenly all of a sudden: the ragged intake of breath, the rough exhalation, almost like the low growl of a dog. *Calm down,* she tells herself. *You know what to do.*

She kicks her flippers again and propels herself further down. She listens keenly to the underwater sounds: the swishes, the glugs, the tinny echoes, the breathing: in and out, in and out. And then, nothing. Luella goes to breathes in, as she has done a hundred times already, but there is no air. She tries again, but she still cannot find a breath.

A moment of confusion. She has a full tank of oxygen on her back, doesn't she?

She spins around. Fergus kicks his blue flippers in her wake. She tries, rather stupidly, to get his attention, clicks her fingers. She blinks: once, twice. Her eyes dart about, looking for Benedict. She feels the onset of panic, of end-of-life terror.

But Luella is no quitter. She has never been one to go down without a fight. *You know how to hold your breath,* she tells herself. *You do it every day. You did it on the bloody boat coming over here!* She knows from doing her PADI that she must let the air out of her body as she floats up, that she must blow out bubbles, to avoid bursting her lungs. She doesn't think she is deep enough for the bends, but she is still a long way down.

Luella begins to make her way upwards, her body kicking wildly towards the hull of the boat far above her. There is not much time left before she will *have* to take a breath. She blows out tiny bubbles, feels the sensation of dizziness grab at her as the hull loses its focus like a desert mirage. Then, the water around her turns milky, and she feels the sudden onset of calm. *This is it,* she thinks. *This is it.* Her lungs are empty; there is no more air to exhale.

There is no moment of existential regret for Luella, in which she acknowledges in her final moments that she shouldn't have been such an awful cow to everyone – no moment of divine intervention or angels singing her to sleep. Perhaps there is simply a nagging thought somewhere in her clouding brain that scuba gear doesn't just *fail*, that someone has royally stuffed up here, and that that person will pay!

But this thought doesn't hang around, because it is quickly replaced by the delirium that manifests before one goes under anaesthetic, when everything feels surreal and strangely warm before it all turns black.

11

Kitty

On the beach, Kitty takes a series of deep, contented breaths. She looks up from Agatha Christie's *Dead Man's Folly* and prods the flesh on her arms. She sees the white indent of her finger flood with pink again and grimaces. She would like to go home with a tan, not tan *marks* – she's seen those terrible memes on social media of holidaymakers in Ibiza who fall asleep in barely-there string bikinis and wake up looking like they've been coloured in with a stencil. *Good Lord, no!*

Kitty would rather like to be the colour of Luella St John-Gray: a light golden bronze all over. Oh, what she wouldn't give to look like her! The woman is so refined, so *polished.* Kitty feels like a frightful mess in comparison, all frizz and freckles and deep-set labial folds. There is nothing refined about Kitty – nothing at all.

She puts her book down on the lounger, fanned out and face down, and rummages around in her beach-bag until she finds her Boots sun cream. She turns the bottle upside down and gives it a thump but then returns it to her bag. She won't get any colour at all if she cakes factor 50 all over her, so she will live dangerously. She opens an almost-empty factor 30 instead and inhales the cucumber scent dreamily as she rubs it methodically onto her arms. She smiles at the woman sipping a cocktail on her right, a striking woman with dark skin and hair pulled back off her face in a messy bun – the kind of woman Fergus would say was 'scruffy' but whom Kitty recognises as effortlessly cool: a coffee-drinking, Birkenstock-wearing hipster.

The woman smiles back. 'Hi,' she says. 'Good book?'

'Yes,' enthuses Kitty. 'It's *Dead Man's Folly*. I do love an Agatha Christie. What are you reading?'

The woman holds up her book. '*The Wim Hof Method*,' she says and Kitty nods enthusiastically, even though she has no idea who or what Wim Hof is.

The woman must sense her confusion. 'Ice baths,' she says, and Kitty is no clearer.

'Is that an English accent?' Kitty asks instead, as she did to Luella earlier in the day because it is her go-to, her conversation starter. She always finds it exciting to meet Brits abroad. There's something comforting in it, chatting about a city they both know or at the very least that Kitty has been to.

'It's a bit of a hybrid accent, I suppose.'

Kitty hears a definite slur in the woman's voice and notes the now-empty cocktail glass on the table beside her. She is a little put off by the slurring, because she isn't a big drinker herself. She finds excessive boozing a little frightening, probably because she doesn't feel she is quite cool enough to do it. She'd muck it up, make an awful fool of herself.

'I was raised in England, but I live in Australia,' the other woman says.

'How wonderful. I'm Kitty, by the way.'

'Thomasina.'

'Lovely to meet you, Thomasina.' Kitty smiles again and turns her head away.

'Well, time for a nana nap,' Thomasina says. 'See you!' She stands up and gathers her things.

'Bye!' Kitty watches for a moment as Thomasina walks unsteadily up the beach, before returning to her book.

She tries to read the same few lines three or four times but finds she is gazing over the top of the page, her eyes fixed on the horizon, wondering how Fergus is getting on. He's done several dives over the eight years they've been together, but Kitty hasn't done a single one. She much prefers to read in the sun or go on a hike and check out the native wildlife. Chances are she'll do her walk to the island's volcanic mountain peak alone, since Fergus has little tolerance for climbing or walking or attuning himself to nature. And while Kitty will wax lyrical back in England about the flora and fauna she hopes she will encounter during this trip, Fergus will likely rave about the food and the swim-up bar and drinking whisky at sunset. The things he can show off about. The *luxuries.* Because the fact is, this single week on Loloma Island is far more lavish than the holidays Fergus and Kitty would normally plan. It is a six-star escape they hadn't expected to take.

It all came about rather rapidly, off the back of the article Kitty read in *Tatler*, which in turn prompted Fergus to grab his turquoise credit card and call up Thomas Cook.

Kitty had been waiting to get a filling in one of her back molars at the dentist in St Albans and just happened to pick up the magazine in front of her and peruse the headlines. *NEW YEAR, NEW YOU!* and *BE RESOLUTE:* 20 *NEW YEAR PROMISES YOU SHOULD MAKE* – and then, there it was, on the right-hand side, just under the ad for the winter beauty pages, the headline: *EMBRACING THE GRAYS*. And Kitty flipped open the magazine, thinking she was about to find out something new about dyeing her hair, and there was Luella, dressed in Balenciaga and dripping with festive jewels, discussing her plans for the New Year with her husband-of-almost-a-year, Benedict St John-Gray, who was a specialist in kick-starting foundling finance businesses. Kitty knew Benedict was an old pal of Fergus's, because Fergus had pointed out their marriage notice in *The Times* the year before. He'd told her that Benedict was just Ben Gray when they worked together and had somehow acquired the *-edict* and the *St John-* additions since.

The article, which was essentially a puff piece about how rich they were, said the couple planned to see in the New Year on a remote island in Fiji, which Luella didn't name but which she did say had recently won some prestigious hotel award. Kitty thought it was rather silly of her to have mentioned this, because all anyone (say, a stalker or such) would need to do, if they wanted to find out exactly *which* resort they were to stay at, would be to enter this information into Google. Kitty didn't ask Google, though, because looking at holiday resorts that only the mega rich can afford to go to is generally rather depressing, and plus, there was a sign on the wall of the dentist's waiting area that asked patients to turn their phones on silent, and Kitty thought it best to just turn it off altogether at that point.

So, she put Fiji to the back of her mind and merely sighed and thought to herself what a striking woman Luella St John-Gray was, and what a wonderful lifestyle she must have – but was she truly happy? And she mused on all of this until Dr Arthur opened his door and said, 'Mrs Miller?'

When she got home with her numb, drooly mouth, Kitty mentioned the *Tatler* story to Fergus, and Fergus put the hotel award into Google and came up with the adults-only Loloma Island Resort & Spa and said things like 'Bloody hell, it's pricy!' and 'Fuck me, hasn't Ben Gray has done well for himself?' and 'That could have been *me*!' And then he realised how that must have sounded and said, 'I meant *financially*, Kitty. I'd never be tempted by a woman with more money than me. A total turn-off.' And he patted Kitty reassuringly on the crown of her head.

The following morning, Fergus announced as he buttered his Tesco croissant – less flaky than Waitrose if you're being pedantic, but cheaper by far – 'We're going to Fiji. We're going to book that top-notch resort, Goddammit, and I'll show Ben Gray just how well I'm doing!'

Kitty pushed aside the fact that Fergus *wasn't* doing well enough to afford a holiday in paradise and that the outgoings for this adventure would be far above funds coming in, and instead thought soothingly: *Well, if I'm getting a holiday out of it, I don't care if it* is *a big old dick-swinging contest!*

But the point of the holiday *wasn't* a dick-swinging contest, as Fergus went on to explain over a meal of salmon en croûte later that evening ('Are these broad beans, Kitty?'). He had a plan for them and a very important role for her, his partner in crime.

It was meant to look accidental, bumping into the St John-Grays somewhere: on the plane or on a sun lounger or over a strawberry daquiri at the swim-up bar. It was meant to be a huge surprise, a real 'By Jove!' moment. And it had been, truly it had.

It was perfect – the wonderful double-take from Benedict, the vigorous pump of a handshake, the startled look from the beautiful wife. And it needed to be this way because it would have been too strange, too *contrived*, for Fergus to approach his old chum out of the blue. It would be far easier for them to make it look like a surprise and then for Fergus to casually mention to Benedict over cocktails that he was starting up a business, a dead cert, *a winner* . . . if he could just secure some financial backing. Not a lot of money in the grand scheme of things, but a token amount from a silent investor to, you know, get things up and running, to enable the birth of the business to proceed a little more smoothly, with less stress on the purse strings. A cool nine hundred thousand – not even a million – to launch things off the ground.

'He'll be good for it,' Fergus said as he slid his fork with a crunch into the pastry and through to the salmon. 'He's always been interested in new businesses, and he loves to spend money. It's a no . . .'

'A no-brainer,' Kitty mutters to herself now as she rubs more sun cream on the back of her neck (her idea to burn is somewhat reckless, she realises). Fergus presented this as an investment: a holiday of a lifetime plopped on top of their mortgage in the hope that they might end up with a verbal agreement that could change their lives in the very best of ways. A veritable *you need to be in it to win it* situation.

They had to walk the walk, and that meant booking the holiday (but not the helicopter transfer – they couldn't stretch to that – so she had to 'man up' when it came to the seasickness), and Kitty very much enjoyed hitting up charity shops from Sloane Square to Hampstead with the three-hundred pound budget Fergus had generously given her, grabbing as many second-hand designer outfits as she could find. A Kate Spade beach-bag, a Diane von Furstenberg wrap dress in cobalt blue with a button missing (a snip at forty pounds), a Matthew Williams kaftan from the Givenchy 2020 Resort Collection – the same designer labels

Kitty has always admired on the pages of glossy magazines, but which, up to that point, always seemed far out of her reach.

Kitty puts the sun cream back in her bag and looks up towards the horizon again. It is fun to play at this lifestyle, but she wonders if she would actually want it if it were served up to her on a platter – via a winning lottery ticket, perhaps. Would she grow bored if money was no object and if she and Fergus had nothing left to strive for? Regardless of the answer, it is the lifestyle Fergus dreams of and the very same lifestyle he likes to promise Kitty, as if he thinks she is desperate to live in this manner, as if she is dying for it. As if *everyone* is!

The resort's scuba-boat catches Kitty's eye as she ponders the meaning of life – it is speeding its way through the waves and over the reef. It slows down as it hits the shallower waters, but still seems to be travelling rather fast, given there are both a paddle-boarder and a snorkeller in the water.

Kitty stands up and hops down to the water's edge on the scorching sand, before feeling the cool relief as the sand darkens, waterlogged. *That was a quick dive*, she thinks. *Aren't they meant to be out for an hour?* She squints through her sunglasses at the boat, then blinks as if to clear the lens of her eyes like a windscreen wiper. Is she seeing this correctly? There seems to be only *three* men on board, and those men, she believes, are Sailasa, Filipe and Benedict. She cannot see Fergus or Luella. *How very strange,* she thinks. Did they stay behind in the water? Then she notices Benedict waving his hands in a manner that is frenzied rather than jovial, and Kitty looks behind her, in case he is gesturing to someone else further up the shore. The boat's engine cuts as the prow slides less than gracefully onto the shore, and Kitty sees panic all over Benedict's face.

'There was an accident,' he says, his breath ragged, skin white.

Kitty's hand flies to her chest. 'Not Fergus?' she cries.

Fergus's head pops up from the deck of the boat. 'Calm down,' he snaps. 'I'm fine.'

Kitty's shoulders fall. 'But why . . . why are you on the floor?'

Fergus runs a hand through his hair and nods to the hull of the boat, where Kitty can now see a lifeless figure lying flat on the hull.

'It's Luella . . .' he says, and Kitty's hand flies to her mouth.

12

Sailasa

Sailasa's head swims. *What just happened?*

One minute, they were under the water; the next, he was dragging Luella St John-Gray's lifeless body towards the hull, instructing Filipe to get her up into the boat. Then Sailasa's head was at her chest, her flesh studded with goose bumps and her ribcage motionless with the lack of breathing. He listened more intently than he had for anything in his life, willing there to be a small sign, the softest of heartbeats. He found one. It was faint, but it was there.

Sailasa pressed his lips to hers and took a deep breath. He was a split second away from transferring his full lung of air to Luella's airway when she coughed in his mouth and turned and vomited. Sailasa's body shuddered with relief.

'Where is the medic?' Fergus says to Filipe now. 'I thought you radioed him!'

'He is on his way, Mr Miller,' Filipe tells him calmly.

'Is she dead? Is she *dead*?' Mrs Miller is crying from the beach, and Sailasa holds his hands up, as if to try and stop her, to calm her somehow. His head feels tight, as if his brain is somehow pushing on the sides of his skull, trying to get out.

'Of course I'm not fucking dead,' snaps Luella St John-Gray, standing up slowly and uneasily.

Sailasa blanches as the woman's spittle hits his forearm. He does not want to antagonise her by wiping the skin of his arms, so he leaves the saliva until she has looked away and then discreetly pulls his fingers across it. He has had his mouth on hers, so what's a bit of spittle?

She wobbles on her feet, and Sailasa goes to steady her.

'Get off me!' she snaps. 'Don't you think you've done enough?'

Sailasa smarts at the comment and drops his hands immediately. He turns his head helplessly towards Filipe, sees his friend's face tighten, his eyes locked on Luella. Sailasa shakes his head in confusion, her words a slap. *Don't you think you've done enough?* What does she mean? Surely the woman doesn't believe this is his fault. But then he comes to the realisation that yes, the equipment was his responsibility. Not Filipe's but *his*. He was the one to check it in the dive shed. He'd told them as much on the boat. And at the end of the day, he is the one who runs the dive shed, isn't he? Filipe may be a decade older and infinitely wiser, but his main role is that of environment manager and diving is his secondary job, so of course the buck stops with Sailasa and not with his good friend.

He looks up to see the resort's medic Pau Marama running down the sand with Mr Roko following, and the sight of his boss makes his stomach plunge.

'What on earth happened?' Mr Roko asks, loudly enough to be heard but quietly enough not to alert other beach dwellers of the near-catastrophe.

'Luella very nearly drowned, that's what,' says Mr St John-Gray. The husband's eyes are wide with shock, his lips dry. Sailasa sees the way he clutches at his wife's shoulder and pulls her in close.

'Touch and go,' adds Fergus Miller, and he glances at Sailasa and then Filipe, as if he believes them both to be at fault and is trying to work out who to blame.

Sailasa would like to say *No, don't blame Filipe – it is me who messed up,* but he cannot seem to form the words, so he says nothing.

'How?' Kitty Miller gasps. '*How?*'

'The equipment fucked up,' says Fergus Miller. Finally he jerks his head towards Sailasa. 'He said he'd checked it.'

Sailasa turns to Mrs St John-Gray's dive equipment on the hull of the boat. He hasn't considered what went wrong. He's been too busy attending to the woman, unfolding the ancient foil blanket stashed under a seat to keep her shivering body warm, unscrewing capped bottles of water. He has not yet considered what might have caused the air to cease its usually effortless journey from tank to regulator to lungs.

He reaches out to tank one – Luella St John-Gray's tank – and checks the gauge. It is fully turned on, as it should be. He cannot understand what has happened to this woman under the water. It occurs to him that her regulator may have somehow failed, but he can't see how it would – he had them fully serviced at the end of last month, and besides, regulators are fail-safe.

Mr Miller's head is ruddy and freckled. 'Does your equipment usually fail?' he asks. It is a loaded question, the gun pointed at Sailasa.

'No. It doesn't,' Sailasa stutters. 'I can't see how . . .' His words trail off.

Ahead of him, Mrs St John-Gray finally makes it on jelly legs to the front of the boat. Her hair is matted, as if someone has drawn a comb though it backwards, and her skin is deathly white. Benedict St John-Gray lifts her in his arms and climbs carefully over the side of the boat and down the two steps onto the sand, where he gently seats her a little away from the boat on a sun lounger. Dr Marama sits down beside her and presses his stethoscope to her chest.

'Heartbeat is a little fast but nothing alarming,' he reports. 'I'd like to keep you in the medical room for observation for a couple of hours if you don't mind, Mrs St John-Gray.'

Sailasa swings his own body over the bow of the boat and walks towards the trio by the lounger. 'I'm so sorry,' he says. 'Honestly, I don't know what happened . . .' He hears his own voice trail off.

Mr Roko fixes his eyes on Sailasa, a look that says, *Make yourself scarce.*

Sailasa shrinks back. He thinks about how distracted he was when he was checking the equipment. He'd been thinking about the money, wondering how he could get a quick income, pay off the debt. Had he triple-checked tank two but forgotten to check tank one? Could he have been so preoccupied by his own problems that he neglected to do the very basics of his job?

No, he tells himself sternly. *That can't be the case. I'm always thorough. Always.*

But he realises like a punch to the guts that regardless of how this happened, it will rest on his head, because people (and especially people like Luella St John-Gray) need to apportion blame. His subconscious teases him with a split second of catastrophising: *Christina Cole,* he thinks. *Look what happened to her on Sunshine Island. This is worse than that. This isn't a diamond earring – this is someone's life. Someone nearly* died!

He fits his left fist inside his right, twists it anxiously like a ball joint in a socket. He cannot lose this job. He especially cannot lose this job when he owes so much money. The idea is terrifying. But it is almost less frightening than the next thought that settles in his mind and takes root, bold and firm, like a native pandanus palm. What was the loaded question Fergus Miller asked him? *Does your equipment usually fail?*

No, says Sailasa to himself, *it does not.* Especially equipment that has just been thoroughly serviced.

The only way that Luella St John-Gray's tank would have failed on her is if someone wanted it to.

13

Una

Luella St John-Gray sits in a lounge-chair at reception and shakes off the blanket Una has placed around her shoulders.

'Get this scratchy thing *off* me,' she demands and throws it to the floor.

Una bends to pick it up.

'I implore you to come with me to the medical room, Mrs St John-Gray,' Dr Marama puts his palms together as if in prayer. It's his third time asking. 'You have had a shock.'

'The only shock I've had is the gross incompetence of the water sports team,' the woman snaps.

Una looks at Sailasa. It is an instinctive response. He stands a little back from the assembled group, to Filipe's right, his hands clasped in front of his groin and his head bowed like a naughty schoolboy. Una sees the line between his eyebrows, the dappled sweat on his forehead. It is the same stance he had at his mother's funeral. So much is going on inside that beautiful, gentle mind. She would like to go to her nephew and ruffle his hair, tell him how much she loves him and urge him not to worry, because really, what is the worst that can happen? It's not like he is at fault here. Equipment fails sometimes – that's the truth of it.

'Luella?' Mr St John-Gray touches his wife's shoulder. 'Please listen to the doctor. If he thinks you should rest . . .'

'I am *fine*.' The angry wife yanks her shoulder away. 'No thanks to them . . .' She turns to eyeball Sailasa and Filipe, and Una can see she is shivering and most certainly not *fine*. She is still in shock. 'This is a straightforward case of negligence, and I intend to engage my lawyers immediately.'

'Please, Mrs St John-Gray.' Mr Roko implores. 'I can assure you this has never happened before.'

'That's lovely to hear,' she snaps. 'But it doesn't help me, does it? I almost *drowned*.'

'I understand,' says Roko. 'Thankfully, Sailasa here was able to . . .'

The St John-Gray woman's eyes narrow. 'Able to what? *Help* me? Hardly! He almost killed me. Does the fact he may possibly have prevented my dying – if I hadn't done that *all by myself* – negate the fact he nearly killed me in the first place?'

Filipe steps forward to speak, and Roko glares at him. 'Filipe, you may leave,' he says. 'Sailasa was on safety duty today.'

Filipe looks to Sailasa and back at Roko. 'But . . .'

'*Filipe!* Please leave.'

Filipe seems to come to. He nods and glances at Sailasa.

'Go Filipe,' he tells him. 'It's fine.'

Filipe nods and walks away. Una sees the sweat on the back of his neck as he goes.

Benedict St John-Gray clears his throat. 'My wife is right. She could have died today. How on earth can that happen on a routine afternoon dive?'

Una would like to step forward and say, *Diving isn't child's play, you know! Isn't that why guests sign a waiver when they go on trips like this? Because it's dangerous?* But she knows an outburst like this would not be welcome, so she studies her feet instead and lets the feeling of helplessness engulf her.

'Well, Sailasa?' snaps Roko. 'Speak up.'

'The tanks were full before we left,' Sailasa says. 'I checked them myself before we went out this afternoon. The only thing I can think of is that perhaps someone—'

'And you triple-checked everything?' Roko interrupts.

Sailasa looks at Una, and it almost breaks her heart to see those innocent, kindly eyes so full of angst. He turns to Mr Roko with a nod. 'Yes. I swear.'

Roko steps forward. 'Mr and Mrs St John-Gray, Sailasa is very thorough. He has done his due diligence and checked the equipment, and it appears to have been an unfortunate accident. We will compensate you, naturally,' he says. 'I will have to speak to my superiors, of course, but we will certainly be looking to heavily discount the cost of the holiday in light of what has happened.'

'*Discount?*' Luella St John-Gray laughs. 'Would my husband have got a freebie if I *had* been killed?'

Roko clears his throat. 'Well, I'm sure we could go that one step further and make your entire stay complimentary,' he says.

'That's the very least you can do.' Luella St John-Gray turns to her husband. 'I'd like to go to the bure now. I believe you still have our passports. Please have them returned to our room.'

She stands up and walks off, her stride a little less confident than the one Una observed when she walked into the resort earlier in the day. Her husband follows behind her, clutching the woollen blanket Una attempted to wrap around her just minutes before.

Dr Marama sighs and puts a hand on Sailasa's shoulder. 'Chin up, Sailasa boy,' he says as he turns towards the medical room.

Sailasa looks to Una again, and she gives him a sympathetic smile and a nod of reassurance, one that says: *don't worry, Sailasa, it will all be OK.* He responds with the very slightest nod, an understanding of what she is telling him.

Alone with just Una and Roko now, Sailasa is emboldened. 'Mr Roko,' he says. 'About the equipment.'

Roko sighs impatiently. 'What about it?'

'As I told you, I took all of it, tanks and regulators, to Vita Water Sports in Nadi for an annual service on November twenty-fifth. They were all in good working order, nothing amiss. I went over with them in the speed-boat, and I left them there overnight. They are thorough there, the dive staff – they clean them out, test them rigorously . . .'

'I think we have established this,' says Roko.

'Yes, but . . .' Sailasa pauses to consider his words. 'I wonder if something happened to them, before the dive.'

'What do you mean?'

'I mean, what if someone tampered with Mrs St John-Gray's oxygen tank. It wouldn't have been hard for someone to access the tank, for example.'

'But the tank was fully open when you returned from the dive.'

'Yes . . .'

Roko's nostrils flare. Una can see his jaw working, considering, mulling over the implications for Loloma Island Resort if someone had gained access to the equipment, if someone *had* tampered with it unlawfully. Eventually, he lifts up his chin, pulls a pen out of his top pocket and flicks through his appointment diary.

'Impossible,' he says, before moving on. 'Did they sign waivers before they went out?'

Sailasa nods. 'Filipe saw to it.'

'Fergus Miller, too?'

'All of them.'

'Good. Get them to me with the service details from Vita Water Sports. Let's hope it's enough.'

Una can see Sailasa's brain whirring by the way he clenches his jaw. *Enough for what?* he must be wondering. *Enough to save me from losing my job?*

Roko turns to Una. 'Get the St John-Grays whatever they want from here on in, Una,' he says. 'Consider yourself their personal valet. Free cocktails, massage appointments, cheese platters – just do it all. If they want a palm tree painted in gold leaf, get it for them, for pity's sake. From this point on, whatever that damn woman wants, you get it for her before she's even thought of it herself. Yes?'

Una nods. Understood.

Roko releases a yoga exhale, long and deep.

'Sailasa, head to the staff village and stay there until this has all died down. Help Joana in the laundry or something. Filipe will manage the dive shed. And, for God's sake, stay out of that woman's way if you see her again, all right?'

Sailasa nods. 'Yes, Mr Roko,' he says, and he turns away, but not before casting a final, mournful look at Una as he leaves.

14

Thomasina

Thomasina picks up her phone for a time check. It is 6.30 p.m., and she's a tad thirsty. Must be the hangover. She wasn't going to drink on the plane, but she ordered one halfway through the flight because she needed to. Rum and coke, then another. Keep 'em coming. It wasn't even lunchtime. A drink at Port Denarau Marina waiting for the ferry, an Aperol on the beach! It's not like her to get so royally sloshed (*that* often, anyway), but she was nervous and hadn't really eaten. She needed it to psych herself up. It's been a long time since she has been on Fiji's sacred sand, and she has been longing for this reconnect, her excitement tinged with nerves. She has always felt an affinity for this place, and this time is no different. The way her feet slide through the sand, the way the water caresses her, holds her tight. She wants to embrace it, learn its customs, its language, surf its waves.

Thomasina yawns. Her nana nap ended up being a three-hour sleep, and now she feels she has wasted time. Tomorrow she'll enjoy the surf, book a trip out to Cloudbreak, where the swells are six-foot high on a good day. Some of the best waves in the world, over at Cloudbreak. She glances over at her surfboard, sleek in its cover against the wall, the luggage tag still attached, ready for another adventure. Better than a boyfriend, that board – it's been with her longer than any man has; it has proven more reliable even than family.

Thomasina opens the door of her garden bure and steps out onto the path barefoot, the gardens splayed out in front of her: frangipani trees and hibiscus and a yellow flower of some kind she doesn't recognise. She rounds the corner onto the fork of the sand-grouted path that runs along the beach, past the oceanfront bures and to the pool bar, where she orders a Margarita and eyes it lovingly. It's mint-green in the glass, a combination of tequila, agave and lime.

'Charge it to Bure One,' she tells the barman, whose gold name badge, positioned above his heart, reads *Petero*.

'St John-Gray?'

'That's the one!'

Thomasina scribbles a vague, unidentifiable signature on the piece of paper, adds a generous ten-dollar tip and turns away from the pool area, which is lit a pink-orange thanks to the very last of a sunset she might appreciate if she were someone else. She joins the path back to her bure. She passes the woman she spoke to on the beach, the one with the detective novel, who is also sipping on a glass of something – Kitty or Katy, wasn't it? – and nods to her. She's wearing a yellow sundress and sandals, and her husband looks like the Man from Del Monte in a kind of too-tight linen affair. Thomasina is still in her bikini top and denim shorts. She lives in Byron Bay, after all, spends most of her time surfing at The Pass, half-dressed and with the sun on her nose, the soles of her feet hardened from barely ever wearing shoes.

Inside the bure, Thomasina demolishes the creamy brie and crackers that were left in the welcome basket in the room and finds she is still peckish. She hasn't properly unpacked yet. She bends down and pulls some clothes from her travel rucksack and throws them into a drawer. Then she puts her passport and phone in the safe, just because that's what she has grown up watching people all round her do: put valuables in safes, grasp close things that are shiny or sparkly. Keep them away from prying eyes.

She knocks her *Wim Hof* book off the bed and bends to retrieve it, and out falls a piece of notepaper that says *Fiji Airways* at the top, scribbled with the holiday to-do list she made on the plane.

The writing's a bit wonky, and it doesn't make the most sense. She turns to read the words on the back.

1. *Learn Fijian*
2. *Tackle Cloudbreak*
3. *Handle Octopus*

4. *Wreck dive*
5. *Confront her*
6. *Get her back*

Thomasina stuffs the piece of paper back between the pages of her book and picks up the phone to dial *two* for the restaurant. She can't be bothered to go there herself tonight, to socialise. But she will tomorrow. Tomorrow she will dress up and face the music. She came here with a mission, after all, and she's damn well going to complete it.

'*Bula*,' comes the immediate response.

'*Bula*. This is Thomasina Delana in Bure Four. Could I order a papaya and prawn salad, please, and a large Diet Coke?'

'Of course, Ms Delana,' comes the reply. '*Vinaka*.'

'*Vinaka*.'

Thomasina opens the door to her bure. *I think I'm going to like it here,* she muses as she steps out onto her veranda and breaths in the twilight air.

SATURDAY 30 DECEMBER

Cocktail of the Day:
Sailor's Warning

(Tequila, pineapple juice, cherries, watermelon chunks)

15

Kitty

Kitty can tell Fergus is still a little shaken by the scuba accident because it has manifested itself in grumpiness. He was snappy as hell over breakfast, but Kitty knows not to take it personally. The events of the previous afternoon must have been utterly harrowing for him. It's not every day you look death in the face.

She opts to go for a bush-walk after breakfast.

'Are you sure I can't tempt you?' she asks as she slathers on the factor 50-plus.

'I said no,' Fergus snaps. He pats his stomach and lies back on the bed. 'I need to sleep off all that bacon.'

Kitty doesn't like to point out that Fergus woke up from a nine-hour sleep only about an hour ago. She wonders if she should alert him about his lack of energy – she read in *Good Housekeeping* that lethargy could be a sign of a weakening heart. Not to mention all the fry-ups he keeps consuming. But she decides against it. It wouldn't go down well.

Kitty rummages in her suitcase for her trainers and pops her big floppy hat on her head. She grabs her water bottle and a small Tupperware container she used for grapes on the plane and decides she'll head to the restaurant and pick up one of the delicious scones they were serving at breakfast and nab it for her morning tea. After all, what could be better than a mid-morning snack with a view?

'Close the door on your way out,' Fergus instructs.

Kitty does as told and closes the door of the bure behind her, hanging the *Do Not Disturb* sign on the handle as she goes. She turns left onto the footpath and closes her eyes contentedly. She can smell the salt and the seaweed and the faint aroma of frangipani all around her. She opens her eyes again, smiles, and heads in the direction of the restaurant, which is adjacent to the bar. It is busy with guests still enjoying long, lazy breakfasts, and Kitty creeps in apologetically, picking up a plump raisin scone from the breakfast buffet display and discreetly popping it inside her little tub. She fills her water bottle from a large glass jug that's dripping with condensation, and the ice cubes give a satisfying clink as they hit the inside of the metal bottle. Kitty screws on the lid tight and heads back out.

She passes Dr Marama outside the spa and bids him a cheery good morning, then follows the path around past the spa and the laundry and then the staff village, which is less of a village than a large green building with a big front veranda and a *Staff Only: No Guest Access Beyond This Point* sign. She sees a lesser wooden sign in the shape of an arrow just beyond that says *Bush Track*, and she follows it on an upward incline.

The terrain is rocky underfoot and steeper than she expected, and she stops halfway up for a breather.

'Wow,' she says aloud. 'It's so *hot!*'

Kitty wipes her brow with the inside of her forearm and fans out her T-shirt. Then she unscrews her water bottle and takes a good ten or so satisfied glugs. Then she presses on. When she is almost at the top of the cliff, she sees the little river she read about on the resort's website. She's been desperate to see it. She specialised in batrachology back at the University of Exeter. (She's lost track of the number of confused faces she's been confronted with over the course of her life when she says that word. But it is rather confusing – shouldn't batrachology be the study of *bats* rather than the study of amphibians?) She did her dissertation on it, got herself a first-class degree, which she always downplays in front of Fergus, because really, how useful is it to know about toads?

Those days seem so long ago now, anyway, a very different era of her life, the days when she was young and free. The days before Fergus.

She crouches down and looks left and right along the slow-flowing water – like everything, this lake is on 'Fiji Time'.

'Ah.' She gasps as she sees a female toad lay a long stream of eggs. This time of year is peak egg-laying season for cane toads. Kitty finds it so very fascinating. Females can lay up to 30,000 eggs in one go, and most animals won't touch the spawn because of its venom. It is nature's way of assuring the continuation of the species. No wonder there is an epidemic of cane toads in these parts.

Kitty picks up her Tupperware container and munches on the scone inside. 'Mmmm,' she mutters aloud, holding it out in front of her and admiring it. Fijian scones are even better than British ones.

She sits back and lets the sun claim her face and thinks to herself how utterly idyllic it must be to be a cane toad – alone in the stillness and quiet with no concerns about anything whatsoever, poisoning predators who threaten your existence.

Eventually, she glances at her watch and gets up, clicking the lid back on her container. 'I'll see you at the race later, Mrs Toad,' she calls over her shoulder as she dusts off her behind and makes her way back down the mountain path – a journey that takes a third of the time of the ascent on account of the downward slope.

Kitty almost trips as she bounds down, and when she gets back to the flat, she feels a sense of euphoria, of achievement. She turns to look behind her at the mountain, the height she has scaled.

Back at the bure, Kitty finds a note on the bed from Fergus. *At the beach,* it reads. She pulls off her shorts and pulls on her swimming costume, stuffing her book and water bottle into her beach-bag (she hasn't quite got used to the fact the staff top up your water at the beach on demand!) and pulls the door shut with a click behind her.

'There you are,' mutters Fergus as she settles herself beside him at the beach a few minutes later. 'Good walk?'

'Yes.' She smiles. 'It was very productive.'

They eat lunch on the beach (crab salad for Kitty and a burger and chips for Fergus), and then Kitty reads while Fergus floats on a Li-Lo in the water. At 5.30 p.m. they come in to wash up for dinner. Kitty is starving hungry again by then, thanks to her long mountain walk, but she feels a sense of euphoria at a day well spent.

After a sumptuous dinner (Fergus's crab curry looked to die for), Kitty grips Fergus's arm as they make their way from their table in the beachside restaurant to the bar behind. She watches with wonder as a magnificent Fijian warrior in a traditional grass skirt blows into a large conch shell and lights the last of the flaming torches that illuminate the resort after dark. Beyond him, bobbing on the water, is the scuba-boat and it makes Kitty shudder. She thinks of the young dive man, Sailasa, and wonders how Mr Roko, the resort's manager, will have dealt with him. It seems wholly unfair to make him culpable.

'Poor man,' she says, almost to herself. 'Out of anyone to almost drown on his watch, why did it have to be Luella? I mean, she's not the most amenable woman, is she? He must be terrified of the fallout and what she'll do to him. She'll eat him alive, the poor thing.'

'Well, he should have checked the equipment properly then, shouldn't he?' Fergus snaps. 'You can't have guests popping their clogs all over the island, can you? Eh? It's not exactly what you expect in a six-star resort: scuba with a side of death.'

'I suppose not,' Kitty muses.

The main floor area of the bar has been cleared of tables, and chairs are positioned around a wide chalk circle drawn on the polished wood. There are already a number of guests seated directly beyond the chalk line, and the room is abuzz with chatter, music from the resort's guitarists and the soft sigh of waves launching themselves gently onto the shore.

Kitty stops to take a photo of the bar area, but Fergus yanks her arm. 'Oh, do come on,' he says.

Kitty slips her phone into her bag and pastes on a smile.

'*Bula!*' Mika, the entertainment manager, stands in the middle of the chalk circle. 'Have a seat, please. For those of you I haven't met, I am Mika! Welcome to the Loloma Resort International Toad Race!'

'*Bula*, Mika,' sings Kitty, because she makes a point of calling every staff member by their name. It's her way of showing her appreciation. If she's honest, she isn't entirely comfortable with the level of servitude she is being offered here, although she would never admit that to Fergus. 'We're so excited!'

'Drink?' Fergus asks.

Kitty nods, and he turns and heads to the bar without asking her what she'd like. He knows she'll have an Old Fashioned. At home it's elderflower cordial or just a nice cup of tea, but there's something about being on holiday that warrants a sturdy whisky with a nice sugary cherry on top. Some places make it with orange peel, but Kitty prefers a plump little glacé in her glass.

She heads to her left and choses a table furthest away from the scoreboard – and hence less in the public glare – and pulls out a chair, slanting her legs to the side like she saw Luella do on the boat. Luella looked so elegant, just like The Princess of Wales.

After a few seconds, Kitty realises it's a little uncomfortable on the hip bones to slant like that and reverts to a crossed leg. How does Luella sit like this for prolonged periods? She understands that Kate Middleton has to do it, because a royal can't flash her knickers, but why does Luella? Does she just do it for show? And if she *does* just do it for show, is everything she does undertaken purely because she thinks she is being watched the whole time, like an *actual* royal?

Kitty smooths the front of her dress. She is probably a little overdressed for a toad race, international or not, in her second-hand Vivienne Westwood shift – but then she sees Luella and does a double-take. She is not usually one to criticise another woman's sartorial offerings, but even she can see that Luella's attire is a little . . . *excessive*. She's wearing a gold lamé maxi dress that is so tight it could be painted on (she can see the woman's nipples, for crying out loud!), and she has on some kind of gold turban. She looks like an Oscar statuette. She glides across the wooden floor, her head high, past the sky-high Christmas tree with flashing white blubs, towards the bar.

In short, Luella St John-Gray does not look like someone who cheated death yesterday and certainly not someone who is bothered by it. All eyes are on her, and she knows it. Fergus, who has just arrived back at their table and is about to eat the plump green olive from his martini, stops dead in his tracks. Kitty watches the olive slide off the cocktail stick and plop back into his coupe glass.

'Bloody hell,' he says to no one, and Kitty feels herself squirm.

Kitty stands up to greet the woman, but Luella doesn't seem to see her, so Kitty raises her hand in an enthusiastic wave, then drops it limply and stares, open-mouthed, as Luella walks straight by. *That's odd,* thinks Kitty, *I'm right in front of her!*

Benedict, bringing up the rear as Luella heads to the busy half of the circle, gives Fergus's hand a strong shake and says, 'Hello, buddy! Come and join us, won't you?' Then he says, 'Good evening, Kitty. You look *stunning!*' and Kitty is ashamed to say she feels a flare of swoony heat travel up her neck. It is rather charming to have her choice of outfit validated by a handsome man – especially as Fergus never seems to notice what she wears.

'Thanks, Benny, my man, don't mind if we do!' Fergus snatches the drink he's just presented to Kitty and gives her a stern nod at the back of the St John-Grays. It's couple code for her to gather her bag quick-smart and follow, and even though she would rather stay in the more discreet corner spot, she realises Fergus must have this chat with his generous friend (and when better than over drinks when Benedict is nice and loosened up?). That is what they're here for, after all, isn't it?

As they follow Benedict, she leans in and whispers to Fergus, 'Darling, you must offer Luella a drink!' and nods her own head towards Benedict's back.

Fergus blinks and clears his throat. 'Can I get you and your lovely wife a tipple from the bar?' he asks Benedict. 'My treat. Champagne maybe?'

'Great stuff,' says Benedict, glancing over his shoulder as he walks. 'How about a bottle of the Dommy P?'

Kitty grimaces. Dom Pérignon is the most expensive bottle on the drinks menu. She saw it right there, at the top of the list, and the hotel mark-up is criminal. The only thing that's not included on this holiday is the booze, and it is half the cost at Heathrow duty free. She *knew* they should have bought a few bottles of fizz before they boarded, and she suggested as much in the departure lounge, but Fergus was funny about it because he didn't want to stump up the cash. And here he is, ordering off the extortionate hotel menu. She can almost imagine the bailiffs at their front door now he's putting Dom Pérignon on their hotel tab.

'Done!' Fergus turns towards the bar for the second time, and Kitty notices a single bead of sweat dripping down from the back of his hairline and disappearing into the fabric of his Hugo Boss shirt.

16

Kitty

Kitty turns away from Fergus and steps on something hard as she follows Benedict through the bar. It is a toe.

'Oh gosh,' she says to the woman standing in front of her. She is slender and dressed in some sort of khaki boiler suit. Kitty could never wear something so trendy – and it is linen, no less. 'I do apologise. I'm such an oaf!'

'It is nothing!'

Kitty detects a French accent. *Oh la la!*

'I'm Kitty,' she gushes, holding out a hand. 'Miller.'

'Sofie. Sofie Barthélemy,' says the French woman. She takes Kitty's hand with the gentlest of handshakes.

'Are you from France?' Kitty asks. 'Or from . . . Belgium?' As soon as she's said it, she realises there are at least twenty-something French speaking countries the woman could be from. She feels her cheeks colour. 'Oh dear,' she says. 'I hope I haven't caused offence.'

'No, of course!' Sofie smiles. 'You are right – I'm from France.'

'Oh, how lovely.' Kitty grins. 'Are you here with a partner?'

'No.' Sofie's smile fades, and Kitty realises she's made another faux pas. '*Toute seule*. I am entirely on my own.'

'Golly,' says Kitty with a pang of jealousy. 'How fabulous!'

'I like it,' Sofie admits. 'To be on my own. Men are a little . . . how you say? *Overrated*, don't you think?'

Kitty glances at Fergus, now grabbing the bottle of champagne from the bar, and takes a glug of her Old Fashioned. 'Um, I suppose . . .' she falters.

Benedict turns to them and holds out his hand. 'Benedict St John-Gray,' he tells Sofie. 'Alone, did you say? You're more than welcome to join us.'

Sofie looks at him and smiles. 'Oh no, thank you. I have the toad race and my book, so . . .' She holds up a Kindle dressed in a cork cover. 'But *merci*, thank you. It is very kind of you.'

Benedict nods and turns away again, back to following his wife, and Kitty stands there smiling. 'Well, um, *au revoir*,' she says. 'Enjoy the toad race!'

'You too,' the Frenchwoman says.

Kitty takes a seat to Benedict's right as the willowy form of Sofie Barthélemy glides away, ethereal. After a moment, Kitty turns around to look at the woman again and sees Sofie cast a long glance at Luella in her gold lamé before turning away to converse with what looks like a mother and daughter duo behind her.

Mika, the entertainment manager, taps the microphone. '*Bula*, everyone. Now, this is the moment you've all been waiting for!' He bangs his fingers on a Fijian drum. 'It's time to meet the toads for tonight's race!'

Kitty clasps her hands with excitement as Mika holds up a big green bucket, which he promptly pretends to drop, causing an excitable squeal from the seated guests, Kitty included.

Mika laughs. 'Each toad is named after a country and wears a coloured elastic band around their middle to identify them. Shortly, we will invite you to bid on the toad you think will make it across the chalk line first. You will get to study the toads' form when I tip them out in just one second. Study them closely, and bid on the one you think will win!'

'Dear God,' says Luella. 'Did I really stay alive for this?'

'Come on, darling.' Benedict puts his arm around her with a grin. 'It's just a bit of fun.'

Fergus returns with an ice bucket and the champagne in one hand and a tray with three glasses on the palm of the other. Kitty understands she will need to drink slowly – there is obviously no Dom Pérignon allocation for her.

Fergus sets the ice bucket and glasses down on the table behind Luella's chair. 'Luella, may I?' he asks, passing her a glass.

She waves her hand. 'Not tonight,' she says. 'I need something a little *stiffer*.'

Fergus colours at the way Luella says the word: slowly and with clear pronunciation, eye contact held at all times, making Kitty feel invisible.

Then she says, 'Fergus, be a darling and order me a Dark 'n' Stormy. Tell the bartender it has to be El Dorado or Diplomático. I cannot *abide* cheap rum . . .'

'His name's Joji, I believe,' mutters Kitty, who has mentally added the cost of a Dark 'n' Stormy to their next mortgage repayment. In a resort this luxurious, nothing comes cheap.

She watches as Fergus scuttles back to the bar and feels a flash of irritation at the woman who looks like a statue and is commanding her husband to wait on her while making innuendos about turgid penises.

'Now this is important, so please take note,' Mika continues. 'Before I release the toads so that you can study their forms, I will issue a warning. These cane toads are *highly poisonous*, so do not touch them. You must stay behind the white chalk line *at all times*.'

Benedict grins. 'Well, that certainly ups the stakes.'

'So exciting,' Kitty enthuses. 'Such marvellous creatures. Did you know that cane toads were introduced to Fiji in 1936 by the Fiji Agricultural Department as a biological control agent and that they can live for over a decade? Some can live as long as . . .'

'You learn something new every day, eh?' Fergus interrupts as he returns from the bar, and Kitty feels the familiar sting of humiliation. He turns to Luella. 'Your drink will be here in *un momento*.'

'*Grazie*,' replies Luella.

Mika raises his voice to cut across the chatter. He holds up the bucket with rubber-gloved hands and takes out a toad with a blue band round its waist. 'The toad that comes first will win forty per cent of the cash, the second toad will win thirty per cent of the cash, and the third toad to cross the line will take home twenty per cent,' he shouts across the crowd. 'The remaining ten per cent will go to the Loloma Conservation Fund.'

Mika drops the toad back into the bucket. Luella inspects her nails and looks out to the moonlit sea, which suggests to Kitty that the woman thinks this is all a little beneath her.

'At Loloma Island Resort, we have planted over nine hundred square metres of staghorn coral on numbered cement markers that are attached to steel posts under the water. We aim to plant coral the area of a football field eventually, thanks to the dive team who dedicate a great deal of time to this project.'

'When they're not trying to kill people . . .' quips Luella.

'They didn't mean to!' Kitty cries. It is a reflex response, and she immediately regrets it when she sees Luella's eyes narrow and fix on hers.

'You're sure they "didn't mean" to almost kill me? Well, that makes it all OK then.' Her voice is cold.

'I was just . . .' Kitty begins and then stops. She knows she will not beat Luella in a battle of words.

'So, to start, this is the toad who will race for Fiji.' Mika holds up a handsome amphibian, this time with a red rubber band around its middle. 'The other toads are listed on the board.' He gestures to the large chalkboard in front of him and points at each listed country, one by one. 'We have toads representing the UK, the USA, France, China, Australia, Korea, Spain, Brazil, Germany and, of course, Fiji.'

Fergus leans in. 'Ah, the Jerries got a look in, did they? No surprise there. Hey, Benny, you'll like this one, eh! What do you call a grumpy German?'

No one answers.

'A *sauerkraut!*'

Kitty is aghast! She can't take him anywhere. 'You can't say that, Fergus,' she gasps. 'It's not *woke!*'

'Who's going to arrest me, eh?' Fergus says. 'The Gestapo?'

'Fergus!' She turns to Luella and Benedict. 'I'm so sorry. I do hope Fergus hasn't offended you . . .'

Benedict shakes his head and bites down on a grin. 'You haven't changed a bit, Miller. Got me into a lot of scrapes back in the old City days.'

Fergus laughs. 'You mean I got you *out* of a lot of them.'

Kitty looks to Benedict with a relieved smile and expects him to offer a grin, but his smile has faltered.

'All in the past, mate!' Benedict takes a sip of his drink. 'And anyway, the Germans aren't all bad . . .'

'Better than the Frogs . . .'

'Oh no, on the contrary. I worked in Paris for two years after I left London. Top city. Got it all, culture, food, romance . . .' He looks at Luella.

Fergus burps discreetly and blows the gas out of the side of his mouth. 'Shame it's full of French people, eh?'

'*Au contraire*,' says Benedict. 'The French are delightful, and they make damn good cheese. And wine. You can't beat a good Châteauneuf-du-Pape . . .'

'I quite agree, Benedict,' Kitty says. 'I had a wonderful French teacher at school called Madame Blanchet. She gave me the most delicious recipe for French Onion Soup.'

'How delightful for the breath,' says Luella, piping up for the first time.

'We've taken the ferry to Bordeaux a couple of times,' muses Kitty, trying to ignore Luella's scathing remark. 'Of course, I had to take a few anti-sickness pills before I got on board. It was a tad rocky. Have you ever done it?'

'The ferry?' snorts Luella. 'Good God, no. We fly.'

'Talking of boats.' Fergus leans into Benedict. 'You'll want to jump on board my new biz venture once I tell you all about it, old chap.'

Benedict nods. 'Now, that is enticing.'

'Damn right. The ship's about to leave the dock, and you won't want to miss your place on the voyage . . .'

'You're in shipping?' Luella asks Fergus.

'Shipping? Um, no, it's just a metaphor,' says Fergus. 'It's actually a fintech company – we're going to change the world of personal investments, shares and pensions. I'm telling you, it's the future of investment.'

'Sounds fascinating,' says Luella drily. She takes her cocktail, without thanks, from a female bartender whose name badge reads *Ana*.

Kitty feels the need to smile broadly at the young woman as compensation for Luella's rudeness. 'Thank you,' she simpers.

'I'd love to chat about it.' Benedict smiles. 'Let's have a good old chinwag after the toads have done their thing. The betting's about to start.' He turns away.

'Of course, Benny, my man, of course!' Fergus says. He raises his glass and winks at Kitty. 'Here's to the toads.'

Kitty feels all agog with possibility. 'Well, isn't this exciting?' she chirps, then adds, 'The toads, I mean,' lest her jumpiness should be confused with anything other than anticipation about the racing amphibians. 'Toad-tastic!'

Luella splutters into her Dark 'n' Stormy.

'I've got another one for you!' Fergus makes his fingers into a gun. 'What's the difference between a frog and a horny toad?'

No one answers, and so Kitty takes it upon herself. 'Tell us, Fergie!' she begs.

'One says *ribbit, ribbit* . . . the other says *rub it, rub it*!'

Benedict shakes his head with an amused smile. 'Oh, Miller, that was bloody terrible.'

Luella, her mouth twitching with distaste, takes a sip of her cocktail.

Mika lifts up the bucket of toads. 'I am going to release the toads for a practice run,' he shouts over the hum of excited chatter. 'Please study the form of the toads and choose which one you would like to bet on for the actual race.'

He tips the bucket upside down, and ten angry toads spill out, whipping their fellow bar patrons into an excitable frenzy. Kitty grins as the toads leap here, there and everywhere. A moment later, the German toad leaps desperately for the chalk line, crossing before all the others and followed in hot pursuit by the Australian amphibian.

'That's the one!' Luella screams, suddenly excited. 'We're going to bet on the German one. Fastest by a golden mile.'

'Don't be afraid to bet big,' Mika calls out. 'And remember, the toad race happens twice a week, so if you do not pick the winner today, you could win big next time!'

The betting commences. The mother and daughter team secure the Australian toad for $160 – which Kitty cannot quite believe, because it seems an absurd amount of cash to part with for the promise of nothing – and the teenage daughter, dressed in some kind of indecent crop top, walks around the chalk circle and hands over the cash. She writes *Ellie & Alice Chen* and *Bure 5* on the chalkboard alongside the listing for the Australian toad. The mother stands up and walks over to Mika, stuffing some crisp notes into the smaller tub beside the toads.

Benedict bids on the German toad, and the bidding gets up to 180 Fijian dollars. Luella sits upright in her seat. 'I *really want* that toad,' she tells Benedict, her eyes narrow.

Fergus, who has pulled out of the bidding for the German toad, says, 'I actually think Brazil is faster. Much better form. Better legs on him.' He nudges Benedict on the arm. 'Just like Brazilian women, eh, Benny?' He mimics the curve of a woman's hips with his hands. Then he tips the dregs of the champagne bottle into Benedict's glass.

It starts to get heated. A young honeymooning German couple who introduce themselves as Klaus and Isabelle Fuch also *really want* the German toad, but Luella isn't one to back down. Kitty thinks World War Three is about to erupt over it. The Fuchs move forward over the chalk line and crane their necks every time the bid goes to Benedict and Luella.

'Back off mate, this isn't Poland,' barks Fergus.

Luella now sits on the very edge of her wooden chair and tells Benedict, 'More! Bid *more*!'

As she watches this statuesque and frosty woman, Kitty is suddenly hit with a flash of what Benedict sees in Luella. This passionate version of Luella, a version where she isn't turning up her nose at some poor staff member or rolling her eyes at a comment she deems too stupid to engage with is, thinks Kitty, beautiful. Her flushed cheeks and her playful smile as she fist-pumps the air make her seem well, *human* – as if there is no one else in the world but her.

Benedict smiles. 'But it's seven hundred dollars, Luella.'

'I couldn't give two *fuchs* . . .' Luella laughs.

Fergus emits a high-pitched giggle, too.

At 800 Fijian dollars, the Germans concede victory to the allies, and Luella fist-pumps again. Kitty works out the conversion rate in her head. 800 Fijian dollars is 300 *hundred pounds*, and Kitty feels almost tearful that this woman can spend so much money so frivolously when they have scrimped so much to come here, that everyone in this resort seems to have the capacity, and the inclination, to throw away money like it is rubbish. She doesn't belong in a place like this. *They* don't belong in a place like this – so why in God's name does Fergus want this life?

Kitty sips her Old Fashioned and blinks back the tears as the St John-Grays' bid is sealed for $800. *Part of it will go to the conservation fund,* she tells herself. *It's for the regeneration of the reef. It is not wasted money!*

Fergus enters the bidding for the French toad, but to Kitty's relief, pulls out at $95. He then places a bid of $75 on the North Korean toad, which he ultimately wins because no one else wants it, and when all the toads have been purchased and money handed over in cash to Mika, the actual race begins.

The German toad romps home, of course, crossing the chalk line first. Mika leans in with a gloved hand, snatches him up and pops him in the bucket before he can mount the front of Luella's patent heels.

'Bravo,' Luella shouts. 'Bravo, you slimy little bugger!'

Fergus seizes his moment. 'Here's an idea. How about you put those winnings, plus some, into my start-up, Benny, my man? Can't fail. Fintech and AI are the way of the future.'

As soon as the words are out of his mouth, Kitty can tell he has pushed it too hard. Benedict looks warier than before, less engaged, and Luella's eyes practically flash with anger. Kitty puts her hand on Fergus's knee and gives a warning squeeze.

'Sounds intriguing, Fergie, old chap,' says Benedict, carefully. 'How about we head to the bar and talk about it?'

'No!' snaps Luella. 'Not a snowflake's chance in hell. There is no way you are investing *my* money in some dodgy start-up.'

Kitty feels a pang of anxiety.

Benedict looks awkward. He glances between Luella and his old friend.

'Come on, darling,' he says. 'Let me hear Fergus out. It's the least I can do. He's saved me from a few drunken scenarios in the past, haven't you, buddy?'

Fergus smiles awkwardly and places his hand under his chest. 'Well, I suppose I . . .'

Luella dusts off her hands. 'Not happening,' she says and stands up. 'Absolutely no security in fintech. None at all. A huge risk. *Huge*. Why on earth would I take that gamble when there is very little chance of a healthy return on my investment?'

Fergus clears his throat. 'Well, that's the thing,' he says. 'By my calculations, the return would be incredibly healthy. Let me explain . . .'

Luella holds up her hand. 'It's a no,' she snaps.

Kitty looks at the woman who has just spent the cost of hers and Fergus' fortnightly grocery bill on a cane toad and feels pure, unadulterated anger. Fergus still has a persuasive smile pasted on his face, but it is cracking at the corners, and his right eye has started to twitch.

Benedict gives an apologetic smile. 'Sorry, buddy,' he says. 'The boss has spoken.' He leans in, kisses Luella on the lips, then turns back to Fergus. 'I'm sure you'll find another backer, Fergus, mate, but do you really need one? It'll only take a couple of mill to get off the ground, and I'm sure you have that much stashed away. I mean, you're obviously doing very well for yourself these days . . .'

Fergus smiles thinly, and Kitty reaches for him under the table, holds his arm for a few seconds, feels the race of his pulse. He snatches his hand away, and she flinches.

'No biggie, mate,' Fergus says, his voice flat. 'I was only mentioning it for your benefit really. Didn't want you to miss out. The fact is, it's going to make millions . . .'

Kitty bites her lip helplessly as she looks to her husband and thinks of the fifteen thousand pounds they scrimped for on three different credit cards to pay for this luxury holiday. The sum was nothing short of vulgar.

She thinks of the bills – gas, electricity, TV licence, water – she'll have to defer when she gets home, of the Dom Pérignon and the cocktails and the North Korean toad, and the money Fergus gave her for the op shop so she could at least look the part. All now completely wasted. She stares into her husband's hang-dog face with a look of sympathy for his plight, because that's what she is expected to do as the doting wife. But in her head she curses him because she knew this was never going to work.

17

Luella

Luella exits the bar to enjoy a Vogue Slim in peace. She perches on a rattan chair by the seawall, while the guests watch the muscular barman in the bright shirt grinding the plant root in a giant mortar and pestle, before straining it through some kind of dirty-looking cheesecloth. He uses a halved coconut shell to scoop out some of the brown watery liquid, which looks like it could be straight from a portable toilet at Glastonbury, and hands it out to guests one by one.

Benedict and his now-forlorn little friends sip from their coconut husks, Kitty grimacing as she tastes the marinated tree-roots, Benedict nodding appreciatively and handing over his shell for more. The barman dips it back in the bowl to scoop up more of the brown water, which Luella thinks is most unhygienic. She doesn't want to wake up with a hangover *and* Covid.

Benedict leans into Fergus, and Luella can imagine what he is saying, her ever-polite husband. Something along the lines of: *I do apologise, old chap, but Luella is* very *selective about the start-ups we decide to back. No offence. I'm sure your project is* full *of potential . . .*

Potential, my arse, Luella thinks.

She turns and watches the sea gently lapping the shore in the moonlight, the volcanic walls of Snake Rock standing proud against the incoming tide. The water looks so inviting, so calm, but Luella knows first-hand just how perilous it is beneath the surface.

She takes a drag of minty smoke deep into her lungs just because she can (even though she is aware she shouldn't). She reflects on the unsettling thought she had on the boat from the mainland, about her death – a prophecy that almost actually happened. Was she dead, just for a second? Or close enough to death to negate the premonition she had, so that it was true for just a sliver of a second and now she is safe with plenty more life to live? Yes, that's it! She can thank Hans for all the breathwork she's done at the yoga studio in Knightsbridge over the last year. If it hadn't been for her learnt ability to hold her breath, the diving trip might have ended entirely differently.

Come now, Luella, she tells herself on the inhale, as the minty smoke travels down her oesophagus. *Don't be morbid!* She is certainly not one to dwell on it, to curl up in her twee Fijian mud hut lamenting the devastation that could have been, because the fact is she *is* alive, and she has never felt more invincible than she is right now in this moment, in her gold lamé Elie Saab evening gown!

At the bar, the insufferable Fergus Miller holds his coconut shell aloft for a top-up, and Luella watches him with narrow eyes. She imagines that this vulgar little man with his tasteless jokes and blubbery beer belly will get royally drunk now, drown his sorrows in the free kava until the early hours. Maybe he will attempt to initiate the same conversation about his dodgy start-up tomorrow in the sober light of day. It isn't the first time and it won't be the last that some dubious personality from the past has sleazed up to them, begging for a handout. They've seen it all: the sommelier from their favourite Mayfair restaurant begging for funds to set up a wine bar; the tiny blonde Pilates instructor asking for sponsorship to do an extortionate hot yoga course in Los Angeles; the estranged former school 'friend' wanting $500,000 to send her ten-year-old daughter to Mexico for cancer treatment when Luella knew there was nothing that could be done for the poor child. And each time Luella wondered this: why should she? Why the hell *should* she?

And now Fergus Miller, on their romantic holiday to Fiji. As if the Millers has *just happened* to turn up at the same resort, and *just happened* to have an enticing business proposition at the ready. Christ, they must think Luella was born yesterday. It's so very tedious but, sadly, not remotely unexpected.

It amuses her, really. Why on God's green earth would Luella invest her money in some unreliable financial scheme invented by a man who looks like he cannot look after his own health, let alone that of a fledgling business? And frankly, she is shocked Kitty Miller has it in her to fly all the way to Fiji to beg for a handout. The Millers' investment in their money-scrounging scheme has been sizeable, she'll give them that – six stars sizeable – and it is for this reason and this reason only that she will not deny Benedict the pleasure of his old chum's company tonight. But tomorrow she'll insist they shake off the hapless Millers.

Luella stubs out the cigarette on a clam shell embedded in the seawall and lets the butt, smeared with bronze lipstick, drop to the ground – partly because there is no ashtray but also, and more importantly, because she is paying for people to clean up after her.

She gets up and makes her way back to the bar, enjoying the eyes on her as she moves her hips slowly, like a model on a catwalk. And as she does, she comes face to face with Kitty, who is holding up a jug of kava and wearing a smile.

Luella's eyes narrow. What has happened, she wonders, to make Kitty Miller so chipper? Has Benedict offered them a lifeline? Perhaps he has vowed to *talk to Luella* or to *take a quick look at the business plan* to placate his pathetic old pal? Or perhaps the Millers have simply popped their disappointment on hold, hoping for another chance to bring up the loan when they perceive Luella to be more drunk or simply more amenable. *Fat chance,* thinks Luella. She never loses control. Never.

'Anyone for a little top-up?' asks Kitty. 'You must try the kava, Luella. It's very unusual, but apparently it really loosens you up.'

Ah, she was correct then.

Luella takes an empty water glass because she draws the line at coconut shells and holds it aloft for Kitty to serve her the kava. She raises it to the group. 'Evidently I need loosening up,' she says.

'Oh, golly, no, I didn't mean . . .' The other woman's cheeks redden. 'I just meant it loosens one up in *general* . . .'

'It's certainly got a kick to it,' coughs Benedict.

'Hallucinogenic,' says Fergus. 'The Fijians love it. They drink it every night. Get the roots of the tree from the mainland. It's a bit of a ritual, like us Londoners going down to the boozer for a pint or five.'

Kitty pokes her bottom lip with a cocktail stick she's acquired from somewhere. 'My lips feel numb,' she whines. 'Is that meant to happen? I hope I'm not having a stroke.'

Benedict laughs. 'That's what happens. Then after about fifteen minutes, the happy vibes start, and then it really kicks in and you get a proper high. Apparently, it's a kind of anaesthetic feel, a bit like heroin.'

Kitty looks alarmed. 'Golly. Is it even legal?'

'Of course,' snaps Fergus. 'Would they serve it in a resort like this otherwise? It's harmless. It's a *plant*.'

'So is opium,' snips Luella. *You stupid man.*

Benedict snorts with laughter, and Fergus glowers. He holds his sizeable stomach with his hand and grimaces. Luella, pleased with her opium observation and her husband's overt amusement, surveys her companions now as they sniff and sip the kava.

'*Bula.*' The barman sets another jug on the table. 'You like the kava?'

'Oh yes, Joji,' says Kitty with a hiccup. 'But, um, how long until the effects wear off?'

'Not until tomorrow,' he says. 'But don't worry, it will make you sleep well.'

Kitty frowns. 'Well, it's certainly making me need the little girls' room,' she says.

She gets up from the table, and as she does, she knocks an empty champagne glass onto the floor. It shatters, and glass shards scatter under the chairs.

'Oh, for Christ's sake, Kitty,' snaps Fergus.

'I'm so sorry, Joji.' Kitty winces, ignoring her husband, as though she's used to being chastised. 'I'll clean it up!'

'No worries, Mrs Miller.' The waiter turns towards the bar. 'I will do it. Don't touch the glass, please.'

Kitty ignores him and bends down to pick up the shards, then deposits them on the table.

'Didn't you hear the man? Just *leave* it,' says Fergus. 'He said he'd deal with it.' He motions a thumb towards the barman's retreating back and puts his hand out to stop Kitty, just as his wife brings up a large, curved shard coloured with red wine sediment.

'Fuck!' Fergus exclaims and turns over his palm. It is a clean cut, about an inch wide.

Luella rolls her eyes. These nauseating people! 'I hope you've had a tetanus shot,' she says. 'God only knows what kind of germs there are in the water here.'

'It's exceptionally clean water,' says Benedict in a tone that is rather too abrupt for Luella's liking. 'It is filtered by reverse osmosis.'

'Even so . . .' The panicked little mouse stands up. 'Come on, Fergie. Let's take you to the doctor's room to get you looked at. You'll need some antiseptic.'

'It's just a scratch,' mumbles Fergus.

'Surely the doctor's office will be closed at this time of night,' says Benedict. 'It doesn't look too bad, but you should probably put something on it. Perhaps chuck some alcohol on?'

'Yes. I was about to suggest that.' Kitty makes Fergus cup his palm and pours on the kava.

'Yow!' yells Fergus. 'That'll do the trick!' He dabs his palm with a paper napkin.

'Seriously?' Luella can't quite believe her eyes. 'That stuff's been strained through a washcloth . . .'

Joji returns with a brush that looks like it's made of palm leaves – which Luella imagines isn't that effectual, but whatever – and begins to sweep the glass into a steel dustpan.

'A large plaster, please, Joji, if you have one,' Benedict says to the barman, who nods and retreats again with the collection of shards.

'Are you all right, Fergie?' Kitty coos.

'I am fine,' Fergus slurs like the seasoned alcoholic Luella has deduced he most certainly is with his ruddy face and *that* belly. 'Absolutely peachy.'

Luella watches him as he pushes the table back and stands on the spot, wobbling. The sweat on his brow is rather excessive, even for this particularly humid night.

She and Benedict exchange glances: Benedict's apologetic and Luella's despairing.

'You sure you're OK, Fergus, mate?' asks Benedict. He leans forward in his chair and holds an arm out instinctively as Fergus lurches forward and falls towards the square table, his face perilously close to the ornamental candle in the centre.

'Fergie?' The wife's voice is shrill. She leans over her husband, her face right up in his.

His fist contracts into a claw as he grips at his chest.

'Fergus?' Kitty cries again as if she is demented.

Luella's hand flies up to her mouth.

Kitty turns to the bar area, arms flailing. 'Somebody help him – somebody *help* him!' she cries as the table slides to the side and her husband falls, motionless, to the floor with an almighty thud.

18

Thomasina

Thomasina wonders for a moment if she's walked into some kind of weird murder mystery party. A man lies motionless on the mahogany tiles of the bar floor, while a group of people, dressed up to the nines, stand glued to the spot with colourful cocktails and open mouths. She doesn't remember seeing *that* on offer on the entertainment tab of the website.

She went to a murder mystery party once in Cornwall, when she was living in the UK: *Titanic*-style, a dead maid lying on the parquetry flooring with fake blood all over her white shirt, eyes open. It was fun, drunken.

The scene in front of her now is also drunken, but it is in no way fun, and it takes only a second for her to realise this is no amateur dramatics society production.

A woman falls to her knees, her shrill voice yelling, 'Help him! Oh my God, *help him!*' and 'Fergus wake up! Oh God, wake up, Fergus *please!*'

It takes Thomasina a moment to realise it is the woman from the beach, Kitty, the one who didn't know about Wim Hof. It seems her husband or partner or whatever he is to her has had a heart attack. Got to be his heart, looking at the size of him – he isn't exactly a walking picture of health. The poor woman's Sunday-school smile has been replaced by a look of despair. She pulls at her hair, her eyes darting here, there and everywhere, helpless.

Thomasina momentarily parks the fact she is here to settle old scores, because even she draws the line at confronting the enemy when a man lies dying – or dead – on the ground. Besides, she has waited this long to even out the playing field, hasn't she? What's a few more minutes in the grand scheme of things?

She takes a step forward, considers jumping in to help. She helped a guy at Wategos Beach one time when he had a heart attack in the surf. She pulled him in on her board, and, God, it was hard because he was huge – tall and muscular and not the usual candidate for heart issues – but she did it: she got him onto the sand and gave him mouth-to-mouth as they waited for the ambulance. He made it, she learnt later – went home to his family, a wife and four children. Got stents put in, good as new.

But now, here in the bar, someone has beaten her to it, hopscotched her procrastination. A woman in a khaki boiler suit and sandals, weaving through the group of assembled guests, all blonde hair flowing and bangles jingling. She falls onto her knees beside Kitty.

'*Je suis médecin*,' she shouts in French. Then she clarifies in a thick French accent: 'I am a doctor.'

She waves her arms to denote that she needs space. '*Rapidement!*' She turns to the wife. 'Please. A name?'

The wife is confused and says, 'Kitty,' before simpering, 'I mean *Fergus*. His name is Fergus. Fergus Miller. Please help him! He has high blood pressure . . .'

'Fergus?' the woman shouts in the man's ear, and there is nothing delicate about it. 'I am Dr Sofie Barthélemy. I am an emergency doctor.'

She puts her ear to the man called Fergus's chest and listens. At the same time, she holds his left wrist in her own left hand and counts.

Thomasina would probably not have picked Sofie to save her own life because she is so waifish, a bona fide hipster. She looks like she'd be more at home bagging up organic vegetables in Carrefour.

'*Rien*,' the doctor says and then seems to remember once again that her audience is mainly English-speaking. 'There is no pulse. Please, some space . . .'

She waves her arms again, and the gawping crowd of guests step back. Hands hover over mouths. Faces are pale with horror. Drinks remain un-sipped. Thomasina realises she is doing the same;

her fingers splay across her lips, and her eyes watch on, wide, as Sofie Barthélemy begins chest compressions. Her tiny arms are totally misleading – the woman is a powerhouse.

Fergus's white belly wobbles, and his shirt rises slightly with every pump, and still the French doctor pummels away, counting in French. When she gets to '*trente*', she pulls her long hair around to the side, bends low and breathes into his mouth twice.

A Fijian woman leans forward and ties up the doctor's hair with a scrunchie as she positions her hands, fingers intertwined, on Fergus's sternum and starts pumping again.

Kitty begins to wail now. 'Why's it not working?' she yells. 'What's happening?' She turns and falls into the chest of the hotel manager. 'Somebody *help* him!'

Thomasina looks away from the scene and casts her eyes around the room. She can't look anymore. She sees a half-full wine bottle – Australian Shiraz – and a used, empty glass on the vacated dinner table to her left. She helps herself to a glass, wiping the lipstick-stained rim with her finger and thumb first. She can't do death without some kind of anaesthetic.

She looks up to see a staff member watching her, the man who took the scuba-boat out. The other guy called him Filipe. Their eyes had locked at the welcome meeting.

'Oh,' she says and feels her skin flush with embarrassment. *Caught out.* He holds up a hand and smiles gravely. *Your secret's safe with me,* the look says. Thomasina nods a grateful *thank you.*

A man in a pink Hawaiian shirt spins into the bar area and runs over to the fallen man and the doctor.

'Dr Pau Marama,' Thomasina hears him tell the French doctor.

She looks up between breaths, before standing up to let the Fijian medic take over. Dr Marama, with fresh energy, plunges violently into Fergus's fat-covered sternum. '*Dua. Rua. Tolu. Va . . .*' He counts to what Thomasina presumes is thirty in Fijian and plunges two decisive, strong breaths into Fergus's lungs, before starting over.

Five, maybe ten minutes later, Dr Marama, whose cheery printed floral shirt is utterly out of place given the gravity of the situation, stands up, steps away from Fergus, and instead looks at his watch.

'Time of death: 9.50 p.m.,' he tells Mr Roko. He turns to the wife, who sobs into her husband's motionless chest. 'I'm so very sorry, Mrs Miller,' he says.

19

Luella

She has just witnessed a man dying right in front of her, and it has disturbed Luella to her core. She will never get over seeing this – never! Almost as disturbing is Kitty Miller, who is on her knees beside the body of her husband, rocking back and forth and screeching like a stuck pig. It is all too much to bear!

'Oh, Benedict!' Luella gropes for his arm and takes deep breaths: in through the nose, out through the mouth. This is not how her holiday was meant to go.

She feels something she assumes must be anxiety: a quickening of her heart, a clammy sensation on her palms. For a few seconds, Luella feels she needs an exit, an oar to grab to help her from the quicksand. Her knees buckle slightly.

'Are you OK, my darling?' Benedict leans in close, partly in a measure of affection, but mainly, Luella assumes, so as to be heard over the infernal sounds of Kitty Miller's labouring howls.

The woman is feral. She screams her husband's name over and over: 'Fergus! Fergus! Fergus! Fergus!'

Luella wants to block her ears and shout: *Make it stop! I don't want to hear it!*

The Fijian doctor steps towards Kitty and attempts to lead her away, presumably to get her out of the vicinity of her dead spouse and offer her something for the shock. Luella would like some of that something, too. A little Valium, perhaps. She wraps her arms around herself, suddenly aware of the thin fabric of her lamé dress. This is all so awful for *her!*

'Come on,' Dr Marama tells Kitty Miller as he leads her away by the hand. 'Come to the medical room and lie down. We will look after your husband.'

Look after? thinks Luella. *We're a bit past that.*

Kitty shakes her head. 'No,' she screams. 'I won't leave him!'

The French doctor in her cheap linen jump-suit kneels beside her and takes Kitty's hand to pull her gently up.

'No,' Kitty cries, but there is less conviction in her tone now.

A voice in Luella's head tells her to step forward and to intervene, to lead Kitty Miller away, but she does not do it because the one telling her not to do it is stronger. Instead, she stares ahead, Benedict's arm warm on the small of her back.

Sofie Barthélemy – who Luella notices is slim and incredibly striking in a sort of anaemic way – seems to sense her gaze and looks up, now holding Kitty Miller's hands. The Frenchwoman's eyes lock onto Luella's for a moment too long, as if she is trying to communicate with her, to share in the shock and grief of this heinous moment with Luella, a stranger. It is unsettling, *unnerving* somehow.

Luella blinks pointedly and looks away. She can barely soothe herself, let alone pacify this woman.

'Darling?' Benedict says again. 'I asked if you are all right?'

Luella pouts. Of course she is not all right! She has seen a man drop dead in front of her eyes and witnessed the horror of mouth-to-mouth and chest compressions, and it's all rather confronting. She would like to point out that she was almost given the same treatment yesterday by the incompetent diver. It was nearly her, this spectacle – except she is now the voyeur, and so no, she is not *all right* – she is really rather shaky and could do with a sizeable nightcap. She does not wish to hang around here while they do whatever they will do to Fergus Miller now he's dead. It's all rather unsanitary. And in this heat, too!

Luella watches as Kitty Miller is led away by both doctors, her face red and blotchy. Kitty casts her eyes back over her shoulder as she walks, her face contorting with agony as she sees the lifeless corpse of Fergus on the floor.

Luella closes her eyes. 'I'd like to go back to the room,' she says, and Benedict nods. 'With a drink.' She makes towards the bar.

'I don't think they're serving drinks right now, in light of . . .' Benedict says. 'Come on – I'll fix you something in the bure.'

Together, they make their way through the gathering of guests and away from the body, which the head cleaner – Uma? Iona? *Una?* – is in the process of covering with a white sheet that looks suspiciously like a tablecloth.

Luella lets herself be led away, under the thatch of the bar and into the night – and that is when she sees her.

She recognises the long hair, the dark skin, the lips that curl up at the sides – not in a smile but a smirk. The small black mole in the corner of her mouth that's always been there. *It's not a mole, Luella – it's a beauty spot!* And the misleading brown eyes that tell everyone a different story to the one Luella knows.

She feels an unwelcome shiver trickle from the nape of her neck to the very tip of her coccyx. She blinks, lest she is imagining it. Isn't that what the kava does, after all? Makes you hallucinate, see things that aren't there? And the stress of the dead man – together, these things are forcing her mind to play tricks on her!

But no. Thomasina is indeed here, holding a glass of red wine with a faint lipstick stain on the rim, her head tilted to the side and an unpleasant smile on her face. Lashes still long, a few more lines around her eyes perhaps, but unmistakably Thomasina.

'Hello, Luella,' Thomasina says, sarcasm sweating from her pores. 'How *are* you?' She looks over at the bar. 'Not at all well by the looks of it!'

Luella does not like surprises, and this is one of the worst – especially given she has just witnessed the traumatic death of an old friend of her husband's in front of her very eyes. How dare Thomasina intrude on this moment of shock and grief? She feels her nostrils flare, as hot anger trumps the shock of Fergus's demise and rises up through her neck to flood her brain. *This is not happening.*

'What the *hell* . . . ?'

'Well now,' Thomasina says. 'That's not a very nice way to speak to your big sister, is it?'

'Thomasina, hello.' Benedict steps forward to envelop Thomasina in an awkward hug, and Luella feels a sense of confusion. Why is he treating Thomasina in this familiar manner, as if he has spoken to her before, when in fact they've definitely never met? And why does her sister shrink at his touch as if she thinks Benedict finds her attractive, as if he's *pawing* at her? She should be so lucky! Pretty, yes, but groomed? Refined? Heavens, no.

'Let me rephrase it then,' Luella spits. 'What brings you to this extortionately expensive luxury island, Thomasina, when you don't have the funds to pay for it? The same island I *just happen* to be on, enjoying a well-earned break?'

Thomasina fakes surprise, gazing dramatically between Luella and Benedict – the same thing she used to do as a child when the pair of them were hauled in front of their mother for arguing.

'Oh,' Thomasina exclaims, eyes wide, mouth puckered in a pout. 'Didn't he tell you?' She nods towards Benedict.

'Tell me what?' Luella looks up at Benedict. She hates herself for taking the bait. This is what her sister *does!*

'You really don't know?' Thomasina's accent has lost any semblance of British public schooling since she moved to the Southern Hemisphere after Daddy's death. It is now has a distinctly Australian inflection, an uncouth varietal of speech that Luella does not like. Sentences that should have full-stops at the end now sound like questions.

Thomasina looks at Benedict with a smug smile.

'Tell me what?' Luella demands again. If there is one thing she hates, it's being kept in the dark.

Benedict clears his throat as if he is about to make a speech, and Thomasina laughs.

'Oh, that is the sweetest thing. He is *scared* of you, Luella!' She turns to Benedict. 'Are you scared of your wife, Benedict? Are you worried she'll make you sit on the naughty step?'

Luella feels a sense of fear. 'Have you two . . . *met*?'

Thomasina folds her arms and fixes her smug gaze on Luella. 'Get with the programme, Sis. Benedict here emailed me out of the blue and invited me to tag along on your lovely holiday, because he thought we could make amends, to stop us being "estranged". He did it out of the goodness of his heart, bless him. Tracked me down and invited me to be your VIP. And I must say, I could get used to this. The cocktails are just divine . . .'

Luella feels the anger turning from simmer to boil. She stares up at her mountain of a husband. No, no. Benedict wouldn't do that. He wouldn't *dare*.

'You think you're going to convince me that Benedict asked you to come here and you just jumped at the opportunity? No chance. What is it you really want, Thomasina? Or shall I just guess . . . ?'

'Luella,' says Benedict quietly. '*Please*.'

'How else would I afford all of this, if it wasn't for your darling husband?' Thomasina opens her arms out wide and gestures around her: at the sea, the vast reception area, the stylish bar that's now empty of all guests except a dead one, whose head and feet are bookends at each end of the white sheet. 'Although, if I'd known I was about to walk onto the set of *Death in Paradise*, I wouldn't have bothered.'

Luella's pulse bangs like the crescendo of 'Bohemian Rhapsody'. 'Benedict?' she asks. 'Did you invite her here?'

Benedict sighs and reaches forward, takes Luella's hands. She knows then that what Thomasina is saying is true: he did invite her. He invited her only sister, her half-sister, the sister she hates – the *disinherited* sister – to join them on their romantic holiday, for some reason she cannot even begin to fathom. She pulls her hands away from his.

'I did it for you,' he says, as if he can read her thoughts, her immediate need for an answer. 'I thought that in a tranquil location, somewhere neutral and beautiful, you might be able to sort things out between the two of you. She' – he gestures at Thomasina – 'is all you have left now, Luella. Life is too short. A man *died* tonight.' He runs his hands through his hair. 'A man I knew.'

Luella's nostrils flare. 'You didn't know he was going to die when you booked her ticket though, did you?' She stares him down. Benedict has betrayed her. She doesn't care that Thomasina shares her DNA; she doesn't care if her only sibling is alive or dead, because she knows *exactly* why Thomasina is here, and it's the same reason everyone else wants to cosy up to her! Her sister must have been rubbing her hands together when she got Benedict's email. A chance to get her hands on Luella's cash.

'It was business class, too,' chirps Thomasina. 'Lovely service on Fiji Airways. Unbeatable . . .'

Luella feels her neck burning with anger.

'I'm sorry,' Benedict pleads. 'Truly I am, but I did it for both of you. I just wanted the two of you to get together and realise that a lifetime of hatred isn't worth it. You are more similar than you both think . . .'

'How the hell would you know?' snorts Luella.

'Similar? Oh *please* . . .' Thomasina shakes her head. She turns to Benedict. 'You told me she would be open to talking,' she snaps. 'But she's the same as she's always been. This is so screwed-up. *She* is so screwed-up.' She turns down the fork of the path that leads to the garden bure.

Luella cannot resist. 'I'm not so screwed-up that I managed to get myself left out of the will, though, am I?' She turns down the other path to her sister, towards the pool bar, while Benedict hovers between the two forks. The satisfaction she gets from the retort is like a tab of speed. 'You only have yourself to blame.'

Thomasina turns back, fixes her eyes on Luella in a way that is most unnerving. 'Drop dead, Luella,' she says, and then she turns her back and walks away, towards the bures.

Luella continues down the path, kicks her heels off.

'Luella!' Benedict calls after her. 'Luella, *please*.'

'No!' She spins around. 'How dare you? I will never forgive you for this.'

He does not move. He will not follow her now; she knows this. He will go to the beach, and he will wait there until he has ascertained she is calm, and then he will find her and try to make amends. It is always this way when they argue, Benedict the peacekeeper – Luella hates this about him.

Luella stomps towards the pool bar, still desperate for a drink. She looks around for someone to make her one and when she doesn't find someone, she steps inside the bar area and unscrews the lid of the Diplomático bottle and pours herself a glass. *Fuck it,* she thinks. *I'm paying enough for this place, aren't I?* She downs it in one and slams down the glass on the marble bar top.

Luella rejoins the main path and turns right, following it towards her bure. The straps of her patent designer heels swing from her fingertips as she navigates the cool cobbles. Something rustles in the bush beside her, and she feels irrationally spooked. *What is this place?* She wants to be back in London, where everything is easier and she's not surrounded by dead guests and incompetent hotel staff, where she can get a Goddam soya latte that doesn't taste like puke. Where there is no psychopathic sister and no disloyal, do-gooding husband.

They will leave early, she decides. Yes, this is her plan: she will suck it up until after New Year's Eve (because if she leaves now, what will she tell everyone when she gets back home? That she spent New Year on a *plane* instead of in paradise?) and then they will pack up and head home to the UK, and Thomasina will crawl back into whatever hippy-infested hole in Australia she climbed out of.

Luella reaches her bure and pushes the little white card against the door panel, and a green light and a single beep welcomes her inside, where the air is crisp and cool. The corners of the bedcover on both sides have been turned down, the curtains have been fully closed and the lamps beside the bed turned on to give the room a dim orange glow. She puts down her heels and peels the turban off her head. Her hair tumbles around her shoulders like caramel-coloured silk. She lifts her hands and tousles it, holds onto her temples for a moment and hisses, 'Shit! Shit!' How dare Benedict do this to her?

Luella sighs long and deep, casts an eye around for more menthol cigarettes on the coffee table, but she cannot see any. She will try her suitcase when she is undressed, and when she finds a pack, she will smoke every single last one here in the room right in front of the little sign that tells her: *We are made of thatch. Please don't smoke.*

Oh, jog on!

She pulls off her gold clip-on earrings and puts them on the glass-topped bedside table – and that's when she sees it: a piece of notepaper with *Loloma Resort & Spa* printed on the top.

It wasn't there before, she is sure; she recalls seeing a notepad in the dressing-table drawer, not beside the bed. She leans in, studies the writing. The words are in black ink, but there is no pen nearby – not one that she can see when she casts an eye around the room, anyway. The handwriting, which is unrecognisable, is strangely childlike and purposefully clear: each letter is inscribed in bold, block capitals.

She takes in the words and feels her hair lift off her neck, an unpleasant shiver whisper across the tops of her bare shoulders.

It reads simply: *YOUR TIME'S UP.*

20
Una

Una stands with her feet buried in the cold sand where the beach meets the concrete of the resort and watches the body of Fergus Miller, encased in a black body bag, being carried to a boat by two sombre members of the Fijian police force. The silence as Fergus leaves the island is disconcerting (departing guests usually leave to the goodbye song) and so is the presence of policemen in uniform at midnight.

She wonders what these men had been doing before they got the call, before they were sent to Loloma Island Resort to retrieve the lifeless body of an unfortunate English holidaymaker. Had they been in bed with lovers or wives? Drinking kava? Playing cards? Had they been desk-bound at Nadi police station, doing admin, coffee cups full to the brim to stop their eyelids from sliding shut? Did they tut when they got the call and learnt they would have to leave the mainland and head an hour across the ocean? And they *did* have to come, because Loloma Island Resort does not have a designated place to store corpses, and tomorrow morning, the sun will bake this little island, and death will become pungent and suffocating. Just like the hapless mongoose Una found rotting behind Bure Two.

It is nothing new, a guest dying. She's seen it four times before: two failing hearts, one stroke, one drowned. But Fergus Miller was the youngest by at least fifteen years, and now here he is, making his final journey in a plastic ziplock bag. It is tragic, and Una feels for Kitty Miller. She has been there herself, facing the death of a loved one, albeit not so suddenly, and the memories of that cannot help but wash over her as she stands here looking on. She feels an overwhelming urge to comfort Kitty Miller and to tell her it will be all right – that grief does takes time but that it abates eventually. Not fully, but a little. She would do it, if it was at all appropriate to approach a guest in such a frank and personal way.

Una waves off the boat as it turns around and begins its return journey to Nadi, although this time to the city hospital and not the airport. Even though Dr Marama suspects Fergus Miller died of a heart attack and has told the police as much, an autopsy will likely be performed in order to release the body to the local Fijian undertakers. From there, Fergus Miller will be buried either in Fiji or embalmed and repatriated to the UK.

Una makes her way up to reception, where Mr Roko is furiously typing into the computer.

'Una!' He smiles wearily. 'Thank you for staying up. Could I ask you to do one more thing? It is rather sensitive . . .'

'What is it?'

'Could you check on Mrs Miller on your way back to the staff village? Pau Marama is dealing with a nasty infected mosquito bite in Bure Seven, so I'd be grateful if you could swing past and perhaps see if she needs anything.'

'Of course,' Una says as she makes to leave. Perhaps she will offer some words of comfort to the bereaved Englishwoman after all. But first, she must speak to her boss about a matter that's closer to home. 'Mr Roko? Jose?'

'Yes, Una?'

'It's about Sailasa.' She needs to be confident the service receipt from the dive shop and the waiver signed by Luella St John-Gray are sufficient to save Sailasa from any fallout from the incident on the beach yesterday.

'What about him, Una?'

'You know Sailasa is a good boy,' Una says firmly. 'He would never cut corners.'

'I know that,' Roko says, his voice pained. 'I know that, Una. I will try my best for him, but if the woman makes a formal complaint to management about him, my hands will be tied, due diligence or not. Who knows – perhaps Mrs St John-Gray will let her complaint go after what happened tonight. There is nothing like a sudden death to put things in perspective and make people reassess their . . . priorities. We will just have to wait and see.'

Una bites the skin on the inside of her cheek.

'Look,' Roko says, his hand on her shoulder, seeming to sense that she is unsatisfied with his response, 'I promise I will do my best for Sailasa, but at the end of the day, I have to act appropriately.'

Una swallows back the urge to challenge her boss. What does he mean by that? That he may need to let Sailasa go? Christina Cole's story takes seed in her mind once again: the young woman packing her bags, a lost diamond earring, a lost job and then a lost baby. *The guest is always right.*

Una turns away before she says something she will regret. She makes her way up the beachfront pathway, almost in a daze with tiredness and emotion. The torches have not yet burnt out; they still throw orange light at her feet and will do until the early hours. The resort is quiet, eerily so, as if the death of Fergus Miller has cast a spell over the place, throwing everyone into a state of emotional exhaustion and willing them to sleep.

Following her instructions, as she always does, Una heads towards Bure Three, Kitty Miller's room. At this end of the island, away from the heart of the resort, the sea is wilder, and Una listens as swell mounts rock. Then come the voices. They get louder as she approaches. She hears a woman's distant cry and the louder sound of a man's voice trying to soothe her.

She quickens her step. 'Hello?' she calls. 'Mrs Miller?'

Benedict St John-Gray steps out of shadows of Kitty Miller's veranda, and Una almost jumps out of her skin.

'Oh, thank God,' he says. 'Una. Can you help me? I was just on my way back to my bure, and I heard her crying. Well, it was more like wailing than crying. I knocked, and she didn't answer. I wonder if you might check on her, Una?'

Una is confused. Was Benedict St John-Gray attempting to call to Kitty Miller through the door? She looks into his face. The smell of alcohol seeps from his skin.

'I was out walking,' he says. 'My wife and I, we . . . we had a disagreement.'

'I understand,' Una says, although she doesn't.

'Fergus was a friend of mine, you see,' he says. He runs a hand through his hair, agitated. 'I feel partly responsible for her, for Kitty. I mean, I barely know her, but . . .'

'That is very kind,' Una tells him without conviction. 'Now, if you wouldn't mind letting me just get to the door, I think it's best that I go in and check on her myself.' Sidestepping the man, she knocks gently. 'Mrs Miller? Mrs Miller? Is everything all right?'

'Tell him to go away,' Kitty Miller calls out through sobs. '*Please!*'

Una opens the door with a bleep and a flash of a green light and steps inside. She pulls the door to almost-closed and whispers through the crack. 'You can go now, Mr St John-Gray. Thank you for your concern.'

The man hesitates, as if debating what to do next.

'Thank you,' Una says, firmly now. 'I will send for help.'

Benedict St John-Gray scratches his chin and, seemingly reluctantly, turns back towards his own bure. Una watches him leave, puzzled.

On the bed, lit by a small reading light, is Kitty Miller, changed now into a nightdress. She is small in the middle of the giant bed, and all around her are her husband's clothes: shirts, swimwear, shorts. She holds a shirt in both her hands as if she has been smelling it.

'Mrs Miller?' Una says. 'I just came to check on you. Is there anything I can get for you? Are you hungry?'

The woman doesn't speak at first, just stares at her hands, as if she is viewing them for the first time. And then she looks up at Una. Her vibrant eyes are now pale, watery.

'I want to die,' she says, calmly now. 'Do you hear me? I just want to *die*.'

Una picks up a glass of water on the bedside table and hands it to Kitty. 'Perhaps have a sip? I'll refill it for you shortly.'

'Thank you, Una,' she whispers. 'I just want to close my eyes and for it to all be gone.'

Kitty Miller turns over, and Una sits with her until she is asleep, which is not long. Ten minutes, maybe a little more. Then she gets up from the side of the bed she has respectfully perched upon and folds up the pile of clothes that are strewn on it, empties the bathroom bin and wipes the sink – little things that are her job, of course, but that will also make a difference to Kitty Miller when she wakes up, small gestures that may make what she is going through just a fraction more bearable.

She sees two masks on the coffee table, one lovingly created with feathers and sequins. It's interesting, she thinks, how the guests have stored their masks. Sofie Barthélemy's delicate silver mask sits on top of the fridge, Luella St John-Gray's on the hook in the wardrobe ('Don't put it just anywhere,' Una heard her tell her husband. 'It's Treacy. Philip must be *hung!*'), then Kitty Miller's magnificent homemade affair propped with rather less ceremony on the coffee table alongside a pirate mask she assumes belonged to the late Mr Miller. Una feels she should move them somehow, or at the very least one of them, so they are not a reminder to Kitty when she wakes up that she is not one of two anymore, no longer half of a pair.

Una has of course never been married herself, but she understands grief better than anyone, and how the smallest of items or memories can trigger a plunge into despair. She remembers seeing one of her sister Adelina's favourite hair clips soon after she died, and the pain was too much to bear. She barely knows Kitty Miller, but she feels for the woman, feels a connection that comes from knowing the agony of intense grief – those desolate first days when nothing, not one solitary thing, provides comfort.

Una moves the pirate mask to the shelf under the coffee table before creeping out of the bure and closing the door quietly behind her.

She hears the voices before the door is closed, and, even though she is loath to listen in on a lovers' spat, she cannot help it. Benedict's voice is thunderous, and although the words he says are tender, their delivery seems fraught with angst, a kind of desperation that seems to whip up the breeze and carry them from the secluded veranda of Bure One to where Una now stands, two bungalows along.

'Listen to me!' he says in a loud whisper.

'Leave me alone!' It is Luella, making no attempt to lower her voice. 'What were you thinking, asking *her* here?'

'We'll just get rid of her . . .' Benedict is louder now, rising to his wife's level.

'How? She's not going to leave voluntarily. I'm going to tell her to get the fuck off this island.'

'We'll fix everything tomorrow. I'm right behind you, darling. We're a *team*.'

A sob. 'I hate you.'

The reply: 'I love you. You're my *raison d'être*.'

A slap. A gasp. A sob. 'Oh, Benedict,' says Luella. 'I'm sorry.'

'It's all going to work out, darling.' Benedict's voice is loud and clear. 'Please. You need to trust me.'

Silence falls now, and Una imagines man embracing wife, holding her face to his chest to absorb her sobs. Who are these people? And why does the island seem to be rotting, bleeding with them on it?

She hurries along the path towards the staff quarters and, once on her bed, falls into the deepest of sleeps, until vivid dreams of dead bodies on square tile floors and drowning women and her own sister, Adelina, lying cold in the funeral home cruelly wrench her awake, her throat aching with suppressed emotion and her body drenched in cold beads of sweat.

SUNDAY 31 DECEMBER
NEW YEAR'S EVE

Cocktail of the Day:
Sweet Revenge

(Bourbon, vanilla chai, coffee)

21

Kitty

Kitty turns onto her side, allows her eyes to adjust to the cylindrical glimpse of ocean through the crack in the linen curtains. She watches as the waves curl ever so slightly to the left in the breeze. She wonders what time it is. There is no one on the water that she can see – at least not in the tiny gap she is privy to through the glass front of her bure door. It could be 8 a.m. or 4 p.m. for all she knows.

Her head is thick, as if she is hungover; a dull thud beats inside her temples in time with her pulse. Her mouth is dry, the corners collecting a sticky white residue, and her throat aches from screaming her dead husband's name.

Kitty hears the scrape of a rake on the pathway outside and flinches. It is the gardeners raking up the fallen palm leaves, the mandarin-orange leaves of the Beach Cordia and the blood-red hibiscus flowers (fresh blood, not old). This is the kind of attention to detail, the touches they are paying for. *They*? Except Kitty is no longer a *they* but an *I*.

She closes her eyes and sees it: the toad race, the smashed glass, the bloody hand, the kava thrown on the flesh of Fergus's palm. The wobble of his body as he stands up, his hand above his heart, fingers digging into his flesh as if he means to extract this living, beating organ with his own fingernails. The bend of his body at the waist as it falls onto the table like a sun lounger collapsing in on itself, folding in half. Fergus on the cold floor, shirt open to reveal a pale, motionless chest. A Frenchwoman. A pair of tiny hands kneading at the fat on Fergus's chest like dough. And at the heart of it all, at the very centre of the commotion, of life switching to death with the click of a finger: Luella St John-Gray, impassive.

And now it is New Year's Eve, and Kitty is alone in the world. She will have to learn self-sufficiency. She will need to find herself as just Kitty Miller and not *Mrs* Kitty Miller the wife, and how will she do that? She can barely remember the person she was before she married Fergus. She doesn't know what she likes and what she dislikes anymore – it has been *they* for as long as Kitty can remember.

She rubs her eyes. She wants to sleep, to go to a place where her brain is switched off and her mind is not visited by the corpse of her husband, motionless in a hospital morgue.

Oh, Fergus! *Throwing a pity party, Kitty?* he'd say if he was here now. *For God's sake, woman, get out of bed and stop brooding. It's nauseating.*

Kitty laughs bitterly. Perhaps there is some part of her that feels a small sense of *relief* – relief that she won't have to pretend to smile when she's the butt of her husband's jokes, that she will no longer need to pretend to be proud of his offensive 'banter'. The guilt these potent feelings bring hangs off her like a lead jacket.

'Oh, Fergus,' she says again as she turns away and blocks out the light. 'I'm so sorry. You didn't deserve it. You really didn't.'

22

Thomasina

Thomasina chooses the cushioned chair on the terrace facing the sea not because she is in the mood for contemplation but rather because it is the only place in the resort with phone reception. Ignoring the fact it is frowned upon to check one's phone here in paradise, she scrolls blindly through social media, checks the weather forecast for the next five days along with the surf report back home in Byron Bay, and googles *The 10 most useful words and phrases in Fijian*. The first is *bula*, of course, followed by *kerekere* (please), *vinaka* (thank you) and *moce* (goodbye). She says each of them in turn, lets the words fall off her tongue. She loves the sound of them and the way they somehow comfort her.

Ahead of her, she sees the mother and daughter who travelled to Loloma on the ferry. She hears the teenager say, 'But it's so creepy. What if he haunts us all in our bures?'

Thomasina takes a sip of the latte in front of her. It was going to be a coffee or a Corona. But even though it is late morning and not an unreasonable time of day for a cocktail, she can't quite face it today. Her hangover from last night is a punishment – one not even hair of the dog will fix. She used to be able to fight on through the morning after, but not these days, not now she's entered her forties. As a twenty-something in London, it was all about excess: parties and drugs and living it up. Since moving to Australia, to Byron Bay, her lifestyle has dramatically changed. These days she tempers her (mostly light) boozing with self-care: surfing, yoga, meditation and, recently, the ice baths.

The meditation has always been a challenge. What Thomasina knows about herself is that she finds it confronting to be alone with her thoughts for too long. When her head is quiet and her mind is empty, Luella seizes her chance and leaps into her mind like a steely assassin, even though it's been three years since they last saw one another. When she thinks about her younger sister and considers the bitterness she knows she has locked away inside her, it makes her anxious. She does not want to feel this way, to hate someone. That's probably why she moved to the other side of the world (out of sight, out of mind?) and more specifically to a town where self-development and positive energy thrives – where even the main road sign on the way into town declares: *Cheer up, slow down and chill out.*

Now that she has seen Luella again, she will need to work hard to focus, to not let the bitterness derail her, to weave its hungry way into her psyche like a worm in an apple.

She thinks of Benedict, and her eyes narrow. Why did he really invite her here? He said in his email that Luella missed her, that she wanted to make amends, but it is not a repentant Luella she encountered last night in that brief, toxic moment outside the bar. She doesn't understand it – the email was so persuasive. She can only assume her half-sister's sycophantic husband wanted to score points by seeming to do the right thing. A sort of: *Look! I've invited your long-lost sister here because I care about you* so *much!*

Thomasina shrugs to no one. What does it matter anyway? As it happens, the invitation from Benedict was timed so perfectly that Thomasina jumped at it anyway, because actually, she needed to see Luella for an altogether different reason – one that didn't involve reconciliation.

She puts her phone down on the table and looks out to the beach. Speak of the devil. To her right, a floral kaftan billows in the breeze, and its wearer marches forward with purpose. Luella seems taller than she was last night, more imposing, as if she has drawn her body up for battle. Her face is set in a scowl. She reminds herself to stay calm, tells herself it doesn't have to end badly. She has a chance to try a different approach and perhaps resolve things satisfactorily for both her and her sister.

She steels herself. 'Hello, Luella.'

Luella does not sit, just looms over her in her gaudy kaftan, hands bolted to her hips. 'What are you really doing here?' she snaps. No pleasantries. 'Spit it out.'

There will be no playing nice, evidently. 'What do you think I'm here for?'

'Oh, come now, Thomas. No need to play games.'

When we were kids, the games always ended in tears! So much of life shared. So much love between us once, now only bitterness.

Joji arrives with a drinks menu. '*Bula*, Mrs St John-Gray,' he says. 'A cocktail?'

'Too early for a Corpse Reviver?' Luella glances over at the spot on the floor where Fergus Miller's body lay. She lets out a single peal of laughter. 'Too soon?'

Joji looks horrified but says nothing.

'An espresso with a shot of rum.' Luella pushes the menu into Joji's chest. 'Diplomático.'

Thomasina offers Joji a half smile.

Luella sits down and leans forward, her elbows on the table and her fingers interlinked. 'I am not stupid, Thomasina,' she says evenly. 'The nasty little note that was waiting for me in my room last night has got you *all over* it. Good to see you're as deeply unhinged as ever.'

'What note? I didn't leave you a note.'

'Don't play dumb, Thomasina, darling. You're no angel now, are you?'

'I think your memory is a little warped, Luella.'

Thomasina knows who is the unhinged one here. She never said she didn't play her hand badly in the past. She didn't say she wasn't to blame for some of the bad blood between them, but she was never *evil*. She was never mean.

'Things change,' she tells Luella. 'People change.'

'Well, not really, Thomas, because here you are, following me to a ludicrously pricey island and allowing my husband to pay for you, which by default means I'm the one footing the bill. And then writing me twisted little love letters to help me get to sleep! You've always been a little obsessed with me, haven't you, Thomas?

Perhaps you could make it your New Year's resolution to move on with your life.'

Thomasina smiles and shakes her head. She must be insane if she thought for one moment that Luella might be reasonable. She studies her sister's face, sees the cheekbones puffed out with filler, the plumped-up lips, fine lines eradicated with Botox at the age of only thirty-six. Despite the lack of general expression, the smugness is somehow still there, covering her skin like an expensive foundation.

'So, now you've demonstrated that you are more than happy to travel for money, let me ask you this . . .' Luella continues. 'How much is it going to take for you to get off this island and get out of my life for good?'

Thomasina feels the anger warming her skin. She looks down to see she has ripped her drinks coaster into tiny little squares. She didn't even realise her hands were moving.

'Come on, Thomas – don't be shy. How much for you to get off the island? *How much?* I'll transfer the funds right now.' She gets out her phone, holds it up to her face. 'What's your price? Name it, because I know that's what you are here for.'

Thomasina sniffs. 'I just want what is rightfully mine, Luella, that's all.'

Luella laughs, and it is an ugly sound. 'And there we have it!'

'You stole from me.' Thomasina feels a familiar bubble of hatred in her chest. It is like a burp she can neither swallow down or release, so that right now it is merely stuck, rigid and aching, above her heart.

'Well, if I did,' Luella chirps, 'there is no one here to concur, is there? It's over three years since Daddy died and my memory isn't what it was! I guess we'll never know, will we?'

'Dad's lawyers would concur.'

'How?' Luella snarls. 'I had power of attorney over Daddy's finances, did I not? In the eyes of the law, you were in charge of his health and I was in charge of his money.'

'And so you saw to it I got *nothing*?'

Luella inspects her nails. 'That's what he wanted.'

'That's a lie, Luella, and you know it.'

'Prove it, then. The law is the law, Thomasina.'

The thing is: Thomasina doesn't want the money – not the pounds in a bank account, not the designer clothes and the hangers-on. She just wants the heirloom she was promised by her mother: the pendant with the single solitaire her stepfather proposed to her mother with. He'd called it the Thomasina Diamond in honour of his new daughter.

'All I want is the necklace, Luella.' She hears the angry tremor in her voice.

'Well, I'm sorry, Thomas, darling, but you can't have it.' She pushes the chair back, stands up and slides on her designer sunglasses. 'Well, as lovely as this chat has been, I have a spa appointment to get to. I hear Ema does a decent shoulder massage. I mean, it's hardly the spa at the Mandarin Oriental, but *when in Rome* and all that.'

Luella walks a few steps away before she stops and turns around. 'If you would like a treatment, please do book in for something. A nice, calming hot stone massage, perhaps? You look as though you need one. My treat, of course.'

Thomasina looks at the marble ashtray in front of her and imagines, for one fleeting second, smashing it into the back of Luella's skull as she walks across the tiled floor towards the beach. Wiping the smug smile off her sister's face. She pictures Luella's body crumbling like a wax candle, sticky blood spilling forth from her skull and pooling around her silken hair, her already pale eyes losing their colour.

She reaches out and lets her fingers caress the cool, grey marble as her younger sister, her last remaining blood relative on earth, picks up her coffee from Joji's rattan drinks tray without a word of thanks and strides purposefully away, her bejewelled kaftan wafting arrogantly in the breeze behind her.

23

Luella

Luella locates Benedict on the beach. A bucket of icy water and a bowl of fresh fruit sits on the table between the loungers, and Luella sets her rum-infused coffee down beside them and slips off her kaftan. Her spa appointment isn't actually until this afternoon, but it was useful to have an excuse to get away from Thomasina.

Benedict turns to her. 'You know how sorry I am,' he says. 'I hate fighting with you. I just wanted the two of you to work it out. I made a huge error of judgement.'

Luella wants to make him beg.

'I love you, Luella, and, like I said last night, I invited her here purely because I know you care about her.'

'I do not!'

'Christ, Luella, you talk about her in your sleep!'

'I do not!'

'You do, darling. Whatever's gone on between you, the fact is Thomasina is your sister . . .'

'*Half*-sister.'

'Half-sister but still your sister. She's your only living relative. Do you really want to be estranged from her forever? I just figured that Fiji is so close to Australia and it would be a chance for the two of you to iron out your differences. Darling, I did it for you.'

'And what do *you* stand to gain from a happy little family reunion, Benedict? Thomasina only came here to try and get near to my money.'

'Luella, we've been over this. I just thought . . .'

'She wants the diamond necklace,' Luella cuts in. 'The one that belonged to Mummy. That's what she's here for.'

'You brought it with you? Darling, I don't think our travel insurance covers—'

'She's greedy. Always has been.'

'Well, it's not as if she can get near to your father's money, darling.'

'*My* money.'

'That's what I meant. Christ, Luella!'

'Well, she could. Everything goes back into the family trust if you and I both die and she's the only one left. She's probably hoping to get us both up onto one of those rickety helicopters . . .'

Benedict smiles. 'Oh, darling, come here.' He crouches again and pulls her towards him. 'The last thing I want to do is upset you. I mean what I said last night – we'll get rid of her. I'll tell the Roko man we're not paying her bill.'

'Ugh!' She bats a hand at Benedict. 'I don't want to talk about her anymore.'

Luella turns on her side, annoyed. She is on holiday in paradise and does not want her precious days in Fiji ruined by Thomasina – she's already had to put up with someone dying in the bar.

She pulls off her kaftan, and rummages in her bag for her sun cream. What can she do to Luella other than write her nasty notes? *YOUR TIME'S UP*? Yeah, right. Luella isn't remotely scared by Thomasina's little joke because she grew up with them: from the benign *LEAVE MY STUFF ALONE* notes to the more venomous, *I HATE YOU*s. So this is nothing earth-shattering that will have Luella reaching for the Xanax bottle. But, being human, she lets herself go there for a second, lets the niggle of the thought simmer gently: what if it *wasn't* Thomasina who left the note? What if it was someone else who had found their way into her bure?

She blinks away the thought. This is what Thomasina wants: to unnerve her, to get under her skin.

Luella's Cartier Love Bracelets jingle together as she aggressively rubs sun cream into her left forearm. She thrusts the bottle into Benedict's hands. 'Do my back?' It's tantamount to offering an olive branch.

Benedict smiles and gratefully shakes the bottle. She closes her eyes as his warm hands caress her back, his fingers slipping beneath the strap of her costume as he covers her skin. Damn it!

He wipes his hands on a towel, and the massage is over. 'Mind if I take a kayak out before the wind picks up?' he asks. 'I'm keen to have a snorkel.' The mild breeze is already steering the current slightly to the left, but Benedict won't worry about that.

'How long for?' A girlish pout. 'I'd like some time in the bure before we get ready to go out tonight . . .'

Benedict grins, picks up on her suggestive lip-puckering. 'An hour? No longer, I promise. Relax and enjoy your book, and we'll have lunch when I get back. I know you've got the spa booked this afternoon, but after that, we can go to the bure for as long as you like . . .'

'Fine.' Luella turns away. She feels a hot pang of desire for her husband. The sexual chemistry between them is still as explosive as it was the first time they went to bed together, and Luella is glad of it. Yet for them, it is more than just a physical connection. She trusts Benedict in way she's never trusted anyone before – he couldn't give a toss about the money, and this in itself is a powerful aphrodisiac. That, and his beautiful body.

'Perhaps I'll wear the diamond in bed,' she says. *You're forgiven.*

Benedict laughs. 'I'd prefer it if you wear absolutely nothing!'

Her winks at her and heads off down the sand. She smiles and picks up her book, wafting her face with it like a fan. She stops to look at the cover; it's the one everyone's been raving about, a Reese's Book Club pick, but she is reading it only because that's what you are *meant* to do on holiday, not because she particularly enjoys reading as a pastime. In her busier-than-average life, she does not have the available head space for make-believe. She flips the book open anyway and attempts to read the first few lines before closing it again.

She sits up, bored, and looks around, her mind wandering to what tasks could keep her occupied instead. She decides she will busy herself by lodging a formal complaint with the resort's manager about the appearance of the note: it means Thomasina had unauthorised access to her room – and how else would she have got in there but for the maid? Luella demands way more of a six-star resort than maids handing out room keys to strangers or neglecting to shut bures securely!

She stands up decisively and slips her designer kaftan over the back of the lounger so that no one will steal her spot in the sun.

Reception is unattended when she arrives a minute later. She taps her acrylic nails impatiently on the polished desk. Why is no one at on the front desk at midday? Have they all buggered off for a siesta? She smashes her hand down on the little silver bell six times: *ding, ding, ding, ding, ding, ding!* Still no answer.

Oh, for pity's sake, she thinks. Where is everyone? Surely they can't all still be attending to death administration. Didn't that all happen *yesterday*? Even in death, Fergus Miller is proving to be a fucking irritant.

She walks around to the side of the desk and steps inside the small room adjacent to reception, which she knows is the manager's office – but Roko isn't there. The computer screen sleeps and beside it, the corners of some paperwork, held down in the middle by a large shell, flap in the mild breeze whipped up by the rattan above the desk. How this place is meant to be six-star is beyond her! She's had better service at M&S on High Street Ken.

She decides to make her way towards the dive shed instead – there is usually some unauthorised gathering of staff *there* at peak times. She marches down the slope that connects reception to the beachfront and arrives at the back of the hut. She throws a cursory glance around, but when she sees it is only *him* there, the negligent dive boy, she backs away.

But it is like he has a sixth sense, and he turns around with a start. He is wearing a wetsuit, rolled down to reveal a very defined six-pack, which, Luella will admit, is rather distracting.

'*Bula*,' he says. His eyes are pathetic, as if they're pleading with her.

'Why are you wearing a wetsuit?' she asks. 'I thought you'd been suspended from diving.'

'I'm not taking guests,' he says, his voice cool. 'I'm planting coral with Filipe.'

'Very worthy. Do check his oxygen tank, won't you?'

The man moves from one foot to the other, awkward. 'Mrs Saint John-Gray . . .'

'It's *Sin-jun*!' How many times must she tell people this?

'My apologies.' He holds up his hands. 'Please, Mrs St-John Gray. I swear I was not at fault. It was just a freak accident.'

'Is that what it would have said on my autopsy report? "A freak accident"?'

The man looks afraid, and Luella is enjoying it. Well, why the hell not? His negligence, his problem! It was very nearly hers – or rather Benedict's problem, because that's who would inherit all the pesky issues that go with a dead body on a remote holiday island. So why not watch the dive boy squirm a little?

'I just wanted you to know . . .' He sighs, and Luella wonders how many times he is going to implore that he *just wants* her to know her near-drowning wasn't his fault. '. . . that I did my due diligence. Everything was checked on the mainland only last month. I have the receipts.'

Due diligence! Receipts! Ugh, if she hears it one more time! If he just shut up about it, she might be more inclined to forget about the whole sorry affair.

But he won't shut up. 'The only thing I can think of,' he continues cautiously, 'is that someone may have tried to sabotage . . .'

Luella regards the dive boy, feels the breeze cold on her neck. 'Are you trying to suggest someone tampered with my equipment?'

The man bites his lip and looks at his bare feet. He doesn't speak.

'How *dare* you! Would you like to know what I think? *I* think that you had the equipment checked at some back-alley dive shop on the mainland and now you're trying to pass the buck.'

'Vita Water Sports are a PADI-certified business,' he says. 'We wouldn't go anywhere else. The safety of our guests is paramount at Loloma.'

'*The safety of our guests is paramount at Loloma*,' she parrots in a baby voice, and then she laughs. 'It's almost funny.' She sighs and smiles at the dive boy, who stands with his hands together in prayer. She can see he is somewhat relieved by the softening of her face. He thinks she's going to say to him: *Well, in* that *case, let's forget about the fact I ran out of oxygen and nearly lost my life and go drink some kava together.* He thinks that with this ironic smile of pure amusement, she is going to roll over and accept her near-death experience and allow him to blame it on some mystery nemesis she has here at the resort: the bogey-man lurking in the shadows of the palms!

Like hell she will!

If Luella were really to think about it, to contemplate the three incidents and their alarming synchronicity – the scuba-equipment failure, the untimely death of Fergus Miller, the sinister note on her bedside table – it might occur to her there is indeed something afoot of which she is at the very heart. But she doesn't think about it. Because right now, she is enjoying this honey-soaked moment of absolute power, momentarily forgetting the old adage that it corrupts absolutely.

The diver bites his lip, takes a deep inward breath and then he asks her, 'Will you . . . will you uphold your complaint, Mrs St John-Gray?'

He looks so pathetic. She sighs. Enough is enough. She splays her right hand across her collarbones, tilts her head and smiles at him, looks deep into his pleading eyes.

'Oh, you dear boy.' She tilts her head, eyes him side on. 'You're damn right I will.'

24

Sailasa

Sailasa runs his tongue over his teeth and spins away from her, giving her only his broad back. He knows it is rude to turn his back on a guest, but he fears he may do something he will regret if he does not look away. He has never struck a woman and he never will, but he knows he has the power to say something right now that he will not be able to take back, and he fears this would only be ammunition for a woman like Luella St John-Gray.

'How dare you turn your back on me!' she snaps, and he turns to her once more. 'Did you know that I personally *know* the CEO of Neptunian Resorts Worldwide? And that if you're still working on this island by the end of the week' – she glances at his name badge as if to emphasise he is no one to her – '*Sailasa*, then someone's head will be on a spit.'

What has he done? He has just made things worse. Now Luella St John-Gray does not intend to go simply to Mr Roko but right to the top, to head of the resort's parent company. He has dug his own grave with his insolence, and he knows it (his mother always berated him for his quick temper), but he cannot stand being treated like this. He has only ever tried to do his job well!

'I sincerely apologise,' he says through gritted teeth.

The woman's cheeks are flushed, her eyes wild. He thinks about Kitty Miller, whose husband lies dead on a slab and who is confined to her bure by grief. And this woman here, who is so privileged and only thinks about herself. *She is a narcissist,* he thinks. *Unhinged.*

They regard one another for a second too long, both of them, shoulders high, chins jutted forward. Then he thinks of his wages, his salary, how Mrs St John-Gray may lose the impetus to do this as the revelry of New Year kicks in, how she may just be toying with him because she is bored. He needs to hold on, wait it out. He cannot let his pride get in the way right now; there is just too much at stake.

He drops his chin. 'I did not mean to be rude,' he says. 'My sincere apologies.'

The woman raises an eyebrow, drops her key card on the floor at Sailasa's feet. She looks at the card and then at him, and she waits. There is only a single beat before Sailasa bends and picks it up.

Luella St John-Gray takes it from his hand wordlessly and turns away.

Sailasa finds Una in the laundry with Joana. They are counting out bed-sheets – huge white squares of luxury threads for king beds that are folded into weighty squares. The vast room is stifling as usual. The back wall, which is lined with giant, industrial washing machines, almost vibrates with the hum of multiple spin cycles, to the accompaniment of Chris Brown's 'Under the Influence' on the radio. To the left of the door is the hotel's lost property basket, always overflowing with guests' goggles, flippers, books and odd sandals.

He nods to Joana. '*Bula.*'

'*Bula*,' sings Joana.

'Ah, Sailasa.' Una appears from behind her cleaning trolley, where she is stacking the square sheets. 'Roko has asked for us to swap jobs tonight, so you'll need to do the evening turn-down service in my bures . . .'

'Swap? Why?' he asks, but of course Sailasa already knows why. Roko still wants him kept away from the guests.

Una sighs and ignores the question. 'I'll be on the beach serving champagne, and you need to do my bures. All four please, around ten o'clock. Straighten the beds, hang up towels and put the lights on as usual.'

'Sure.' Sailasa nods. He will not fight it. Roko is right, he needs to stay away – especially after the run-in he's just had with Luella St John-Gray. In his head he hears words: *You're damn right I will,* and all he sees is the smirk on the woman's face, the false smile, the trickery. 'That's fine with me.'

'Good,' she says, eyeing him as if she's suspicious he is not putting up a fight. She knows he loves being on the beach with the guests on New Year's Eve. 'Bures One to Four, yes?'

Sailasa nods at his own feet. 'Yeah.'

She studies him further and then puts her hands on her hips.

'Right, what is the matter?' She doesn't miss a beat, his all-seeing aunt. 'What has happened now?'

He does not reply.

'Sailasa!' Una's voice is like his mother's, the same reedy sound. She turns to Joana. 'Joana, give us a minute please?'

'Una, I run the laundry . . .' Joana begins, but then she stops. 'Fine,' she says and heads into the drying room, where six industrial ironing boards are lined up and the smell of washing-powder infused steam hangs constantly in the air. Sailasa likes the smell because it reminds him of home. His mother used to work in the laundry before she trained as a teacher, and he often sticks his head in here when he is looking for Una, and it always comforts him. But not today.

'What is it?' Una asks. She pulls him further away from the drying room door, out onto the pathway outside the sliding door of the laundry. 'Roko hasn't told you to leave, has he?'

'No.' Sailasa shakes his head. 'I mean, not yet, but she is going to get me fired.'

'The St John-Gray woman?'

He nods. 'She told me she would.'

'You spoke to her?'

'Just now.'

'Sailasa, no! I told you it was a bad idea to go near her.'

'I know!' He balls his fists and then unclenches them, once, twice and three times. 'But she came to the dive shed.'

'You weren't even supposed to be at the shed.'

'I thought Roko would be OK with me planting coral because it doesn't involve talking to guests.'

Una sighs. 'He told you to stay away from the main resort.'

'I messed up, OK?' Sailasa's voice cracks, and Una's softens.

'What did she say to you?' Una asks. 'Exactly, I mean. What did she say *exactly*?'

'That she will upholding the complaint with Mr Roko and that she's going higher, to Neptunian Resorts Worldwide – that she knows the CEO and I'll be lucky if I'm still working here at the end of the week.'

'What did you say to her to get that response? Did you provoke her?'

'No!' It isn't *really* a lie. Sailasa knows anything would have infuriated the woman. Turning his back on her isn't a crime.

'Well, why on earth did you speak to her in the first place?' Una fumes. 'You should have stayed away!'

'I told you,' he cries, indignant. 'She came to the desk. I didn't look for her. I just thought if I could explain to her that it wasn't my fault . . . if she saw I was, you know, a real human, she would help me.'

'Human? *Human?* Sailasa, the woman is not human. You've just made it worse. For pity's sake, how could you be so stupid?' Una taps her temple.

Sailasa feels as if she has slapped him across the face. His shoulders slump; his hands reach up for his head. He cannot help it. He begins to cry like a child. The sense of despair threatens to envelop him. He is only twenty-two, and he still feels ill-equipped to handle adulthood most of the time.

'Oh, my boy!' Una steps forward and holds out her arms, and Sailasa bends down and lets her comfort him. It is an awkward stance for both of them, because Una is so much smaller than him, but he wraps his arms around her just like he did when he was a boy.

'It's OK,' Una tells him. 'It will be all right.'

They stay this way for maybe a minute until Una pats him on the back to denote it is time for him to pull himself together.

He stands back and sees the wet patch his tears have made on the shoulder of her uniform, turning the colour of the fabric from pale green to dark.

'I can't lose this job,' he sniffs. 'I need the money.' He hesitates, plays with the woven leather bracelet on his arm. 'The thing is, Una: I'm in trouble.' He watches the way her eyes flinch. '*Serious* trouble.'

Una sighs and nods, gestures for him to walk beside her. As always, it is Una leading the way and Sailasa following gratefully. How could he ever have resented this familial show of guidance, of comfort? He vows to himself he will never begrudge it again.

'I'll take my break now,' she says and leads him out of the laundry and towards the empty engineering shed behind it, the place where furniture is adjusted and electrics are fixed, where props are being stored for New Year's Eve.

He follows, silently, his step in time with hers. They take a seat on the wooden steps that lead up into the shed, and Una looks at him expectantly.

'I owe some money,' he tells her. He cannot meet her eye and instead fixes his gaze on the tiny white tick on the front of his right sandal.

Una blinks twice. 'Go on,' she says.

25

Una

'Fijian dollars, not American,' Sailasa tells her, as if it will soften the blow to know his debt is in their native currency.

Una isn't stupid; she knows how much 6,000 Fijian dollars is – it is a fortune, the equivalent to almost 3,000 American dollars! It is a debt that's almost unfathomable. Una cannot imagine being that much in the negative.

'Good God, Sailasa! *How?*'

He hangs his head. 'I borrowed it from a guy in Nadi. And now he wants it back.'

Six thousand dollars! Not six hundred, six *thousand*!

'Why? What do you need that kind of money for?'

'I'd rather not say.'

'Sailasa. You cannot tell me this and refuse to say why!'

Una gets up and paces. She does not know what to think. People do not borrow that kind of money for nothing. Sailasa must be involved in something shady: drugs or laundering or some such. She can't quite fathom it – or the fact she does not know her nephew as well as she thought she did. She understands the folly of youth, but this is something else. Is this the same boy who always did the right thing, who played by the rules while others didn't? Who cared more for his mother and his aunt than any other child she's ever known, could never let them down? Who was honest to a *fault*?

'Well, you'll need to work out a payment plan or something,' she says, as if it's as easy as that, as if it's a bill for groceries he owes. She is offended he is not being altogether honest with her, and it has made her less inclined to help.

'It's not as simple as that,' Sailasa tells her. 'He's not a nice man, the loan shark. I'm trying to get the money together, giving him most of my pay and tips.'

'Who is he?'

'I just know him as Lemeki. I don't have a last name. I keep holding him off, but he's . . . his henchmen have threatened me. If I lose this job, Una, and I can't pay him, they'll kill me.'

Una feels as if the sides of the world are caving in, as if she's being crushed. She has little in savings herself, so it's not like she can bail him out. Neither does she have connections with local gangsters whom she can call on to sort out the bad guys. She felt her darling nephew was clutching at straws with regards to Luella and his job *before* he mentioned the money, but now . . .

Nevertheless, she puts her hand on Sailasa's knee, because it is her job to offer comfort in lieu of his mother, in lieu of Adelina, however confused she is about his reasons. She promised her sister it would be this way.

'It will be all right,' she says. 'I will speak to Mr Roko.'

She does not tell Sailasa she has already done this and that Roko has told her that his hands are tied if Luella St John-Gray makes good on her threats. They are now reliant, she and Sailasa, on the warm will of a woman with a cold heart. They are puppets on a string.

'Keep doing what you are doing,' she says. 'Pay as much as you can. I have $400 in tips I can give you to keep him off your back. Did you spend all the money you were loaned?'

'Yes.'

'Right,' she says, leaning forward, her hands decisively on her knees. 'If I am to help you, you must tell me what for!'

Sailasa looks at her, eyes empty.

'*Now*,' she presses.

'OK,' he says, conceding defeat. 'I'll tell you what it was for. It was for *Tinaqu*,' he says. *Mother*. 'It was for her treatment, to send her private. Her operation – that's how I paid for it. It wasn't on the insurance like I told you both. But then we lost her anyway.'

The tears spring to Una's eyes readily. He did it for his mother, her sister. He gambled his life on hers, and now hers is gone and his is on the brink of ruin.

'Oh, Sailasa.' She pulls his head into her chest. He *is* that boy. Beautiful, kind (to a fault), generous, naive. 'Why didn't you tell me?'

'Because you would have told me not to do it, Aunt Una. You would have said *Tinaqu* wouldn't have wanted me to get into debt.'

'That's because the odds were so against her,' Una says softly. 'Your mother wouldn't have made it anyway, and she knew it. You do realise that?'

'But I gave her more time with us. Don't you see? I gave her six months. We had her for *six more months.*'

Six months of pain followed by seven more for Sailasa, of grief *and* fear. And for Una, too. Months that made Una reflect that, in losing a sister, she may as well have lost a limb. Months that had made her realise she was adrift at sea. No children of her own, no husband, no sister. It was only Sailasa and her need to cater for his grief, to soothe it like ointment on a sore, that carried her through.

Una strokes Sailasa's hand now, rhythmic and slow. She thinks about how she can solve this problem. She counts the ways. She could ask the staff to donate their tips until they can be paid back; she knows many of them would do it. She could crowdfund – isn't that what it's called? Go online and set up one of those accounts that relies on the kindness of strangers – ten dollars here, another ten there – she has seen it done before! Maybe she could ask Roko to put out a plea on social media on behalf of the resort, just like he did for food hampers following Cyclone Winston in 2016? Maybe she herself will speak to Luella St John-Gray and thus destroy that particular piece of this ugly Jenga game – the one that hovers on the top menacingly and threatens to bring down the whole tower.

Una gets up, brushes the dust from her skirt. 'I have some ideas. Just keep your head down, and I'll come back to you when I've worked something out.'

Sailasa nods. 'Thank you, *Aunt* Una.'

She sighs. 'Don't worry about doing my turn-downs tonight, OK? You have too much on your mind. I'll ask Letitia or Kelera to do it.'

'No,' he tells her. 'I want to do it. I want Roko to see I'm trying.'

She nods. 'OK,' she says. '*Vinaka.*'

Una bids Sailasa a farewell and returns to the laundry to collect her cleaning cart.

'All OK?' Joana asks her.

'Fine,' snaps Una.

She pushes the cart briskly along the cobbled pathway towards the gardens, her mind buzzing with adrenaline. How did she miss it? How? Una sees *everything* – but she didn't see this. How did he manage to keep such a big thing hidden? That poor boy, drowning in worry. She slows down as she passes the kidney-shaped swimming pool, where American pop music hums from the poolside speakers, and Petero stands drying glasses with a tea-towel.

'*Bula!*' she calls. *Nothing to see here!* She travels past the spa, where the fragrant scent of coconut oil wafts forth from the arched entryway dotted with yellow hibiscus blooms. As she rounds the corner close to reception, Una almost takes out Sofie Barthélemy, who is heading towards the reception area.

'Oh.' Una starts. 'I'm so sorry! I wasn't looking . . .'

Sofie smiles. '*De rien,*' she says, holding up her hand. Una doesn't speak French, but she can tell by the woman's smile and the acquiescent hand gesture that she is not remotely fazed by the collision.

Thank God for guests like Sofie Barthélemy, Una thinks as she lets down the break with her foot. She watches the woman walk away, her Kindle in her left hand, a large floppy hat on her head and a long, white, bohemian sundress grazing the floor in her wake like the train of a wedding dress.

'Una!' Mr Roko beckons her from his office door. 'Slow down with that thing before you injure someone. I don't want another corpse to dispose of, especially not on New Year's Eve. Have you found someone to do your turn-down service tonight?'

'I have,' she says. She volunteers no more information, and nor does Roko ask for it.

'Good. And while I've got you, Una, when you're serving the champagne tonight on the beach, just make sure you keep everyone topped up the whole time, especially the St John-Grays.' Roko leans in. 'God forbid the woman goes dry.'

Una notices that Roko's nails are bitten down to the quick and his cuticles are angry and red. There is a sense of jumpiness about him.

'I'm relying on you to keep everyone happy, Una,' he says with a sigh. 'God knows everyone's anxious enough after what happened last night. Let's keep them nicely fed and watered so it's not the first thing they put on their reviews.'

Una nods. 'Of course.'

'I mean, a man keeling over at our bar, Una! It beggars belief! In all my years of service, that was certainly the most shocking thing I've ever seen . . .'

Una would agree with him there. She can hear the silence in the resort today as guests take in the enormity of what they witnessed in the bar.

'Anyway.' Roko seems to snap back to the present. 'We need to get on with things. Be careful with that trolley, won't you? And thank you, Una.'

'Of course.'

Una departs Roko's office with a renewed sense of unease, as if she has caught Roko's jitters. She negotiates the bend and continues along the pathway on the beach side now. She notices Thomasina Delana hovering around outside Bure One on the path up ahead and wonders if the young woman is lost, but just as she is about to call out to enquire, the door of Bure Five opens and the Australian guest Alice Chen steps out. Her daughter Ellie wears a tiny string bikini that Una thinks is a tad inappropriate for a teenager, and Una isn't even a prude, not by a long shot.

'I thought I heard you, Una,' says Alice Chen with a broad smile. 'Would you be able to replace some towels before we head off to lunch? Ellie's already washed her hair twice today, and they're all soaking wet! That's fifteen-year-olds for you. I mean' – she pauses here – 'I feel bad even asking after what happened last night. New towels are hardly important in the grand scheme of things, are they? His poor, poor wife – I can't get her face out of my head. It's just devastating.'

Una bends down and pulls two fresh towels from the side of her trolley, even though they are meant for the bathrooms in her own bures and not Kelera's. It means she'll need to make a trip back to the laundry. 'It is indeed terrible, Mrs Chen. I do hope you are still able to enjoy your holiday.'

The woman smiles. 'Thank you, Una,' she says and closes the door, and Una hears her say, 'For God's sake, Ellie, there is just no fabric to it.'

Una carries on down the path and up towards Bure Three, where she will start her round today. She is later than usual on account of last night's sad events – she usually cleans at breakfast rather than at lunch – but the restaurant had been strangely empty first thing and Roko had suggested she wait. Everything is topsy-turvy today. Ordinarily, she would start in the garden in Bure Four, where Thomasina Delana usually resides, but she is keen to check on Kitty Miller as soon as possible, so she walks away from her usual starting point. As she does, she glances ahead for Ms Delana, wondering what she's up to, but the woman has now disappeared.

At Bure Three, it is evident Kitty Miller has not heard the rattle of cleaning fluids and teeny-tiny luxury body care products on approach as most guests do (it is a flaw, thinks Una, not to have created a cleaning trolley that doesn't wake the dead), and so Una knocks gently on the glass of the door. When there is still no answer, she takes the master key and beeps it open.

The inside of the room is dark, because the curtains are closed, and it smells of body odour and sleep and ever so slightly of damp, on account of the seasonal rain showers they had last week.

And there, wrapped up inside the sheets, is Kitty, so still that for a moment Una fears she is dead, too. She watches, concerned, until there is a discernible rise and fall of her chest, a slight movement of the nightdress she is wearing.

She puts her hand on Kitty Miller's brow, and the woman's eyes flicker open but only for a second. She groans and turns over and pulls the covers over her head, and Una takes that as a sign that the diminutive widow is still in the land of the living and that she doesn't have to worry about her having died of a broken heart. It isn't a silly fear – Una's read about it so many times: one spouse dying and the other following shortly after, grief affecting the muscles of the heart.

Una does a cursory clean-up of the room. It is still tidy, of course, from the previous night, but Una refreshes the water jug Kitty Miller has drained, mops up a small spillage on the bedside table, fashions the end of the toilet roll into a point and clears a few brownish blonde hairs from the plug hole. Sand has blown onto the deck and under the door of the bure, and so she sweeps the deck first and returns for the debris back inside the room, then mops her way backwards, as she always does, out of the door, closing it with a soft click.

She glances at her wristwatch. It is 1.30 p.m., a safe time to continue to Bure One without having to face the woman who is making Sailasa's life hell. At this time, most guests are already at lunch or are finishing up their first stint of the day on the beach, with the energy required for sun-worshipping at its peak thanks to a good sleep and a morning coffee. It is the afternoons when guests retreat to their bures for siestas or sex. Not everyone remembers to put the *Do Not Disturb* sign on the door, and Una has been mortified once or twice when she's inadvertently woken a guest or stumbled on a scenario that looks like it is straight out of a Mills & Boon novel.

Still, she doesn't need to worry this time. As she passes the beach on her left, hand-on-head under the coconuts, she sees Luella St John-Gray prostrate on a lounger, her hat over her face, her husband dragging a kayak up the sand behind him. She tells herself she will clean the room in record speed just in case one of them should return and speak to her. Una will always make nice when she has to, but it is through a clenched jaw when she's peeved or resentful. She fears even that will be hard now she knows how much Luella St John-Gray's actions have impacted, and are still impacting, her beloved Sailasa.

Inside the St John-Gray bure, there is an aroma of coconut oil, which Una presumes is a suntan product of some kind. A slight shimmer catches her eye in the sunlight from the bathroom window, and Una sees the most magnificent floor-length gown hanging by a wooden hanger from the very rafters of the room. It is a tiny size and covered from top to toe in intricately woven blood-red sequins in a herringbone pattern, like the scales of a fish. Una runs her fingers down the sequins and reaches inside the neck of the gown to look at the label. It says Valentino. Una's hands dart away, understanding immediately the value of the garment.

The shoes positioned at the foot of the gown have a red sole and are identical to ones she has seen in Kitty Miller's bure, although Luella's look brand-new and Kitty's look scuffed and old. Hanging alongside the dress, just inside the wardrobe, is Luella St John-Gray's Venetian mask. Una saw it yesterday but didn't stop to take in its opulence. It is made of gold filigree, decorated at the scalp with silk flowers, beads, braid and lace. Twelve thin spikes of lightweight gold with delicate rhinestones at their tips burst forth from the top like on America's Statue of Liberty. And how free is Luella with her wealth and her devil-may-care steamrolling of other people's emotions? Una feels a sudden and overwhelming sense of hostility to this woman who has every single thing but wants to take Sailasa's *everything*.

She moves into the bathroom at the back of the bure and avoids the temptation to clean the toilet rim with Luella St John-Gray's electric toothbrush. Everything on the countertop reeks of opulence: tubes and perfumes in domed glass jars and tiny plastic pots with French names she doesn't recognise and others, like Chanel, that she does; a space-age Dyson hairdryer with nozzles and tongs with an adaptor plug fixed on to the end of the wire. On the side of the sink are two diamond stud earrings with their backs attached. Una carefully moves them to the side of the sink-top, well away from the danger of the plug hole – she does not want to pay the same price as Christina did for a split second of negligence. She cleans around them and checks they are still there when she has finished with the basins and again when she has replaced the towels, just to be sure.

Next, she empties the bin. On the floor beside it, she finds a piece of paper, not just screwed up and tossed to the floor but rolled tightly with an angry fist. Una unravels it, her curiosity unfurling with it. The notepaper bears the Loloma Resort & Spa logo at the top, and the message is written in jet black ink: *YOUR TIME'S UP*, in capital letters. The word *UP* is underlined with the messy scribble of an angry hand.

Una turns it over and it takes her only a moment to realise it is a threat. Time is up for what? This is not a loving note, signed with a kiss; it is an ugly scrawl, a threat. Someone is intimidating either Luella or Benedict St John-Gray, and the recipient has dismissed the warning by tossing it in the bathroom bin.

Una hears a man's voice from the doorway and jumps. 'Hello?' She shoves the piece of paper into her pocket just as Benedict St John-Gray appears in the bathroom.

'Mr St John-Gray!'

'Hello, Una.' His skin is goose-bumped from the sea, water weaving in tiny rivers through the hairs on his chest. His eyes, alive with adrenaline from his underwater adventure, are circled with the imprint of a tightly fitting scuba-mask – a bright red figure of eight lying on its side across his tanned skin. He does not look like a man who is being threatened or intimidated. Quite the opposite, in fact.

'Did you have a good snorkel?' Una asks him.

Benedict looks at her and smiles with his eyes. 'Killer,' he says.

26

Luella

Luella leaves the beach at around two o'clock after a bowl of ceviche fish and heads straight for the spa, where she spends the next few hours. First is a hot stone massage, which she follows up with a full body scrub and finally a mani-pedi.

All conversation with her therapist is swiftly nipped in the bud. 'I'd rather not talk,' she tells the older Fijian woman, whose own nails could frankly do with a paint. 'I'm here to relax.'

'*Vinaka*,' says the woman with the name badge that reads Ema. Thankfully, she does not speak for the rest of the treatment.

'Would you do that one again?' Luella points at a red fingernail that Ema has just worked on. 'There's a bubble.'

After she is scrubbed and massaged, which is a bitch on her sunburnt calves, Luella returns to the bure, has a little siesta followed by a spot of oral sex (taking, not giving) and then showers ahead of the New Year's Eve masquerade party. She is a light eater but already feels she is tipping the scales after two days of Fijian food, which is dripping in so much coconut cream and butter it should be illegal, so she announces to Benedict that she will forgo dinner.

'On New Year's Eve?' asks Benedict, incredulous. 'It's a six-course menu with a traditional Fijian lovo!'

'A piece of meat cooked in the ground?' She grimaces. 'No, thank you.'

'Darling, you'll starve.'

'Good.' She looks at herself in the bathroom mirror and then turns to Benedict. 'Am I thinner than the French doctor?' It's something that's been bothering her. Usually, she is the most attractive, the slimmest, woman in a room by a golden mile, but here on Loloma, she feels the unpalatable sting of competition. 'Some people would think she's rather attractive . . .'

Benedict laughs. 'The French doctor? Where did that come from? I can assure you: she is not in the *least* bit attractive. You, on other hand . . .' He pulls her in and nuzzles her neck. '. . . are utterly perfect!'

'Terrible taste in clothes,' muses Luella. 'But that's the French for you, isn't it? They have absolutely *no* idea about fashion.'

She pulls on a black lace Simone Pérèle thong, sprays herself with Galop d'Hermès and then sets about applying her make-up: primer, foundation, translucent power, bronzer, eye shadow, liner and mascara – in that exact order. When she is ready, she turns to the Valentino gown hanging from the wooden rafters above the door. This will be its first outing, and Luella knows no one else will be dressed in anything like it. In her general sweep of the resort, she has found none of the other guests to be in possession of her innate sense of style.

'Pass me the Vally, Benedict.'

Benedict – who, she jokes to her friends, is actually her own personal *valet* – carefully unhooks the clothes-hanger from the rail and passes her the weighty bejewelled Valentino gown. It is as regal a dress as they come, with its high neck and red sequins. Blood red. Sensual, breathtaking, outspoken.

She slips it on. 'Do me up?'

Benedict slides up the zip at the back and kisses her shoulder. She turns around.

'You look magnificent,' he says. 'You'll be the belle of the ball.'

Indeed, Luella *feels* magnificent, invincible. She turns to look at herself, takes in her own beauty. And then she slides on her Venetian mask with its regal gold filigree and spikes like coronation sceptres. When the mask is on, she can see only her eyes and her red lips in the reflection, but she knows that every single person in the resort will know exactly who she is and that every one of them will acknowledge her beauty.

At 7 p.m. they leave the bure. As they head further along the path to the main resort, they pass the second negligent scuba instructor, Filipe, wearing a grass skirt as he lights one of the torches beside the pool area. Luella keeps her eyes forward, refusing to meet his as he offers her and Benedict a rather pathetic '*Bula*'.

At the terrace, the nosy maid called Una is standing in something other than her customary snot green, handing out drinks. Luella cannot abide places where the staff have twenty roles – just give them one, for pity's sake. Talk about jacks of all trades and masters of none!

She holds forth a tray of champagne flutes. 'Welcome!' she sings. 'Champagne?'

'Dom Pérignon?'

'Of course,' says the maid.

Luella nods and reaches for a glass with her spare hand. She notices the maid cast an admiring glance at the diamond tennis bracelet on her wrist.

'Do call us Benedict and Luella, please,' Benedict says. 'In case you haven't already guessed who we are under these masks!'

'Welcome,' says the maid again. 'I must say, your masks are incredible. Are you the Phantom of the Opera?'

'I am indeed,' says Benedict. He turns to Luella. 'Una was in the bure when I returned from my snorkel, darling. She was doing a brilliant job.'

'Wonderful,' Luella says and glances away. Pesky chit-chat. She will never see this woman again in her life after tomorrow, so what is the point? Benedict doesn't know she intends to bring their flights forward and that in twenty-four hours they will be en route back to London.

The terrace is busy already. Everyone turns to look at Luella when they enter, of course, as they should. The Chen woman and her pouty daughter sit in glum silence overlooking the water. The daughter, who must be all of fifteen, is dressed in some slutty spandex number that leaves nothing to the imagination. The French doctor leans against the bar in a long, silver slip-dress that Luella thinks looks vintage, and over it she wears a long, bohemian kaftan. Her dark blonde hair sits in a low bun at the nape of her neck. *Hardly party-wear,* thinks Luella. *Talk about dressing down!* But then again, Luella muses, the woman is a doctor, after all, and it's been Luella's experience that doctors are mostly dowdy creatures with nothing much to them aside from their intellect. There is no sign of Kitty Miller, but this is no surprise (or great loss) as far as Luella is concerned. The woman's husband met his maker only last night – she's likely dosed up to her eyeballs on medication.

At the long table perpendicular to the bar, a group of moneyed locals sup expensive whisky and laugh uproariously. The luxury yacht they must have arrived on bobs up and down a few metres from the shore, a measure to denote their collective importance. Luella watches Benedict salivate as it simmers on the water.

'Bloody nice boat,' he tells Luella, as if she gives a single toss. 'Mind if I go a bit closer and take a look?'

Luella gives a murmur of consent and watches as he jogs onto the beach. Now *she* is a tragic single like the Frenchwoman, standing in the middle of the terrace. She twists the stem of her champagne flute between her fingers and listens to the soft whisper of the white foam as it grazes the shore.

'Hello.' Madame Dowdy appears in front of her, her gaze intense and her eyes alarmingly pale and glass-like.

'Yes?'

'You are Luella.' It is not a question. The Frenchwoman gazes out to sea. 'I noticed you in the bar, when Monsieur Miller . . .' She stops. 'A tragic circumstance, no? It is not the holiday his poor wife was hoping for.'

Her accent is not as thick as Luella remembers it when she saw the woman frantically thumping Fergus Miller's sternum. There is a slightly British twang to it, nestled somewhere, hidden between the *ze bar* and the *trageec*. Luella does, in fact, *parle français*, but frankly she cannot be arsed. She will save that for the boutiques of the Rue Saint-Honoré or when she is sipping a luxurious *chocolat chaud* at Angelina on the Place du Carrousel.

'Tragic indeed,' Luella drawls as she takes another sip. The glass is almost empty.

'I wanted to introduce myself,' the Frenchwoman says. 'It is hard travelling alone.'

'Of course,' Luella offers. She is not good at this. 'Your dress?'

'Vintage Saint Laurent.' *Son-Larron.* 'And the kaftan from All Saints. I have a mixed taste,' the Frenchwoman finishes. 'Eclectic – is that the word? I like to add the designer with the more fashionable . . .' *Fash-un-arb.*

Luella, who is pleasantly surprised to learn that the woman's slip-dress is Saint Laurent, would very much like her to know that she herself is wearing Valentino haute couture – but the humourless doctor does not ask. Instead, she sips her own champagne and smiles, studies Luella's face. Luella remembers the woman looking at her this way last night, trying to work her out, to read her face as if she were a book.

Luella cannot help herself. The woman needs to know that she, too, understands fashion, that she lives and breathes it. 'This is Valentino,' she says, her palms open, as if to introduce the dress. 'Haute couture.'

The other woman seems nonplussed. *Moi non plus.*

'Well,' she says, with a shrug. 'You look good.'

Valentino Couture? Just *good?* Luella feels the side of her mouth pull up.

'The truth is, Luella, I know who you are already. Our paths crossed once, overseas, a long time ago.'

Luella closes her eyes. *Here we go.* The top half of the woman's face is hidden by a thin silver sequinned mask, but Luella knows it is a complete fact that she never saw her before in her life until she observed her pumping at Fergus Miller's obese ribcage. But Luella is not worried about her memory failing her, because she has heard it all before, the old *remember me?* and the *you'll never* believe *it, but we've met before!* It is almost always followed by: *my poor dog is dying . . . can you spare some cash?* These false exclamations are as old as Luella, as clichéd as the tired expression *don't I know you from somewhere?* and they *always* precede a dig for money, a blatant request for money.

'I don't think so,' Luella says. 'Now please, I would like to enjoy my drink.'

'Luella, I would just ask a moment of your time . . .'

'No, thank you. I would like you to *leave*.'

'Luella, *please*!' The doctor grabs her wrist, and it is not a limp grab. The woman has strength. Of course she does – she pumped at a grown man's chest last night, broke his ribs!

'Get off me!' Luella snatches her hand back and holds onto her own wrist where the Frenchwoman's fingers have left an angry red mark. She glances to her right to see the Fuchs staring at her. She glowers at them and watches them shrink forward into one another. 'Who the hell do you think you are?'

'I'm sorry,' the Frenchwoman says, but Luella is not listening.

She turns and walks away without looking back. She kicks off her shoes when she reaches the beach and bends down to pick them up. When she stands again, Thomasina is in front of her.

'Oh, for God's sake,' she spits. 'From one bloodsucker to another.'

'Nice to see you, too,' Thomasina drawls.

'And how are you, Thomasina?' Luella hears herself purr. 'Sent anyone any sinister love notes lately?'

'Funnily enough, I haven't. It's not my style. Have you arrived at a beach party ludicrously overdressed recently? Oh . . .'

Luella runs her tongue over her top front teeth and turns away. Why must she keep fending off these vile limpets? Fergus, Thomasina, and now the Frenchwoman whose name she doesn't even know!

'Just a quick spot of admin, and then I'll disappear.' Thomasina flicks her long dark hair over her shoulder.

'Spit it out.'

'I'd like to know where you've stashed the diamond. *My* diamond.'

'*Your* diamond?' Luella lets out a high-pitched laugh and notices Ellie Chen staring over at her. The teenager looks her up and down and laughs, before whispering something to her mother. Luella wonders if the sulky teen is going to come over and ask Luella to put some money in her piggy bank.

'Yes. *My* diamond. The Thomasina Diamond?'

'It's just a name, Thomas, darling. It doesn't denote ownership.'

'Luella, please.' Thomasina drops the sarcasm for a rare moment. 'You know I didn't contest any of it – any of the money, any of the will.'

'Of course you didn't – you wouldn't have had a leg to stand on! He wasn't your real father! Of *course* I was going to inherit all of it. That is the strength of blood and DNA.'

'And having power of attorney.'

'Well, yes. That too.'

'He was my father, too, Luella.'

'It's not the same,' Luella tells her. 'You never had the bond biology brings.' Even as she says it, Luella knows it is not true. She knows her father loved Thomasina immeasurably, but that is immaterial now that he is gone.

Thomasina's eyes are glassy. 'Just do the right thing, Luella, please. Give me the necklace, the one thing that is rightfully mine, and I'll go away. You'll never have to see me again, I promise.'

Luella feels her lips turn up in a smile. 'You want me to give you a jewel worth 200 grand just like that?' She clicks her fingers with a crisp snap. 'So you'll "go away"?' She makes quote marks with her fingers. 'You live on the other side of the world, for crying out loud! I never have to see you anyway. I've offered you cash to sod off and leave me alone, haven't I?'

Thomasina begins to cry now. False tears. The tears of an actress. 'It was my mother's, Luella. Please!'

'*Our* mother's. We are both our mother's daughters, and according to law, she and *my* father – not yours but *mine* – wished for me to inherit everything when he died. Anyway, what do you even want it for, Thomasina? Don't you enjoy living "off grid" or whatever it is you do? Haven't you abandoned all your worldly possessions?'

Luella inspects her nails. There is a chip in the varnish already, and she will have to go back to the spa tomorrow and demand a repaint, which she will not be paying for. It irks her no end when you pay for a service and you do not get recompensed with quality. Of course, Luella's stay here at Loloma is now completely free, but that's not the point.

Thomasina has regained her composure. 'I live in a town. I'm not a nomad!' She sighs and cocks her head to one side. 'Luella, please . . .' It is the begging face: the same one she used to put on when she wanted to borrow make-up or a magazine or a pair of shoes, or when she wanted Luella to vow not to tell their mother she'd sneaked out of her bedroom window again. 'I promised Mum,' Thomasina finishes. 'I gave her my word I'd look after it.'

'"Promised Mum"?' Luella is tiring of this ridiculous conversation now. 'Mummy thought you were a lost cause.'

Luella watches with satisfaction as her sister's nostrils flare. The calm before the storm. The quiet before the maelstrom of revenge, a torrent unleashed. But Luella does not care – she has seen it before time and time again: the anger, followed by the repentance and then the acceptance, the quiet. Thomasina will rage and then go away to Australia again. So she will deliver the blow she knows will get her irksome sister off her back for good.

'It's too late,' she says, as simply as she might order a coffee. 'I don't have it anymore.'

Thomasina's lower lip quivers. 'What do you mean?'

Luella looks down at her chipped nail once more and shrugs. 'I sold it,' she says.

27

Una

'Una!' Alice Chen enthuses. 'Would you mind?' She hands Una her empty champagne glass, and her daughter, Ellie, hands over what looks to be a half-drunk glass of Coke.

'Thanks, Una,' says Ellie.

'Una, how is Mrs Miller?' Mrs Chen asks. 'Such an awful thing to happen.'

Una nods gravely. 'Mrs Miller has been grieving in private, in her bure. I do believe both Dr Marama and Dr Barthélemy have been attending to her.'

'Poor thing. If it was me, I'd need to be drugged up to the eyeballs,' says Mrs Chen. 'You'd hardly want to be gallivanting around the beach in a masquerade mask, would you?'

'I believe not,' says Una.

'Do you have any New Year's resolutions?' Ellie asks, changing the subject entirely. 'Do you do that stuff here in Fiji?'

'We do, but I don't, not really,' says Una. 'Maybe to read more books.'

'Me too.' Mrs Chen laughs. 'Surely you're not working all night, Una? Will you get to celebrate after your shift?'

'In the staff village, yes,' says Una. 'It's always a happy time.'

The trio's contented moment of silence is filled with a shout, and Una turns to her left to see Thomasina Delana and Luella St John-Gray in some kind of verbal altercation on the beach, anger charging between them like lightning bolts. Una can see it in their postures, the angry jut of both their necks, the rigid gesticulating of the hands. She is confused – what are these women to one another?

Then it becomes achingly clear: Thomasina Delana has darker skin, but their height, their postures, the upturn of their noses, is almost identical – so much that Una is quite thrown by it. Why had she not noticed it before?

Alice Chen turns to her right and follows Una's gaze. 'I've been a marriage guidance counsellor for twenty-five years,' she says after a moment, 'and I recognise when two human beings hate one another.'

Una does not respond – it isn't her place.

'*Fight, fight, fight . . .*' Ellie giggles, jostling against her mother.

Mother and daughter move closer along the beach towards the action. Una cannot be seen to be a voyeur, so she says goodbye to Mrs Chen and Ellie and turns away towards the bar with the empty glasses. But intrigue makes her stop, and she sets down her tray of glasses on a table and tucks herself behind a wooden pillar in the restaurant to watch the women on the beach. She leans in. If she focuses very hard, she can just about hear their conversation above the muffled noises of the party.

'You didn't, Luella,' Ms Delana cries. 'Not even you would stoop that low.'

Luella St John-Gray holds up her palms. 'Calm down, Thomasina,' she says. 'It's only a necklace. I mean, it *was* only a necklace . . .'

'You're bluffing,' snaps Thomasina Delana.

The Chens are rooted to the spot just ahead of Una, Ellie with an excited smile on her face and her mother with a look that's somewhere between amusement and horror.

'No? Well, here's the proof.' Luella St John-Gray produces her phone and lights up the screen. She scrolls dramatically for a moment while the other woman waits. There's an impatient shuffle of feet in the sand.

'Here you go. The receipt: £202,000 at Christie's in London,' Luella St John-Gray snarls. 'Right here on my email. See?'

Thomasina Delana steps forward and glances at the screen. She gasps and then lifts her palm and swipes the phone out of Luella's hand. It flies a couple of metres through the air and lands in the sand at Ellie Chen's feet. Ellie bends to pick it up at the same time as the arguing women turn to look in the direction of the mother and daughter, noticing their prying eyes for the first time.

Luella St John-Gray marches down the sand. 'Get off my phone,' she says, snatching the device from Ellie's outstretched hands. 'It's private. How *dare* you!'

'Chill *out.*' Ellie pouts. 'I'm not interested in *old* people stuff anyway.'

'Oh, piss off back to nursery,' snaps Luella St John-Gray and stomps back across the sand towards her opponent.

Una half expects Alice Chen to make some kind of protest, but she simply opens her mouth and closes it again.

Thomasina Delana is on the sand now, her knees drawn up to her torso and her head in her hands. Eventually she looks up. 'Please tell me you are lying,' she begs.

'Why would I be?' Luella St John-Gray looms over her, the stance of a bully. 'The proof is right here in my hand.'

'But it's all I have left of Mum.'

Sisters, thinks Una. *I knew it!*

'Rubbish,' the St John-Gray woman replies. 'You still have her pre-surgery nose and her irritating habit of seeing the best in people. Surely that's a legacy, of sorts.'

'But why, Luella? Why would you do it?'

'Because it was mine to sell!'

Ms Delana jumps up. 'No! No, it wasn't!' she spits. 'God, I hate you. You are so full of spite. I wish you *had* died in there . . .' She gestures to the sea, now flood-lit with moonlight.

'Well,' says her sister, brushing her hands off and turning away. 'We can't have everything we want, can we?'

Una watches Thomasina Delana as she gets up and flees from the bar towards the pool area, and as she glances at Ms Delana's retreating back, she wonders if the sister who has been wronged hates her more glamorous sibling so much that she might leave her a threatening note? Her hand instinctively reaches inside her pocket for the screwed-up piece of paper.

'Guess what her phone screen said?' Ellie Chen whispers to her mother as she passes Una. 'Get this – it said *CHRISTIE'S AUCTIONS & PRIVATE SALES*. And then *SOLD* and a helluva lot of zeros.'

'Crikey,' says Alice Chen. 'She sold her sister's jewellery! From their mother!'

'Whoa, that's so fucked.'

Una waits for mother to admonish daughter for her language, but instead Alice Chen says, 'Yes. My thoughts entirely, Ellie. My thoughts entirely.'

Una takes her drinks tray to the main bar and then heads on towards the pool area. The pool bar, with its rows of liquors and spirits, is closed due to the beach party, and the area is dark, save for scattered fairy lights. Una glances around and sees a figure hunched on a sun lounger.

Una takes a step forward and offers a soft, 'Hello? Ms Delana?'

The other woman jumps. 'Oh!' she says and wipes her nose with the back of her hand. 'Una.'

'I just wanted to check if you're all right. Can I help?' Yet again, Una realises she should not pry into the affairs of guests, but she has always found that people *want* to confide in her. It is a gift of hers, Adelina always said, this ability to bring comfort.

'Oh, not really.' Thomasina Delana pauses. Then she sighs. 'Oh, what the hell. It's obvious to everyone anyway. My sister is the devil.'

'Your sister.' Una is not a good liar, so it is not a question. She can't pretend she doesn't know.

'We couldn't be more different, could we?' the other woman says. 'She's my half-sister, actually. My father was Fijian. He was in the Parachute Regiment in the British Army.'

'I did wonder if your surname was Fijian. It's certainly a South Pacific name,' says Una. 'How did your parents meet?' She cannot help but ask the question – especially if she thinks she can help Thomasina Delana in some way.

'They met in London and were very much in love, but he died in the Falklands War when I was just a few months old. He was from Lamu, near Suva.'

'Really?' Una touches the goose bumps on her left arm with the fingers of her right. 'What was his name?'

'Joseph Delana. My mother married her boss, Frederick Walsh, a year after my father died. They went on to have Luella. Luella and I both grew up as Walshes, but I reverted back to my real father's name after my stepfather died. I guess I wanted to pay homage to my birth dad.'

'That's special,' says Una.

'I felt weird about changing it at first because I was so close to my stepdad,' Thomasina continues, 'but it just felt like the right thing to do.'

Una smiles. She feels an immediate kinship with this woman. Her own father had served for Britain in World War II, interned in a prisoner-of-war camp run by the Japanese. She has had generations of relatives serve in the British Army.

'We haven't been close since we were kids, Luella and I,' she explains. 'We're too different – different priorities, you know?'

Una nods. 'All families argue,' she says, ever the diplomat, even though she senses this is more serious than a mere exchange of words.

'God, I don't know why I'm boring you with all of this,' Thomasina Delana says. 'You're just easy to talk to.'

Una smiles. 'Well, that is nice of you to say. Is there anything I can do for you? To help?'

'That's kind, but I'm fine.' She shakes her head and looks Una directly in the eyes. 'I just wish she wasn't so spiteful, Una. She is evil, pure evil. I know I shouldn't say this, but I hate her. I hate Luella so much.'

Una nods as if she understands, even though she does not. She loved her own sister deeply and feels Adelina's loss every single day. That's why she holds onto Sailasa so tightly, and he to her.

'Can I get you anything?' she ventures again. 'A glass of water? A cocktail? Today's special is called Sweet Revenge. It has coffee and bourbon . . .'

Thomasina laughs out loud, her wet eyes sparkling. 'Sweet Revenge? How apt. Yes, thank you, Una – I'll try one of those.'

'Of course. I'll have Joji make one at the main bar and bring it to you. Would you like it here or in your bure?'

The other woman smiles. 'Thank you, Una. I'll have it here. I'm all right now,' she says. 'I appreciate you checking on me.'

Una smiles and turns towards the bar.

'Una?'

She spins around. 'Yes?'

'Do you believe bad things happen to good people?'

Una picks up the drinks tray and holds it flat against her chest, thinks of Sailasa. 'Yes,' she says. 'Yes, I do.'

Thomasina lets out a long sigh. 'Why is life so unfair?'

'I don't know,' says Una. How do you answer something so profound? 'But I do believe in karma. What goes around . . .'

'. . . comes around. Yeah. I hope so.' Thomasina gets up. 'Thanks again, Una.'

'You are welcome, Ms Delana. But please say *vinaka* instead of *thank you*. You are Fijian, after all.'

Una is rewarded with a pretty smile. 'Speaking Fijian is on my list of things to do this holiday, Una. Thank you – I mean, *vinaka* – for reminding me.'

Just before midnight, Una sets down her champagne tray on the bar for the last time and heads along the pathway towards her four duty bures to give the decks a quick sweep. Her feet ache after a long day, but the job needs to be done. The gentle north-westerly has brushed sand onto the verandas of the oceanfront bungalows, just as it always does.

She starts in the garden at Bure Four – Thomasina Delana's bure. It is set back from the others in the garden but still proves an unfortunate victim of windswept sand from the beach. When she gets there, she notices the front door is slightly ajar.

'Hello?' she calls through the open crack. 'Ms Delana? Una here!'

There is no answer, so she steps inside, just to check Sailasa's turn-down service is up to her standard. She trusts him, of course, but she is incredibly thorough, and it is a known fact that not even the other maids, Kelera and Letitia, have standards as high as hers. Plus, if Sailasa has accidentally left the door open, then there may be other things he has missed, as well as the annoyance of a sandy entranceway.

Una realises immediately that Sailasa hasn't been in this room. The bed-sheets are still wrinkled and a wet swimming costume lies in a heap on the floor next to an open beach-bag. There is, as suspected, sand everywhere. Una feels panic swelling in her chest, her pulse quickening. Of all nights for him to forget! She hopes it is only this bure he has neglected to check. Did she ask him to do only the beachfront bures, and not this one, which sits a little behind her other three? It crosses her mind. But no, she is certain she instructed him to do all four of her bures while she was on champagne duty, and he assured her he would.

Ugh! she thinks now. *I should have asked Kelera!* She should have known Sailasa would mess it up with his mind elsewhere, on loan sharks and faulty scuba tanks and Luella St John-Gray. But there is no point in worrying about that now, because she has work to do, and fast.

She sets about straightening the bed, pulling it taut and tucking the corners under so the sheets shine. She carefully folds the corner back on the side she knows Ms Delana sleeps on, next to the bedside table with the water bottle and the book that's open, face down, bending the spine. She lifts up the book, which is called *The Wim Hof Method* and appears to be about a handsome bearded man who likes sitting in ice. She notices the library sticker on the spine and thumbs the pages. She can't remember the last time she found a library book in a bure. The books brought to the island by guests are normally pristine, purchased at great cost from airport bookshops all over the globe, with price stickers in various currencies: American dollars, Australian dollars, Euros, British pounds.

In her haste, she slams the book down on the table rather ungracefully, and as she does, a piece of paper with the Fiji Airways crest slides out of somewhere towards the end and sails elegantly down to the floor. Una bends to retrieve it and sees it is a list that reads:

1. *Learn Fijian*
2. *Tackle Cloudbreak*

3. *Handle Octopus*
4. *Wreck dive*
5. *Confront her*
6. *Get her back*

She studies the words in front of her. Instinctively she pulls out the balled-up note that is deep inside her pocket and unfurls it, holding it open above Thomasina Delana's cryptic list. The writing is different, aside from one tiny thing – the crosses of the capital Ts in the word *TACKLE* on the list and the word *TIME'S* on the note in her hand have an almost identical calligraphic flourish.

'No,' she laments. She does not want the threatening note she found in the St John-Gray bure to have been written by Thomasina, not now she feels a kinship with the woman. She would like to think the striking Anglo-Fijian is too gentle of spirit for these kinds of antics.

But then again, what does she know? How can you ever tell what's going on inside another human's head, even the ones who seem empathetic and kind? Especially when the proof is in front of you, as it is for Una now. At this very moment, it is achingly clear that this note and the one she found in Luella St John-Gray's bathroom bin have been written not only by the same pen but the very same hand.

28

Kitty

It is the noise that wakes Kitty, the voices that cry out together, like the sinister chanting of a cult. The second-long pauses in between the words they shout are deafening in their silence, and Kitty wonders if she is imagining it until they start up again. She realises then that it is numbers she can hear: 'Seven . . . six . . . five . . .'

Kitty touches her hair, feels the grease. The Valium Dr Marama gave her has worn off. She can smell the stench of her own armpits, stronger than she could have imagined, the yeasty smell of a dirty scalp, the sour scent of her unwashed skin. She has been in her room for twenty-four hours.

'Four . . . three . . . two . . . one!'

Then cheering, flashes on cameras followed by bright splashes of colour through the linen curtains, and bangs like gunshots: neon pink, silver, purple and gold exploding in the sky and then trickling down against the black backdrop like glitter. Fireworks.

It is officially a new year. One of the first inhabited places in the world to herald it in. Twelve whole hours before Kitty's friends and family will celebrate at home in England. She will need to call Fergus's relatives and break the news about his passing: his brother, Callum, in Edinburgh; his sister, Jayne, up in Dundee. She dreads the task and wonders how long she can put it off for.

The chanting turns to cheering, to whoops of delight. Kitty hears one single peal of laughter, and she recognises its provenance: it is Luella St John-Gray, whose husband is still alive. He has not, unlike Fergus, met an early demise. The anger that floods Kitty now comes in the form of pain – a stab of vitriol, pungent and tangy, that rises up inside her, acid against the tender flesh of her windpipe.

Luella! The way she told Fergus, and by default Kitty, too, a *cruel* no – wouldn't even hear them out. 'Not a snowflake's chance in hell' she said. 'There is no way you are investing *my* money in some dodgy start-up!' And Kitty felt the rapid pulse thumping in her husband's wrist when she put her hand there to comfort him. His blood pressure at boiling point. It was Kitty who watched as Fergus placed his palm over his chest and rubbed it, as if to soothe or dislodge some kind of discomfort there, some kind of dull ache caused by trauma and stress. And then she watched him stagger forward and cease to breathe. An undignified death on a cold floor.

Kitty hears the laughter, the revelry outside, the shameless vitality of living men and living women. Of Luella St John-Gray.

She turns onto her side in the bed and puts a decisive toe out onto the slatted wooden floor.

29

Luella

The fireworks fizzle and die like a bad orgasm and the cries of 'Happy New Year!' are done and dusted. The best part of the night, if she can call it that, is over, and Luella is bored.

Benedict, still in his Venetian mask, leans against the beach bar, speaking limited German with the two boring Fuchs. Alice Chen wears a mini mouse mask, which Luella considers incredibly lame, and sips a cocktail while her rude adolescent daughter screeches 'Happy Fijian New Year!' to her friends on FaceTime. Luella is forced to listen to the squealing of spotty adolescents with nauseating Australian accents on the other end of the video call. A couple Luella hasn't seen before who must be on their honeymoon given their frequent bouts of tonsil hockey, swap drinks for a taste. *Ugh, germy!*

At the edge of the water, the group of Fijian VIPs prepare to board their yacht again, downing the very last drops from the champagne glasses handed to them by one of the male waiters. It's all so *parochial!* Luella is not in the least bit interested in speaking with any of these people. Dull as ditch water, all of them.

She hugs her champagne and allows her mind to rewind and relive the satisfaction of her earlier interaction with Thomasina. Like a feral cat, her half-sister has slunk away to lick her wounds, which means Luella can finally relax, knowing she won't be pounced on again with some God-awful attempt at a guilt trip. She twiddles the stem of her glass between her fingers.

Behind her, the bright lights of reception glow alongside the muted candlelight of the restaurant and the bar beyond. Two figures are having some kind of altercation, and Luella sees it is Una and the dive boy. Una gesticulates wildly, and he grovels with his hands in prayer. Luella watches them for a moment, the almost unusually straight back of the cleaner who spends her day bending over beds, and the tall, stooping figure of the barely-man. They are obviously talking about her, because he looks across at Luella and glances quickly away. Then they hurry off together down the path towards the bures.

'Happy New Year, Mrs St John-Gray!' It is the resort's toadying manager, right in her face. 'Did you enjoy the fireworks?'

Luella smiles sweetly. 'Yes.' *Not really. She's seen better in her own back garden.*

'Wonderful.' He grins. He holds out his hand nervously and passes her an envelope, which reads: *LSJG. Bure One.* Luella does not recognise the handwriting, but she knows for a fact this is Thomasina's doing. 'I believe this note is for you,' he says with a bow.

Luella inspects the envelope with her initials, just as they are on her monogrammed suitcase. 'Where did this come from?' she asks.

'One of the maids, Kelera, found it on her cleaning cart,' the man replies. 'I thought I'd give it to you now rather than drop it into the bure. You know, just in case it is urgent.'

Luella grits her teeth. She ignored the first note, screwed it up and threw it into the bathroom bin. She rips open the envelope.

It reads: *SNAKE ROCK* 12.15 *a.m.*

She senses the nosy manager reading the words over her shoulder, and so she pointedly pulls the note to her chest and says, 'Thank you, Mr Roko. Is that all?'

'Yes, thank you, Mrs St John-Gray,' he mumbles and slopes off.

Luella's head whips around to look for her sister, but she is nowhere to be seen. Stupid, stupid Thomasina. Does she really think Luella is going to be intimidated by a couple of idiotic notes? It is laughable. But at least a confrontation will liven up the party, and at Snake Rock, no less – a forbidden destination for guests after dark. *Bring it on!*

She turns to Benedict, engrossed in telling the Fuchs about some boat trip he once took on the Rhine. *Yawn!* 'I'm going for a walk,' she tells him.

He nods, distracted. 'Have fun,' he says and launches back into his story, which pisses Luella off to high heaven. *Wunder-fucking-bar,* she thinks. Some New Year's Eve this is. If she'd wanted to hang out with a bunch of Germans, she would have gone to Berlin.

At least she has this sparring match with Thomasina to keep her entertained. She gathers up the hem of her dress in her right hand, turns and marches down the shoreline towards Snake Rock, the cold sand between her toes, the straps of her heels swinging from the tips of her fingers. She looks across to the bures that line the beachfront, and she thinks she sees Kitty Miller standing on her veranda, glaring at her as she makes her way across the sand. *Doesn't the woman know she's meant to be wearing a mask?*

When Luella reaches the halfway point between the main resort and Snake Rock, she hears a rustle behind her, the sound of footsteps crunching the sand.

'Luella?' The voice is softly accented.

Give me strength, thinks Luella. *What the hell does the Frog want?* She speeds up, pretends the wind has drowned out the sound of the other woman's calls.

'Luella, stop!'

Her patience is a cord that has now snapped. 'Oh, for God's sake, leave me alone,' she hisses. 'I do not wish to speak to you. I have enough friends already.'

The Frenchwoman stops dead. Luella feels pleased and carries on without her.

She reaches Snake Rock and climbs over the craggy structure to the beach that sits in a U-shape. She makes her way down slowly, avoiding the fossilised oyster shells imbedded in the sides that julienne your feet. As soon as she lands on the soft sand, she realises that, despite her efforts, she has indeed still lacerated her feet and will need to put antiseptic on them when she gets back to the bure. She feels a flash of anger at the Frenchwoman for forcing her to hurry across the rocks just to get away from her.

She sits down with just a sliver of moonlight as her vision, and that's when it occurs to Luella that deep inside the embrace of the rock, she cannot be seen. She is hidden entirely from the main part of the resort and cannot observe the revellers on the beach, nor they her. She can hear them, a faint hum. This is why they pick this spot for marriage renewals, because in daylight and at sundown, it is picturesque and provides a privacy screen from the bikinis and the beach volleyball on the other side.

'Luella, can we talk?' It is the French doctor again, although now her voice has taken on a hard edge.

For pity's sake, thinks Luella. *Why don't you just fuck off?*

'I must talk to you,' she says, insistent now. Her accent seems more French somehow; it's like she's from that terrible old programme Luella used to watched with Thomasina and their mother when she was a child: *'Allo 'Allo*. The policeman who said, *Good Moaning*.

Luella sighs and looks up at the doctor. Her face is hidden under her small silver mask, but her eyes shine in the moonlight and her pupils are narrow. 'What is it? Do you want my money? *Quelle surprise*.'

There is a laugh and a shake of the head, and Luella hears the word '*Non*,' and there is a pang of something, of déjà vu or recognition or some such sensation. It is something in this woman's smile, the way her top lip stretches out thinly over teeth that have the slightest of gaps. It throws Luella, floods her with a sensation she does not like, something like fear.

'Then leave me the fuck alone,' Luella snaps. 'Who are you, anyway?'

'My name is Sofie Barthélemy.' The doctor pulls down her mask and smiles grimly. 'You really don't remember me,' she says. 'Do you?'

30

Una

'How could you just forget?' She could murder Sailasa in cold blood. He promised he'd go to the bures at 10 p.m. They cannot be caught turning down beds at gone midnight!

Thank goodness Una remembered when she did and that there are now two of them to get the work done at this very late stage, and that Kitty Miller's door wears a *Do Not Disturb* sign and doesn't require an evening service. Small mercies.

'Oh, Sailasa.' She sighs. Sometimes, it is just far easier to do a job yourself, rather than entrusting it to someone else who will promptly forget and you'll end up having to do it yourself anyway.

'I'm sorry!' Sailasa laments. She can tell he is panicked, in fight-or-flight mode. 'I meant to do it, and then something came up.'

Una looks out to her left, sees Sofie Barthélemy scurrying along the sand after Luella, who is storming ahead towards Snake Rock. Luella turns to say something to Sofie that halts the doctor in her tracks temporarily. It's a relief the two women are safely away from their rooms – it will give her and Sailasa time to do what they need to.

Una lets out a long sigh. She cannot stay angry with him, this boy, this child who is actually a fully grown man but will always be a boy to her. Twenty-two but a baby in her eyes. Her nephew, her heart. 'It's fine,' she says. 'Let's just get it done quickly now, yes? I'll do Sofie Barthélemy's room while you do Bure One, OK? And make it fast.'

'Got it.' Sailasa nods and heads off down the path.

Una clicks open Sofie Barthélemy's door. The room is tidy and neat. Clothes hang in the closet with an inch-wide gap between them; products line the bathroom sink in perfect symmetry, mostly French: Clarins face wash, Embryolisse moisturiser, L'Oréal shampoo. Una turns up the air-conditioning, switches on the bedside lamps and folds over the toilet paper into a triangular point. She sprays some coconut, lime and mango room spray around the place and pops a new frangipani flower in the foot-bowl outside the front door.

This takes – what, four, maybe five minutes max? Usually, she would take longer, perhaps do a sweep or replace one or two of the towels, wash all of the sand from the bottom of the shower with the showerhead and not just the most offending parts. But tonight, they are rushed, she and Sailasa, her partner in crime.

Una turns to the bed, and it is with the reading light now on that she notices the indent of two heels on the right side of the bed – the side on which she knows Sofie Barthélemy does not sleep. More interestingly, the dents are at the very end of the bed, suggesting they belong to someone tall: a man. She smooths the bed with her hands, pulls down the top quarter of the top sheet (it's called a *turn-down* service for a reason) and steps back. There is a lump under the sheet now. Una puts her hand under and rummages to straighten the secondary one below, pulls out a black, lacy negligee – the kind of item a woman would not wear if sleeping alone. She carries it to the laundry bag that hangs inside the closet and turns back to the bed.

Una feels as if she has overstayed her welcome. She closes the door and hovers under the third palm on the left, waiting for Sailasa. Was that a figment of her imagination, she wonders, the indent of a man's feet in Sofie's bed? Is she getting confused in her state of tiredness? She has worked until midnight the last two nights, after all. She shakes the thought off and turns to her right to see the slender figure of Luella St John-Gray clambering over Snake Rock and back towards the heart of the resort, her long hair coming loose from its bun.

Una cannot see her face, but she can tell by the way she is walking that the woman is more rattled than usual – as if she's been exposed to something behind the rock that has unsettled or frightened her.

Una hides behind the palm and clutches the trunk with both hands as she peers around it and watches the woman hurrying down the beach, her mask on and the hem of her dress and the straps of her shoes both dangling from her left hand. When Luella St John-Gray reaches her husband, she pulls him away from Klaus and Isabelle Fuch to whisper something discreetly in his ear.

Benedict St John-Gray smiles and nods, and Una wonders if the wife has offered him something of the carnal kind – not that her spouse is in any fit state to oblige. He holds up his hand with a discernible wobble as if he is telling her, *You go and I'll be along in five minutes.* Una doubts that very much – just from the way he is trying to get the attention of the barman for a nightcap.

Una glances anxiously towards Bure One. *Come on, Sailasa,* she begs silently. *What is taking you so long? What the hell are you* doing *in there?*

31

Sailasa

Sailasa turns down the corner of the sheets as Una has shown him, plumps the pillows and moves to the bathroom. Toilet paper folded into a point? Tick. Toilet seat down? Tick. Towels folded and rehung? Tick. He gives the bathroom vanity a quick wipe, and as he does it, he sees something move, and then he hears a smash.

'Shit!' he hisses. A jar, of face cream he thinks, has broken into twenty, maybe thirty pieces, the letters that made up the word *CHANEL* flying off into some far-flung corner of the bathroom. '*Shit!*'

He grabs a towel and gathers it all up, feels a piece of white ceramic slice the base of his right index finger. The blood drips on the floor, and he winces as he wraps it in the side of a small white hand towel. He is in panic mode now, and he is not thinking at all clearly.

Una had warned him to get the rooms done before midnight, but then he received the text message and it threw him. *Sailasa,* it read. *You're running out of time for your next payment, and I'm losing my patience.* There was a skull emoji after it.

Sailasa couldn't tell Una this was why he'd forgotten about the rooms. It would serve only to worry his doting aunt even more.

At last, when Sailasa is satisfied there is no more cream or blood or shards of white, he hurries towards the bure's entrance, flicking off the lights on the way. He glances over his shoulder at the room as he races forward to the door, and when he turns, he gasps.

There, in the doorway, is Luella St John-Gray. She is still wearing her Venetian mask but is somehow unkempt, wild even.

She gives a gasp of outrage at the sight of him.

'I'm so sorry, Mrs St John Grey,' Sailasa pleads. 'I'm here to do the turn-down service . . .'

She steps into the room. In the darkness, Sailasa can see the woman's eyes through the holes in the metal filigree. They are dark, full of fear. He wants to tell her not to be scared – he is here to make the bed, to make a pretty V-shape with the toilet paper, to pick up and replace wet towels, all at Una's request, and not to attack her. He sees the eyes look down at the white hand towel in his right hand, now red with blood.

'Get *out!*' She says it slowly, as if Sailasa is stupid.

'Mrs St John-Gray . . .' he says. He can hear his own voice now, hear his boyish tones packaged up in a hard edge. 'I can explain. I was cleaning the bathroom, and I dropped a pot, a face cream of some kind . . .'

He watches as the woman points behind her, out of the doorway behind her and into the night. He takes a step towards it as she has directed him to and then hesitates.

'Please . . .'

'I said, get out!' she hisses, *spitting* it, like she did on the boat. 'Get the *fuck* out!'

It all happens so quickly. Sailasa feels the heat rise up through his neck and into his head, anger taking over his body as if he has been injected with the stuff right into the softest part of his arm, the place Dr Marama told him was the called the median cubital, the biggest vein. It pulses now with despair and rage. All of him pulses.

He steps forward, left hand now raised high above his head. He floats up to the ceiling then, an outsider looking in, and watches in horror as his hand comes swiftly down.

MONDAY 1 JANUARY
NEW YEAR'S DAY

Cocktail of the Day:
Karma Killer

(Triple sec, dark rum, peach brandy, pineapple juice, orange juice, grapefruit juice)

32

Una

Una is up early, despite the late night. She has to be – she's rostered on shift today. Not that she minds. It's not as if she's the wildest one in the staff village. She ate a very late dinner, a traditional New Year's Eve feast with the others, and then she left the young ones to party. She was in bed with a cup of tea by 1 a.m., no time to even reflect on any resolutions for the year ahead. She makes one now: to help Sailasa get out of the mess he's in – to pull her family close, or what is left of it: this nephew of hers who has become like a son.

Una makes her way along the path that links the oceanfront bures, collecting champagne glasses from the veranda tables as she goes, and smiles at the sight of Benedict St John-Gray lying in a hammock, his long legs hanging awkwardly over the side. He's still dressed in his suit trousers from last night. His shirt is unbuttoned, and his bow-tie hangs undone around his neck. She tiptoes past and carries on along the path.

Beyond him, the resort's gardeners comb the beach with long rakes, gliding up and down the sand by the rock, smoothing the countless footprints and sand-hills created the night before. Una can see the sweat on their brows as they eradicate all the signs of a good night, transforming the beach from party to paradise once more.

Once she has collected the glasses, Una begins emptying the water pails on the verandas of each of her bures and refilling them, adding a hibiscus flower to the top. Back outside Bure One, the handle of the pail clangs against the side of the bucket, and Benedict St John-Gray sits bolt upright.

Una holds up her hands. 'Mr St John-Gray,' she says. 'My apologies.'

'No bother,' he yawns. 'Happy New Year, Una.'

'And to you, Mr St John-Gray. I hope you enjoyed last night's party.'

'I certainly did,' he says. 'A little too much, judging by the fact I slept outside.' He grins and scratches his head.

Una smiles. 'Well, it was a very balmy night. The perfect night to sleep under the stars.'

Benedict St John-Gray gets up with a wobble and walks the two metres across the sand to the veranda where Una stands. He feels in his pockets. 'Oh,' he says. 'It's a good job you're here. I don't appear to have my key card.'

Una picks up the lanyard round her neck and clicks open the door for him.

'You're a gem, Una – an absolute gem.'

He steps inside.

Una collects a rogue teaspoon from behind the outdoor chair and is making to walk off when she hears a raised voice.

'What the hell? *Luella?*' He appears on the veranda. 'Una?'

Una turns back. 'Is everything OK?'

'Well, not really. Have you seen my wife?'

'This early?' Una asks, her face a quiz. 'No, I haven't seen anyone outside of the staff village – aside from the sand-rakers over there. Could she have gone for a swim?'

'No. She doesn't do that. She's not a morning person.'

Una ponders on it for a moment. She hasn't seen a soul this morning, aside from the gardeners. 'Your wife returned here last night, though?'

'Yes,' says Mr St John-Gray. 'Her dress is here, on the floor. Look.' He gestures to the mass of shimmering red by the left side of the bed, which Una can just see through the open door, and points to the mask on top of the bar fridge.

'I don't understand it.' He scratches his head again.

'I'm sure she'll turn up,' Una offers brightly. 'You can't get lost on Loloma. It's impossible. The island is too small . . .'

'No,' Benedict St John-Gray muses. 'You're right – I don't suppose you can. But it's just . . . it's more than a little out of character for Luella.'

Una studies his face and watches as his eyebrows pull together into a frown. A man suffering the effects of a rollicking New Year's Day hangover.

She smiles again. 'If I come across Mrs St John-Gray, I will tell her you are looking for her.'

'Thank you, Una,' he says.

After lunch, Una heads to the laundry to reload her cart and refill her bottles of cleaning fluid for tomorrow's routine. Joana talks at her, almost non-stop, until Una snaps and tells her, 'Joana, you know how to give a woman a headache!'

Joana shuffles off huffily, and Una folds, loads, pours and ponders. There was something a little off about the St John-Gray bure earlier. She thinks of the hammock, the Venetian mask, the Valentino gown and the sand on the veranda. What is she grappling for? What is it that's vexing her?

And then it comes to her: it was the bed. Benedict St John-Gray slept in the hammock outside the bure, but the side of the bed usually occupied by Luella St John-Gray – the left – was as neat as her husband's side, the sheets almost as taut. It was as if her side had been only briefly lain on, *on top of* the sheets, before the inhabitant had thought better of it and taken themselves off somewhere else entirely.

33

Thomasina

Thomasina is at the pool bar drinking an early afternoon Fijian beer when the resort manager, Jose Roko, appears beside her.

She's already seen him once today; he hammered on her bure first thing to ask her if she had seen Luella. 'Mr St John-Gray can't locate his wife,' he explained with an apologetic grimace as Thomasina stood at the door in her pyjamas. 'She doesn't appear to be anywhere at the resort.'

Thomasina just shrugged. Why on earth was he bothering her about it? What did she care where Luella had swanned off to? It wasn't as if she could have gone anywhere far on a tiny island in the middle of the Pacific.

'Seriously?' she asked, annoyed. 'How am I meant to know? She's probably gone for a walk.'

She checks her watch now: 12.15 p.m.

Roko greets her with a bow of the head. 'Ms Delana.'

'Has my sister turned up yet?' she asks in a bored voice. It is a formality, the asking of the question, because Thomasina does not really care. The Thomasina Diamond is gone because Luella sold it at Christie's in London, and so Thomasina doesn't give a fuck where her sister is.

'That's actually what I'm here for,' says Roko gently. 'I wanted to let you know that I have filed a missing person report in response to Mrs St John-Gray's disappearance.'

Thomasina turns to him. 'A missing person report? Really?' How typical of Luella to whisk up so much drama. 'Isn't that a little over the top? She's only been gone a few hours.'

'We do not think it is over the top,' says Roko gravely. 'I have contacted the surrounding resorts, and I'm afraid no one has seen your sister. Filipe and some of the other staffers have also scoured the bush-land and the walking track now, and they still haven't located her. I'm duty-bound to report her missing.'

He shifts from one foot to the other. 'Ms Delana, we are a waterlogged resort, and with that comes risk.'

Thomasina nods. 'Well, thanks for letting me know,' she says, realising that the manager is actually taking Luella's disappearance seriously.

'I will, of course, keep you informed of any developments. But please do let me know if I can help in any way.'

'Thanks,' she says. 'I will.' Thomasina swallows down a sip of her beer along with a strange feeling of foreboding that has settled, like heartburn, in the centre of her chest.

Roko pauses. 'Ms Delana, might I ask you . . . ?' He pauses. 'We would like to keep this as low key as possible here on the island,' he says. 'For Mr St John-Gray's benefit, as well as out of concern for the other guests – and of course for yourself, too.'

Thomasina raises an eyebrow. Of course he wants to keep it on the down-low. A dead man one day and a missing woman the next? It's hardly good for business. Come to Loloma and you, too, could go missing! *It's all about the money,* she thinks. *How ironic. But I'll give him this: he's good at playing concerned.*

She gathers up her bag. 'Thanks for the update,' she says. 'If there's nothing else, I think I'll go for a swim.'

'Of course.' Roko stands up and offers a funereal bow.

When she gets to the beach, Thomasina feels an almost desperate urge to immerse herself in the waves. She pulls off her T-shirt and shorts and leaves them behind her on the shore with her bag, then walks to the water's edge and wades in. When she is deep enough, she dives forward and feels the tepid saltiness revive her. There is nothing so calming, so cathartic as immersing herself under the water. It holds her in its grasp like nothing or no one ever has. It is even more meaningful here, in the place her father was born.

She plunges beneath the waves and holds her breath, cleanses herself of the bitterness she felt when Luella told her she'd sold the diamond. *She's not worth it,* she tells herself. *Life is simpler when you learn to accept an apology you never got.*

When she comes up for air, she hears the radio from the beach bar spewing out the nineties hit 'Baby, I Love Your Way' by Big Mountain. She turns towards the sound and sees two staff members bouncing over the waves on a jet ski to retrieve an empty kayak that bobs up and down by one of the buoys. Over at the reception, a group of staffers point towards various island landmarks as if they're about to launch some kind of search party and they are divvying up spots to check.

Thomasina plunges under the water again and opens her eyes. *Things are so much less complicated under the sea*, she thinks.

Thomasina was two and a half when her baby sister arrived. She vaguely remembers it. She has no recollection of her early life: of living in Esher as a newborn baby and scraping by, left in the arms of neighbours while her mother rode a train and then a red double-decker bus into work every day. Her first memories are of the giant Belgravia home with the metal gates and the plush white carpets and a bedroom larger than a McDonald's outlet. She had her own dad, Joseph, who was dead, and then Freddie, who treated Thomasina as his own – before *and* after Luella came along.

Both girls were spoilt, both adored – Luella strangely less so by their father because she hadn't come from nothing like Thomasina had (and like he himself had, years before her). Freddie had built up a logistics chain in the south of England, first one fleet of lorries and then another in the north, until they were everywhere. You couldn't do a loop of the M25 without seeing at least five of them, with their big green canopies and the words *WALSH-BERGER* in yellow. He did it despite the shackles of his alcoholic business partner, Christopher Berger, until ultimately he got rid of the weak link and went solo, claimed the dynasty as his own. After that, the trucks just said *WALSH*. When he was in his mid-sixties, he sold the company for millions. Freddie, or just Dad as Thomasina and Luella knew him, had quite literally supplied the logistics to provide a roof over their heads, and then some.

Within two years her mother was dead from terminal cancer and her father had been diagnosed with vascular dementia, the aggressive kind. And when he died, Thomasina was left with nothing. The terms of his will stipulated that everything would go to Luella.

Thomasina hadn't cried over the loss of the money itself because, in those very early, happy years when it was just her and her mum, she had learnt it wasn't money that made you happy; it was love. But she mourned the loss of heirlooms, of photos, of her mother's jewellery, for the comfort they might have brought her, for the memories. And she knew *exactly* how it had unfurled, the financial abandonment: it had been down to Luella and her cruel manipulation of a mentally infirm man.

Thomasina closes her eyes, falls back onto her back and floats, feeling the sun burning her face. She hears her name, and she pulls her body upright, rubbing the salt from her eyes.

Benedict stands on the wet sand, close to the water. 'Where is Luella's diamond?' he barks from the shoreline. 'What have you done with it?'

What the hell?

Thomasina stands up and wipes her cheeks with her palms. She squeezes the water from her ponytail with her clenched fist and wades through the waves towards him. In the distance, she sees Filipe milling about by the dive shed. She turns back to Benedict – she in a tatty old bikini, and he in a preppy pink polo top and shorts. He glances at her chest, the pervert, and she pulls her bikini over herself more.

'What are you talking about?' she calls back.

'Don't play dumb, Thomasina!'

Benedict runs his hands through his hair, his face red. She has always suspected there is a *side* to him: aggressor, creep. The way he touched the small of her back when he hugged her the other day, the way his eyes danced over her body.

'The box is in the bure but not the necklace. That's what you came for, didn't you? To Fiji? To steal from my wife?'

Thomasina stares at him. 'What the hell . . . ? *You* invited *me* here! And why did you do that, Benedict? We both know it wasn't so I could make up with my sister and play happy families again.'

'It was, you ungrateful b—'

Thomasina laughs bitterly.

Benedict takes a step forward as if he might hurt her. His face is ruddy and bloated and his face contorted with anger. '*Where is it*, Thomasina?' he hisses. 'Tell me now.'

Thomasina feels a sudden flash of panic, standing here half-naked in the water in front of a man who is incandescent with anger. Benedict takes a step forward and she scans her periphery for someone, anyone. Then she sees Filipe walking down the sand towards her, his eyes trained on Benedict. She exhales through her mouth.

'Is everything OK, Ms Delana?' he calls out as he closes in on Benedict.

'Fine, thank you, Filipe, but perhaps if you could wait here for a moment, that would be wonderful. I wanted to run something past you, about. . . about the diving trip to the Salamander Shipwreck?'

Filipe looks from Thomasina to Benedict and back again, and he nods.

Benedict ignores him and takes another step forward. 'Don't dick about, Thomasina,' he says through gritted teeth. 'I want you to tell me where you've put the diamond, and I want you to tell me *now*.'

Filipe takes a step forward, too, and it emboldens her.

'Didn't my sister tell you, Benedict? She sold it at Christie's. She *auctioned* it. She showed me the receipt on the beach yesterday evening. Take it up with her, not me. Or perhaps just check your bank account – that's if Luella has actually allowed you access to it . . .'

Benedict shakes his head. 'Bullshit. She brought it here – she told me so. Now, I suggest you hand it over.'

'Are you not *hearing* me, Benedict? I saw the receipt of sale with Christie's clearly marked on the top.' Thomasina taps her temple with her finger. 'Ask Alice Chen and her daughter – they saw it, too. Luella hurled her phone at the poor kid.'

Benedict runs his hands through his hair, offers up an angry smile. It's as if he hasn't heard her. 'Thomasina, do you understand me? I want that stone *back*.'

Thomasina glares at him, a challenge. 'Shouldn't you be more concerned about Luella, Benedict? Or is it just the diamond you're worried about?' She squeezes more water from her ponytail angrily. 'You make me sick. Perhaps she's finally taken off because she's realised what a leech you are!'

'I love my wife!' Benedict shouts in protest. He turns away from her and walks a few steps before slumping down on the very same wooden sun lounger on which Thomasina saw Luella applying designer sun cream yesterday.

'I love my wife,' he pleads again, only this time his voice cracks. He puts his head in his hands and begins to sob.

Filipe and Thomasina exchange a glance, and Thomasina shakes her head. He won't be getting her sympathy vote.

She looks up to see a woman on the beach path in giant sunglasses and a hat with a brim that flops down over half of her face. For a second, from her position in the water, Thomasina thinks it is Luella. But the accented voice, when the woman calls out, is unmistakably Sofie Barthélemy's.

'What is going on?' Sofie calls out to Thomasina and Filipe as she clocks Benedict slumped on the sun lounger.

'He is . . . distressed,' says Filipe. His eyes meet Thomasina's. 'His wife is. . .' he stops.

'What Filipe means to say is that Benedict's wife, my sister Luella, has disappeared.'

'Disappeared?' asks Sofie. 'How?'

Thomasina shrugs. 'Search me. It's quite the mystery.'

Sofie looks from Thomasina to Filipe. She steps off the path and hurries down the beach, stopping after a few steps to kick off her sandals. She sits down beside Benedict, picks up his wrist and places a finger on his pulse point and looks to the sky as she counts. 'His pulse rate is fast,' she calls out to Thomasina, as if

Thomasina remotely cares. 'I had better take him to Dr Marama's office.'

She turns to Benedict. 'Monsieur St John-Gray,' she says softly. 'Will you come with me?'

Benedict looks up at Sofie and seems at first confused.

'Monsieur St John-Gray?' she offers again.

Eventually, he seems to come to and answers her with a small nod.

'Filipe, would you?' Sofie gestures to Benedict, and Filipe steps forward and grabs an arm. Together they hoist Benedict up. Once he is upright, he shakes Filipe off and allows Sofie to lead him away like a child – the slender bohemian doctor, who hours ago was dancing on the sand in a thin slip of a silver dress, somehow taking an equal share of the weight of this six-foot-something man.

'Is everything alright, Ms Delana?' Filipe asks when he arrives back on the shoreline.

'Crocodile tears,' she says as she steps out of the water and scoops up her belongings from the sand.

They walk together side by side back to the dive shed.

'Roko told me about reporting Luella missing,' she says. 'But I imagine the police can't do much at this early stage. She's only been gone for a few hours.'

'No,' says Filipe. 'It's likely they'll investigate as soon as possible,' Filipe says. 'A few months ago, there was some bad press about the police waiting twenty-four hours before they began looking for missing persons. The commissioner even held a press conference to confirm that they *do* always begin investigating earlier.'

'I don't see any police boats.'

'They will file the report first, and then they'll come.'

'How do you know?'

'My cousin's in the police. That's how they do it.'

'Oh,' says Thomasina, looking to her right and out to sea. 'Anyway, tell your cousin not to get too excited. Luella's like a bad penny. She'll turn up.'

They reach the dive shed. Filipe picks up a snorkel that's been left on the desk and drops it in a bucket of disinfectant.

'You and your sister. You do not seem. . .' He looks away from her and stops.

'What? Say it, please.'

'I don't want to speak out of turn.'

'It's OK – go on.'

Filipe pulls at his earlobe, hesitant.

'It's fine,' she says. 'Really.'

He sighs. 'You do not seem very . . . close.'

Thomasina smiles. 'Luella and me? I don't mind talking about it, but it's just a case of where to start. We are different as adults, but we were worlds apart as kids, too. She always felt she was better than me, somehow. I think it's because my stepfather preferred me. He adopted me as a baby after my real dad died. He was Fijian actually.'

'You're half Fijian?'

'I am.'

Filipe smiles. 'I can see it now. You look like a Fijian girl.'

Thomasina grins. She likes the comment; it sends a shiver of warmth through her. 'My stepdad, Luella's father, brought me up. We went through so much together. He never said it, but it was kind of obvious I was his favourite. I think he loved me more than Luella because I'd lost my biological dad. You know, adversity and stuff.

'We had such a strong bond. Luella hated it. I was bullied a lot at school for looking different, and she was the driving force behind it.'

Filipe nods, like he is processing it all. 'Was it always like that?'

'Pretty much, although I screwed it all up at some point – I took the bullying out on my parents. I was awful to them, and I regret it so much. But even during that time, I had a better relationship with them than Luella did. Dad thought she was entitled and rude. They didn't see one another for a while – Dad and Luella – until

Mum was dying and Dad was at the beginning stages of dementia. And then Luella swooped.'

'Swooped?'

'*Swooped.*'

They were in their parents' living room, a shrine to their mother since her death. Their dad's lawyer had suggested it: power of attorney. 'It's advisable in cases of dementia to get power of attorney over the subject's health and finances.'

Dad wasn't in his right mind most of the time, but he had lucid days and he was deemed well enough to sign the forms.

'Daddy, we are sharing the power of attorney job,' Thomasina told him. 'Luella will do one and I will do the other.'

And because Thomasina was, to all intents and purposes, the full-time caregiver for her father, she took the health role. She wanted to be able to decide where and when he was treated – and how. Luella took control of their father's property and finance.

He had asked them to divide the assets in accordance with his will after he was gone – he'd told them immediately after their mother died – but when he was in the throes of dementia, Luella changed the will and disinherited Thomasina, the half-sister, the sister she never regarded as *whole*. That included keeping her mother's pendant from her. ('Make sure the diamond goes to Thomas,' had been one of the last things their mother said when the cancer turned terminal and they started imagining the unimaginable. 'It's hers.')

Thomasina challenged it at first – of course she did – but she was warned off by Luella's lawyer every single time ('cease and desist!') and everything had gone silent for two years, until Benedict emailed Thomasina and told her Luella was keen to make amends on the island of love.

'You know he invited me here?' Thomasina tells Filipe. 'Benedict.'

'Why?'

'Well, that's just it,' she says. 'It makes no sense.'

'Maybe he had good intentions,' Filipe says. 'Maybe he is angry because he is worried about his wife.'

Thomasina smiles. 'That's generous of you.' She looks into his face and is suddenly aware of the sound of her own voice, how much she has talked *at* him.

'God listen to me!' she says. 'What about you? Do you have any brothers and sisters?'

Filipe studies his own palms. 'I have a sister,' he says. 'She lives in Nadi. She's having a tough time trying to have a baby at the moment. It just isn't happening for her and her husband.'

Thomasina can see the sadness in his eyes, recognises him as a man who cares deeply about his family. She is learning that this is the Fijian way. 'So I guess shit happens in all families, doesn't it?'

Filipe nods. 'It sure does.'

34

Una

The day is almost over. Una has cleaned all four bures immaculately once again, swept each of the guest verandas and restocked her cart with clean linen and shampoo bottles, when it occurs to her that she has not yet seen Sailasa. It is New Year's Day, of course, and a lot of the staff worked late cleaning up after the party and afforded themselves a lie-in – but Una does not think Sailasa was one of them. She distinctly remembers him mentioning he was on the early shift with Filipe, just as she herself is.

Something in the pit of Una's stomach does not sit right, and it can't be her lunch because she had a plain old ham and cheese sandwich like she always does. She doesn't know what it is that's irritating the lining of her gut other than some kind of instinct that something is afoot. A woman has vanished from the island, and even though there is likely a very good explanation for it (a clandestine jaunt to another island, perhaps?), Una feels a distinct sense of unease.

As she returns some rogue beach towels to the laundry, she entertains herself by trying to piece together a jigsaw: a note that was *clearly* written by Thomasina Delana; the imprints of a man's feet in Sofie Barthélemy's bed; Luella St John-Gray's Valentino dress tossed aside on the floor of her bure; Sailasa's failure to show up for his shift . . .

She takes her phone out of her pocket and scrolls down her *called* list. His name is the second number. It rings out, and she catches her breath with the momentary euphoria of hope when the dial tone stops for a fraction of a second, but she frowns as she realises the pause is merely his voicemail kicking in. 'This is Sailasa. Leave me a message!'

She doesn't leave a message as his automated response instructs her to but decides she will go to the staff quarters and find him in person instead.

She ditches her trolley outside the Chens' bure and continues along the path that weaves a figure-of-eight towards the staff quarters. Halfway along, she bumps into Sofie Barthélemy.

'Oh, *pardon*!' The woman's head is down, and she does not laugh frivolously about the accidental collision like she did the last time.

Una tilts her head to look at Sofie's face, an instinctual thing, and sees the purpling of a bruise on her cheek and the red line of a cut. There is make-up over both, to suggest the doctor does not want anyone to notice, but Una cannot help herself – it is a fault of hers, this overfamiliarity; she is well aware of it.

'Your face, Dr Barthélemy!' she says in a gentle voice. 'Are you hurt?'

Sofie's shrinks backwards and lowers her head, but Una notes the tears in her eyes behind the oversized sunglasses.

'Dr Barthélemy,' says Una gently. 'What happened to your face?'

The doctor hesitates. 'It was . . .' Her voice is shaking.

'Yes?'

'*De rien*,' says Sofie Barthélemy, waving a hand at Una. 'Nothing, please. I thought I covered it well, but obviously I did not.'

'It looks painful,' Una ventures.

'If you must know, Una' – Sofie Barthélemy lets out a long sigh – '*Madame* St John-Gray slapped me.'

'Slapped you?'

'Yes. At Snake Rock last night.'

Una recalls seeing Luella St John-Gray marching back along the sand away from the rock, and now it makes sense. She was angry, and this is why. 'Was there a reason?' she asks.

The doctor shifts from one foot to the other. 'I needed to talk to her about . . . some business. It was nothing too important, but she took offence to me, and then she hit me.'

Una wants to ask more. What business? Why would a benign chat, a 'not too important' discussion rile up Luella St John-Gray so much she would lash out at the Frenchwoman?

Una opens her mouth and then shuts it. It is not her place to ask questions. She is a cleaner, and Sofie Barthélemy is a paying guest.

'I'm very sorry to hear that,' she says to the doctor instead. 'I hope it is not too painful.'

'It is fine,' says Sofie. 'I am not expecting an apology from Madame St John-Gray.'

No, thinks Una, *and there won't be one forthcoming if the woman can't be found.*

It is as if Sofie Barthélemy reads her thoughts. 'Is there any update on her whereabouts, Una?' she asks.

'I don't believe so.'

Sofie Barthélemy turns to leave but then stops. 'You know, Una, I am a firm believer that people with evil in their hearts do not win in life. Do you believe this too?'

'Very much so,' says Una.

The doctor's gentle features seem to morph into something harsh. Her lips thin out. 'I do not wish anything bad upon Mrs St John-Gray, but I do believe she will get her payback for the way she treats people.'

Una is not sure she should be condoning this with a woman missing, but nevertheless, she nods sympathetically and hands the doctor a fistful of leaves from the Island Musk bush. 'This is how we traditionally treat ailments on the island, Dr Barthélemy,' she says. 'It is our traditional medicine. You may find it eases the bruising.'

Sofie Barthélemy holds out her left hand and takes them with a small smile. '*Vinaka*, Una,' she says.

Una, burning with intrigue about the confrontation between the French and English women, continues towards the staff village in search of Sailasa. She passes the ageing frangipani tree outside the green and white building, with its offering of pink blooms and potent aroma, and the sign that clearly states: *Staff Only: No Guest Access Beyond This Point*, and she pushes open the swing-door that leads first to the kitchen and then through to the main staff dormitories.

Una sometimes wonders what guests would make of the staff village, with its peeling paint and tiny rooms and bright, colourful washing strung up on lines and over balconies – a place that is far less luxurious than the bures she services but that has so much more colour, so much more soul.

It is stiflingly hot, even at this late stage in the day, and Una pulls her dress away from her chest a few times to fan herself.

Sailasa's room is at the end of the corridor, the last in the row. She knocks on the door once and stands back. Then she knocks again, this time leaning her ear against the wooden door painted the colour of evergreen. In the silence, the clang of her gold hoop earring against the wood is almost deafening.

'Sailasa?' she calls softly. And then, 'Sailasa!' An urgent rap of her knuckles on the door. 'Sailasa. Wake up!'

Una puts her hand tentatively on the aluminium door handle and slowly turns it, a sickly feeling settling over her. Her hand flies to her mouth.

'Oh God,' she whispers as she takes in the scene in front of her: an empty room with a bed that has not been slept in.

One thing Sailasa never does in the morning is make his bed, but as she stands in the doorway of the dorm, she sees it is perfectly made, and she knows it is perfect because she herself made it yesterday afternoon. She passed the open door and saw the messy bed and tutted to herself before going inside and plumping the pillows, stretching the sheets taut and tucking them with vigour under the curved corners of the single mattress. Una knows she is a soft touch when it comes to Sailasa – *everyone* knows it. There's no way Sailasa both slept in this bed last night and also made it this pristine again afterwards.

'Making his bed again?' Kelera asked yesterday, with a shake of her head as she passed on her way to the spa. 'That boy doesn't know he's born.'

'You mind your own business, Kelera Vatubua.' But Una smiled. 'I like to spoil him.'

But the fact is: there is no girlfriend on the island whose room her nephew might have stayed in, and the woman he is sweet on is back home in Nadi. She feels sick. Has Sailasa fled? And if so, *why*?

Una closes the door quietly and leans against it, her hand to her chest. Anyone aware of Sailasa's financial problems, as Una herself is, might think he's been driven to do something stupid and then to run as a consequence of his actions. What if something happened in the St John-Gray woman's bure?

Una! she berates herself. She will not allow herself to entertain thoughts such as this. She spins around and steps back into the corridor just as Joana steps out of the dormitory opposite.

'*Bula*,' Joana chirps.

'Oh, *bula*,' Una tries to sound casual. 'I was just looking for Sailasa.'

Joana fans herself with a copy of the *Fiji Sun*. 'I haven't seen him since last night.' She peers over Una's shoulder through the open door of Sailasa's room. 'You been making his bed again?'

Una ignores her. She can smell the inky print of the paper Joana waves in front of her face.

'The dive shed?'

'Yes, he's probably there,' Una says. She must act like nothing is wrong, which is a hard task since her legs are now wobbling as if she is fresh from a boat. 'I'll go there now.'

Una continues along the corridor towards the front door that will take her across the garden, past the laundry and then alongside the spa, towards the heart of the resort.

'Wait,' calls Joana. 'Has the missing woman turned up yet?'

'Not that I've heard.'

'Roko said earlier that they've filed a missing person report. Gives me the chills,' Joana says.

'Why?'

Joanna looks serious now. She hugs herself with her arms. 'Someone died two nights ago and now a woman has disappeared into thin air on an island you cannot get lost on. It just feels . . . eerie. Don't you agree?'

'It's just an unfortunate coincidence,' says Una firmly. 'Fergus Miller died of a medical episode. The woman isn't *dead*. The missing person report is just a formality. It hasn't even been a day yet – Mrs St John-Gray will probably show up soon enough.'

Probably.

'Well, Roko's pretty concerned,' continues Joana with a shrug. 'The sea was treacherous last night. Maybe she went for a swim and didn't come back? Or maybe someone wanted rid of her . . .'

Una rolls her eyes. 'You've watched too many detective shows.'

But of course, Joana is right. There *is* something decidedly eerie about a death and a disappearance in quick succession. And the fact that Luella St John-Gray can't be located on an island as tiny as Loloma is very worrying indeed.

Una shakes off the thought – for now. Idle speculation amongst the staff will not help Una find her nephew and that is her top priority right now – not a guest who's gone walkabout.

Joana clicks her tongue on the roof of her mouth. 'Well,' she says. 'I hope you find your Sailasa!'

The look on Joana's face and the proximity of Sailasa's name to speculation about the whereabouts of Luella St John-Gray bothers Una so extremely she can almost taste it. She tells herself there is no reason why anyone should suspect a link between him and the missing woman. She herself doesn't think the two disappearances are linked – *does she?*

She takes only a few steps before she hears Joana's voice again. 'He seemed upset in the laundry yesterday.'

Una squirms. Joana must have been listening to them when Sailasa was telling her about his debt.

'He might even be relieved when he finds out she's missing. The woman can't have him fired if she has disappeared, can she?'

Una stops in her tracks. She wants to turn around – oh God, how she wants to! – but she will not give Joana the satisfaction of an emotional response.

'No, but her husband can,' calls Una over her shoulder. '*Sota tale.*' *See you later.*

The sports desk also sheds no light on Sailasa's whereabouts. Una only sees Filipe pulling each of the yellow-nosed kayaks back up the shore to the dive shed against the red backdrop of the setting sun. She looks at him and shrugs. He understands what she means, shakes his head. *No,* he is saying. *I haven't seen him either.*

To her left, the restaurant, now in the midst of the first dinner sitting, is strangely animated. Una skims the tables of guests for Sailasa, but he does not appear. She stands in the entrance and casts her eyes around, sees heads leaning in around tables and at the bar, hears the words 'missing' and 'drowned' and 'dead' – some are questions; some are fact. The news of Luella St John-Gray's disappearance is clearly out, and it is on the guests' dinner tables for consumption. They feel the same as Joana – that the death of a man followed by the disappearance of a woman is not what they want from their holiday in paradise. There is, quite rightly, an aroma of edginess in the dining room, as potent as that of tonight's lobster bisque.

Ahead of Una and a little to the right, Mr Roko stands at a table, reassuring Ellie and Alice Chen. She hears him say, 'We suspect Mrs St John-Gray is visiting a nearby island,' and: 'People do decide to leave the island from time to time.'

But Una knows Roko doesn't believe his own narrative. His reassurances are just damage control, lip service. Perhaps they are what Loloma's nervous guests want to hear.

Una turns away and begins her journey back to the staff village. Petero, dressed in warrior attire, lights the torches, the twilight ritual that marks the island's journey from day into night.

'Where are you, my boy?' she whispers to the trees.

She is at a loss. Joana *is* right. You simply cannot get lost on this island, because it is too damn small. If you are not here, then you have voluntarily departed – or indeed left in the unfortunate manner of Fergus Miller – and Una knows Sailasa could do it if he wanted to without a single soul knowing. He is the strongest swimmer she knows: he could swim the kilometre to busy Totoka Island in an hour if he swam fast enough. He has raced Filipe there enough times on transfer mornings when the water is flat, arms in front crawl, legs kicking wildly. He wouldn't be out of place on Totoka, brimming as it is with families and hundreds of staff. Staffers would just assume he was new at the resort; guests wouldn't know any different. From Totoka, he could catch a boat to anywhere.

But in order to do this, to embark on this swim alone, Sailasa would have to have done something shameful, something that made him run.

TUESDAY 2 JANUARY

Cocktail of the Day:
Bloody Sunrise

(Tequila, blood orange liqueur, orange juice, grenadine, maraschino cherries)

35

Sofie

Sofie wakes up at 5.45 a.m. and sees the first of the dawn's orange light filter through the gap in the curtain pulled across the glass door of her bure. She rolls over onto her side and tries to sleep, but she cannot.

Sofie waits for fifteen minutes until the skies are devoid of any signs of night and she knows the arrival of the men who rake the sand in front of her bure every morning is imminent; then she slides out of bed and to the bathroom. There, she pulls on her swimming costume, throws a linen slip-dress over it and creeps out of the door.

The warmth of the morning light hits her like a furnace. She crosses the cobbled pathway carefully, a toe-stubbing hazard if her feet are anything to go by, and heads to the beach, where she closes her eyes and breathes in. The men in green shirts rake the sand far away to her left.

Sofie bends down, touches her toes and stands up straight again. Then she turns right and walks towards Snake Rock, climbing carefully over the volcanic stone. The craggy stone presses into the pads of her feet, like stepping on glass, and she berates herself for not bothering with sandals.

She climbs down the side of the rock, crosses the sand in the middle of the rock's U-shaped curve and then makes her way over the other side of the snake and down onto the beach. She gazes out to sea. The soft stuff is separated from the wet by a wavy barrier of the ocean's natural flotsam and jetsam: seaweed, shells, hermit crabs. She watches a crab scurry along to her right, on its way somewhere urgently, its shell cumbersome behind it. *Where are you going?* she wonders. She follows the creature's path to the foamy shore. She is further down the beach when her eye catches on something – something long and almost flesh-like poking out from behind a solitary mound of black rock to her right, moving back and forth with the tide. She takes a step into the water and squints, and that is when she sees it.

A body, head to the side. A body with wrinkled skin and goose-flesh. A body that could be *any*body with long, light brown hair because the face, at least what Sofie can see of it, is so disfigured. Part of the cheek is gone, the soft flesh eaten away by something – a sea creature of some kind: a reef shark or a crab. The forehead is covered with angry red abrasions from being dragged in and out across the shoal on the tide.

Then Sofie sees the eyes – eyes that are opaque now, almost transparent in their whiteness. The eyes of this . . . this *being*, are the only thing that remind her that this bloated lump of flesh was once alive, breathing, thriving.

'*Mon Dieu!*' she screams.

Sofie turns away from the body. She has seen plenty of corpses in her time, but they are usually in clinical surroundings and are rarely this deformed. The appearance of this disfigured, half-eaten woman on the sand is grotesque and shocking, even for a medic.

She turns and clambers back along the jagged rock, slashing her feet in the process, unable to tread carefully this time in her haste to get help, then races along the sand and onto the cobbled pathway. She stubs her big toe twice violently, does not notice the prints of blood she leaves in her wake as she runs.

The sand-rakers are gone, and she cannot see anyone, anyone at all, until there is someone, a tall man sitting on the sand in a yoga pose, his hands offering a sun salute. It is the manager, Jose Roko.

'Monsieur Roko!' she calls as she propels herself towards him.

He turns, his contented smile turning to horror.

'There's a woman lying dead on the sand,' she says in a whisper. 'By the rock. I think it's Luella St John-Gray.'

She does not look at Mr Roko after she has said these words or register his reaction. Her empty stomach begins to convulse, and she turns and vomits nothing but yellow bile onto the shiny, sun-streaked sand.

36

Una

Una looks at the dead woman. She is mangled, bloated, her face and calves hacked away by reef sharks. The sight is grotesque, and she turns away. *What is happening here?* Two deaths within four days on Loloma island, the island of love. It is something that would have seemed unfathomable to her a few days ago as she watched the boat come in with smiling guests.

Roko holds a handkerchief up to his mouth and nose, even though there is no smell, nothing yet, only the always-present smell of salt-water spray and seaweed.

'Let's get a sun tent up to cover the body.' He turns to Dr Marama. 'Pau, please stay here with her while I contact the police and inform Mr St John-Gray.'

Roko turns to leave, and Una sees his face has drained of colour and his brow is thick with perspiration. She looks at his hands and notices they have a slight tremor. It is no surprise. The sight of Luella St John-Gray's mangled body is certainly confronting.

'Una, please man the reception desk until Nunia's shift starts,' Roko instructs, glancing back. 'We need someone practical.'

In other circumstances, a compliment like this might have filled Una with a warm glow, but not now. She cannot get her mind off Sailasa. Her nephew's whereabouts occupy her every thought, and now there is a dead body to deal with – the body of a woman whose bure her nephew visited just after midnight on New Year's Eve.

Una returns to the resort's central building and stands behind the polished desk, her brain a scramble, but no one will leave her alone. News is travelling around the staff quarters – and fast – and one by one, her colleagues sidle over to her and demand more answers.

'A dead body?' Letitia whispers as she stands at reception with Kelera, both of them clutching fresh towels that Una suspects did not really need to be brought up to this end of the resort at this particular point in time. 'Una, was it *her*?'

Una nods.

'And does the husband know?' Joana asks.

Una nods again. 'Roko has spoken to him.'

Kelera leans in, eyes wide. 'What did she *look* like?'

She fields the questions expertly ('She looked dead, Kelera!' and 'How am I supposed to know how she died? Do I *look* like a pathologist?') except the one she can't answer: 'Where is Sailasa, Una?'

This one makes Una stutter. 'He is out somewhere . . . running errands,' she tells them. 'He'll be back soon enough.'

Joji brings her a cup of tea with extra sugar, and Una waits. It is only seven o'clock in the morning, and guests are now beginning to appear. She braces herself for what she knows will be an onslaught of questions, guests wanting to know how soon they can leave, requesting to call the various airlines to see if they can bring forward their flights. Two deaths and a near fatality on a routine dive is enough to make even the most devoted of holidaymakers want to vacate their bures in paradise.

'Una?' Mrs Miller appears, and Una thinks it must be the first time she has left her bure since her husband's death. She wears an expression of pure shock. 'I just can't believe it,' she says, her red eyes hidden behind large sunglasses. 'I wondered what you were doing standing all the way down there, by Snake Rock, you and Mr Roko. I saw you from my window. And then Sofie Barthélemy told me on the beach path just now – she was very shaken up, poor woman. How utterly awful. I'm so sorry you had to witness it, too, Una.'

Una feels gratitude for the generosity of this woman, who saw death up close herself less than three full days ago. Imagine thinking of Una's feelings at a moment like this!

'*Vinaka*,' says Una. 'You are very kind. It is so good to see you up and about.'

'Life goes on, apparently.' Kitty Miller smiles sadly. 'I'm supposed to be going to the mainland today with the doctor, but I don't know if it will happen with everything else going on.'

Kitty is likely off to view her husband's body at Nadi Hospital, something Una herself did when she went to visit Adelina. And even though she has been gone for months now, Una still refers to 'visiting' her sister, as if they will have tea and cake together at the grave-site and chat about life as they loved to do when she was alive.

Una observes Kitty Miller now and sees the same confusion in the woman's eyes as she felt after her own bereavement: a sort of bewilderment at life itself and her role in it. Una feels an almost gravitational pull towards Kitty at this moment – she is probably the same age as Una, give or take a year or two – and she almost feels the urge to embrace her, but it wouldn't be appropriate. 'You are very brave,' she says instead. 'Please come and talk to me whenever you need to.'

Pau Marama, who is evidently now off guard-duty, approaches the reception desk and greets Kitty first, then Una. 'Mrs Miller, shall we?' he says. It looks like their trip will be going ahead.

'I'll be back at lunchtime,' he says to Una, keeping his tone mellow in the presence of a guest. 'Mr Roko has asked Sofie – I mean Dr Barthélemy – to keep an eye on Mr St John-Gray while I'm gone.'

Una nods. 'Best wishes to you, Mrs Miller,' she says.

'Goodbye, Una.' Kitty smiles an empty smile and walks down the beach with the doctor. She hitches up her black sundress – aptly chosen, thinks Una, given her state of mourning – and holds her sandals in her left hand as Filipe takes her right to pull her up into the boat.

Una thinks of Adelina again and the ripple effect on her family of her sister's death, and now Luella St John-Gray will leave behind a legacy of grief – for her husband, at least. Will Thomasina be grief-stricken like Una was for her own sister? She cannot say.

Her imagination is already taking on a mind of its own. Did the aggrieved sister with the sold jewellery make good on the sinister promise she made on hotel notepaper in black ink?

At 8.30 a.m., as the nose of a police speed-boat edges over the reef and into the pale turquoise bath-water of the resort, Una dials Sailasa's number once again. His phone has now been switched off.

'Where are you, my boy?' Una mutters to herself and stashes her phone under the reception desk.

Down on the beach, Mr Roko waits on the sand as the police boat slides onto the shore. He steps forward and shakes the hands of the four police officers in their regulation blue uniforms and berets as they disembark. They do not come up to reception but walk immediately down the beach towards Snake Rock, away from the breakfast bustle, where news of the demise of Luella St John-Gray filters rapidly across the buffet stations.

Ellie Chen appears at the front desk. She pulls out her AirPods and throws two navy passports down on the desk, jolting Una away from her contemplation as she watches the policemen make their way across the sand.

'Hey, Una,' Ellie says. 'We need to get a flight back to Sydney, like ASAP. My mum needs to get home – she's, like, completely losing the plot. She's having major panic issues what with two dead bodies and stuff. I don't want to go, but I can't stay in a bure with my mum when she's freaking out, either. She's gone, like, *totally* crazy.'

Una gets it – she does. This isn't exactly the relaxing setting the Chens were expecting. 'I understand, Ellie,' she says. 'Let me see what I can do. Fiji Airways, yes?'

Ellie nods and puts one AirPod back in.

'Let me talk to the airline while you're having breakfast.'

'That'd be great.' Ellie makes to leave and then turns back and eyeballs Una. 'How did it happen anyway? The Luella woman, I mean. Did she drown?'

Una detects a wobble in the young woman's voice. She realises Ellie is just as eager to leave the island as her mother.

'Probably,' she says, because she would rather sow this seed in the teenager's mind than the alternative. Roko would certainly prefer it, too. 'Although, in truth, I really don't know.'

But she does know. Una sees *everything*. A drowning doesn't present a body so bloody, so hacked, even if it has encountered the grabbing jaws of the perennially prowling reef sharks. Drowning is peaceful, isn't it? Or at least that's what she has heard. And Una saw with her own eyes that there was nothing peaceful about the washed-up, broken corpse of Luella St John-Gray.

37

Thomasina

Thomasina steps out of her bure at just gone 9 a.m. after a long lie-in. She walks the short journey from her bungalow to the beachfront pathway, where the pricier villas sit overlooking the shore, regal and perfectly maintained. There is an eerie silence but for the moving figures to her right, just beyond where the black volcanic rock stands up, fearsome and imposing.

Men in blue uniforms and berets circle a small marquee with the words *Loloma Island Resort* on the side in a sweeping font, no doubt used when families request some shade from the blazing sun. Why station it there, she wonders, on the very edge of the water? Have they found something there? An injured dolphin or shark?

And then she realises – call it an instinct born of whatever DNA they share – that her half-sister lies under the shade of that tent. They have found Luella.

Thomasina does not approach the scene, but neither does she turn away. She merely stands, devoid of emotion, as the men in blue circle the tent.

Then she turns and walks, robotic, towards reception.

Una is behind the desk, and they lock eyes.

'It's Luella, isn't it?' she says.

Una breathes in deeply. 'Yes,' she says. 'Yes, it is.'

'How?'

'We do not know. I would advise you . . . not to go over there.'

'It's OK,' Thomasina says. 'I don't want to.'

'It was decided not to wake you until . . .'

'Did Benedict decide that?'

'Mr St John-Gray said he would inform you himself.'

Thomasina smiles bitterly. 'Well, surprise. He didn't.'

Una blinks. Thomasina wonders if Una thinks she is being unfair, expecting a bereaved man to do the death knock so soon after learning of his wife's death.

'I suppose that sounds heartless,' she says. 'When he's grieving and all.'

'Grief does strange things,' Una replies diplomatically.

'Well, thank you for your honesty, Una,' Thomasina says as she turns away. 'I appreciate it.'

Una nods. 'Take care of yourself, Ms Delana.'

Thomasina walks towards the beach, but turns left, away from the rock, and finds a spot in the shade. She stares ahead, arms and legs on autopilot, and thinks of her sister, wonders what her last thoughts were, if she knew she would meet her death in the water. Luella has always been a strong swimmer, but she had to work at it, to practise, unlike Thomasina. Thomasina's limbs are made for the water; even at the age of five or six, they bent over in a crawl so naturally, so effortlessly, and they have become only stronger.

She remembers the family holidays in Cornwall when she learnt to surf: plunging herself into the waves despite the cold water, while Luella swam neatly and then returned to the shore, where she would sit primly atop a blanket, her body in a model pose, hoping the local boys would notice her. The beginning of a lifelong feeling that everyone was looking at her, that she was the centre of everybody's world, the star of her very own *Truman Show*. Thomasina, on the other hand, never really cared.

And even by then, Luella hated her, though Thomasina tried and tried.

It was constant: the time they went to the cinema and Luella left her in the bathroom, and she hadn't known what screen and what row; the time Luella buried their dead white rabbit in the garden without waiting for Thomasina to get back from her school trip; the time she put Thomasina's beloved teddy bear in the garden bin and watched from the window as the rubbish truck came along and swallowed him up; the time she cornered Thomasina's sixth-form boyfriend and suggested he screw *her* instead.

Every day, something new, a new jibe, a new *cut*, until Thomasina left for Plymouth University and got away from it all, lost herself in surfing and drinking to blot it all out. There was not a single moment of kindness, and their parents did nothing about it. It was the only thing she never understood about them, why they just let Luella be.

'It's just the way she is!' they would tell her. 'She doesn't *mean* it! She'll grow out of it, you'll see!' They wanted this person they had created together out of love to be perfect – or at least to come good when they realised she hadn't been made that way.

Thomasina asked Luella once. 'Why do you hate me so much?'

There was no denial. No, *Of course I don't hate you, Thomas! How could you* say *that?* In its place was simply the acceptance of Thomasina's question as fact.

Thomasina gets up and walks for a bit, kicking up the sand. She ambles without direction until she finds herself at the dive shed. She doesn't really know why, only that she is looking for company. The shed is empty, and so she sits on the bench outside and waits.

That's when she sees him up at reception: the bent-over figure of her brother-in-law. Benedict holds a passport in his hand, and Thomasina wonders if he is planning to leave the island. Surely he is not allowed to go so soon?

His head is cast down, as if he is looking for something on the floor, his stubble overgrown. He wears a thick blanket around his shoulders, which looks ridiculous given the heat that is already sweating the island of moisture, hours before midday. He glances up slightly and sees her, and his eyes register shock and then anger. His shoulders tense, his back straightens, and he shakes off the blanket, like his wife did after the scuba-diving incident, marching purposely towards her. Sofie Barthélemy scurries behind him, cooing, 'Monsieur St John-Gray . . .'

'What did you do to her?' He jabs his finger at Thomasina. 'I know it was you!'

'Excuse me?'

'You killed her – I know you did. That's why you really came here, isn't it? You had to get rid of her to get the diamond back, didn't you?' he spits.

Thomasina almost starts at the word. *Killed.*

'You seem remarkably well-informed about the circumstances,' she says evenly. 'I had assumed my sister drowned. Who said anything about murder . . . ?'

The tiny French doctor holds up her hand and murmurs, 'Stop. Please.'

Thomasina ignores her and nods towards Benedict's right hand, which grips a maroon passport. 'Are you planning to leave? Making a hasty escape, are you?'

'I need it to formally identify my wife,' Benedict growls. 'Your *sister!*'

'Your wife? Don't you mean your *benefactor*?'

Benedict grits his teeth and moves forward, his chest puffed out, but the tiny doctor with the strong arms pulls him away.

'*Non!*' she shrieks. 'No!'

Benedict lets himself be held back, but he does not take his hate-filled eyes off Thomasina.

38

Sofie

Inside Bure One, Sofie hands Benedict St John-Gray a sedative, which he swallows down with water. If his pulse remains high, she will administer something stronger: something that will temporarily allow his adrenaline to fall and his muscles to relax – something that will allow him to forget.

Sofie scans the bure. She sees the dead wife's clothes hanging lifeless in the closet. No one to wear them now. Gowns, jumpsuits, minidresses, shorts, sarongs, all neatly stowed. The long gold dress the woman wore the night Fergus Miller died is not so chic without a body in it. It hangs limply, the lamé folding in on itself. Luella St John-Gray had wanted her to know she wore haute couture, and now Sofie can see it all. Money spent on dresses the woman will never wear again.

She feels her cheekbone where her bruise still shines. It is yellowing now, the purple fading to grey, but it is still tender, swollen. She thinks back to New Year's Eve, to Luella threatening her on the beach. She closes her eyes and sees the woman's angry face. She doesn't care that Luella did not recognise her; Sofie is not precious like that. A good deal of time has passed, after all, so she did not really expect her to know – didn't expect a fanfare and a hug and a *Oh my dear, Sofie!* But *mon Dieu,* the woman was so cold, so *English*! Luella didn't want to hear her out or to listen to a story that was meaningful, valid – a story that connected the two women indelibly.

Sofie watches Benedict, now almost asleep. She was taught during her medicine degree to detach herself from patients, to remain aloof, but she is too sensitive for that, too loving. She wants to save everyone she comes across, the good ones and the bad. She fights the urge to kiss him on his forehead in front of the open door of the bure, to tell him it will all be OK, to make him all hers, just like she did when she was a lover in another life, before it all changed.

She gets up and slips out of the bure, drawing the curtains as she goes to make the room conducive to sleep despite the morning light, but she does not want to disappear completely in case he should need her, so she sits at the little table outside. She scrolls on her mobile phone, even though the reception at Loloma is not the best.

'Sofie?' Pau Marama walks towards her down the cobbled path.

'Dr Marama, you're back. How was Nadi?'

'Fine, but . . .' He is flushed, his face filled with concern. He doesn't ask after the health of Benedict St John-Gray. 'Sofie, you didn't happen to take something from the cabinet, did you?'

'The cabinet?'

'Yes, the glass cabinet in my surgery. It is where I keep the harmful medications – morphine, ketamine . . .'

'You keep ketamine? *Here?*'

'A small amount, in case I have to operate in an emergency.'

Sofie sits up straight, concerned. 'No, I haven't opened it.' She knows better than anyone the devastating effects of that particular drug on humans – not least the awful incidences of drink spiking and sexual assault. In the emergency department of the Pitié-Salpêtrière Hospital, she has treated dozens of poor young girls who have suffered the effects of the tranquilliser, some even dying. It is a horrible drug and one she is used to cleaning up *after*, not administering.

'I still have the Valium you gave me for Madame Miller and Monsieur St John-Gray, and I have not needed any more,' she says. 'Why do you ask? Is something missing?'

Dr Marama scratches his head, and Sofie sees the minuscule beads of sweat start to form on the bridge of his nose.

'The ketamine,' he says. 'It is no longer there. Someone has unlocked the cabinet and removed it.'

39

Kitty

The sun streams down on Kitty's face as she sits in a cosy lounge-chair in the bar area. It is almost lunchtime now, and the resort is a hive of activity. Maids push carts, while uniformed policemen in blue shirts and shorts march about purposefully – and yet strangely, it is quieter than she has heard it before. There is a hush of macabre shock that whistles down the wind, deafening in its silence, as if everybody is moving about in a grandiose mime sequence.

Filipe talks to a young man at the bar in hushed tones as the other dries glasses with a tea-towel. At reception, two policemen speak with Dr Barthélemy. The fact she is wearing a stethoscope makes Kitty fear that yet another person has taken ill. Mr Roko nods earnestly from the other side of the desk as Sofie caresses the rubber tubing with the fingers of her left hand. Kitty sees that all the fingers are bare and wonders if Sofie has ever been married. She must be in her late thirties and is certainly a catch. There are not enough thanks Kitty can offer her for trying to save Fergus's life.

The thought of Fergus makes Kitty's eyes fill with hot tears, but underneath the layers of self-deprecation, Kitty knows this: she is worth something, and she is strong enough to get through this period of grief. She closes her eyes momentarily, lets the sun shine on her face. Lets it heal her.

Up ahead, the sun throws shards of glitter on the sea, and for the first time since she has been in Fiji, Kitty sees the true beauty of it. Life is all around her. It is in the water, under the sand, in the lazy sway of the palms. Colours are suddenly more vivid than she's ever seen them, and she takes it all in: the vibrant green leaves, the sand that's the exact colour of bread dough, the kaleidoscope of blue as the sea unfurls. How did she not notice before? It's as if Fergus's death has allowed her to see more *life*. She has heard it can go one of two ways after someone dies: you either withdraw with terror that you are next in line for the grim reaper, or you become grateful of the life you have yet to live. Kitty is somewhere in between.

She sips the sugary tea and shuts her eyes again, lets the warm sun flood her closed eyelids with orange light.

When she opens them, she sees Una heading from the reception area and into the bar with an empty mug. Kitty recognises the look on her face, because it is the same look of melancholy she imagines she wears herself. She feels the comfort of the other woman pull at her like a magnet.

'Una?'

The kindly maid waves. She places the mug behind the bar and then walks over. '*Bula*, Mrs Miller. May I ask how you are?'

'Oh, do call me Kitty, *please*, Una.' Kitty twists the wedding band on her finger. 'It's been a tough morning, I'm afraid. Dr Marama and I went to the Births, Deaths and Marriages Registry at the Ministry of Justice in Nadi to get my husband's death certificate.'

Una sits down and puts her hand on Kitty's, and Kitty feels comforted.

'They decided toxicology reports were not necessary, even in light of the discovery of poor Luella St John-Gray, because Fergus already suffered from atherosclerosis.'

Una nods. 'Blocked arteries?'

'Yes. It would have been an expensive endeavour to send samples across to Auckland for testing and so they didn't bother. That's fine with me. I knew it was his heart. I always thought that's how he would go. He was on statins to lower his cholesterol, but he still didn't eat well. I was always telling him to stop with the cheese.' Kitty blows her nose. 'But gosh, "myocardial infarction" just sounds so . . . clinical. A broken heart would have been better.'

Una offers a sad smile. 'I am so sorry for your sudden loss, Mrs . . . *Kitty*. I lost my older sister recently, so I know a little of how you feel, although her death was not sudden. We were very close.'

'Oh, Una.' Kitty reaches out for Una's hand. 'I'm so very sorry. What was her name, your sister?'

'Adelina. She was wonderful. She was a teacher at a primary school on the mainland, in Nadi.'

'Teaching is such a noble profession,' says Kitty. 'You must have been incredibly proud of her.'

'I was. Adelina was forty-four when she died. Several months have passed for me since losing her, but for you it is very fresh. You must allow your Loloma family to help you in any way we can.'

'Thank you – that is very kind.' Kitty releases Una's hand and picks up her teacup. 'I'm going to be fine. I mean, I wasn't fine when I was at the hospital this morning, and nor was I fine at the government office. Sobbing rather pathetically, I'm afraid – tissues galore. Poor Dr Marama, the dear man, had to deal with me. Men are never good with crying women, are they? He didn't know where to look! But no, I am all right. I didn't think I would be in the hours after Fergus . . . you know, but I'm glad, in a way, that it was his heart and that it was quick. He wouldn't have known about it, you see. That's what Dr Marama says. And really, in terms of death, you can't ask for more than that, can you? He would have preferred a heart attack to any other way. Certainly not cancer – all that time in a hospital bed and having people fuss around him. He hated hospitals and doctors, *despised* them! God forbid he would have had to use a bedpan or anything so *dehumanising*.'

Una smiles sadly.

'Although to die in front of all those people – that *would* have humiliated Fergus. He was a very proud man, my husband,' Kitty says. 'Very proud indeed. I think it was his Scottish heritage. They're a very proud race, the Scots. They don't like anyone fiddling with them.'

Kitty looks out to sea and fingers the necklace she wears with the little golden frog on it, a nod to her days studying biology at the University of Exeter. Those were some of the happiest and most carefree times of her life, although she didn't realise it at the time, as few students do. 'So I suppose what I'm saying is, it's a relief, actually. I am relieved. There – I said it.'

'I'm glad you have some comfort in that. Men can make tricky patients.'

'They can indeed. They're built differently to us.'

They sit in silence for a moment or two, until Kitty speaks again. 'Thank you, Una, for checking in on me while I was resting. I know you came into the bure because Mr Roko said you had, and my water jug had been refilled. Plus, the room was so tidy. I very much appreciate it.'

'Of course,' says Una. 'It's my job.'

'I know it is, but you really do seem to go above and beyond. It's not your job to care for people, too, to check in on them, is it?'

'It is nothing, really.'

Kitty looks out to sea. 'Is someone doing the same for Benedict St John-Gray?' she asks. 'You know, looking out for him?'

'Yes, the two doctors,' says Una. 'Sofie Barthélemy has been very kind, giving up her holiday time to look after him. It's lucky in some ways that she is here alone, because she's been very helpful to Mr Roko and to Dr Marama.'

'That's good. I feel I should reach out to him.' Kitty frowns. 'Benedict, I mean. But he and Luella were so dismissive of Fergus on the night he died, and I was very upset by it.'

'Dismissive?' Una asks.

'Yes. Fergus asked if Benedict and Luella wanted to invest in his new company, a fintech venture, and Luella all but laughed it off. She was positively *mean*. It was so humiliating for poor Fergus. I don't think his heart could cope.'

'I see,' Una says, and Kitty sees the woman's pupils narrow as if she is thinking. 'Well, I'm sure Mr St John-Gray would understand you keeping your distance given your own circumstances. You have both lost a loved one, but it is not your job necessarily to console one another.'

'No,' ponders Kitty. 'I suppose it isn't.'

The two women sit in silence for a moment.

'Where is Sailasa? The lovely chap from the dive shed?' Kitty asks, and she sees Una flinch. 'I just heard Mr Roko chatting about him, that's all.'

Una sits up. 'Oh?'

'Yes. To another man. A man in a suit with a Panama hat. They both seemed very concerned.'

Kitty sees a flash of panic wash over Una's face.

'He's my nephew,' says Una. 'He—'

'Gosh, I'm so sorry.' Kitty feels she has intruded somehow. 'I hope I haven't spoken out of turn. I just . . . well, what I'm trying to say is that I hope Sailasa is just over on the mainland on his break or something and that Mr Roko didn't end up letting him go after the awful scuba incident with Luella.'

Una fidgets in her chair. 'I think Sailasa was feeling a little unwell . . .' She stops. 'It's nothing to worry about. He should be back on the island soon.'

'Well,' says Kitty, unconvinced, 'do pass on my regards.'

'Of course.' Una stands up. 'I had better go. Mr Roko has called a staff meeting in the laundry to discuss the police investigation. I meant what I said, Kitty. I am here if you need anything. I know what it is like to go through this awful thing.'

Kitty feels genuine gratitude for the offer, because she sees that it comes from the owner of a good heart. 'Thank you, Una.'

Una leaves, and Kitty watches the waves land on the shore again and again and thinks of how normally life continues after death. The waves still dance; the sun still shines; the birds still sing. Kitty sees nothing but life in front of her, the colour flooding the darkness. She thinks of Luella, the gold lamé dress, the matted hair as she climbed off the scuba-boat, the cruel dismissal of Fergus's ambition, his lifelong dream.

She breathes in the salty air and lets it revive her, and when she stands up, she realises this is the most alive she has felt in forty-eight hours, because she acknowledges somewhere deep inside her insular cortex – a place so remote and private that surgeons can't even access it or compute what goes on inside – that in Luella St John-Gray's untimely death, life has intervened and given the mean-spirited woman a dose of something Kitty firmly believes in: karma.

40
Una

As Una hurries to the all-staff meeting in the gardens under the cluster of luscious palms, she tries Sailasa's phone again. It is still switched off.

'Sailasa!' she hisses under her breath. 'What are you doing?'

She wonders for a terrifying moment if the loan shark, this dangerous Lemeki character, has got to him. But why would he, unless Sailasa had stopped paying entirely?

'Ah, there you are, Una!' Roko smiles, interrupting her panic. She hopes it wasn't showing on her face, for Sailasa's sake. 'Now we can begin.'

They stand in a group inside the laundry, and Una surmises this is because Roko does not want the laundry team to fall behind with their chores. *If there's time to lean, there's time to clean!* Why not work *and* listen to a briefing?

Inside the sweaty warehouse, the huge washing machines and industrial dryers still churn. Four pairs of hands led by Joana still fold and press while they lend an ear to Roko and the police detective, who stand side by side at the front of the semicircle of staff. Sofie Barthélemy, positioned to the left of the men, wears the stethoscope still, while Pau Marama clutches the kind of clipboard doctors hang on the end of hospital beds.

Mr Roko introduces the detective as Emori Roy, and Una immediately recognises him as one of the VIPs who came in on the boat to celebrate New Year's Eve before sailing home in the small hours. He wears a cream linen suit with a Panama hat and a lazy expression that suggests he is somewhat annoyed to have had to come all the way back to the Mamanuca Islands when really, he could be at the Shangri-La playing golf.

The Panama hat suggests this is the man Kitty saw with Roko discussing Sailasa's whereabouts, and Una feels a distinct sense of unease. She wraps her finger around the note in her pocket that implicates Luella St John-Gray's sister. She will present it to Emori Roy if she has to, whether she feels a kinship with Thomasina Delana or not.

'*Bula*,' says Detective Roy. He waits for the forty or so staff to murmur hello in response. 'I will not make this too long and painful. What we have here at Loloma Resort is a dead woman.'

Una sighs. Talk about stating the bloody obvious.

'There will need to be a post-mortem done immediately, of course, but at this stage, we believe the death of Luella St John-Gray was suspicious. There is bruising on the deceased woman's back that denotes trauma.'

Eyes dart about, and voices begin to raise.

'Quiet, please,' snaps Roko. He takes a step forward. 'This news has been relayed to the guests and to the woman's next of kin. Before we go any further, I would like to stress that none of you are to discuss the details of this case with the guests or outside of our island. There will be harsh consequences if it happens.'

Una sighs. As soon as the post-mortem is made public, the news will be all over the *Fiji Sun* in a flash: *Death in Paradise*. A six-star murder, no less. There is no way news like this can be kept out of the media.

Detective Roy clears his throat. 'First things first. Does anybody here know the whereabouts of a diamond necklace like this?' asks Roy. He shows a photo of a close-up of a woman's neck. A large diamond hangs at the end of a thin gold necklace. 'The husband of the deceased has listed it as missing from the crime scene.'

Una looks around and sees her fellow staff members shaking their heads and offering up blank expressions. She surveys the group, looks for a chink in someone's armour – but she cannot see one. She feels another stab of panic. A missing diamond *and* a missing Sailasa? The stakes have just doubled.

'The box containing the diamond, which was on a simple gold chain, was still in the safe. This is why the husband of the deceased believes the necklace to be missing,' continues Roy. 'He is unsure whether the safe was locked or unlocked at the time.'

Roko glances at Una, and they share a look that means something, although Una is not sure quite what. She has not seen that expression on his face before. It looks a little like he might be asking her what the hell is going on. She shakes her head. *I don't have a clue.*

'No one? OK then.' Detective Roy nods and begins to pace theatrically past the drying machines. 'Dr Marama has also confirmed that there is a bottle of sedative missing from the island surgery,' Roy continues. 'If any of you know the whereabouts of this drug, could you please declare it now?'

There is silence once more, and Una scours the crowd for the second time.

'I will ask again. Has anybody seen a glass medicine bottle like this?' He pulls out another piece of paper from his breast pocket to show a small brown glass bottle with a metal top. The label on the printout is too small to read. Una notes rows of shaking heads. 'We think the drug in question may have been missing for as long as forty-eight hours. The last time Dr Marama recalls seeing this bottle was on Sunday 31 December, which was New Year's Eve.'

Detective Roy turns to Roko. 'Once more, no one knows a thing! Well, can anyone answer me this? Has anyone seen Sailasa Latu?'

Una's stomach plummets as if she is on a rollercoaster.

'We believe Mr Latu left the island in a hurry, and we have reasons to question his whereabouts,' Roy says.

'No!' Una exclaims. 'Sailasa is not a thief or a murderer. He has a valid reason for leaving . . .' She does not know what that reason is, but she knows it to be true.

Mr Roko holds his hand up. 'Una, *please!*'

'We will investigate what that reason is,' says Roy, scribbling on his notepad. 'In the meantime, if anyone hears from Mr Latu, would they please make it known to myself or Mr Roko? I will be staying in Bure Five. Please stop by if you have any information.'

'The bure has been vacated by the Chens,' confirms Roko. 'They are leaving the island shortly.'

Thankfully, Una managed to find two seats on a flight home to Sydney. They weren't first-class, but Ellie Chen insisted her mother would take anything to get away from the island.

Una feels a hand tap her shoulder lightly, and she realises Kitty Miller is standing beside her. 'Kitty,' whispers Una. It feels strange to use a guest's Christian name. 'What are you doing here?'

'I need to keep busy,' says Kitty. 'Otherwise I'll . . .' She sniffs, and Una realises she cannot tell Kitty Miller what to do. It was her poor husband who started off this chain reaction of oddities, and so Una does not want to argue with her.

'Then it's fine,' whispers Una.

'That man in the hat.' Kitty looks over at Detective Roy. 'That's who Mr Roko was talking to about Sailasa . . .'

'I guessed as much,' says Una.

Mr Roko clears his throat, noticing Kitty for the first time. 'Um, Mrs Miller, this is very strictly a staff meeting,' he chirps. 'I do not wish to be rude, but I don't think it's entirely appropriate that you . . .'

'I want to help,' interrupts Kitty. 'No one said guests *couldn't* come along!'

'Yes, but . . .'

'I'm a bereaved woman, Mr Roko, and I strongly feel . . .'

'Very well.' Roko holds up a hand, because he knows that, unfortunately, the guest is always right.

Una feels a moment of euphoria, a checkmate moment.

Detective Roy begins again. 'Until we have investigated the incident, I would ask you all to stay away from Snake Rock and the beach beyond it. There should be no reason for anyone to go there. It has already been cordoned off. In the coming hours, you will all be spoken to individually about the events of the last few days, but if you have any information to offer in the meantime, please bring it to my attention or inform Mr Roko.'

'In other words,' says Roko. 'It is business as usual. We still have guests to look after. Now, are there any questions?

Mika steps forward. 'Detective, are there any links between the two . . .' He looks at Kitty Miller. '. . . *incidents*?'

Roy shakes his head. 'No. It seems what happened to Mr Miller was a health-related episode as far as the pathology report goes.'

Una squeezes Kitty's hand, and Kitty squeezes back.

Joana raises her hand. 'What will happen with the St John-Gray woman's body?'

'The same as any death on the island,' Dr Marama says. 'Now that forensic officers have attended the scene, the body will be removed in the next hour or so and taken to the pathology unit at Nadi Hospital.'

'Right then.' Roko looks at his watch. 'Are there any more questions?'

The silence and shaking heads denote there are indeed no more questions, and so Roko nods and turns to his left. 'Dr Barthélemy, would you like to say a few words?'

Everyone turns to look at Sofie Barthélemy, who stands in the door of the laundry. Behind her is the island's largest beach hibiscus tree. Una recalls her mother treating sores and boils and sprained ankles with leaves from the tree. She would place them over the swelling area and gently strap them overnight. Somehow the clinical form of the pretty doctor is all wrong set against this natural, herbal backdrop.

The Frenchwoman, who is wearing large sunglasses that succeed in hiding her nasty bruise, clears her throat. '*Bula*,' she says. 'Please call me Sofie – *docteur* is too formal for this setting. I'm sorry I must present to you in these difficult circumstances. Since Dr Marama will escort the body of Mrs St John-Gray back to the mainland today, I will replace him in his office for the afternoon and tonight. Please refer guests to me for treatment for any medical issues. Thank you.'

'No,' says Roko. 'Thank *you*. You have gone above and beyond the call of duty, and we are truly grateful for all you are doing here on the island, Dr Barthélemy.'

Marama and Detective Roy offer grave nods.

'Well, if that is everything, then you may all return to your posts,' announces Roko. 'As I said, it's business as usual. We want to make sure the guests continue to have the best time they can, help them forget about everything that's happened. I don't want people all over Tripadvisor next week talking about dead bodies and missing jewellery. We are here to help people *forget* about their problems, not to make more for them.'

He clears his throat. 'I do not like to say this, but I must reiterate that discretion is required here, and if I hear there has been gossip outside of the staff village about the goings-on here at Loloma, there will be severe consequences. Thank you all for your time.'

Roko turns to leave, flanked by the two doctors. Detective Roy studies his notepad as the staff members file out and return to their stations.

'Are you walking back towards reception, Una?' asks Kitty.

'No. I want to speak to the detective about Sailasa.' She approaches the detective. 'Excuse me? Detective Roy?'

The detective's eyes snap up. 'Yes?'

'Una. Una Simpson.'

'Mrs Simpson, *bula*.'

'Ms, actually.'

A heavy man-sigh. 'How can I help you, *Ms* Simpson?'

'It's about Sailasa Latu.'

'What about him?'

'I meant what I said just now, about him not being a murderer or a thief. Sailasa is my nephew, and I can assure you he is a kind, hard-working young man who . . .'

'. . . was about to have his livelihood and reputation ruined by the murder victim?' Roy offers.

Una puts her hands on her hips. 'No! I mean, *yes*, but there is absolutely no way he would have killed her. However, there are plenty of other people in this resort who disliked Luella St John-Gray enough to get rid of her.'

'Including me,' announces a voice.

Una and the detective both turn to see Kitty, who has appeared at Una's side.

'Oh?' says the detective.

Kitty's pasty skin turns scarlet. 'I don't mean I actually killed her! I was being hypothetical.'

'I found a note,' blurts Una, desperate to protect Sailasa. 'In the dead woman's bure. It said, "Your time's up".' Una hands over the crumpled ball of paper.

Roy takes it with his fingertips as if he doesn't want to sully evidence.

'I think it was written by—' Una begins.

'You know who wrote it? So you've had it analysed for DNA?'

'No, but—'

'Well, how about you leave your theories to the professionals then?'

'But it's a *threat!*'

'"Your time's up",' ponders Roy. 'Your time's up in the shower? Your time's up in the spa?' He offers a strained smile. 'Thank you, Ms Simpson, but I'm not sure of the relevance—'

'But it's evidence!' Una cries. She is treading a line between guilt and desperation. Guilt that she is about to throw Thomasina Delana under the bus, but desperate to save her nephew. Dear, sweet Sailasa.

'Well, in that case, Detective Simpson, would you like my badge?'

Kitty's shoulders straighten out. 'Of course she isn't a detective,' she snaps. 'And that kind of sarcasm is utterly uncalled for. For your information, Una sees everything in this resort, and you should damn well listen to her.'

The detective smiles and holds up his palms in a gesture of amused surrender. 'Well, thank you, Ms Simpson and Mrs—'

'Miller. Kitty Miller,' Kitty says.

'Miller?' says Roy. 'The wife of Fergus Miller?'

'The *widow* of Fergus Miller,' Kitty snaps.

'I am sorry for your loss, Mrs Miller,' says Roy. Then he sighs. 'Ms Simpson and Mrs Miller, I will indeed take your thoughts on board,' he says. 'In the meantime, if you see anything that has a *serious* relevance to this crime, then do not hesitate to make it known to me. Otherwise—'

'Serious? What about the note?' Una interrupts. 'Is that not serious enough?'

'*Otherwise*,' Roy continues, ignoring her, 'I will just continue doing what I have done for the last thirty-five years.'

Una swallows down a ball of fury. He has completely underestimated and undermined her, and Kitty, too, it seems.

'Fine – then I will prove Sailasa is not guilty,' Una says, nonchalant, and then kicks herself because the fact is she cannot prove a damn thing while her nephew is God-only-knows-where, and she will not be able to do so until she establishes exactly where that is.

'You are obviously very fond of Mr Latu,' says Roy. 'You are his aunt, yes?'

'Yes, but regardless of that—'

Roy holds up his hand. 'It's wonderful you want to help,' he says. 'It really is.' He taps his pen on his notepad and flips the lid of the little square pad shut. 'But the simple fact is this: people who are not guilty do not run, Ms Simpson, do they?'

41

Thomasina

Thomasina lies back on a sun lounger outside the dive shed and stares out to sea. The beach is more or less empty today; there seem to be fewer guests, and the ones she does see are downcast, edgy even. She isn't surprised. News travels fast.

Detective Roy met her at the restaurant earlier, just as she was finishing lunch. She wasn't able to stomach much. He invited her to Roko's office, told her about Luella's death being suspicious.

'Thank you, Detective Roy,' she said when he told her. All she could focus on were the dull brown walls and the eighties-style ceiling fan in the office – nothing like the opulence of the bures themselves. One thing for the staff, another for the guests.

She felt a sense of disconnect. The words 'ketamine' and 'drugged' and 'testing' washed over her. They sounded like white noise from a TV set, the insipid buzz of interference on a radio channel.

'So, you think she was drugged and then drowned?'

'We are investigating that possibility, yes.'

'Right.'

'Do you have any questions, Ms Delana?' Detective Roy asked.

She shook her head, picked up her beach-bag. Some of the contents spilt out and so she bent down to stuff them back inside: factor 50 sun cream in a lemon-yellow bottle, tortoiseshell glasses, her Nike baseball cap.

'No,' she said and left.

He called after her. 'We will, of course, keep you updated at every stage of the investigation, Ms Delana.'

As she walked away from the office, away from reception and to her cool, air-conditioned bure, she felt the detective's eyes on her. She didn't turn back to look at him; instead, she counted her steps along the path to the bure in Fijian: *dua, rua, tolu, va.*

Then she stepped inside the bure and closed her eyes and leant against the inside of the door. 'Fuck,' she said aloud. '*Fuck!*'

Now, on the lounger, Thomasina lets the breeze tickle her skin. She closes her eyes and lets the warmth coat her like a blanket. She feels a strange sense that her father is with her, that he knows she is here – that he is glad of it. She feels, for a moment, that she is home.

She sits up and looks around her at the empty beds on the beach. She has her pick of the best spots, but something – or someone – has drawn her to the end of the beach near the shed once more. She sees Filipe walking casually towards her, although he hasn't noticed her yet. Mr Roko, the resort manager, closes in behind him, his stride brisk and efficient. She watches as Roko leans in and says something, and Filipe nods and pulls himself up straighter.

Stand up straight, is what she imagines the suited man has said. She blinks, tries to catch Filipe's eye, but he seems wholly distracted, his thoughts somewhere else entirely. His jaws clench and unclench like the beat of her own feet on the path: *dua, rua, tolu, va . . .*

'Hey.' She stands up as Filipe arrives at the shed. '*Bula.*'

'Thomasina!' He seems shocked to see her there.

'You look miles away,' she says.

'I'm sorry?'

'I mean, you look like you have the weight of the world on your shoulders. Is everything OK?'

'I'm fine.' He doesn't meet her eye. 'I'm so . . . I'm sorry about your sister,' he says.

'Don't be sorry,' replies Thomasina, her face tight. 'I'm not.' She feels a flash of guilt for having said it, but she can't help the way she feels.

Filipe doesn't reply. She suspects he probably doesn't know how to. How do you react to a statement like that? A woman who doesn't even care that her own sibling is dead? He shifts on his feet, inspects his toes.

'Where's everyone been?' she continues, despite his silence. Behind the dive shed, she sees ten or so staffers returning to their positions in the restaurant and bar. The chefs filing through the double doors of the kitchen in chef's whites and black Crocs for the kitchen floor. 'The staff, I mean.'

'All-staff meeting,' he says. 'At the laundry.'

'Hot day to be in the laundry.'

He nods. 'It was.'

'Was the meeting about Luella?'

'Yes, but I can't talk about it. I'm sorry.'

'Why?'

'Because Roko doesn't want the news getting out. Not good for tourism.'

Thomasina gives a wry laugh. 'So you all know she was murdered, then?'

'The detective told us.'

'Did they tell you who they think did it?'

Filipe glances back towards reception, as if he's afraid Mr Roko is going to step out and admonish him. He says loudly, 'I'm sorry, I cannot talk about it,' and then he takes Thomasina's arm and leads her around to the side of the shed where they can't be seen. She closes her eyes for a second at the tenderness of his touch and lets herself be led.

'They didn't say,' Filipe whispers. 'But they're trying to cover all angles. They think . . .' He pauses. 'They think the diamond necklace has something to do with it.'

Filipe knows all about the diamond. Thomasina thinks back to the scene on the beach – Benedict raving at her about stealing it, and Filipe standing by, knowing she might need him at any point if Benedict lashed out.

'He's still maintaining to the police that Luella brought it with her?'

'Yes, and they're looking for it.' He pauses and then says, 'I can't be found out talking about this. I could lose my job. I'm sorry.'

Thomasina nods. 'I know. Thank you for telling me,' she says. Then she looks at him. 'I don't know why, but I really feel I can trust you.'

'You can,' Filipe tells her.

They lock eyes for a moment before Filipe steps back anxiously towards the shed. He casts another glance up towards reception. Then there is a rumble and squeak of wheels on cobbles as Alice Chen and her daughter Ellie appear, dragging their own suitcases. They haven't even waited for the porters – that's how desperate they are to get off the island.

'Don't you think . . . ?' Filipe begins and then stops.

'What?'

'Don't you think it feels like the whole island has gone mad?'

Thomasina laughs wryly, her eyes filling with tears. 'Yes, yes, it does. But don't you see? That's what Luella did, Filipe. She drove people to madness. And for someone on this island, it was enough to kill.'

WEDNESDAY 3 JANUARY

Cocktail of the Day:
Sea of Confusion

(Pear brandy, Amaro Sfumato, rum,
Chartreuse, passionfruit syrup, lemon juice)

42

Sailasa

Sailasa knows downtown Nadi like the back of his hand: the pastel-coloured homes that line the roadside, broken up by lush, green pines; the bustling shops selling electronics and groceries; the banks, the nightclubs, the restaurants on Queens Road, with their vibrant canopies. Posters on walls selling phone plans and Coca-Cola and real estate. He walks briskly along Queens Road, passes the Vodafone shop, Steps Karaoke Night Club, Namaka Pharmacy, the Western Union Exchange – all the places he has walked by before, in another world.

It feels strange, to be on the run. He has seen it on TV and in the movies enough times, watched characters looking over their own shoulders at every step, terrified their evil deeds will catch up with them. Yet now here he is, doing the same, hoping that what he did on New Year's Eve at Loloma will not catch up with him.

A police car squeals down Queens Road, and Sailasa pulls his Adidas bucket hat as low down as he can. It's hardly *Reservoir Dogs*, but it makes his heart leap nonetheless. Today, Nadi is bustling with shoppers and tourists, and he feels he has some kind of safety in numbers. He passes Vita Water Sports and looks in the window, shakes his head at the irony. He wishes Filipe were with him; they'd exchange a knowing glance if he was.

But no, he is not with Filipe or Una or anyone. Sailasa is alone, pure and simple.

He feels he has changed in a matter of days from an innocent boy to a world-weary man, as though he has made a judgement so fatal, so flawed that it has aged him. Yet he still does not know how to behave. He raised a hand to a woman; he intended to hurt her. He saw the anger in her eyes, the way she sneered at him through the slits of her mask, and it made him snap. And even though the line between reality and make-believe is pretty distorted in his head, he knows exactly what he has done, and he cannot go back there again.

He feels bad about Una, because she put her faith in him. He knows she will be looking for him, worried sick, but he cannot call her. They will know he has run by now, and they will be waiting for him to make contact – Una will be duty-bound to report what she hears, and he will not put her in that position. He may have done the wrong thing, but he has not changed in temperament; he has not lost his capacity for guilt. He just snapped – that was all; acted on an impulse that was alien to him.

Besides, if he were to call Una, he knows she would only say something sensible, tell him to come back to Loloma on the next ferry and face the music. He feels a flash of annoyance. She is not his mother, even if she is the closest thing to it now. He cannot return to Loloma and protest his innocence, because that would be a barefaced lie.

Sailasa does not know what to do. He is a wanted man, rolling in debt. But not a wasted debt. He would do it over and over to have his mother back, even for a single minute.

They told him she had only a year, maybe eighteen months if she had the operation.

He read there was a surgeon in Suva who could operate on tumours that close to the spine, so he tracked down Lemeki through a friend of a friend at another resort, a guy who knew a shady gang in downtown Nadi. He borrowed the full amount, and they went to Suva. His mum had the operation and it bought her six more months with him.

But then those six months were up and he was left with no mother and no money. Minus money. Minus thousands. He used the last of it to cremate her, scatter her ashes at Shell Village in the islands where she'd grown up, and he told Una the money was from saving up his commission on fishing trips, his lifer savings. He said goodbye to her with nothing and no one except Una, and afterwards Una scooped him up and guided him and helped him put one foot in front of the other. But he was struggling with the repayments, struggling to stay afloat.

And then Luella St John-Gray arrived at Loloma Resort & Spa and made everything worse still with her cold heart and her intention to ruin him.

Sailasa passes the newspaper seller on the corner now and picks up a copy of the *Fiji Sun*, his head down and his eyes to the ground. He unfolds the paper as he walks, surveys the headline blaring out in red and white – and, like a punch to the guts, the breath leaves his body.

EXCLUSIVE! WOMAN WASHED UP AT LOLOMA

By Aseri Naituku

The *Fiji Sun* reports today through trusted sources that a woman's body has been washed up on the shores of Loloma Island Resort, Mamanuca Islands. The woman has not yet been formally identified but the body is thought to be that of a guest at the resort who was reported missing in the early hours of New Year's Day . . .

Sailasa closes the paper. He wants to be sick; he wants to cry; he wants to find a bathroom and defecate. His body feels as though it is not his own, and something is taking over him, a heat born of extreme panic. His heart thunders in his chest. *Her body has been found.*

Somehow, he continues to walk, to put one foot in front of the other. When he reaches the front door of the apartment, he takes out a key from under the doormat with shaking fingers and lets himself into the room. He closes the curtains and sits in the dark, alert like a fox to the noises on the outside. His adrenaline has peaked; his eyes see more keenly. The stakes have become even higher: now, not only are the baddies after him but the goodies, too.

What have I done? He thinks back, sees the blood. He cannot quite remember how it all unfurled and how she got hurt – it is all so unclear – but there is a voice in his head telling him: *Now you're for it! You're going to get what you deserve.*

Sailasa will not sleep tonight; he is a watchman. But he also knows that if he closes his eyes, he will see her open ones. Luella St John-Gray staring at him, stunned, a maroon pool of blood growing at her temple.

43

Una

Una passes the downcast figure of Benedict St John-Gray as she wheels her trolley along the path. Even though he is heading towards the main heart of the resort, he appears to her directionless, a man with a grey cloud above his head. Benedict St John-*Grey*.

'Mr St John-Gray,' Una ventures. 'Would you like me to clean your room?'

He barely looks at her, just offering the slightest of nods.

She opens the door of Bure One and steps inside. It is silent, as the bures always are at lunchtime, but for the whir of the air-conditioning unit on the wall. She is grateful to have started her shift later again today, to be servicing the bures at lunchtime and not breakfast. It somehow makes for a shorter day.

She turns towards the wardrobe on the left side of the bed, its sliding door fully open, and allows her eyes to run along the clothes that hang up side by side. She lifts a hand and runs a finger along Luella St John-Gray's garments, feels the textures: sequins, satin, crochet. Labels Una has heard of but never worn, labels she often sees in the bures she cleans: Chanel, Chloé, Balenciaga, Stella McCartney, Alexander McQueen. The red sequinned dress, the Valentino gown, is nowhere to be seen, presumably removed by the police, but Una's eyes catch on a tiny red sequin shimmering up at her from the wooden panelling at the bottom of the wardrobe.

She stares at it for a while and then picks it up and turns it over in her fingers. Mr St John-Gray will pack up his wife's clothes, she has been told. Some things are too personal to be removed by another hand.

Una tries to focus as she gives a rudimentary clean of the bure, but of course all she can think of is Sailasa. Now that Detective Roy has her nephew in his sights, Una's senses have become akin to those of a fox. Everywhere she turns, everywhere she *looks*, she hunts for something that will exclude her nephew from suspicion.

In front of her, make-up is strewn across the whole of the vanity unit, some of it in the sink. Una bends down to straighten the rattan waste-bin, which has been emptied by the police. Something nicks her skin: it is a piece of white ceramic, from a tile or a jar or something. On it, there is the word *HANE* in minuscule print. Una recognises it immediately as the middle of the word *CHANEL*, the small print on the back of the jar near the ingredients. She knows it because she has come across jars like this on sink-tops many a time.

Her eyes scour the area for more fragments, and she finds some in the bin, one balancing on top of the tissue box on the shelf under the sink. She thinks back to turn-down on New Year's Eve. Did Sailasa knock something off the vanity? Is *that* why he was taking so long in the bure? Una reluctantly imagines the scenario: Luella coming back and finding Sailasa in the bure, the woman admonishing him for the breakage, threatening him once again. It would be enough to make anyone lash out . . .

Una flicks the idea away with a shake of her head and proceeds to wipe the marble sink area vigorously. *Sailasa, as if!* There plenty of other people here on Loloma who disliked Luella St John-Gray; Kitty was right to tell Detective Roy this fact.

She runs it all over and over in her mind, her brain scurrying down a million rabbit holes, as she mops the floor and closes the door behind her.

She heads to Bure Four now, the temporary home of Thomasina Delana, and knocks on the glass of the door. 'Housekeeping,' she calls.

When there is no response after a second knock, she lets herself in as she usually does. The room smells of coconut and sea water, and the wardrobe is a hotchpotch of sundresses and sandals and a colourful kaftan with a label that says *Arnhem* inside it. The bed is littered with debris: a pair of cut-off denim shorts, a bikini, a stick of surfing zinc, a shell necklace, a sarong. It is as if Ms Delana has produced an extra suitcase from somewhere, as if her clothes are multiplying! The contrast is extreme to Bure One, to the sterility and perfection of her sister's room.

Una thinks back to the list she found inside the book she was reading about the man named Wim Hof who swims in ice. The book is no longer here, and Una wonders if Ms Delana has taken it to lunch with her to read. She bends over to untuck the bed-sheet, and the book falls out. She picks it up and flicks through it for the list again, and the slip of paper with the Fiji Airways logo obediently slides out of the book and flutters down to the floor.

The words are still there: *Learn Fijian, Tackle Cloudbreak, Wreck dive, Get her back* . . . Una takes out her mobile phone and snaps a photo, then places the note back inside the book, and the book on the bedside table.

Then she scours the room for more. If Thomasina Delana *did* write the other note, the one Una found in Luella St John-Gray's bure, then perhaps Una will find something else that implicates her – something that will take the heat off her nephew.

What am I missing? she wonders. *Think, Una. Think!*

In the bathroom, where she can't be seen from the path, Una studies the photo on her phone. Wreck dives are not massively popular with guests, but Sailasa and Filipe have taken several visitors to dive at the sunken passenger ferry known as the Salamander Shipwreck and to the underwater site of the downed B-26 World War II bomber – both of which rest on the ocean floor of this tropical archipelago. Una wonders if Ms Delana will still do a wreck dive now, after all that has happened. The water was so hostile to her sister, after all.

As Una scrubs the toilet, the words play in her head. *Wreck dive, dive wreck.* She thinks of Luella's dive on that very first day, which indeed turned into a wreck – sabotaged by someone, perhaps, rather than by faulty equipment?

She stands up, toilet brush in hand. 'Wreck dive?' she asks herself. 'Handle Octopus?'

Una's jaw drops open, her heart rate quickens.

Handle Octopus? Wreck dive?

Una is no scuba-diver, and she would never claim to be, but she has learnt some things from Sailasa. And one of those things is that the part of the diving gear that supplies air to the body from the tank, the regulator, is colloquially known by an entirely different name. It is known amongst divers as *the octopus.*

Suddenly, Una sees the list in a whole different light. Does it mean something else? Did Thomasina in fact intend to *wreck* Luella's dive? Did she plan to engineer a slow and breathless death for her cruel sister in the waters off Loloma? Did she tamper with the octopus regulator or some other part of the diving equipment, before Luella climbed into the boat?

Handle Octopus. Wreck dive.

Then the final words: *Get her back.*

Una almost trips in her speed to get onto the veranda. She pulls the door shut and steps out onto the path, almost crashing into Kitty Miller on the way.

'Una!' Kitty exclaims. 'Whatever's wrong? You look like you've seen a ghost.'

Una looks at Kitty. She has a choice to make, and in an instant, she makes it. *I trust her,* she thinks. *I like this woman, and I trust her.*

'You won't believe this, Kitty,' she says, her voice a wheezing with euphoria. 'But I think I've found something. I think I've worked it out.'

44

Kitty

'Whatever is it, Una?' Kitty asks.

She's been feeling teary and has stepped out for a walk, the looming cloud of overwhelm above her head, and it was as if the weather has sensed her mood and performed accordingly: a charcoal sky for a dark and melancholy mind. And now here is Una, outside Thomasina Delana's bure, evidently rattled, yet pleased to see her. Kitty's heart lifts.

'What's wrong?' she repeats. 'Una?'

Una's breath is shallow. 'It's a wish list, Kitty,' she says. 'Thomasina made a list of things she wanted to do, and I found it in her book. She was using it as a bookmark.'

'I see, but what's the relevance . . . ?'

'Shh, listen,' says Una, and Kitty closes her mouth. 'Take a look.'

She produces her phone and holds up the photo to Kitty, who leans back. 'I'm afraid I'm not good with small print,' she says.

Una jabs at the screen. 'See? "Learn Fijian, Tackle Cloudbreak, Handle Octopus, Wreck dive . . ."' Una reads. '"Confront her. Get her back."'

'Confront her?' Kitty looks up, eyes wide. 'Get her back?'

'*Exactly*,' says Una. '*Get her back!*'

'Hmm,' says Kitty thoughtfully. 'I mean, I do agree this note is a little on the combative side, Una, but it doesn't mean Thomasina *killed* her. I mean, if you think about it, 'Get her back' doesn't necessarily mean revenge – it could mean Thomasina wants Luella back in her life. You know, to get her back in that sense, to make amends. It could mean anything.'

'Yes, but what about this? Handle *Octopus*. *Wreck* dive?'

'So she wants to see a shipwreck and an octopus! So what?'

'No, but, Kitty, think about it. The octopus is another word for the regulator in scuba equipment! What if Thomasina was saying she wanted to *wreck* the dive Luella was going on, and tamper with the octopus?'

Kitty's mouth drops open. 'Wow,' she says.

Una looks pleased. 'Then of course there's the other note,' she says.

'The one you showed Detective Roy at the laundry? "Your time's up"?'

'Yes,' Una tells her. 'I think Thomasina Delana wrote it.'

'How do you know? Did you see her writing it?'

'No.'

'Then couldn't it have been anyone?'

'The Ts,' says Una.

'The tease?' Kitty is confused.

'No, the *letter* T.' Una sighs, reaching into her pocket and unfurling the rolled-up note from the St John-Grays' bure and holding it alongside the photo on her phone. 'The one on the "Time's Up" note is identical to the one on the wish list. *T*ackle and *T*ime! See?'

Kitty studies the photos and feels a surge of adrenaline. 'Oh yes,' she says. 'It is the same!' Then she looks up at Una. 'Why didn't you tell Detective Roy you think Thomasina Delana wrote the note?'

'I was about to, but he wasn't listening.'

'How did you work it out?'

'I noticed the likeness on New Year's Eve when I first saw the wish list in Thomasina's bure.'

'Snooping?' Kitty gasps. 'Una, you mustn't!'

Una's shoulders square. 'I wasn't snooping,' she snaps. 'I stumbled across the evidence!'

Kitty holds up her hand. She does not want to offend this gentle woman. 'Una, I didn't mean . . . you've obviously onto something here. It's incredibly impressive.'

Una's shoulders drop again.

'Do you, um . . . ?' Kitty treads carefully. 'Do you maybe think you should have left the note in the bin, though? It could be construed as – by *some* – as, you know, stealing evidence?'

Una leans in. 'It's not stealing, Kitty,' she says. 'Even Detective Roy didn't suggest that! It's *borrowing* for the sake of illustration. To prove that someone else may be responsible for a crime that people seem set on pinning on my nephew!'

'Oh, Una,' says Kitty, who understands perfectly what Una is trying to do. 'I'm sorry if I offended you.'

'You didn't,' says Una.

'But I do think you should tell Detective Roy what you found inside the book. He may have pooh-poohed the note, but the list is another thing, and this is evidence in a murder investigation.'

'Yes, I know,' says Una. 'I will pass everything I find along to Detective Roy in due course, but before I do, I need to make sure I have concrete evidence. We need to find out more in order get Sailasa exonerated from this investigation. We need something *solid*.'

Kitty feels a warm flush at the word *we*. She looks at Una and nods. She is part of a team again, and it makes her feel warm with relief.

'Roy is hell-bent on framing Sailasa, I'm sure of it,' Una adds. 'If we can give him some solid findings, some more proof, he'll have to listen to us.'

Kitty nods. She opens her mouth to speak, shuts it and then opens it again. She needs to tread with caution when it comes to this topic. 'Now, Una, I am just playing devil's advocate here,' she says, 'but Sailasa *does* appear to have run from the scene. Is there any chance that he might have, um . . . ?'

Una's eyebrows, expressive and welcoming at all other times, knit together in a death hold, and Kitty is silenced.

'Understood,' she says and holds up a defensive hand. 'Like I said . . . I'm just playing devil's advocate.'

Kitty is prepared to trust Una's judgement, to accept that this case is not as straightforward as it might seem, because she knows Una does not suffer fools gladly or otherwise. And even if her thoughts did creep in the same direction as the detective's (surely even Una would not have blamed her for that), Kitty does not want to be on her own, dwelling on her loss, missing her husband.

And anyway, there is new evidence now, evidence that proves there is a new suspect in the murder.

'Well, if we *are* playing devil's advocate,' says Una, 'we should consider who else could have written the notes if not Thomasina?'

Kitty feels her forehead. 'Which way does it slope?' she asks. 'The writing? Does it slope to the left or to the right?'

'Why do you ask?'

'Oh, it's probably nothing,' says Kitty.

Una eyes widen, and she stares off to the left as if she's in some kind of trance.

'Una?' Kitty feels a keen sense of alarm. Is her friend having a funny turn? She steps forward to touch her, but then Una turns back, her eyes alive and the beginnings of a smile on her face.

'Of course!' she says cryptically, leaving Kitty more confused than ever. 'Kitty Miller, you're an absolute genius!'

45

Thomasina

Thomasina returns to her bure after a lunch of grilled fish and swaps her sandals for trainers. Una has clearly been in while she was in the restaurant – the bed is made, and the towels folded. Her book has been placed on the bedside table and a fragrant white and yellow frangipani flower placed on top. She picks it up, stuffs it into her canvas tote, grabs her baseball cap and her water bottle and shuts the door behind her. She has not done the bush-walk yet, but she overheard Kitty Miller telling someone or other that she'd done it on the second day, and that from the top of the steep hill, there is a stunning 360-degree view of the island.

Thomasina needs to be somewhere private to gather her thoughts. She has not yet managed to do it in the twenty-four hours since Luella's body was discovered. She still hasn't quite convinced herself it has happened, that her sister is no longer of this life, and if she wasn't in the resort – if she hadn't witnessed the furore of the search and the dramatic discovery of Luella's body – she wouldn't believe it was possible at all.

Now that everyone knows Luella was her sister, they will probably be expecting – hoping, more likely – to see some remorse, some grief, from Thomasina. But still, she won't, she *can't* cry for Luella. Can't give them the satisfaction. *Let them think I'm cold!* How can you cry for someone when you have wished they were dead? And God knows, Thomasina wished it enough times.

She sweats her way up the vertical incline, hears the rustle of lizards darting back into the undergrowth. Her head throbs, and her calves ache, but in some ways, she enjoys the pain, the slightly solitary fear of it. The burning of muscle and the thumping in her chest is some kind of punishment for what she has done, for the bone-aching resentment she had for Luella.

She wanted to give her sister a chance, somewhere deep down. In her head (perhaps not in her heart) she thought that maybe, just *maybe*, they could resolve their issues positively, that Luella might smile and say, 'Of course, Thomasina, darling, here's the diamond back – it *is* rightfully yours after all' and that no one would get hurt. But they *had* both been hurt – Thomasina emotionally (because bitterness is surely an emotion, isn't it?) and Luella physically. And who did Luella have to blame for that but herself? If only she'd just been *nicer* about it, more courteous, then karma may not have come for her, hunted her down. If only she had explained *why* she didn't want Thomasina to have what was justly hers, if she'd given a valid reason. *If she'd just been more damn likeable.*

But, in her heart of hearts, Thomasina knows none of this would have been possible, because it wasn't in Luella's make-up to be nice – not as a toddler when she would bite anyone who crossed her path, leaving ugly white teeth marks; not as a child who wouldn't share so much as a crayon, let alone a bag of lollies; not as a teenager who sniped about her friends and flirted shamelessly with their boyfriends; certainly not as an adult, as bitter and vindictive as she was. Thomasina couldn't have made it right, whatever way she played her sister.

She makes it to the peak. She is sweating under her arms, on her stomach, in her hair. She wipes away the moisture on her abs with her T-shirt and swigs from her water bottle. Then she settles herself by the little river and watches the tadpoles darting about in the warm water. Her surroundings are so idyllic and so unspoilt, aside from a rubber hospitality glove wedged under a rock and an empty plastic Coke bottle, and Thomasina wonders if she has ever been this close to paradise. It is the perfect place for the little ceremony she is about to conduct, a ceremony of closure.

She puts her hand in her bag and pulls out two things: her book and a plastic lighter with a picture of a palm tree and the words *Fiji Time* on it. She flicks through her book and pulls out a piece of Fiji Airways notepaper.

Thomasina runs her thumb along the metal spark-wheel three times until there is a flame. The paper takes straight away, and she holds it between her thumb and index finger until it is all burnt away and there is nothing left but the smallest corner and a handful of black embers.

She closes her eyes. Time to forget. Time to move on. Time to *live.*

'Goodbye, Luella,' she says, and she lets go.

46
Una

'Una?' Roko calls to her from the door of his office as he sees her approach on the path. 'How are you getting on with your bures? All cleaned?'

Una strides past him, Kitty in tow. 'Almost. Mrs Miller wants a quick tour of the bush-land behind the rock,' Una calls in her wake. 'I'll be back in fifteen minutes to do Two and Three!'

Roko mumbles something, and Una ignores it. She takes her sandals off as she leads Kitty onto the beach and holds them in her hand, kicking up sand with the brisk movement of her feet.

Kitty run-walks beside her. 'What exactly are we looking for?'

Una's hand reaches into her pocket again. She wouldn't have chosen this uniform herself – she much prefers the 'bula'-style shirts and shorts worn by the majority of the resort staff – but something can really be said for the deep pockets. She pulls out a red sequin.

'We're looking for more of these,' she says. 'This is from the dress Luella St John-Gray was wearing on New Year's Eve.'

'I didn't see it,' says Kitty, suddenly morose. 'I was in my room.'

'Ah, of course. Well, that's what we're looking for. Sequins from Mrs St John-Gray's red Valentino dress.'

'Valentino?' says Kitty. 'Fancy.'

'Come on, Kitty. *Look*.'

'Really, Una. You shouldn't keep moving evidence,' Kitty says again, looking to her left and right as if she's being caught on CCTV.

'Calm down,' says Una. 'It's only a couple of sequins.'

When they get to Snake Rock, Una climbs up barefoot and begins to scour the nooks and crannies in the rivulets of the rock face, bending down to pick up another sequin.

'Your feet, Una,' Kitty warns.

Una bats a hand. 'I grew up climbing on rocks like these.'

Kitty, in a pair of practical Crocs, follows, scouring the watery pools of the rock face for shimmering red.

'So, you think Luella came here on New Year's Eve, when she was wearing the red Valentino dress?' she asks.

'I know she did,' says Una. 'I saw her walking towards the rock with Sofie Barthélemy behind her. They stayed there for a few minutes, and then Luella stormed back towards the main resort. She looked incredibly agitated. She was walking faster than usual, and she was holding her dress in her hands like this.' Una gathers up her skirt in her left hand and walks a few steps.

'So, if you know she was here, why are we picking up sequins?'

'I'm looking to see *how many* we can find.'

Kitty sighs. 'Una, I really don't understand.'

'Don't you see? I already have six,' Una says. 'That's a lot to fall off a designer dress, isn't it? Unless there was some kind of rough and tumble here, and they were ripped off.'

'Oooh,' Kitty enthuses. 'You think there was a tussle?'

Una smiles. 'I know there was, Kitty. I saw Sofie Barthélemy the next day, and she had a huge bruise on her cheek. She told me Mrs St John-Gray struck her. I saw it with my own eyes. Sofie admitted that the woman had done it. You may think what I'm going to say is crazy,' Una adds as they walk along the sand. 'But I have a theory about all of this. I have to service the bures now, but we will reconvene tomorrow morning.'

'I can't wait that long,' laments Kitty.

'Well, you'll have to,' instructs Una. 'I just need to think it all through a little more.'

Kitty nods. 'Fine,' she says and turns to leave. 'Bye, Una.'

'Goodbye, Kitty.'

Una heads straight for her cleaning cart, which is still discreetly parked on the grass verge next to the pathway between Bures Two and Three. She is as thorough as ever over the next forty-five minutes, changing Sofie's sheets, folding clothes and sanitising the bathroom from top to toe.

She is just doing her last sweep of the veranda, relieving it of sand and fallen leaves and coconut husks, when she hears footsteps and panting on the path beyond. Nunia is racing towards her, her blouse flapping as she runs, her face awash with concern.

'Una,' she says, breathless. 'It's about Sailasa.'

Una closes her eyes, says a silent prayer.

'They've found him,' Nunia says.

47

Sailasa

Sailasa watches the rain beat down on the window of the holding cell. He can smell the reheated lunch of the police constable at the front desk – some kind of curry, he thinks. Chicken, perhaps? It doesn't smell like fish.

He feels like shit, here on this uncomfortable plastic chair facing a wall. To his left, windows with bars and to his right, just bars – bars that offer a tantalising glimpse of the front door.

He has been at this police station in the old government building on Koroivolu Lane once before. It was last year, in February, when the tourist crowds were starting to thin down and the rain lashed the palms and the wind and flash-flooding turned everything milky-grey. He was doing his shopping at the Shop 'n' Save on Queens Road – a can of Fanta, a frozen pizza, that sort of thing – when he saw something sparkling at the bottom of his plastic shopping basket: a big central stone and two smaller ones beside it, all on top of a little gold band. A tourist's ring, for sure, stuck in between the angry red slats. He tried to put the ring on his little finger for safekeeping, but it didn't even fit there – that's how small it was. A tiny band with a large rock, fit for the smallest of hands, the slenderest of fingers. He thought about leaving it in the store, with the cashier, but he didn't know if it would find its way back to the owner that way (how can you *really* ever tell if someone's trustworthy or not?) and he figured that if it wasn't claimed, he might end up with a share of the booty. And so he tucked it deep inside his wallet and he took it to the police station on foot. He handed it over to the desk clerk there, a woman in her forties, about his mother's age, he thought, who smiled at him and said '*Vinaka!*' and offered him a cinnamon biscuit.

Today, no one offers any kind words or smiles or *vinakas*. Today, they *tut* and *tsk* and ignore his repeated requests for water. Eventually, a constable brings a plastic cup and pushes it through the bars. The water, which is warm, sloshes over the sides. He wants to tell them, *I came here of my own accord – I handed myself in! I did the right thing!* But they do not care, because he is already guilty in their eyes. He was the man they were looking for, the one who ran from Loloma Island, and whether he gave himself up or he was captured on a wild chase through the streets of Nadi makes absolutely no difference at all.

But even though it saddens him, he cannot expect anything else, because it's his comeuppance, to be snubbed and to suffer.

He raised his hand to her in anger.

He deserves everything he gets.

48

Una

'Can I speak to him?' she asks Detective Roy.

Adelina would turn in her grave if she knew Sailasa was falsely implicated in this . . . circus. And even though Sailasa is at the police station in Nadi, Una will not be swayed from her conviction that he is innocent.

Detective Roy sips Lipton tea from a dainty white cup, which he places back on its saucer to address Una. He sighs. 'Your nephew will be allowed a phone call later on today.'

Una folds her arms.

'Ms Simpson,' says Detective Roy. 'Una, if I may?'

Una looks up at the tall detective. 'You may *not*.'

The detective nods, sheepish, and clears his throat. 'Ms Simpson, we have reason to believe Mr Latu may have been involved in the death of Luella St-John Gray.'

'On what *grounds*?' she asks.

'Two types of blood were found in the woman's bure. We suspect one was Mr Latu's and the other Luella St John-Gray's. I will have confirmation of that imminently – as well, I expect, as confirmation that both blood types were also found on the body.'

'Why would you think it's Sailasa's blood?'

The detective sighs. 'Because he was seen by a guest entering her bure on New Year's Eve very shortly before she returned to it. And no one saw him leaving.'

Una could lie here. She could say *she* saw him leaving. But where would it leave Sailasa if she was imprisoned for perverting the course of justice?

The smug detective picks up the teapot in front of him and tops up his cup. 'I feel bad for you, Ms Simpson – I really do – but I'd say it's a rather cut-and-dried case.'

Una laughs loudly, and even she can hear how false it sounds. 'Well,' she says, 'I hope you don't jump to massive conclusions on *every* case you handle.'

'Only the ones where it is obvious.'

'What is obvious about this?' says Una. 'What if he just cut himself in the bure? The presence of blood doesn't mean Sai . . . that whoever the blood belonged to killed her or that they stole from her.'

'Ah yes, thank you, Ms Simpson – you just reminded me that I'd forgotten to mention the theft of the diamond.'

Una scowls. 'I expect you've hanged a few innocent men in your time.'

'Not really, since the last person hanged in Fiji was in 1964.'

'I've told you,' Una says, steadfast. 'Sailasa wouldn't do something like that.'

'Wouldn't isn't the same as *couldn't*.'

Una sighs, angry. She knows they will not find DNA on the woman's body from Sailasa – she has faith at least in this – yet she is frightened for him. The only saving grace in this God-awful scenario is that she is starting to form her own picture of what happened on the night of Luella St John-Gray's death. Like a barrister in a court of law, all she needs is a little longer to collect her evidence before presenting it to the jury.

THURSDAY 4 JANUARY

Cocktail of the Day: Secrets Revealed

(Cointreau, pineapple juice, sparkling water, lime juice)

49

Kitty

Kitty takes the path away from the resort to the bush-track, the same one she took on the first day when she climbed to the peak. She passes the staff village and sees Filipe emerging from what she assumes are the dormitories. He is holding a plush grass skirt and a long strip of cloth with brown and white geometric shapes that the male warriors wear as a sort of cummerbund. She opens her mouth to say hello, but Filipe seems distracted and doesn't acknowledge her. He is without the amiable smile he wears when he is customer-facing and instead appears downcast, angry even. Kitty turns away and walks on towards the bush-track.

Walking has always been the way she processes things. She woke up earlier this morning wanting the sheets to swallow her up, a grey cloud hovering above her, despite the bright-yellow sunshine outside. She had to force herself out of her bure, to pull her trainers on with defiance and face the day before it consumed her.

Now, she is glad she did. She climbs higher still, towards the peak, up and up until the whole of the Mamanuca Islands lie outstretched before her, like one of those prints you see in fashionable beach houses. She stops, bends her back and puts her hand on her knees, a standing cat-cow pose, and casts her eyes up to heaven. She cannot see a single cloud in the sky, only blue. The air is muggy and humid, and it is only ten o'clock.

'Oh, Fergus,' she says. 'What on earth am I going to do with you now?'

She called the insurance company after dinner last night – at the start of the working day in the UK. She needed to know how she was going to get Fergus home. The woman on the line, on her first call of the day, was apologetic. 'I'm so sorry for your loss,

Mrs Miller,' she said in a strong northern accent (Manchester? Kitty has never been good with accents), 'but your husband did not take out travel insurance for your trip to Fiji.'

Kitty burst into tears. 'Nothing?'

'I'm afraid not, Mrs Miller.'

'But we are loyal customers,' Kitty begged. 'We get our home cover through you and our car insurance. Is there anything you can do for us? I've just lost my husband!'

The woman sounded like she was all of eighteen, fresh out of school. What a job to be doing, dealing with people who had messed up their insurance and wanted a favour from a stranger without the authority to grant one.

'I'm so sorry, Mrs Miller,' she said.

Kitty sobbed then, tried to form a reply, and she knew the woman felt bad.

'I understand how devastating this must be for you, Mrs Miller,' the voice on the end of the line said, 'but sadly, there really is nothing I can do to help at this stage.'

The kindly officer at the Birth, Deaths and Marriages Registry on the mainland at Nadi mentioned the options for the uninsured when she visited with Dr Marama on Tuesday. It was either a funeral and cremation on the island (the least costly option) or an extortionately expensive repatriation flight to the UK, followed by a cremation, which would have been Fergie's preference.

Now, Kitty stares out ahead of her, trying to gather her thoughts and form a plan. What can she do if the £4,000 she needs for the funeral home in Nadi to make arrangements (and that's without the flights!) isn't there? She and Fergus – and it pains her to admit it – gambled everything they had on this holiday. They spent every last available penny in the coffer and then on top of that they borrowed on multiple credit cards to make up the balance: a red one, a black one, an orange one, a turquoise! They were already maxed out. Kitty has only £1,800 in her 'secret emergency fund' (her friend Meredith has always said that all women should have one in case of divorce: *You want to save enough to buy a car!*) but that paltry sum is not enough to pay for anything.

'What am I going to do?' Kitty asks aloud.

Would Fergus have taken *her* home if she had been the one to tragically died on their luxury holiday? Would she have expected him to? She thinks that the answer would have been no on both counts.

She throws a stick over the edge of the cliff and watches it flutter down towards the water.

She has decisions to make, tough ones, and decision-making is not her forte. She wants to do her best for Fergus, but the fact is, he is gone. What does it matter if he is cremated here in paradise or flown home to England by Fiji Airways via LAX in a box underneath hundreds of unsuspecting holidaymakers? In some respects, Kitty feels it would be unfair to bundle Fergus up like this, in the pitch dark, for the twenty-four hours it will take them to get back to Heathrow, alongside barking dogs and battered suitcases full of sand and dirty washing. And how on earth would Kitty even survive the flight herself, knowing as she would that he was down there, when on the outward journey just one week ago, he was by her side in seat 63B supping red wine and reading the *Daily Mail*?

'I'm so sorry, Fergie,' she says. 'Life is so unfair.'

Kitty turns away from the precipice and begins to walk, her feet pressing down hard on the dusty pathway lined by wart ferns, copperleaf and scented evodia, with its lemon-yellow flowers. She pushes her muscles to the point of pain, a sort of self-flagellation, she supposes. Punishment for not having a better plan.

She trips and stumbles on a tree-root exposed overground. Kitty is exposed, too, raw to the elements, battered to the point of pain. She looks up, sees what she recognises from her guidebook as a Fiji woodswallow land on a branch overhead in her nest to feed her young. By the river, she observes fresh rows of sturdy toad eggs, some tadpoles already. *It is the circle of life,* she thinks: life stops for some and continues for others. Death is inevitable; longevity is not a promise. She closes her eyes and breathes in the stillness. Not a single sound, not so much as a murmur of the breeze.

And then she hears it: a rustle behind her, the snap of a branch underfoot. She turns, but there is nothing but a desolate dirt track and a gecko looking up at her, questioning her, from a rock. A skid on the track.

Kitty's heart speeds up, and she is frozen to the spot. But she sees nothing. She walks on, faster now, the mothering bird and sticky eggs and the tadpoles long forgotten, instead replaced by an unfamiliar sense of panic. *What am I doing?* she wonders. *It was a mistake to come up here, so far away from everyone.*

Another crack, a snap. Kitty sees something in her periphery, a movement, sly and fast. It is too quick for her, this apparition, this thing behind her.

She feels something around her neck, something like a rope, fabric of some kind. She reaches up instinctively to grab it and catches a glimpse of the familiar brown and white geometric fabric that has become a tourniquet twisted angrily about her throat. Kitty's fingers are trapped against the flesh of her neck as the tourniquet, the noose – if that's what it is – is pulled and twisted over and over until her own fingers press crudely, painfully against her windpipe.

Her remaining arm flails as she grabs, in blind panic, at nothing, her eyes staring as she struggles with all her might to catch a breath.

50

Una

'Ms Simpson?' the detective calls to her across the empty bar area.

Una spins around. She does not like his face, this detective with his sarcasm and his smug smile. 'Yes?' she asks with a distinct lack of enthusiasm.

'I shouldn't tell you this until it is official,' he says, dabbing his forehead with a napkin. 'But I will. Use it to comfort yourself, perhaps.'

Una looks into his eyes, hopeful as a hungry dog. *Give me something,* she pleads silently. *Anything.*

'The post-mortem results for Luella St John-Gray suggest she was injected with ketamine and then suffocated in the sand. The drug leaves the system fast, but traces were found in her hair, and sand was found in her lungs. The bruising on her back and neck is consistent with being held down.'

'The missing ketamine? That's how she was killed?'

'It looks that way.'

'And Sailasa?' Una asks.

'Mr Latu believed he had accidentally killed Mrs St John-Gray in her bure and offered a full confession. He even corroborated where we could find blood in the bure. He was ready to take full responsibility for the murder.

'However, pathology tests have shown Mrs St John-Gray died from a fatal ketamine overdose and not from a bang to the head. Mr Latu made no mention of the ketamine in his confession. In fact, he was barely aware of what the drug was for and was confused by the mention of it. I have had vast experience of interviewing murderers and murder suspects, Ms Simpson, and my belief is Mr Latu did not administer the drug to Luella St John-Gray.'

Una's relief tastes like sweet, sweet milk. She has known all along Sailasa is innocent – she believed it before she had her own theory about the death of Luella St John-Gray – but *they* didn't know; Roy didn't. They wanted to catch the scared boy who ran simply because it looked like he had something to hide and not because he actually did.

Roy must sense her reassurance. 'It is not over for your nephew, Ms Simpson,' he says, not unkindly. 'There is also the case of the missing jewel.'

Una opens her mouth to protest but decides it is not worth it. She has faith Sailasa's innocence will be proven when it comes to the gem, too.

'I do appreciate your patience. We just want the right man for the crime.'

'Or woman,' Una says.

'Well, yes,' says Roy. 'Or woman.'

'Where is Sailasa now?'

'Mr Latu has been released while we investigate further. I'm sure you will hear from him, soon enough. He should be collecting his belongings about now.'

'Thank you,' Una says, 'for letting me know.' She cannot be uppity now, because she recognises the gruff detective was merely doing his job. She just has to trust that he did it properly, and, it seems, he has.

He nods, and Una gives him a small smile as she turns to leave. She senses him watching her walk to where the tiles turn to parquetry flooring.

'Your nephew is lucky to have you,' he calls after her as she hurries towards reception.

Una feels the right side of her lip turn up.

The office door is already open as Una approaches it and Roko leans out.

'Una? Have you seen Filipe?'

'No . . .'

Roko turns towards reception. 'Nunia? Where is Filipe?'

Nunia shakes her head and offers a quizzical look to Una. 'No clue, sorry.'

'Damn it. Is everyone missing in this resort?' Roko mutters, tutting. 'I have guests wanting to scuba-dive and now not only do I have no Sailasa, but my only other competent diver appears to have also gone off for a stroll somewhere also.'

Roko turns away from Una and leans across the reception desk. 'While I'm here, could I please have the passport for Ms Walsh please, Nunia? The detective wants it.'

'Who?' Nunia asks.

Roko sighs. '*Mrs* St John-Gray.'

'I don't understand.'

'The dead woman, Nunia – come on! Her passport was in her maiden name, and her maiden name was Walsh. You do have it in the safe behind the reception desk, do you not?'

'Luella *Walsh*?' Nunia asks, tilting her head to the side in contemplation so far the frangipani behind her ear drops onto the desk. 'But . . . wasn't that the name of the woman who got Christina Cole fired from Sunshine Island Resort?'

Una feels the hairs on her neck stand up. She wraps her arms around herself to protect against the sudden onset of cold, the chill that permeates her entire body. She knows what Christina went through, the impact it had on that poor girl and on her entire family. And the reason she is well aware of how the family suffered is because she knows Christina's brother.

She knows him very well, in fact, because he works with her right here, at Loloma Island Resort.

51

Christina

Christina looks out of the window overlooking the marina and cradles her stomach where the baby was. It was easy to get pregnant the first time around, but since she lost the baby three years ago, she has not fallen pregnant again.

The doctor blamed stress for her loss – not the pressure of working at Sunshine Island Resort itself but the trauma of what happened after the earring fell down the plug hole. She still wakes up covered in sweat sometimes, her nightmares full of the memory and how it all unfurled.

It was a morning like any other morning on the resort: a helicopter transfer due at eleven; the smell of lunch preparation surrounding the entire complex, maintenance up trees lopping down coconuts; Jone the engineer fixing the headboard on the bed in Bure Seven. That had made them all laugh – it was creaky, and the woman had complained.

Christina was in Bure Two, cleaning the bathroom, listening to Jone banging the nails in. They chatted a bit while he was there (something about his eldest getting a prize in school, something about her last pregnancy scan at Nadi Hospital, general chit-chat about kids) and maybe Christina wasn't paying as much attention as she should have as she sprayed the shiny black marble vanity with the double sinks and the brass taps with eucalyptus cleaning spray.

She polished and wiped and admired her own swelling belly in the large round mirror, and then somehow the little diamond stud slipped down the side of the sink, as if it had a life of its own. It was fast, like a little child on a water slide, and it lodged itself in the sink. Christina swore then, tried to grab at it with her salmon-painted pinky fingernail, to coax it out of the little gap.

'Come on,' she willed it. 'Come on.'

But the damn thing didn't listen, and down it went. She yelled to Jone to come into the bathroom, in tears, panic rising in her. He immediately radioed for Ovini, the plumber, who came running from the staff quarters and promptly opened up the plastic pipes under the sink, thinking the tiny earring might have been resting, pausing for breath on its adventure in the U-bend. But it had gone, gone far away – it was probably far out to sea by then, Ovini told her – and Christina knew that the only honourable thing was to come clean: to tell the manager that she'd messed up and that she was sorry, truly sorry, and what could she do to make up for it? She would work extra shifts for free, she would write a letter to the woman, anything to keep her in long-term employment now she would soon have a little mouth to feed!

And while her manager was sympathetic, Luella Walsh was horrid, *vicious*. The way she accused Christina of theft in front of everyone was devastating – the way the woman stood there and waited until the resort manager publicly fired her, and then watched her leave on the boat with her suitcase and handbag while her peers looked on and saw it, saw her crying with humiliation. The woman had known she was pregnant; it was obvious from her swelling belly. The woman had not been particularly interested, Christina realised, but nonetheless, she knew Christina needed the money for her growing family. She tried to hold her head high as she climbed into the boat, but as the vessel started to navigate the choppy water and she held onto her belly, Christina felt the sobs envelop her.

Four days later, with nothing but worry to support her, she started to bleed – just a little bit at first, just spots in her underwear, but then a lot, followed by an awful lot, soaking through towels, and the doctor confirmed what Christina already knew: that the baby could not be saved. She was too far gone to miscarry naturally at twenty-four weeks, and so she went into hospital, they put her into labour.

When she came out, the woman with the earrings had moved across to Turtle Cove Resort, and was visiting the spa twice a day and sipping Pina Coladas by the infinity pool. And Christina's brother, in particular, was incandescent with rage. He wanted to rip the woman's head from her shoulders, he said. He wanted to kill her, tear the lining from *her* womb. It was only Christina's begging, her tears, that stopped this show of macho, alpha-male behaviour. Instead, he went out and got drunk in Nadi and punched a brick wall over and over until you could see the raw bones of his knuckles.

And then, like the sun emerging from behind a dark cloud, they all moved on. They managed to find their way over it. One hundred days of mourning in Fiji and then you must let go, and Christina forced herself to look forward with hope rather than looking back with despair.

Three years passed, and Christina was learning to accept her lot in life. And then the phone rang two days before New Year's Eve.

'Baby brother,' she sang into the handset. 'Don't you have some coral to plant?'

'She's here,' is all he said. 'On the island, at Loloma.'

'Who?'

'Luella Walsh.'

Bumps sprung up on Christina's arms and legs; a shiver travelled up her back. Luella Walsh was not a name she ever wanted to hear again. Not here, not in Fiji, not on her territory, where she felt safe.

She heard her voice falter. 'Are you sure it is her?'

'It's her, Christina,' her brother said. 'She's married now, but I took her passport for the diving waiver form, and it had her maiden name on. It is her.'

Christina clutched her stomach. She had hated the woman once, but she had taught herself to stop, because bitterness wouldn't help her get pregnant again. Hatred is not what Jesus expects of her. But here was her beloved baby brother, his voice filled with anger and adrenaline in equal measures.

'You haven't done anything stupid, have you?' she asked him. 'You mustn't, Filipe. I'm begging you. *Please.*' She realised her hand was shaking. 'I don't need you to fight my battles for me.'

But even as she said it, she knew her brother would not, *could* not, comply. Protective to a fault: the kind of brother to act first, think later.

'You know I cannot promise that,' Filipe replied.

52

Sailasa

Una answers the phone after just one ring.

'Sailasa!' He can imagine the relief on her face. But her relieved tone swiftly hardens. 'Where have you been? Why didn't you call me?' she asks.

'I was worried they would trace my phone.'

'Why? When you had nothing to run from?'

'I did, Aunt Una.' He pauses, ashamed of what he is about to say. 'I . . . I raised my hand to her, to Mrs St John-Gray.'

'Raised your hand to her? What are you talking about?'

'I didn't mean to hurt her. She turned and banged her head on the edge of the door.'

'Oh, Sailasa!'

'I'm sorry,' he says. And he *is* sorry, but he will only relieve himself of his own guilt if he tells her the rest. The full truth. But not now. Not until he has made it right. 'It was an accident, but I promise you, that's how it happened. She hit her head, and I panicked, and I just ran.' He begins to cry. 'I am so sorry!'

'You don't need to be sorry,' Una says. 'Sailasa, the bang to her head . . . It wasn't your fault, any of it. We worked it out, you see. Kitty Miller and I.'

'Mrs Miller the guest?'

'Yes,' Una clarifies. 'We know who killed Mrs St John-Gray . . .'

She breaks off mid-sentence, and Sailasa hears a sharp intake of breath.

'Kitty?' his aunt calls, shrill.

'Una?' Sailasa calls into the handset. There is no reply – all he hears is a tinny voice far down the line, crying out for help.

'Mrs Miller, dear God,' a voice that sounds like Roko's shouts. 'Someone get her a chair!'

Then Nunia: 'I'll call Marama!'

'Kitty? What happened?' Sailasa hears his aunt cry.

'My neck,' the woman herself says, breathless. 'He . . . tried to strangle me on the bush-track.' She stops, as if she is struggling to get her words out.

Someone, although Sailasa can't work out who, can be heard saying, 'Who did? Who was on the bush-track with you?'

'Filipe,' Kitty Miller eventually manages to say. 'He's still there.'

PART TWO

The body judders slightly as the speedboat jumps from wave to wave. But the neck is still with rigour and is not floppy. The woman in the bag does not feel the jolts, or the cool of the breeze as the boat moves. The body she honed for two hours every day in her plush home gym is useless now – all those sessions futile, pointless.

Her vile death has been sanitised and removed from the luxury island she arrived on mere days ago – no corpses and no decay, just music and food. The show must go on! But it is no less pungent in the nostrils of the guests and staff who tread its beaches. There is still the smell of fear, as ever-present as the salty aroma of the sea.

The husband weeps freely. The sister plunges her body into the ocean that uncovered her half-sibling's gnawed-at remains, lets the water wash over her as if it is filtered and clean. The widowed woman distracts herself from her hatred of the dead by stepping inside the investigation. The young diver hides himself away, wracked with guilt at what he has done. His fearful aunt swallows down her disrespect for the murdered woman and instead hunts around for clues, sees them in everything.

For the man on the mountain who wrapped his hands around a woman's neck, it is too late for reflection or regret.

One of them knows. One of them knows why and where and how.

There is motive everywhere: hatred, revenge, and of course, the obvious one: money. Because the very idea of a flawless forty-five-carat brilliant-cut diamond, if it did indeed make it onto the island, would be enough for anyone to kill for. Wouldn't it?

SIX DAYS EARLIER

FRIDAY 29 DECEMBER

53
Filipe

Filipe waits at the dive shed with Sailasa for the guests. It is 2.50, and they're scheduled to get going at 3 p.m.

Sailasa is saying something about Luella St John-Gray, about how he hopes she's cheered up. 'You checked their passports?' he asks.

'Yes,' says Filipe, spreading a patch of wet on the floor with his toe. He cannot look his friend in the eye, so he'll stare at the floor. He does not want to give anything away. 'I wrote their passport numbers on the waivers. All they need to do now is sign.'

He was forced to swallow the anger when he saw the name on the passport: *Luella Walsh*. The name sang at him, taunted him, the letters dancing smugly before his eyes. He called his friend Ma'afu at Sunshine Island and asked him to go through the guest records and check a passport number. He needed to know it was the same woman. He needed to know his suspicions were real, that he wasn't just *hoping* it was her.

He wrote the number of the document on the dive waiver form with shaking hands. *You ruined my sister's life* was what ran through his head on loop.

Breathe, he tells himself now. 'I've just added Fergus Miller, Bure Three,' he tells Sailasa. 'He caught me at reception and signed up.' *Just breathe*.

'He's on his own?'

'Yeah. I'll carry the tanks down to the boat.'

'*Vinaka*. OK, tank two for Benedict St John-Gray, tank one for his wife, and three for Mr Miller. I'll take tank four.'

Tank one for his wife.

Filipe nods. He picks up tanks one and two and makes off down the beach towards the boat. They are heavier today, for some reason – they must be, because Filipe's heart is racing, and he is dripping with sweat.

As he lifts them over the hull, Filipe glances towards the dive shed. Sailasa is not looking; no one is.

He reaches for tank one, Luella St John-Gray's oxygen tank, and turns it to the almost closed position.

54

Thomasina

Thomasina watches the scuba-boat bob up and down on the waves. She sees Luella in the distance pulling up her wetsuit over her arms – her and her lechy husband, a man Thomasina has taken to calling 'The Octopus'. She saw him eighteen months back, at the Eurostar terminal in London when she was visiting the UK, groping a woman who wasn't Luella, his hands running up and down her back. She knew it was him, because the pair of them had done some story in *Hello!* or *OK!* or one of those mags, with the headline *Luella's New Love!* Thomasina had stared at her loved-up sister in print, and then this new man, flavour of the month, and she'd tried to work out whether or not he was genuine. And then, a few months later, there he was with his slimy hands all over another woman. Thomasina looked away because it wasn't her business, and Benedict certainly wasn't the first playboy Luella had eventually tamed, but the nickname she made in her head for him has stuck.

She wanted to go on the 3 p.m. dive – she was planning to pop up, creepy-style, like Mia Farrow in the 1978 film *Death on the Nile*: 'Hey, y'all – remember me?' and watch Luella's face recoil. To see the horror on her younger sister's face. But she is a little drunk right now, and it is not the time to either scuba-dive or confront her venomous little sister. They wouldn't let her anyway, the dive guys – not when she can barely walk straight.

As much as Thomasina would like to be generous, and as much as she would like to think she has the strength of character to forgive Luella, she cannot. She feels nothing but hatred for her sister, and at the heart of it, distaste – distaste for Luella's greed, her meanness, her malignancy. Luella knows their mother's diamond – the Thomasina Diamond, always referred to within the family affectionately as another woman, a character, an extra member of their gang, a *she* – is not Luella's to keep. It is Thomasina's; it is named after *her*.

She sips her cocktail and pulls out the piece of notepaper she's using as a bookmark inside the Wim Hof book she's reading. She scans the list she wrote on the plane:

1. *Learn Fijian*
2. *Tackle Cloudbreak*
3. *Handle Octopus*

At the words *Handle Octopus*, Thomasina let out a sigh. He'll have to wait until she finds her opportunity.

Thomasina reads on:

1. *Wreck dive*
2. *Confront her*
3. *Get her back*

She shakes her head and slips the paper inside her book to mark her place. Her holiday to-do list was perhaps a little misjudged – a little too dramatic and drunken. She needs to be a good deal more subtle if she wants to get what she wants from her narcissistic younger sister.

Thomasina sighs and stretches in the sun as she watches her sister's boat become a dot against the reef. She had better sober up before dinner. She glances over at the woman on the sun lounger beside her, all fizzy hair and freckles, and meets her eye by accident. She smiles.

'Hi,' says Thomasina, 'good book?'

After all, a little small talk won't do her any harm.

It's all about biding your time, she tells herself.

SATURDAY 30 DECEMBER

55

Kitty

Kitty enjoys a feeling of sheer bliss after her mountain trek, and even Fergus is amiable for the rest of the day. However at dinner time, his irritability returns.

'For God's sake, hurry up,' he growls. 'I'm hungry!'

He stands at the exit to the bure as Kitty fiddles anxiously with her earring. It always takes her twice as long when she knows he is waiting for her. Her nerves kick in and stand to attention, keeping her on edge.

At dinner, Kitty orders a raw fish salad and Fergus orders the Fijian crab curry, which smells utterly divine. It arrives while he's in the loos, and Kitty dips her spoon in for a taste. It is delicious, so creamy and flavoursome.

'What are you doing?' snaps Fergus as he sits down.

'Sorry, Fergie, I had to try it, and now I've got serious food envy,' Kitty grimaces. 'Swapsies?' She looks at the salad on the woven placemat in front of her.

'I don't think so,' says Fergus. 'Eat your own dinner.'

Later, in the bar, after the toad race, Fergus clutches his stomach, complaining that his heart is palpitating.

Kitty leans in. 'Fergie, you know you shouldn't have had so much spice,' she says.

'Stop fussing, would you?' Fergus snaps. 'I'm fine.'

But the pain seems to get worse as the night wears on.

'Should I call the doctor?' she whispers into his ear when the kava comes out.

He grimaces. 'No.'

'Then at least let's get you to the bure to rest.'

'Oh, for Christ's sake,' he hisses. 'I'm not a fucking child.'

Kitty puts her hand on his wrist, feels for his pulse, but he snatches his arm away.

'Fergie, my darling,' she whispers. 'It's not worth getting this stressed about. It's only money.' She fishes in her brain for the saying about being the richest corpse in the graveyard, but she only remembers it much, much later.

And by then it is way too late, because fifteen minutes later, Fergus falls to the ground, his hand gripping the glutinous white flesh above his heart.

56

Thomasina

Thomasina sits on the chaise-lounge under the window inside her bure with a very expensive club sandwich in front of her and a beer to wash it down. She saw Luella on her way back from the pool bar and hid behind a tree as she watched her sister glide towards the restaurant in her ridiculous gold dress, her chin tilted upwards in that arrogant way Luella has. She felt nothing but hatred and distaste. *Vulgar,* she thinks. *That's what you are. Ostentatious.*

She takes the small rectangular notepad out of her shoulder bag and brings the black ink pen to the paper. She writes *YOUR TIME'S UP* in bold strokes, changing up her handwriting, of course. She looks at the words she has written and thinks: *Now* that *should play with her head.*

Thomasina gets up from the chaise-longue now and looks at the note. A pang of something flushes her arms with goose bumps. Guilt, perhaps? Is *this* the woman she is? She bites the inside of her cheek. *Am I the kind of woman who leaves a note for her sister suggesting she's about to die?*

She sighs, her shoulders collapsing inwards. But then she thinks of Luella and what she has done to her, and her shoulders open. She never came here for reconciliation. She came for resolution, and maybe, in some part, revenge. Maybe it's the beer talking, but in this moment, Thomasina's decision is made, and she takes a step forward, the note in her palm. She opens the door of her bure and walks alongside the garden towards her sister's.

Her plan is to slip the note under the door and make a hasty retreat, but then she sees one of the maids on the beachfront, with a skeleton key that opens all of the rooms.

'Sorry,' Thomasina says, her shoulders shrugging apologetically, her hands a steeple. 'I locked myself out of my bure. Can you help?'

The maid, whose name bag reads Kelera, is busy counting the tiny designer shampoo bottles on the top of her trolley, in the middle of her night-time turn-down service of the beds.

'Of course,' Kelera says. 'Which bure?'

'This one.' Thomasina smiles, nodding to Bure One. She reasons that if Kelera knows Bure One is not hers, Thomasina can pretend she is simply lost in the dark and found the wrong path – it's her first day on the island after all and it would be easy to feel disoriented. But the maid walks over to the door and clicks it open.

'Thanks,' Thomasina says.

She leaves the door a fraction ajar, in case she needs to get out quickly, and creeps across the cool stone floor. The room is almost icy cold thanks to the whirring air-conditioning, and she feels a shiver down both arms.

At the bed, she instinctively turns left and puts the note on the left-hand bedside table, where Luella's things are, predictably, neatly stowed: a jar of face cream, a grey satin eye mask. Luella always slept that side as a child, demanded it whenever she stole a spot in their parents' bed – why would things change now?

She takes a moment to survey the room: an interior that's ornate with beautiful and charming Fijian workmanship, yet dripping with materialism and sequins and feathers and labels torn off brand-new clothes with so many zeros. Champagne bottles and jewellery and first-class airline pyjamas folded neatly into squares. Waste, abandon, gluttony, all under one exquisite tapa-cloth roof. Thomasina does not waver. She turns and clicks the door shut.

Outside the bure, she feels a flush of satisfaction of a job well done. She turns down the path towards her garden bure, then stops under the shade of the second palm on the path. She leans her back against the tree and feels the soft sting of heat behind her eyeballs.

'What the fuck are you doing?' she whispers aloud as she lifts up her hand and wipes the tears angrily away. *Get a grip!*

Thomasina hears a scream, and then another, the crying of a man's name ahead of her in the bar area. She steps onto the path and hurries towards the heart of the resort, and as she walks, she sees the formation of a circle in the bar, guests huddled in to view something.

She joins the back of the crowd and strains to catch a glimpse of what's going on, what the commotion is about, and that's when she sees it: a dead man lying in the very centre of the floor.

57

Sofie

Sofie's arms still hurt from pumping Fergus Miller's chest, and her knees are sore from kneeling on the floor. She is exhausted and emotional. She feels as though she has failed Mr Miller, that perhaps she could have done more to save him. She has done chest compressions on exactly thirty-one patients now, and she has saved only fifteen: she had a fifty-fifty success rate before tonight, and now she is hovering towards the failure end, and she does not consider that particularly impressive for an emergency medic.

She has always felt an overwhelming need to help men, in particular. It's not that she does not like women, but it is something that is inbuilt in her psyche, the need to save struggling men. She feels pity for them, stripped bare of their dignity, men who were once great but find themselves at their most vulnerable, men arresting on hospital gurneys clutching their chests, men who are bleeding or beaten up or bruised. She understands it is a result of what she saw in childhood: her father, a once great man, reduced to poverty, to nothingness, to vagrancy, a life on the street, a lonely death – a once great man reduced to a pitiful mess in front of the woman and child he had vowed to protect.

And now Sofie has spent her life trying to protect those women – women and their children – by raising up these lifeless husbands and fathers and bringing them back from the dead. But she couldn't do it for Fergus Miller. For his wife Kitty.

Sofie sighs and rolls her sore wrists. She tells herself sternly that she will not beat herself up about it now. She tried her best with the man, didn't she? She has been trained to understand that life is fleeting and that people die. Death, *la mort*, is as natural as birth, and she has been instrumental in both ends of the life cycle during the short course of her career. And while it is never nice to witness a person's demise, especially in such shocking and sudden circumstances as Fergus Miller's, she understands it is necessary for people to die for life to continue. *Ne sois pas en colère contre toi-même. Don't be angry with yourself.*

Sofie takes off her make-up and sits on the side of the bed. She knows she will not be able to sleep; there is too much going on in her head: images of the man's gaping mouth, the noise from the contents of his stomach sloshing around as she pounded at his chest.

Her hair is still wet with sweat from the effort she put in to saving him, and she touches it with the tips of her fingers. She is too tired to shower but too alert to sleep. She lies back and listens to the sound of the air-conditioning unit whirring above her, a gentle hum she finds mildly comforting.

Then she hears the sound of raised voices from a neighbouring bure and realises quickly that there is an argument going on. She creeps to the window and opens it a crack. She hears the soft hiccup of a woman crying and then a man's voice. It has a deep, almost baritone sound. Masculine and manly. The woman's voice is softer, and she can only hear the odd word, but she hears Benedict, as clear as day.

'We'll just get rid of her . . .' he tells her, then a few moments later: 'We'll fix everything tomorrow. I'm right behind you, darling. We're a *team*.'

He says, 'I love you. You're my *raison d'être*.'

Sofie blanches at the tender French words. *The reason for being.*

'It's all going to work out, darling.' Finally, he begs, 'Please. You need to trust me.'

Sofie listens to the words of love, which sound harsher in English than they would do in French. She moves away from the window. She is tired, so tired, yet her brain is wired and electric with adrenaline.

She could not save a life tonight. Her life–death rate is out of balance by one.

She climbs back into bed, pulls the sheets over her head to blot out the pleading voice of the husband in the bure next door and falls into a fitful sleep.

SUNDAY 31 DECEMBER
NEW YEAR'S EVE

58

Kitty

Kitty knows very well what the autopsy will say: it was Fergus's heart. He had high cholesterol and high blood pressure (and God knows he should not have eaten that delicious-looking Fijian crab curry with all the coconut cream). No one could accuse her of not trying to help. Hadn't she limited his red meat intake? Hadn't she boldly put her hand over his wine glass on those occasions he was pushing himself over the limit? Wasn't it her who booked the doctor's appointment to get his cholesterol checked and got him on the statins? Hadn't she looked after him well, damn it?

Anyone could see that with the high blood pressure and the calcium deposits, Fergus was simply a bomb waiting to explode. The situation the previous night alone – the excessive drinks, the spicy meal, the shock of Luella's refusal – had together provided the acute stress that lit the match. Poor, poor Fergus!

Kitty rolls in the crisp white sheets of her bed, her head aching as the Valium wears off and her reality unfurls before her. She is in limbo, somewhere between devastation and a strange kind of euphoria. She can recognise that she has not been happy for a long time. She cannot remember the last time she laughed, really laughed, or the last time she felt desired. But, like Stockholm syndrome, she still doesn't know how to live without Fergus.

She feels she needs to speak to Luella, to confront her – to tell Luella her role in all of this. She reaches for the Loloma Resort & Spa notepad and an envelope from the desk drawer and writes *SNAKE ROCK* 12.15 on it. On the envelope, she writes *LSJG, Bure One*. She peers round the curtain drawn across the glass of her bure door and waits for her chance.

At around 10 p.m., she opens her door and slips the note onto Kelera's cleaning cart outside. She will meet with Luella at the out-of-bounds rock, and she will blame her for what happened to Fergus, and she will get all of this grief and anger and hurt right out of her system and put it on someone else.

The effort of this decision exhausts her, and she lies back down on her bed, lets herself slip into sleep.

At ten minutes past midnight, having been woken by the countdown before her phone alarm, Kitty pulls on her second-hand New Year's Eve gown and her Venetian mask, and walks out of the bure, closing the door and hanging the *Do Not Disturb* sign on the handle. She has not brushed her teeth for more than twenty-four hours.

As she stands on the veranda of her bure, she sees Luella heading towards Snake Rock, glancing over her shoulder. Kitty puts one foot in front of the other in the direction of the rock to follow – but then she notices another person, a woman, hurrying behind Luella, calling her name. She watches from behind a palm until she sees the woman is Sofie Barthélemy, her long hair flowing down her back.

She has missed her chance. Kitty cannot confront Luella with the French doctor there, so like a cat in the shadow of a dog, she slinks back a few steps to her bure and lets herself back in, closing the door on her anger for another day.

59

Sofie

'You really don't remember me,' she says to Luella. 'Do you?'

Sofie feels the bitterness swirling in her chest. How easily Luella has forgotten!

'Oh, for God's *sake*,' Luella balks. 'Should I?' She turns away.

Sofie feels the sting of cuts on the soles of her feet from clambering over the rock, but the hot anger in her chest is stronger. It beats in time with her pulse: *Je-te-déteste-je-te-déteste-je-te-déteste.* 'Was your father like you, Luella?' she spits. 'Or do you take after your mother?'

Luella spins around. 'What do you mean?'

'My father knew your father, Frederick Walsh.' Sofie spits the words.

'Your father? I think not.'

'Oh yes. They worked together a long, long time ago.' She twiddles a lock of hair in between her finger and thumb, teasing.

Luella's lower eyelid tremors slightly, and Sofie feels the thrill of one-upmanship.

'My father was Christophe Berger,' she says. She studies Luella's face, notes the lower lip twitching. 'Now do you know who I am?'

Luella swallows down the shock she was clearly trying to mask and smiles. 'Ahh, I see. So, you're little Sofie Berger, are you? My, oh my.' She looks at Sofie with narrowed eyes. 'You're quite the antithesis of the chubby little redhead you were circa 1996 aren't you?'

'And you're still as venomous as you were back then.'

Luella sniffs. 'Barthélemy? *Very* exotic. Did you choose a pretty new name to throw me off the scent?'

'Not everything's about you, Luella,' Sofie laughs bitterly. 'I was married for a while in my twenties. It didn't work out.'

'Oh dear! Man trouble? I can't say I know too much about *that*, but why don't we paint our nails and talk all about it?'

Sofie paces the sand. 'Do you know, Luella, that when Frederick Walsh forced my father from the business – *their* business – we lost everything. Your father gained everything.' Sofie sweeps her arms around.

'Christophe Berger was an alcoholic who couldn't do his job,' snaps Luella. 'That's why my father got rid of him.'

'Frederick *drove* him to alcohol,' Sofie hears the tremor in her own voice. 'He pushed and pushed him. He took from him, always taking. And then you, Luella. *You* told your darling Daddy that I was evil to you, that I bullied you, and that made poor old Daddy Walsh even more determined to get rid of my papa. He would have done anything for his two little girls. We had to uproot our lives and move back to Paris.'

'*Comme c'est tragique*,' says Luella. 'Do continue . . .'

'You know how my father killed himself?'

'Pray tell.'

'From the rafters of our garage in Paris. He'd been living on the streets, but he came back to kill himself. He came *home*. I was the one who found him. Can you imagine what that does to a child?'

Luella turns away. She speaks to the air in front of her. 'What do you want, Sofie? Money, like all the rest of them? I notice you're not following poor little poverty-stricken Thomasina all over the island.'

Sofie's eyes cloud over with a fog, a short-sightedness, a need to hurt Luella St John-Gray, to wipe the self-satisfaction off her face.

'Yes, money would be nice,' says Sofie. 'I'm not going to deny that. But it's more than that.'

Sofie smiles this time. '*Je veux me venger*,' she says. '*Revenge*.'

Luella rolls her eyes, actually rolls her eyes, and Sofie sees it as her cue. She lifts up the syringe filled with ketamine, enough Special K to fell an elephant, and plunges the needle into the carotid artery in the right side of Luella's neck.

Luella's hand comes up instinctively, tries to wrestle with her, but Sofie has had a vast amount of experience injecting people who don't want to have a needle stuck in them. She lifts her forearm up and swipes away Luella's hand firmly, empties the syringe directly into the bloodstream of her nemesis.

'What the hell?' Luella asks. 'What was in that syringe?'

But Sofie ignores her and watches for signs that the drug is beginning to work. It takes less than a minute. In the moments before she passes out completely, Luella attempts to stand up, but her legs give way. Sofie uses the arms she's built up doing weights and saving lives to push the drowsy woman down onto her stomach on the sand.

'Help me,' slurs Luella, her face to the side, her breath making bubbles in the wet sand. '*Please.*'

But Sofie is sick of helping people. She is sick of saving lives. She climbs onto Luella's back, and she pushes her face into the waterlogged sand with all of her strength. She wraps her thighs around Luella's arms. Luella fights at first, until the paralysis is complete and she can fight no more and no more bubbles of life-saving breath come from her mouth. The struggle lasts all of sixty seconds.

Sofie falls on top of Luella's back, exhausted, and allows herself a quick moment there, and then it is time to move – and fast. She climbs off Luella's back and pulls her body as far behind the rock as her strength will allow. Then she kneels beside her, unzips the back of the gaudy sequinned dress. The top half of it is heavy with the weight of water, but the most part of it is dry. She pulls and wriggles the dress over Luella's head, sweating profusely as she does it, shaking out as much of the sand as she can when she has it off. Time is of the essence.

She pulls the dress over her own figure-hugging silver slip dress and zips it up as high as she can with her hand around her back. She switches positions and reaches over her shoulder to pull up the last inch of the zip. Then she fixes Luella's Venetian mask (which, under any other circumstance, she would covet passionately) onto her face and clambers back over the rocks, barefoot.

60

Sofie

Sofie checks Luella's mask is secure on her own face as she hurries towards the terrace, where the party is beginning to peter out. Guests are beginning to disperse now that they have seen the New Year in.

Her heart thumps in her chest. The technical term is tachycardia, when your heart beats faster than normal. She should have taken a beta-blocker. There were plenty in Marama's cabinet, alongside the ketamine she stole.

Respirer, Sofie! She tells herself. *Breathe.*

She needs to pretend for only another minute, and then she will be back inside the room, and it will all be over, and she can be Sofie Barthélemy again. But for now, she is Luella St John-Gray, and she cannot falter.

'*Je suis Luella*,' she mutters to herself as she lengthens her neck and tilts her chin upwards. She holds the hem of Luella's dress in her hand as she saw her nemesis do earlier on in the night, except she actually carries the hems of two gowns in her hand, because her silver Saint Laurent slip is still underneath. Together, along with the shoes, they are surprisingly heavy – especially since the Valentino dress gathered water in the fight with Luella. But the dress underneath is essential to play her new role – Sofie is more waifish than Luella *was*, and without the silver slip, the Valentino would hang off her.

Sofie stumbles in the sand and steadies herself, picks up her pace. She is almost home and dry.

Ahead of her, she sees Benedict talking animatedly to Klaus and Isabelle Fuch. The terrace is lit by dull, orange lamplight – the kind she hopes is dim enough to keep her secret.

Benedict looks up when he sees her. He opens his arms, and her breath skips a beat.

Je suis Luella!

'Luella, darling,' Benedict says and wraps her up.

She leans up on her tiptoes, her warm breath on his earlobe. 'It is done, *mon amour*,' she whispers from behind her mask.

61

Una

Una stands behind a palm tree, waiting for Sailasa to finish turning down the bed in the St John-Gray bure. She taps her foot impatiently. *What the hell are you* doing *in there? You'll be skinned alive if that God-awful woman finds you inside her bure!*

She glances back to where the figure of Luella St John-Gray stands near her husband, the sequins of her gown glinting in the moonlight. The woman who could change the fortunes of her nephew, who holds his future in her manicured hands.

Sailasa, come on*!*

Una watches anxiously as Luella steps away from her husband, her foot-tapping at a frenzied pace. And then it slows. There is something about the way the woman moves with tiny steps, her chin pointed downwards inside her ornate mask with its regal filigree, about the way she grasps the hem of her skirt in her left hand – a hem with a flash of silver in it – the heels of her shoes clasped in her fingers.

Una, she wills herself. *Think*. What is it that's wrong about this scenario? She cannot quite put her finger on it. She leans against the palm, peering around and squinting for clarity, before she remembers and stands bolt upright.

To her right is a bure with her nephew inside, to her left, an angry woman who is running out of patience with him. If Luella St John-Gray reaches her bure and Sailasa is still inside, then it is over for him, Una knows this much. The woman was already threatening to contact the CEO of Neptunian Resorts Worldwide.

Una has a choice to make now: does she run along the pathway and drag Sailasa out of that room, or does she trust in him to get out of there swiftly and also in fate to keep Luella St John-Gray on the beach terrace with her husband and the other New Year's Eve revellers a little while longer?

She chooses the latter, brushing the front of her uniform down, mopping her brow with a handkerchief from her pocket and hoping, very much, for the best.

62

Sailasa

There is blood everywhere. Sailasa can see the cut is deep, possibly deep enough for stitches. It mixes with the thick white face cream on the floor of the St John-Grays' bure. *What the hell is happening to him? Why does he keep fucking up?*

He needs to get out of here, pronto. He needs to clean up all this pinky-red mess and get out of this bure and never mention the pot or the blood or the cream to anyone.

He wraps a face towel around his finger to stop the bleeding and then uses another to wipe up the blood on the counter, but he only spreads it around on the shiny marble surface.

'Shit!' he cries. A drop of sweat from his brow drops onto the vanity and mixes with his blood. With his good hand shaking he turns on the tap and shoves one corner of his cleaning towel under the tap to wipe up the mess. He uses the other corner to dry up the wet.

He scours the floor and the expensive ceramic benchtop for fragments of the jar, then scrapes them into a tiny pile, wrapping them in the bloody cleaning towel. He thinks he's got them all. It is almost 12.30 a.m. now, and he can't be found snooping about in the St John-Grays' bathroom. How would he explain his hand? He'd have to tell the woman he'd broken something of hers, something expensive.

He shoves the towel with the pieces of broken ceramic deep into his pocket. Sweat again drips off his brow and onto the ceramic.

Fuck. FUCK! No time to wipe up sweat!

Sailasa casts his eyes around the bathroom. *It's OK,* he tells himself. *I got it all.* Then his eyes glance up, and he sees himself in the mirror. The man looking back looks unhinged, manic. He feels as though he can see his shirt moving – that his heart is beating so fast it is lifting the fabric up: *ba-boom, ba-boom, ba-boom.*

He blinks away from himself, turns around and exits the bathroom. Then he heads through to the front of the bure, where he flicks off the main lights and makes for the door.

63
Sofie

Sofie gasps as a face appears in the shadows.

The dive instructor is standing in front of her, his left hand up in surrender.

'I'm so sorry, Mrs St John-Gray,' he begins. 'I'm here to do the turn-down service . . .'

Sofie stares. He is out of breath, and his right hand is wrapped in a bloodstained towel. For a second, she forgets herself, steps forward and almost reaches forward to see if she should dress the cut.

But then she remembers who she is meant to be, that she is wearing the mask and the blood-red dress of the woman she has just killed. She wants to turn and run, but she cannot – she needs to be inside the bure. It is part of their plan.

Encountering Sailasa inside Luella and Benedict's bure is not.

Sofie needs to be Luella now. She needs to act. She doesn't care that she will ruin this man's day – why should she? Luella wouldn't.

'Get *out!*' she hisses, affecting her best English accent.

'Mrs St John-Gray . . .' He glances down at his bloody hand, wrapped in a white towel. His forehead is covered in sweat, and his bad hand is shaking, and Sofie realises that he is afraid. 'I can explain,' he begins. 'I was cleaning the bathroom, and I dropped a pot, a face cream of some kind . . .'

Sofie points sharply behind her, out of the door.

Sailasa steps forward, then hesitates. 'Please . . .' he begs.

Sofie embraces the role. 'I said, get out!' she spits, without a trace of her native France. She lived in London for many years; she can put on a half-decent English accent when required. 'Get the *fuck* out!'

She watches the young man in front of her flinch, his face contorting in anger and his left arm rising up high in the air. She barely feels the moment of impact, until a second afterwards, when the pain sets in.

It is, she realises, as a drop of blood trickles down her cheek underneath Luella's ornate mask, penance.

64

Sailasa

Sailasa lifts his hand and goes to grab her shoulders and then stops himself. This is something he will never do; he will never use violence against a woman. But Luella St John-Gray is already turning from him, and as she does, she smashes her face into the open door-frame. Sailasa hears the thud of the wood against her mask, followed by a sort of smash, and at first, he thinks she is OK – that she has been saved by her New Year's Eve costume. But then she groans in pain, and he realises the hard casing of the mask has actually smashed against the wood, cutting her.

She slides her hand under the cracked mask and cradles her cheek.

Sailasa hovers, stunned. It is his fault. If he had not raised his palm to her, she would not have turned in fear of him and smashed her face. He raises both of his hands again now – the good and the bloody – in a conciliatory gesture. He wants to offer help.

'Please,' he says. 'I'm so sorry.'

Tears spring to his eyes. His mother, Adelina, would be so ashamed if she could see him now. He cannot look in the eyes of the woman in front of him in the bejewelled mask as she winces in pain. So he does not stay – he does something far more shameful: he pushes past her and runs from the bure and away from the heart of the resort, through the emerald green undergrowth of the garden and along the figure of eight path back to the staff village.

He slows down on approach. He cannot be noticed acting strangely, although he does not know what on earth he will do now. He has hurt a woman, inflicted an injury. He needs to get out of here, to leave this island immediately.

He creeps past the rowdy staffers drinking kava and swapping stories in the kitchen area and heads along the narrow corridor where the dorms sit side by side like prison cells. He opens his bedroom door and closes it behind him, leaning on the inside for a second to catch his breath. His body is drenched in sweat. He looks down and opens his right palm, to the blood-soaked towel. Carefully, he unwraps the fabric, until his eyes feast upon the contents of the crimson material.

It is not the ugly cut at the base of his index finger he is looking at, but a perfect round diamond on the end of a long, thin golden chain. Enough to pay for everything, to wipe out every debt. It had been lying there, on the ceramic sink top, so close to the edge. He hadn't meant to take it, but he'd been desperate, so desperate. It was a solution for him in that moment, an answer to his prayers.

He looks at it now, blood-stained. A blood diamond. He stares at the glistening stone forlornly as he balances it on the tips of his fingers, the bloody gouge beside it throbbing in perfect time with his pulse.

65
Sofie

Sofie dabs disinfectant on her cheek. The cut isn't too deep, but there will be a bruise there tomorrow – of that, she is sure. She will need to think of a way of explaining it if she cannot cover it with make-up.

She hears the door of the bure open, and Benedict steps inside. He scoops her up in his arms. '*Mon amour*,' he whispers into her hair. *My love*.

'Ah!' She flinches, and he stands back and looks at her, sees her cut cheek.

'Did Luella hurt you?' he asks, reaching for her face.

'No. The dive guy was in the bure when I got back. I turned and hit my face on the door,' she says, and she wonders if he believes her, even though it is the truth. 'He was fixing the room. He thought I was Luella.'

'You're sure?'

'I am sure.'

'Are you OK?'

'I am fine – it will heal. It would have been worse without the mask,' she says. She stands up and turns her back to him. 'Help me take this off.'

Benedict undoes the zip of the red, sequinned Valentino – a task that, in most other circumstances, he would take his time doing. Sofie wriggles out of the dress and lets it fall to the floor. She is left in her silver slip, like one of those acts at Cirque du Soleil where clothes are under clothes are under clothes, and she is Sofie once again. She pulls off the slip, too, wet at the bottom and across the chest from the sodden, salty sequins, and drops it on top of the red one.

Benedict looks at her in the semi-light, her arms, the ripples of her abdomen. 'You are so strong,' he tells her. 'You could do anything.'

'Yes.' She knows it is true. Sofie has always been strong, has always been able; it is part of her make-up. The overweight child always teased, with the veneer of indifference. She pulled on detachment like a cloak after her father died as a way of protecting herself, and it became her strength. She knows Benedict adores this in her – her determination and her fire, her innate sense that there is nothing she cannot handle.

He has told her before that he saw it immediately, her hardiness, the very moment they met at the private members' club in Soho back in 2018. That he was instantly drawn to the self-sufficient, British-born French divorcee. It was what tore him apart when she instructed him to take the job in the City of London and they briefly separated. She went to Paris, the place she'd called home with her mother, the same place her father had been born and had died. They tried to be apart, but Benedict sought her out again, wooed her, pledged his eternal love. She knew she had him for good. *Un papillon de nuit vers une flame.* A moth to a flame.

And he was what she needed. He understood her. He knew she was driven by bitterness; it fuelled her from the bowels up like the furnace of a steam train, and he didn't care. He *admired* it, fed off it. He hated what she hated, and he wanted what she wanted.

It was Sofie's idea for them to track down Luella, for Benedict to start dating her. It seemed like the obvious way to get Sofie's father's money back. And how they've enjoyed spending Luella's ill-gained inheritance together. Benedict would tell Luella he was on boys' golf weekends and whisk Sofie to Paris or Madrid or Rome. They had to be careful. But in Europe, there was less chance of being caught because Luella wasn't particularly known; she wasn't in the party pages of magazines. They had to keep in mind always that Benedict needed to make it to at least five years married to Luella to get a settlement of any worth in a divorce.

Unless Benedict became widowed, of course – in which case, everything Luella owned would go to him. On those terms, of course, as little as a year was fine.

Sofie wavered on the second night, passed him outside the bure and whispered to him that she couldn't do it. She'd been thrown by Fergus Miller's death; she didn't want to be strong again. But he delivered a message of strength to her in the guise of arguing with Luella. A message he knew she would be listening for.

'We'll just get rid of her . . . We'll fix everything tomorrow.'

'I'm right behind you, darling. We're a *team*.'

'I love you. You're my raison d'être!

My raison d'être! Sofie was immediately soothed. He had given her a shot of strength.

Now, Benedict kisses Sofie on her forehead. 'I'll sort everything from here,' he tells her. 'The torches will be put out soon.'

She nods. It is his turn now, time for him to do his part. Sofie sits on the bed as Benedict spies through a crack in the curtain and watches as the torch outside the bure is extinguished by one of the overnight staffers, far less ceremoniously than they are lit at sunset with warriors in grass skirts. It is 2.30 a.m.

Benedict waits for a few more minutes, knowing there are at least two more lamps to go. Then he turns and glances at her and nods before he steps outside.

Sofie races to the glass doors and peers through the curtain. The half-moon is her lover's only guide as he runs, lightning fast, down to the dive shed. She cannot see what he is doing now, but she pictures him in her mind's eye as he pulls a yellow kayak along the sand to Snake Rock, where she knows Luella's body lies in nothing but a lace G-string.

Sofie pictures Luella's cheek half buried in the sand, just as she left it. She imagines Benedict turning her over and grabbing at her arms, dragging her further to the water's edge, struggling and sweating as the water from her hair trickles down his warm back and her wet, sandy legs rub against his groin. She knows Benedict will lie on top of Luella for the last time as he places his body on hers and uses his strong arms to paddle out to the halfway point between Loloma and the nearest island across, Totoka. There, he will slide off and push with all of his might until he hears the gentle splash of her body in the water.

At 3.16 a.m., Sofie sees Benedict's shadowy figure racing up the beach and towards her, across the little path that divides the sand from the bures. She has been lying on the bed, on Luella's side, waiting, but when she knows he's close, she opens the door for him and he steps inside, breathless.

'It is done,' he whispers, and she smiles at the repetition of her own words to him on the beach just after midnight. 'She's gone.'

Sofie feels the relief flood her. 'My love,' she says in English as she rests her head against his wet chest. 'Finally.'

She leads him into the shower, and they make love there. Sofie tenderly washes her lover's body and dries him with a beach towel she will later discard.

'I must go,' she says as she pulls on a T-shirt of his. 'Give me the towels.' She scoops up the beach towels and opens the door. Before she closes it, she hesitates. '*Je t'aime*,' she whispers as she attempts to smooth down the bed.

'I love you, too,' he tells her.

Sofie hops across the brick pathway, heading to the beach. There, she throws both hers and Benedict's wet towels on a sun lounger for the early-morning cleaners to pick up and take directly to the laundry. They could be anyone's, these blue-and-white striped beach towels, and the moment they are lifted from the sunbed, they will be jumbled up and put in the same industrial washing machine together, obliterated of DNA.

At the door of her own bure, Sofie turns back and sees Benedict, dressed in his New Year's Eve attire, climbing into the string hammock in front of Bure One, three hundred yards from the area of the Pacific Ocean where his wife's body floats lifeless and bloated, a favourite spot for hungry reef sharks to feed.

In bed, she closes her eyes, safe in the knowledge Benedict will be woken in under an hour, at the very crack of dawn, by the chatter of the sand-rakers as they move down the beach, combing every single inch and unwittingly eradicating the incriminating signs of their passionate crime: their footprints and the deep groove in the sand where Benedict dragged the cumbersome yellow kayak up to the water, where he left it after disposing of Luella, so the water would wash it of DNA.

And then at sunrise, poor, hapless Benedict St John-Gray will discover his 'beloved' wife has gone missing, never to be seen alive again.

66

Sailasa

It is 4 a.m and Sailasa is pacing his room in the staff village. He cannot sleep; he has not even got in to bed. His mind is too active. He turns the diamond necklace over in his fingers and feels the beginning of a panic attack. He needs to hide the diamond, put it somewhere it can't be found. He can hardly return it to the bure – the St John-Grays will be sleeping, and he cannot risk waking them.

What was he even thinking? He isn't a thief! Thieves never win; everyone knows that. He needs to get rid of the diamond, hide it where it won't be seen, until he can return it again. He considers the possibilities: the mechanics of one of the laundry drums, perhaps, or under a shell somewhere. Too obvious. Perhaps somewhere underwater, under one of the metal markers that breed the regenerated coral? There are dozens of them under the water, screwed in where the coral has disintegrated – each like a trellis for the ocean wall, an underwater nursery for fledgling coral. It is a good plan. It will be safe on the seabed, trapped by the heavy marker, in a place the guests and staff do not go – a location that is the domain of the dive master.

He pulls on his wetsuit and grabs his snorkel and mask, and he makes his way back along the garden path. It is pitch black now the torches have gone out, but Sailasa knows this route like the back of his hand.

There is no time to get an oxygen tank or an octopus, and he can't risk being seen. Tonight – or rather, this morning – he will be free diving, holding his breath while he completes the task. He has a torch on his head, so at least he will be able to see.

He walks into the water by Snake Rock and begins his swim towards the buoy that denotes the presence of the metal number six on the seabed, where he planted coral just days ago. He will tuck the diamond under the number, secure it under the metal wiring. It will be safe there until he can return it to his rightful owner.

He is halfway to the buoy when he sees something floating in the water. At first, he thinks it is the fin of a dolphin, but as he gets closer, he realises it is a human – a human facing downwards. His first instinct is to cry out for help, get help for this reckless (and probably drunken) New Year's Eve swimmer. But he realises by the shape of the body and the way it floats that this person cannot be helped.

He swims closer – the hair and the feminine shape of the body denotes the floating stranger a woman. He pushes slightly and the body turns over, eyes open.

Luella St John-Gray. There is nothing he can do to save her. He turns around and swims as fast as he can back to shore.

When he reaches the staff village, he is dripping with sweat. Luella St John-Gray is dead, and he was in her bure shortly after midnight. Somehow, between then and now, she has met her maker. He thinks back to their encounter in the bure. Did her knock to the head cause some kind of fit when she was in the water?

He touches the large plaster on his hand. His blood is in her bure.

'No, no, no!' he cries, his fist in his mouth to muffle the sound. This is all his fault! If only he'd done the turn-down when Una asked him to!

He goes straight to Filipe's room and rocks his friend's torso with both hands to wake him.

'What?' Filipe pushes him away, sleepy.

'Wake up,' he cries. 'Please, Filipe. I need your help.'

'What is it?' Filipe murmurs.

'Bure One. Luella St John-Gray . . .'

A yawn. 'Yeah, I know who's in Bure One.'

'She's dead.'

Filipe sits up, eyes wide open. 'What? *Dead* dead?'

'Not alive dead! What do you think?'

'You sure?'

'Yes!' Sailasa hears the tremor in his voice. 'She's in the water.'

'What do you mean in the water?'

Sailasa cannot explain it right now. How can he say he was hiding a stolen diamond under the number six coral marker when he found the bobbing body of the missing guest? That is a story for later.

'I couldn't sleep,' he says. 'I was swimming, and I turned, and there she was, face down.'

'You need to call Roko, get the police.'

'No. No, I can't. You see, I was with her earlier – in her bure. I almost hurt her. She was screaming at me, and *I almost hurt her*. I lifted my hand to her, and she hit her head.'

'What are you telling me?' Filipe swings his legs round so that he is sitting on the side of the single bed. 'Start from the beginning.'

Sailasa paces the room as he explains. 'Filipe, my blood is all over her bure. And now she's dead. And with the dive accident as well . . . I have to get out of here.'

Even as he says it, he knows it is not the right thing. He knows he has not hurt Luella and that running will make him look guilty, but staying here and facing the consequences would almost be more dire. He knows how it will look for him. His hand throbs, and he thinks of the broken glass, the blood. His DNA will be everywhere: the tests will confirm that! They will hinder him, not help. A protestation of innocence will not be enough to save him.

'Shit, Sailasa, what have you got yourself into?' says Filipe.

Sailasa gets up and walks to the desk near the window, fingers the rim of a photo of Filipe's beloved sister, Christina. 'I don't know what to do,' he says.

Filipe is silent for what seems like an eternity, and Sailasa feels as though the walls are closing in on him, as if he is waiting to be sentenced for a crime. But then Filipe stands up. He pulls a soccer shirt over his head and puts his feet into his Adidas slides.

'We'll leave now, while it's dark,' he says. 'I'll take you to Nadi in the boat, OK? If we go now, I can get back to Loloma before sunrise.'

Sailasa nods. This is not the time to question Filipe's offer, to ask: *Are you sure you're happy to take me?* He has no other option, no one else he can ask to help. He will not bring Una into this, make her complicit in his crime of theft or the other crime they'll all accuse him of when they find out he was in the dead woman's bure being shouted at mere hours before her death. He will not compromise Una's integrity, her morals, her sweet personality just for his own comfort. She means too much to him for that. Filipe, on the other hand, is savvy, cool, streetwise. He can take care of himself.

He nods. 'Thank you,' he says to his best friend, and they get up to leave, hurrying out of the staff village, Filipe still in his sleeping shorts. The resort is deathly still and shrouded in darkness.

A minute later, they climb on board the white speed-boat with the *Loloma* name and logo on the side, and Filipe brings up the anchor.

Filipe turns to him. 'There is something you should know, Sai.'

'What?'

'We both have this woman's blood on our hands.'

Sailasa looks up, confused. 'What do you mean? Are you telling me you killed Luella?'

'No! God, no. Well . . . almost.' Filipe exhales, his lips pursed. 'It was me, Sai. I was the one who closed off her oxygen tank.'

'I don't understand. Why would you do that?'

'Luella was the one who hurt Christina at Sunshine Island.'

Sailasa looks at Filipe for a long time as cognition sets in. 'Shit,' he says. 'How long have you known it was her?'

'I found out when I prepared the dive waiver. Her passport is in her maiden name: Luella Walsh. Ma'afu at Sunshine Island confirmed it was her. I called him.'

'You did it as revenge for Christina?'

He nods. 'I made a decision in a moment of rage, you understand, when I realised who she was. My sister's baby's life for hers. I wanted her to pay . . . and now she has.'

The boat rocks on the waves, and Sailasa feels a pang of nausea. 'Filipe?' He has to ask again. 'Did *you* kill her? Tonight?'

'I told you, no.' Filipe looks Sailasa in the eye. 'I wanted to. I shouldn't have done it, but I was wild with rage – I was even angrier after she got off the boat and blamed you! I *wanted* to hurt her, Sai – I truly did. But I didn't do it, and I'm glad I didn't. I hated the woman, but I love my sister more, and I realised that hurting Luella would only bring Christina more pain.'

Sailasa nods. He was right about the diving apparatus. He *knew* it had been tampered with; he just would never have suspected Filipe would be the culprit.

'You have caused me a lot of grief, my friend,' he says.

'I know.' Filipe stares at his hands. 'I didn't think you would get the blame. I thought, because you'd had the equipment serviced, it would all be OK, and they'd just put it down to an accident. But I was also thinking with my heart, making snap decisions based on love and rage. I was thinking about Christina and what she went through with the baby. I wish I'd never done it. I'm sorry.'

Sailasa nods. He is not angry. How can he be after what he has done? Everyone makes mistakes; everyone does things out of desperation, and he has learnt the hard way that desperation, like grief, is the price you pay for love.

'I can try and help you now, to repay you,' says Filipe. 'Christina has a room at her apartment off Queens Road if you need a place to keep on the down-low for a couple of days. I will call her and tell her you are coming, OK?'

They drift for two minutes, maybe three. Filipe starts the engine when they are finally past the yellow bobbing buoys that denote the reef, further enough out to sea that the night staff will not be alerted to the noise. The waves, flat and smooth like silk, are lit by the same silvery moonlight that shrouded Luella's body in the water. As the speed-boat begins to pick up pace, Sailasa looks out to the horizon, loath to scour for the woman's floating corpse. Once is enough to see it.

'You went swimming?' Filipe shouts over the noise of the vessel. 'In the middle of the night?'

Sailasa nods. 'Yes,' he says, as if it explains everything.

'You going to tell me why?'

Sailasa looks at Filipe and then glances to his left, at the black rucksack on the polished leather seat. It contains his wallet, a bloody hotel towel and a change of clothes, and, in the front pocket, a diamond worth a quarter of a million American dollars.

PART THREE

THURSDAY 4 JANUARY

67
Una

It is tea-break time for the early waking laundry staff at 9.30 a.m., and Una has to hustle Joana, who is dallying over her copy of the *Fiji Sun*, out of the door.

'Why do you want to get rid of me?' huffs Joana, taking her leave as Kitty strolls in.

'Short-staffed, Una?' Kitty jokes. 'I hope you're going to pay me.'

'Ah good, you got my message!'

Kitty holds up a note: *COME TO THE LAUNDRY AT* 9.30 *A.M. UNA.*

'I certainly did,' says Kitty.

'OK, listen,' instructs Una. Now they are firm friends, Una doesn't need to be as polite as she once was. 'We don't have much time.'

'OK,' says Kitty solemnly. 'Go ahead.'

Una puts her hands behind her back and paces about like she imagines Hercule Poirot does when he's explaining a case.

'So, the sequins on the rocks indicated to me there was some kind of tussle behind Snake Rock, like I said,' Una begins. 'I saw Mrs St John-Gray hurrying back up the beach in her dress, and then the next day Sofie Barthélemy had a cut and a bruise on her face.'

'So . . . you think they fought? Sofie and Luella?'

'I think it was more than that, Kitty. Much more. It was actually something you said to me about the notes perhaps being written by a left-hander that made me work it all out. Do you remember?'

'Of course. I asked if the letters sloped to the left or to the right, because that would indicate whether whoever wrote them was left-handed or right-handed.'

'Yes, well, that got me thinking about Luella St John-Gray. Every time I saw the woman, she was holding the straps of her various shoes in her right hand. On New Year's Eve, I saw her all night gripping the hem of her dress and holding her shoes in the same hand – her *right*. Do you follow?'

'Not yet,' admits Kitty.

'Then when I saw her on the beach, hurrying back to the resort from Snake Rock, she was not only carrying her shoes by her heels but they were in her left hand.'

'Ahh, so you think she was ambidextrous?'

'No, Kitty. Just listen, please.'

Kitty pulls an imaginary zip across her lips.

'Now, consider Sofie Barthélemy,' says Una, pacing again. 'I watched the next day and took note of what she did with her hands. When I saw her with her bruise in the garden, I handed her a fistful of *Euodia hortensis*, or Island Musk, for the bruising, and she took it with her *left* hand.'

'Ahhhh,' says Kitty. 'You think Sofie wrote the notes!'

Una sighs. 'Forget the notes, Kitty! I'm saying Sofie Barthélemy is left-handed, and so was the woman wearing the red dress on the beach.'

'I don't follow, Una. Really, this is all very confusing.'

'What I'm saying, Kitty, is that it was Sofie Barthélemy *dressed* as Luella on the beach, heading towards the resort and carrying the hem of her dress. Luella, I believe, was already dead behind the rock, injected with ketamine by Sofie Barthélemy.'

Kitty's mouth is agape. 'Oh my goodness, I can't believe it.' She sinks into the desk chair. 'But why would Sofie want to kill Luella?'

'For love.'

Kitty jumps up. 'Benedict!' she cries.

'Shh, Kitty. Joana has ears like an elephant!'

'It makes perfect sense,' Kitty whispers loudly. 'You should have heard him at the toad race, Una, gushing about how much he loved France . . .' Kitty explains. 'He couldn't stand Fergus insulting the French.'

Kitty suddenly looks downcast at the mention of her late husband.

'I'm not sure Mr St-John Gray being a Francophile is exactly conclusive proof,' says Una. 'But what *is* proof is the way Sofie kissed him on the terrace when she had arrived back from the rock. When she was dressed as Luella, that is. It would have been caught on the security camera by reception.'

'Yes, but wasn't she wearing a mask?'

'It wouldn't matter,' says Una. 'They'd have a million ways they could identify her.'

'Una, you are a genius!'

Una does not dispute it. 'On New Year's Day, when Benedict St John-Gray told me his wife was missing, I also happened to notice that his wife's Venetian mask had been left on the top of the fridge, when I had expressly heard her tell Benedict that a Philip Treacy mask had to be *hung*. It looked decidedly dishevelled, broken perhaps. Luella would never have shoved it on top of the fridge.'

'Of course!' Kitty coos.

'And there's more. I also saw heel impressions on Sofie's bed made by a man who was at least six foot tall. Benedict St John-Gray is the tallest man on the island by a golden mile. Not even Sailasa is that tall!'

Kitty shakes her head. 'You should be a detective, Una, honest to God.'

'I know,' agrees Una.

'But what about the notes?'

'I was getting to that,' Una says. *Kitty is obsessed with the notes!* 'I think Thomasina wrote them.'

'Those Ts were rather telling, weren't they?'

'They were, Kitty. But I don't think Ms Delana was in any way involved in the murder. The scuba incident perhaps – although there is no evidence that would stand up in a court of law – but not the murder.'

They look at one another, and Una sees Kitty's eyes are shining. It makes her feel a sudden glow, this unlikely friendship, and the way it appears to be easing Kitty's pain – or at the very least distracting her from it so that hopefully, when it returns, it will have blunted, dulled a little.

'We need to set a trap,' says Kitty, folding a towel and putting it on Una's pile. 'I don't think Roy will take any of it seriously unless we get a confession.'

'I think you're right,' Una says, taking the towel Kitty has clumsily doubled over and refolding it.

'I could tell him I know about him and Sofie, and then see what he says,' suggests Kitty. 'I could lure him somewhere by telling him we know his secret and then confront him.'

'We'd have to go together. Safety in numbers.'

'Absolutely not!' Kitty cries. 'Think about it, Una. He's not going to come if he thinks there are *two* people on his case. It wouldn't be safe for him. I could take a walkie-talkie, and you can listen in the whole time, then send someone out to get me if it gets dicey.'

'A walkie-talkie won't help if he decides to push you over the edge. If he thinks you know what he and Sofie did to Luella, he might want to *dispose* of you.'

'Oh, Una, I'll be fine. Just make sure Roy is nearby and you can get him to race up the track if I'm in danger . . .'

'Roy? Race up? Have you seen the size of the man? I don't think he'll be racing anywhere.'

'I think he's quite handsome, Una, don't you?'

Una rolls her eyes. 'What about Filipe?'

'Well, he's gorgeous, obviously . . .'

'No, Kitty, good Lord! I mean why don't we get *Filipe* to look after you. Sort of like a bodyguard. I'll suggest to Roko he sends Filipe up there to collect the toads for the next race, and I'll brief Filipe to keep close behind you.'

'Brilliant.' Kitty balls her fists and waves them in front of her.

'Right, well, how are we going to lure him up there?' Una asks.

'Easy.' Kitty walks across to the laundry's reception desk and picks up a notepad and pen. 'With a note. Isn't that how messages get sent here on Loloma? We'll tell him we know what he and Sofie have been up to.'

'Good idea,' Una says.

'What shall I write?' Kitty chews on the end of the pen. 'This is where I'm stumped.'

Una clears her throat. '"I know about you and Sofie",' she says with a dramatic flourish.

'*Yes!*' Kitty enthuses.

'Then, how about "Meet me 11 a.m. at the top of the bush-track or I'll go public"?'

'Oh, Una, you are so clever.' Kitty scribbles on the paper and then looks up, gesturing to a copy of the *Fiji Sun* on the desk beside her. 'I know, we could cut letters out of the newspaper and stick them on?'

'This isn't a ransom note, Kitty!'

Kitty shrugs and continues writing. When she is done, she hands the note to Una.

'Perfect,' says Una.

'Right,' says Kitty. 'Time for the postman to pay our little friend Benedict a visit.'

68

Kitty

It all happens very fast. One minute Kitty is standing on the bush-track wondering if she has made a huge mistake coming here, if she ought never have suggested such a wild plan to Una – and then something is thrown over her head, something like a rope, fabric of some kind.

She reaches up instinctively to grab it, but it suddenly becomes taut, this fabric, this rope. She sees the end of it and realises it is the fabric belt used for the torch-lighting ceremony, the traditional painted cloth worn about the waist of the warrior as he lights each torch and blows in his conch shell. She remembers seeing it on Sailasa the night of the road race, the night Fergus died.

Her fingers are trapped against the flesh of her neck as the tourniquet – the noose, if that's what it is – is pulled and twisted over and over, until her fingers dig crudely and painfully into the delicate flesh of her windpipe.

She hears more feet now, the rhythmic beat of trainers on the dusty ground, and Kitty cannot quite compute. In her slight delirium, she wonders if it is Fergus, if he has come back to help her – if she is already dead here on the track and she is looking down on herself.

But the voice does not belong to Fergus.

There are two voices. Two sets of feet moving, a scuffle, the sound of men groaning as they go into battle.

Kitty falls to the floor, released from her noose. She pulls the rope away from her neck and breathes in, half of it dust, but there's air, too. She turns, watching as the wrestling moves away from her and towards the less hospitable terrain of the mountain-top. Then they are back again, and they plunge towards her like fighting dogs.

She watches, frozen, as a hand bends down and grabs the fabric tourniquet she has discarded far to her right.

Kitty backs away, hides behind a yellow-flowering beach hibiscus. She peeks through the branches, watches these two strong, fit men struggle and slowly brings herself to her feet. They are well-matched in terms of build, both with almost triangular torsos.

They take their scuffle backwards again, towards the cliff edge, and it is there they seem to entangle themselves and turn around so that they are perilously close to the precipice. A couple more steps of oblivious scrapping, and they will both go off the edge.

'No!' Kitty cries, but she cannot hear any noise come out. It is only a squeak. It is as if her vocal cords have been broken by the rope or her own hands as they grappled to fight the hangman's noose, flattened and broken.

'No . . .' she tries again, and the sound is like a child blowing on a grass reed.

The rope is now twisted in Filipe's hands. He tries to loop it over his opponent's head, but the Englishman is faster. Benedict holds a stone, his trump card, which he smashes against Filipe's head. Filipe stumbles, and Kitty wonders if this is the end of the fight, but then he summons strength from somewhere to haul his body up. He lunges at Benedict, pushing him to the cliff edge before falling backwards on to the track.

Benedict's eyes widen as his right foot catches on the root of a tree, just like Kitty's did just minutes before. Time slows down as Kitty watches from behind the safety of the beach hibiscus as Benedict circles his arms wildly to try and regain balance. The look on his face is of complete terror, an understanding on Benedict's part that if he does not claw his way back to vertical, it is all over for him, this life.

A few seconds later, she hears a man's cry and something that is like a large branch being snapped in half.

Kitty stands glued to the spot, shaking. After a few moments, she takes a tentative step forward, then another, until she is half a metre from the edge of the cliff. She leans forward but cannot see over, and so she shuffles closer still, adrenaline coursing through her. Her footing feels unsteady, and dust wafts up as she shuffles.

She leans forward again now, and that's when she sees Benedict, on his back, his body spread out like a starfish on the rocks below and his head twisted unnaturally to the right.

She steps back and turns to look at Filipe, but sees he is still on the ground, his eyes closed.

'Filipe?' Kitty squeaks, her hand to her neck. She can feel her pulse thudding beneath her fingers. 'Oh God. Just hold on, Filipe, OK? I'll get help!'

Damn it, Una, she thinks. *I told you I should have brought a walkie-talkie!*

She turns. It is something between a run and a scramble. First on all fours, and then up and forward, pushing herself to go so fast that she almost trips over herself, face-plants on the gravelly ground. Around her, dust flies up as she runs, a latte-coloured swirl of particles in her wake. When she reaches the bottom, she hurls herself onto the manicured pathway of the resort, past the spa and the pool and to reception.

Una is at reception on her phone just a metre or so from Mr Roko and Detective Roy, who stand chatting in the door of Mr Roko's office.

'Una,' she pants, and the name comes out as a whisper.

'Kitty?' Una cries, tossing her phone onto a pile of hand towels in front of her, the screen still lit up.

Kitty cries to say that Filipe needs help, but the words come out choked and thin.

'Mrs Miller, dear God.' It is Roko. 'Someone get her a chair!'

'I'll call Marama!' says Nunia, picking up the phone.

'Kitty? What happened?' Una's voice is like a tonic.

'My neck.' Kitty gestures to her throat. 'He tried to . . . strangle me on the bush-track.'

'Who did?' Detective Roy leaps towards her. 'Who was on the bush-track with you?'

'Filipe,' Kitty says, her voice hoarse. 'He's still there.'

'Filipe attacked you?' Roy attempts to clarify. 'Filipe from the dive team?'

'No,' says Kitty in barely more than a whisper. 'It wasn't Filipe who attacked me. He tried to *save* me. It was Benedict. Filipe *saved* me, and he's still up there, and he's hurt. You need to help him!'

The detective spins around in the direction of the bush-track, while Roko instructs Nunia to call Dr Marama.

'Kitty, come on!' Una races behind Roko, beckoning Kitty with her fingers. 'Keep *up*!'

'No,' Roko calls behind him. 'No guests beyond this point. This time I insist. Mrs Miller is in no fit state to—'

'Try and stop me,' Kitty squeaks.

He sighs. 'OK. . .fine.'

Dr Marama joins them on the path, and together they race up the bush-track until Kitty says, 'Just up here,' and guides them a little off the dirt track to the right.

Filipe's eyes flicker between open and shut and he groans softly. There is a bump, the size of an ostrich egg on his forehead. 'I'm OK,' he mutters and closes his eyes again.

Una kneels beside him and takes his hand. 'Just stay still, Filipe,' she says. 'You've had a nasty bump to the head by the looks of things.'

From the cliff edge, the very point where Benedict went over, Kitty can hear Dr Marama saying to Detective Roy. 'He has a broken neck. No chance of survival. I can see it from all the way up here.'

There is the sound of feet scuffing on the dirt track then, and Kitty and Una look up. Sofie Barthélemy stands, out of breath, looking from face to face, with Thomasina behind her.

'What is going on?' Sofie asks, and Kitty fixes her with an angry stare.

'We heard from Nunia that . . .' Thomasina stops as her eyes land on Filipe. 'Oh my God, what happened to him?' She kneels down beside him.

'Benedict tried to kill him,' Kitty says. 'There was a scuffle and then . . .' She pauses. 'And then Benedict went over,' she says.

Sofie steps forward. She looks at Marama and Roy standing by the cliff edge. 'Went over?' Her voice is small, pleading. '*Je ne comprends pas*.'

'Oh, I think you *comprends* very well,' snaps Kitty, and she turns to the Frenchwoman. 'But let me spell it out for you. Benedict went over the cliff and landed on the rocks. *Il est mort*. He is dead.'

Sofie falls to her knees, and the anguished scream that escapes her mouth is deafening. '*Non!*' she cries.

69

Una

Roy stares at Sofie Barthélemy as she rocks on her haunches and pulls at her hair. '*Non, non, non!*' she cries, breathless. '*Oh, mon amour!*'

Thomasina Delana looks up from beside Filipe and fixes her gaze on Sofie. Her brow furrows. 'I don't understand,' she says.

'Can someone please explain?' Roy sighs against the faint hum of the rescue chopper as it makes its way to Loloma's helipad below. 'Ms Simpson?'

'Don't you see?' says Kitty. 'Benedict St John-Gray and Sofie Barthélemy are lovers.'

'*Were* lovers,' says Una.

'More than lovers,' cries the doctor. 'We existed for each other!'

Roy scratches his head.

Sofie Barthélemy gets up and stumbles blindly towards the cliff edge. 'I don't want to live,' she cries.

Marama steps forward and grabs her. 'No,' he says gently.

More gently than the woman deserves, thinks Una.

'No,' snaps Kitty to the Frenchwoman's back. 'You're not getting away with it that easily. You *killed* someone!'

'I tried to save your husband!' Sofie cries.

Kitty looks as though her face has been slapped.

Thomasina stands up. Her face is bleak with grief. She fixes Sofie with a stare. 'You and Benedict killed Luella together, for the money?'

Sofie whips around. 'No!' she cries. 'It wasn't just for the money! We didn't kill her just for that.'

Una looks at Marama, and they exchange a wide-eyed expression. Una indulges in a smile, which she bites down on immediately when she remembers the gravity of the situation.

'Is that a confession?' asks Roy.

'Of course it is,' says Kitty. 'We all heard it.'

Sofie's words are breathless between sobs. 'What we had was worth more than money. Can none of you see beyond that?'

Thomasina takes a step forward. 'Then why?'

'It was about who I used to be. It was revenge for my father. For what your stepfather did to him and the money he stole from him.'

Una glances at Kitty, who stares, wide-eyed, at the steely slip of a doctor. They weren't expecting this.

'*Vous me connaissez*,' says Sofie, wiping her nose on her wrist. She laughs, manic. 'You know me, little Thomas Walsh.'

Thomasina gasps, breathless. 'Oh my God,' she whispers. 'Sofie Berger?'

'*Oui*. It took you a while,' she says.

'You could have come after me,' cries Thomasina. 'I was Freddie's daughter, too. Why didn't you?'

'Because you weren't his real daughter, Thomasina, were you?'

'But I was the favourite.'

Sofie emits an unhinged cackle. 'We didn't want you because you don't have any money, little Thomas.'

'Then why did you invite me here? Why did you want me on the island?'

'To make you a suspect, of course. Certainly not for your money. You have nothing!'

'And now *you* have nothing,' Thomasina cries and points towards the cliff edge. Una steps towards Thomasina and takes her hand. It is clammy to the touch. 'You've lost it all.'

Sofie turns her head away, but suddenly Thomasina is in front of her.

'How did you do it?' asks Thomasina. 'How did you kill my sister?'

'With the ketamine she stole from the medicine cabinet in my office,' says Marama. He turns to Sofie. 'When did you take it?'

Sofie does not answer.

'My guess is that you took it when you came back to the office after Fergus Miller died. Is that correct?'

The Frenchwoman shrugs.

'Then she lured Mrs St-John Gray to Snake Rock with a note that she left on Kelera's cleaning cart . . .' begins Roko. 'I saw the words myself.'

The Frenchwoman shakes her head. 'No,' she says. 'There was no note.'

'There was,' says Roko. 'I passed it to Mrs St-John Gray myself after the fireworks.'

'*Non*,' she says and taps her temple. '*Ce n'était pas moi.* I wrote no note.'

Una sees Kitty shift uncomfortably from one foot to the other, and an odd thought passes through her consciousness. She bats it away.

'Well, I don't think we can trust anything you say, can we?' Kitty says. 'If you're unscrupulous enough to inject a woman with a horse tranquilliser, then you're the kind of person who writes a threatening note asking someone to meet you at the rock at 12.15 a.m. . . .'

Una doesn't recall anyone saying the time on the note, but she'll just forget that little detail. It doesn't matter anyway. What does a piece of paper matter in the grand scheme of things? Thomasina Delana's note doesn't matter, does it? Una doesn't question this one, either.

Instead, she stands up and explains to the small crowd about the dress, the sequins on the rock and how she had guessed it wasn't Luella returning from Snake Rock because of Sofie's left hand.

'This is a lovely story,' says Sofie, her bent body now unfurled. '*Très romantique*. But where is your evidence?'

'It will, of course, be confirmed by analysis of the surveillance camera at reception,' says Roy.

'Ears,' chirps Kitty, who Una suspects has been mulling it over after their chat in the laundry. 'That's how the folk at passport control can tell toddlers from their baby photos. That's how they can distinguish anyone – the ears. They'll be able to tell you weren't Luella, even though you had a mask on. They'll also find your

DNA on the inside of Luella's Valentino dress, no doubt.' Kitty is on a roll. 'And probably all over the scuba equipment you tampered with,' she adds.

'Thank you, Mrs Miller.' Roy sighs. 'But there is no evidence that Dr Barthélemy had anything to do with the scuba incident.'

Roko looks at Una briefly and then turns to Kitty. 'It's my belief it was just a freak accident. I certainly do not believe my dive staff were at fault.'

Una offers her boss a grateful smile.

'Accident?' cries Kitty. 'Benedict was on the boat with Luella, for goodness' sake, and her oxygen suddenly runs out forty-eight hours before his girlfriend actually murders her? I'd say Benedict was very much to blame . . .'

'Mrs Miller, we cannot make assumptions in police work!' barks Roy, irritated. 'Anyway, if you'll allow me to continue . . .' He clears his throat. 'I was informed a short time ago that a syringe has washed up on a beach at Shell Village, three miles north-west of here. A mother caught her child playing with it and reported it to the village chief, whose daughter Joana happens to work in the laundry here at Loloma. It is the same brand of imported syringe used in the resort, and once examined, I expect it will be found to have faint traces of ketamine on the inside.'

Two uniformed officers arrive at the peak and survey the assembled group. They are closely followed by two medics with a stretcher, who kneel down to attend to Filipe.

'Cuff this woman, please, Nagata,' Roy tells the shorter of the policemen. The constable obliges, sliding the handcuffs onto the waifish doctor's wrists and clicking them shut. Her head hangs down, her blonde hair matted and wet from her tears.

Thomasina steps towards Sofie and bends down to see her face under the hair. 'Money,' she says. 'You said earlier that I didn't have any.'

Sofie Barthélemy looks up with a scowl. It has turned her face from serene to ugly. 'What did you say?'

'It turns out I do have money. I've just inherited it,' Thomasina says as she looks into Sofie's dark eyes. 'Thanks to you.'

Una sees the doctor's hands ball into fists. 'Thanks to me?'

'When Luella died, the money was to go to Benedict, but with him dead, too, I inherit all of her money. It's in the will – everything goes back to the family trust in the event of both their deaths. I'm the only Walsh left now. Me, the stepsister. I *am* the family trust.'

The veins in Sofie's neck pulse wildly, and she chews on the skin on the inside of her cheek as she is led down the bush-track and back towards the beating heart of the resort.

70
Thomasina

Thomasina scratches her head as she makes her way back to her bure. There are too many tabs open in her brain. She feels woozy. She stops to steady herself on the trunk of a lazy palm. Una and Kitty rush to her side.

'Are you two following me?' she asks.

'No,' insists Kitty. 'We just wanted to check you're OK, which you obviously aren't.' Then she adds, 'Understandably, of course.'

'This is a lot for you to deal with,' agrees Una.

Thomasina offers a limp smile. 'I'm fine. I mean, I don't know how to feel, if I'm honest. I suspected Benedict of killing Luella as soon as she was found,' she says. 'But I had no idea about him and Sofie. They were very clever I suppose, weren't they?'

'They were,' says Una. 'But they didn't bank on us two being cleverer . . .'

'You did throw us off a little,' says Una cautiously. 'With the menacing note you left her.'

'Menacing note . . . ?' Thomasina begins, and then stops. She sighs. 'How did you know it was from me?'

'Your capital Ts,' says Una. 'They were the same as the one on your to-do list.'

'Wow, Una – I was sure I'd tucked that drunken to-do list inside my book. How on *earth* did you find it?'

Una inspects her own fingernails. 'It must have just fallen out,' she says.

'Uh-huh,' says Thomasina. *Fallen out, my arse.*

'Well, anyway,' says Kitty. 'There's no crime in writing a note.'

'No, there isn't,' Thomasina agrees.

'Unless you had something to do with the scuba incident,' says Una. 'You seem remarkably knowledgeable about scuba terminology.'

'I'm sorry?'

'The octopus?' says Kitty. 'You know, the equipment?'

Thomasina's brow furrows. 'I don't know what the hell an octopus is in diving terms but that's what my nickname was for Benedict: The Octopus. And anyway, Filipe told me Luella must have accidentally closed off her tank and that's what caused the oxygen to fail.'

Una shrugs. 'Oh well,' she says. 'It's all over now.'

Kitty nods. 'What will you do next, Thomasina?' she asks.

Thomasina looks out onto the water. 'I'm going to stay here in Fiji for a while. Island-hop maybe, surf.' It's the first time she's acknowledged her plan, even to herself. 'I suppose I've just come into a lot of money, so I don't really have to worry about heading back to Byron any time soon. I guess I'd like to explore this place, find out more about my father's family.'

'Well,' says Kitty. 'Una and I wish you the best of luck. Come and see us before you leave the island, won't you?'

Thomasina smiles. 'I will,' she says. She's fond of these two busybodies, and she will miss them in a strange sort of a way.

She heads out of the bar and turns onto the beach. She passes the dive shed and sees it's empty. She has almost reached Snake Rock and is turning inland towards her garden bure when a figure jumps out at her from behind a palm tree.

'Filipe, what the . . . ?' She sees the bruise on his forehead and she reaches up to touch it, but he grabs her hand.

'It was just a bit of concussion,' he says. 'I'm fine, really. Come with me.'

She follows behind without even questioning where she's being led. As they approach the laundry, Filipe pulls her into a side room, which she realises is a courtesy room for guests who have vacated their bure prior to travel and who need to shower and change ahead of their airport transfer. It is stuffy and dark, the curtains drawn.

'What are we doing in . . .' she begins. 'And are you actually OK?'

'I'm fine. They checked me over thoroughly at Nadi Hospital. I was concussed but they cleared me to come back.'

'Are you sure you're not still. . ?'

'Thomasina,' says Filipe. It's the first time he has used her Christian name. 'Listen, please.'

'OK.'

He raises his right fist and holds it in front of her, and when he opens it, her breath stops. On his palm sits the Thomasina Diamond, winking at her as if it has enjoyed giving her the runaround. Thomasina looks at the diamond and up into Filipe's eyes.

'My diamond,' she whispers.

'Is this the one you've been looking for?'

Thomasina hears herself laugh. 'Yes! Yes it is.'

Then she frowns. 'But. . . I saw the receipt. Luella sold it.'

'You must have been mistaken, or. . .do you think it's possible the receipt was for something else?' Filipe says.

Thomasina nods. 'I'd say that's entirely possible,' she replies. 'Luella has bought and sold plenty of items at Christie's in the past.'

She blinks, suddenly fearful of what she is about to be told. 'But how do you have it, Filipe? Where did you get it from?'

Filipe sighs. 'I got it from Sailasa,' he says. 'Sai gave it to me.'

'Sailasa stole the diamond?' she asks.

Filipe looks her directly in the eye. 'He had to,' he tells her.

71
Una

Una watches the police boat depart. In any other circumstances, the journey away from Loloma Resort & Spa towards the orange sunset might be viewed as romantic, but not this evening. There is no singing, no pomp and ceremony for the single guest on the white boat with the blue-and-white checks and the words *Fiji Police*. Instead, Sofie Barthélemy sits on a plastic seat, her wrists encased in handcuffs. Her body tilts forward, scorn and anger written on her face. No tears for her lover, who travels to the mainland ahead of her in a thick, plastic bag, his body broken and bruised.

Roy approaches as Una rocks on her heels in the sand.

'You're not going to the mainland with Dr Barthélemy?' she asks him.

'No. Constables Nagata and Tuilevu are capable,' he says. 'I wanted to let you know the lab just called. The results came in on the blood samples in the bure. The blood on the bathroom floor, the taps and the towel rail belonged to your nephew, and its placement was consistent with Mr Latu cutting himself and washing and drying the wound exactly as he told us he did.'

Una nods. Her eyes fill with tears, and she blinks them away.

'The second blood sample, found on the door-frame, was from Sofie Barthélemy, which corroborated your nephew's story about the woman purporting to be Luella St John-Gray – but who was not Luella St John-Gray – hitting her face on the door-frame.'

'And the syringe?' asks Una.

'It was found to have faint traces of ketamine as we suspected,' says Roy. 'Interpol has already run a search on Sofie Barthélemy from her passport number and found footage of her in passport control booths at foreign airports, together with her married lover.

The dates line up with his passport being used, too. One item of footage is at Rome's Fuimicino Airport, one at Milan Malpensa, another at the Eurostar terminal in Paris.'

'The clandestine meetings of two lovers plotting a sinister murder,' says Una.

'It seems that way, Una, yes. Sofie Barthélemy will be jailed for a long time.'

Una nods and smiles. She does not even mind that the detective has used her Christian name. There may now be actual scientific proof, but she and Kitty knew who was guilty without it. Una saw it, all of it – the small things, the minutiae of details.

'Both you and Mrs Miller did a remarkable job,' says Roy.

Una smiles. 'Yes,' she says. 'We did. I do believe we solved the crime faster than you did, Detective!'

Roy shakes head and walks away, but Una sees he is smiling.

A moment later, Una feels Kitty come up behind her and slide her arm through her own. Together, the two women stand like this until the blue-and-white police speed-boat is just a tiny dot on the other side of the reef.

'Gosh,' says Kitty. 'I'm rather relieved it's all over.'

'Me too,' lies Una, because, truth be told, she has enjoyed this adventure.

'I still can't believe I'll be travelling home alone,' Kitty says. 'Fergus didn't purchase travel insurance for the holiday, and the cost of repatriation is beyond my means, so I've decided to have him cremated here in Fiji. Next week, actually. I've pushed my flight to the UK back by a few days and booked into a resort on the mainland. I think Fergus would be happy with the idea of his ashes being scattered here. I'll take some home with me, of course. I might scatter them at an Arsenal match. He loved the Gunners.' At Una's blank stare, she adds, 'A football team.'

Una smiles. 'That's a wonderful idea. You know, Kitty, my three-day break is coming up. I could come and help you bid farewell to Fergus if you'd like me to? I'd hate for you to have to do that alone.'

'Would you? Oh, Una, that would be so kind of you. I really could do with a friend.' Una sees the tears in Kitty's eyes. 'Thank you.'

Una smiles and squeezes her friend's arm. Together, they turn around and make their way up the beach. Kitty wipes her eyes and looks forward.

At the water sports shed, Filipe is cleaning snorkel masks with a cloth.

'Una!' Filipe cries. 'Mrs Miller! *Bula!*'

'*Bula,*' says Kitty, opening her arms to hug him. 'It is so good to see you back here, Filipe, but shouldn't you be resting?'

Filipe smiles. 'I'm fine. Truly. Dr Marama is checking in on me.'

'You gave us a fright,' says Una, embracing him.

'It was nothing. Just a bump and a cut.' He turns to Kitty. 'Did Una tell you Sailasa is on his way back to Loloma tomorrow?'

'Oh, how wonderful,' says Kitty with a clap of her hands, turning to Una herself. 'So Roko agreed that he wasn't negligent with the scuba equipment?'

Una winks and nods. She still has her feminine wiles, and she will use them when needed.

'And Sailasa feels all right about it all?' Kitty asks.

Una smiles. 'He's going to be just fine.'

FRIDAY 5 JANUARY

Cocktail of the Day:
The Resolution

(Vodka, soda water, ice, mint leaves, fresh raspberries)

72

Thomasina

Thomasina steps out of the jeweller's shop in Nadi at around 11.30 in the morning. She checks the time on her phone. She has a boat to catch at one.

'Thank you, Mr Prasad,' she says as she puts the two yellow envelopes in her bag and zips it up. 'My father's letters spoke very highly of you,' she says. 'My mother kept them until her death.'

'We were very good friends in the army,' says Adi Prasad. 'I'm so glad you looked me up. It is a wonderful thing, Google.'

'It is.'

She jumps in a taxi for the short fifteen-minute ride to Port Denarau and makes her way to the Dolphin Café at the marina. She sits at a small round table in a quiet corner, away from the travellers waiting for their resort transfers on the waterfront.

A moment later, her guest walks in.

'Hello, Ms Delana,' Sailasa says.

'It's just Thomasina,' she says. 'I've ordered you a Coke. Is that OK?'

'Sure. Thank you.'

There is a moment of silence.

Sailasa leans forward in his chair. 'Is everything OK?' He twists the silver ring on the middle finger of his left hand.

'Look,' Thomasina says, 'I'll make this brief. I know you took the diamond from Luella's bure on the night she was murdered. Filipe told me.'

Sailasa's eyes widen. 'Ms Delana,' he says, panic-stricken. 'I can explain . . .'

'It's just Thomasina,' she says again, 'and you don't need to explain anything. Filipe already told me.'

Sailasa's skin looks almost grey. 'What . . . ?' He hesitates. 'What did he tell you?'

'Everything about your mother, about your debt, about how you found Luella's body in the water – all of it.'

Sailasa puts his hand to his chest and looks around the café, as if he is expecting a policeman to step out of the shadows and handcuff him. Thomasina watches as his hands come down and stretch across the table towards her, as if he is waiting for *her* to do it instead. It is almost like an admission of guilt, an apology. His brow is wet with sweat.

She puts her hands over his. 'Listen,' she says. 'I have something for you, and I want you to take it.'

She lets go of his hands and unzips her bag. She slides one of the yellow envelopes across the table. 'I don't need it,' she says. 'Not anymore.'

Sailasa looks at her, quizzical. He picks up the envelope and slides his forefinger under the flap. He takes out the money, a thick wad tied by an elastic band. He looks at Thomasina in confusion. Then after a moment, he shakes his head. 'There's thousands here,' he says.

'Five thousand American dollars,' says Thomasina.

Sailasa shakes his head. 'You mean to give this to me?'

'Yes.'

'Why?'

'Because I don't need it, and you do. It will cover your debt with a little left over.'

'No,' Sailasa tells her. 'I can't.'

'You can. It's yours. Use it to pay off your debt – get the loan sharks off your back. Get yourself a foot ahead.'

'But . . . but what about the police?'

'As far as Emori Roy is concerned, my sister sold the diamond,' she tells him. 'The only person who insisted it was in the bure all along was Benedict, and he was an accessory to her murder. This money does not exist as far as the police are concerned.'

Sailasa's Adam's apple bobs up and down. Then Thomasina sees the tears welling in the man's eyes, an almost-six-foot mountain of a man – a man locked in grief and shame and hurt. Her own throat aches.

'I don't know what to say,' he tells her.

'Thank you will do.' She smiles and wipes her eyes. 'I want you to have it.'

'Thank you, thank you,' says Sailasa, and he puts his head on the table and cries.

Thomasina lets him, but only for a minute. She puts $20 Fijian dollars on the table for the drinks. 'That's our ferry,' she says, nodding towards the South Sea Cruises catamaran that's arrived in the marina. 'Shall we go?'

Sailasa blows his nose with a napkin and gets up, hauling his rucksack onto his back. And together they board the South Island Cruises catamaran back to Loloma.

Thomasina steps back from her large, backpacker's rucksack and looks around her bure, her little sanctuary for the last week. It is farewell to Loloma but not to Fiji. She has lost her heart to this place, her father's home – to the sound of the sea as it crawls seductively up the sand; the sway of the green palms and the twice-weekly trips of the maintenance men who scale them and machete down the loose coconuts; the Fijian people with their humour and their warmth and their perpetually sunny outlook on life. And even though she understands Benedict invited her here purely to make her a suspect in her sister's death and to take the heat off himself and Sofie, she is glad she came. The connection she feels with the country of her father's birth is almost unfathomable. The way the sun touches her skin is almost like coming home.

She recalls her first meeting with Luella on the path outside the bar: how Luella's initial reaction to her hardened her with hatred and drove her to creep into her sister's room and leave a poisoned note threatening harm. What was she thinking? Why did she behave in that way?

She realises now that this was just Luella and the effect she had on others. She poisoned those around her, infected them with her aura somehow. It is no excuse for Thomasina's behaviour, but it is the only one she has. Somewhere deep inside, she feels sorry for her sister, a life cut short. It wasn't *all* bad. The time they went to Disneyland in California when they were small and ran around, hand in hand, grabbing autographs from Minnie and Mickey, screaming their lungs out on the rides. The rare times when Luella would invite her to play.

Thomasina only remembers these events because they were rare, anomalies of her childhood. But still, she will carry them with her.

She feels emotion grip her from nowhere, and she lets out a single, solitary sob. 'Oh *Luella*,' she cries. Then she pulls herself up. She has said her goodbyes. She said them on the mountain top when she burnt her holiday to-do list, when she said goodbye to resentment and anger and plots of revenge. It had been a ritualistic thing for her – a way to say goodbye, to wipe the slate clean. A ceremony, of sorts. Bad thoughts swapped for good. She must let it all lie in the past, forget Luella's meanness, forget it *and* forgive it, because that was who Luella was, and what transpired between the two of them was not a result of anything Thomasina herself had done but rather of the woman Luella was. Her sister lived life clutching a golden gun to her chest, and Thomasina always believed she would, at some point, fall on it and shoot herself.

But whatever her complicated feelings for her sister, Thomasina is glad Luella never found out Benedict was in love with another woman and that together, they desired only one another – and her riches. If she had known all of this, the grief alone would have killed her; Thomasina is sure of it. The idea that yet another person in her life was faking their affection for the chance it could make them rich. Luella had trusted Benedict, with her life, ironically enough. She truly believed he loved her, most likely even at the moment of her death.

Thomasina has never wanted the money or the notoriety or the lifestyle. All she has ever wanted is to be anonymous: to travel, to move her body, to feel the buoyancy of the water beneath her. She has only seen the damage wealth can bring, the greed it instils, and this why she has decided she will give the majority of Luella's fortune to charity.

She doesn't know where, just yet, but she's heard about an organisation called Fiji Kids Learning For Life, which aims to break the poverty cycle through education. She likes the idea of Luella's money being put to good use like this. Because that is what life is about, isn't it? Caring and giving and saving lives. Not stockpiling riches and jewels and Thomasina Diamonds.

Thomasina folds a kaftan haphazardly and tosses it into her beaten-up rucksack and smiles. She chucks in her book and make-up bag on top of it and tightens the drawstring tags at the top. In the side pocket is a second yellow envelope – a cash kitty if you will – which will allow her to travel the magnificent South Pacific for a good while longer while she waits for the money from the Walsh trust. When she sold the diamond, Mr Prasad made a bank transfer for the bulk and gave her two envelopes, both with an equal amount of cash.

There is much she plans to do. She still hasn't surfed at Cloudbreak or done the Salamander shipwreck dive – the only things on that silly list, aside from learning Fijian, that actually she truly wanted to do. For Thomasina, it will be a case of life carrying on as normal, an existence that's slightly nomadic, made up of surfing and good friends, and hopefully love if she finds it.

Filipe appears at the door.

'You did a beautiful thing for Sailasa,' he tells her solemnly.

'He needs it,' she says. 'I don't.'

Filipe smiles. 'You are a good person, Thomasina Delana,' he says. 'But I knew that about you straight away.'

Thomasina smiles. 'Likewise,' she says.

They stand in silence for a moment, and then Thomasina suddenly laughs. 'It's all so messed up,' she says. 'Don't you think?'

'What is?'

'All of it. All of the last week. Three deaths here on the island. I can't quite believe it's happened.'

'Me neither,' he says. 'It's been a weird week, that's for sure.'

'Do you think . . . ?' begins Thomasina. She shakes off the thought.

'What? Say it.'

'Well, don't you think it's strange that there were so many deaths? What if they were connected somehow? Luella and Fergus Miller, I mean?'

'Can't be. Fergus Miller's was natural causes. Roko told us.'

'Yeah, I guess.' Thomasina shakes off whatever thought is tap, tap, tapping at her temporal lobe. It is over now, and she has said her goodbyes. It is time to start afresh.

Filipe gestures to Thomasina's rucksack. 'Can I take your bag?' he asks.

Thomasina knows there are porters for that kind of thing here in this six-star luxury resort, and she realises Filipe has made an excuse to come to her. He moves aside, and the room floods with sunlight. It coats Thomasina's shoulders and neck, baptises her in its warmth.

'*Vinaka.*' She smiles as their eyes meet. 'Thank you.'

FOUR MONTHS LATER

FRIDAY 17 MAY

Cocktail of the Day:
Last Word

(Gin, green Chartreuse, lime juice, maraschino liqueur)

73
Kitty

Kitty surveys the living room in her new home in Potten End, Hertfordshire. She loves this little house. It has so much more charm than the red-brick new-build Fergus chose them in the heart of the city. This one is smaller and sits deeper into the countryside, and she has an Aga like she has always wanted and a cat curled up in a basket.

Kitty's new home is close to the magnificent bluebell woods at Ashridge Estate where she used to walk with her mother as a child. The bluebells are in season now it is mid-May, and Kitty loves to walk straight through the fields and see nothing but lilac around her and blue up above. She breathes it all in and listens to the sound of nothing but birdsong and the wind in the high grass of the surrounding meadows. She feels so free here.

The decor is more relaxed in her new place: a soft cream sofa with a sage-coloured woollen throw, an almost-crumbling fireplace with wood in the grate bought from the honesty box at a nearby farm, waiting for winter. Upstairs, there is a brand-new king-sized bed with fashionable amber linen sheets and plump, comfy cushions strewn about – nothing like the angular, masculine slate-grey decor favoured by her late husband.

Kitty has boxed up the staged monochrome wedding photos Fergus liked to have on show, because they are too painful to look at now, these memories of times gone by, and instead she has picked some new prints for her wall: an arty map of London for the sandstone in the kitchen, a 1930s golden-framed painting of a horse from her grandmother's home in the hallway, and a typography print of her favourite Gandhi quote – *Where there is love, there is life* – in the bedroom. Not that there is any romance in Kitty's life, but she is hopeful.

She has placed a framed copy of her degree certificate on the wall above the side table beside her front door. She had always wanted to hang it up somewhere, even if it was just in the downstairs loo, to celebrate what is arguably her greatest achievement: a first-class degree in biology, a Bachelor of Science, no less, from a prestigious, green-welly university – but Fergus never wanted her to. He preferred photos on the wall, or lifeless, angular modern art – nothing that had any sense of Kitty's whims or pleasures or which showed her off as intelligent or free-thinking. Fergus seemed to forget she was educated, preferring to place her in the 'little wife' category and keep her there.

Gosh, Kitty! She feels terrible thinking the worst of poor Fergus and berates herself, affords herself a playful slap by her right palm to the top of her left hand. Fergus may have been a tad controlling, but the poor man was always bumbling about, putting his foot in it, never understanding why people hated him.

He did one thing right, however – he invested in a decent life insurance policy, even if he neglected to secure the travel insurance. It will be enough to help her live a contented life, to never have to worry about having a roof over her head.

She glances across at the framed certificate, at the cream-coloured paper beneath the glass, with the University of Exeter crest embossed in gold type and the words *Bachelor of Science* at the top, followed by her name, *KATHERINE JANE BURTON* and the year: 2002. She loved her degree, every single minute of it. She found it fascinating, even if her peers did not. She still doesn't know anyone else in the 'real' world who specialises in the study of amphibians; she was certainly the only student in her cohort to write her dissertation on the cane toad.

No one else in Kitty's everyday life or even in the vast and bragging world of social media seems to appreciate how fascinating frogs and toads can actually be! Cane toad eggs, for example, come in strings that are so strong you can pull them from the water by hand without them breaking. That's how damn hardy they are, cane toads – how desperate these amphibians are to reproduce. But, despite her best attempts to *try* and convince those nearest and dearest to her to listen to her when she talked about her fascination, no one else Kitty knows would appreciate the exciting fact that these sturdy strands of eggs are so incredibly toxic to humans and animals that you have to handle them with extra sturdy rubber gloves. Or that, *hypothetically*, if the eggs are ingested, the bufotoxins inside them can cause death within a very short time.

Kitty looks out of the window into the garden as her mind wanders to exotic climes where cane toads live and breed, places like Papua New Guinea, Guam, Hawaii and . . . Fiji. She considers the hypothetical fact that if a person were to find these cane toad eggs in a slow-flowing river in the bushy undergrowth of an island, at the top of a mountain on an everyday bush-walk perhaps, and a decent amount of these eggs were to make it into someone's food – say, if they were collected in a Tupperware box that once contained a delicious, juicy scone and then stirred into a very strong-tasting Fijian crab curry – they would, after a few hours, kill the person who ingested them.

First would come gastrointestinal symptoms and then, sometime later, bradycardia and cardiac arrest, all in as little as four hours. Even more rapidly in someone with questionable fitness levels and already calcified arteries. Or if, say, a small amount of the eggs made it into a drink, such as perhaps Fijian kava, and that drink was accidentally thrown on, say, a deep cut made by a rogue broken glass in a bar, and the toxin got straight into the person's bloodstream – well, that would be utterly catastrophic. Death would, *hypothetically*, be almost instantaneous.

It really wouldn't be a pleasant way to go, death by cane toad spawn. It would be a rather embarrassing scenario, too, if the truth got out. But luckily, any human being unfortunate enough to unwittingly consume these toxin-rich eggs would be highly unlikely to suffer the humiliation of their friends and family suspecting they'd been chasing a cane toad 'high'. No, any such death would most likely be ruled a natural demise because medics wouldn't bother checking for something as downright unlikely as bufotoxin ingestion. They'd assume that if it *looked* like a run-of-the-mill cardiac issue caused by overindulgence and the carrying of excess weight in a middle-aged man, then it most likely *was* a cardiac issue caused by overindulgence and the carrying of excess weight in a middle-aged man.

A decisive ruling like this would avoid the hassle and expense of sending tissue samples all the way to Australia or New Zealand for further testing, and save the island resort in question (if, *hypothetically*, that's where the incident were to occur) from losing face.

And if, of course, there just happened to be a repulsive millionairess on the same island whose cruel behaviour had expediated those health issues – because stress narrows the arteries and all that – then it would be downright conclusive. (It might even be an opportunistic time for a grieving wife to attempt to extort some money, perhaps – something that could be engineered by the simple writing of a note suggesting a clandestine meeting after dark. . .)

But anyway, this is all complete conjecture, and Kitty knows she should not dream up things that are completely improbable. It really is rather self-indulgent, and it does not serve to honour the memory of her dear late husband Fergus in any way, shape or form. She blinks a couple of times as if to shake away these thoughts from her head. Fergus always said she had an active imagination, and he was right. Dead right.

Kitty sighs contentedly. She straightens the degree certificate on the wall, picks up the card that screams *Congratulations On Your Engagement!* addressed to her good friend Una Simpson and her fiancé Emori Roy, care of Loloma Island Resort & Spa in Fiji's Mamanuca Islands, and slides her feet into her new UGG boots sent all the way from Byron Bay, Australia by Thomasina Delana.

She steps outside. It is a beautiful day, albeit a little chilly, and she has bluebell fields to visit and post to send. Kitty pulls the door shut behind her, using the handle of her brand-new brass knocker in the shape of a portly toad, and steps out into the brilliant spring sun.

Acknowledgements

Fiji is my happy place, and there is a resort in the Mamanuca Islands called Castaway Island I have visited with my family several times. The layout of the fictional Loloma Island in my mind is very similar to Castaway, as is the upbeat and friendly spirit of the staff and the idyllic surrounds. But that's where the similarities stop. Castaway Island (Qualito) is family-friendly, relaxed and in no way murderous. However, I'd be lying if I said I wasn't inspired by the island and its scenery. I must thank the wonderful staff who helped answer my questions about plants and reef regeneration and cane toads, and thus made this book come alive: Jessie (for the amazing medicinal bush-walk), Mika and Pita (Toad Race Kings), Kalo, Aseri, Sala, Emori, Pau, Steven, Kelera and of course the beautiful Una, who has a huge smile and an even bigger heart.

Lucy Stewart, I could tell from our first call that you completely 'got' this book and the way I write. Thank you for your thoughtful edits – every single one was spot on. They have shaped this book invaluably and made it infinitely better. I can't wait for the next! My thanks to the entire Hodder & Stoughton team in London for being the best publishing gang an author could hope for. Katie Lumsden, I am so grateful for your amazingly detailed copyedits.

To the Hachette ANZ gang, particularly Ellen Tyrell, Cassy Nacard, Eliza Thompson, Alexa Roberts and Nicky Luckie – I am so grateful for all the wonderful things you do for me here in Australia. A special shout-out to the magnificent sales team who have put my books on shelves and into the hands of readers. I'm so thankful for everything you do behind the scenes to get my books into the hands of booksellers and book lovers.

Marina de Pass, I so enjoy our long inter-hemisphere phone calls and our occasional UK lunches and truly appreciate your advice and endless organisational skills. You are the absolute best agent I could wish for. My thanks to you, Helen Mumby, Benedict Clark and everyone at The Soho Agency.

My thanks to Jackie Lai from Pro Dive in Brookvale for taking the time to chat to me about scuba equipment and how it works (and fails). I hope this is definitive proof that I am actually a bona fide author and not a random punter who wants to cleverly off someone in a South Pacific diving mishap.

A huge shout-out to my work wife Vanessa McCausland for the companionship, coffees and car rides. I am so grateful for the supportive and inclusive community of Australian authors I have found myself a part of – it has been life-changing in the very best way. My thanks to Ber Carroll, Petronella McGovern, Maxine Fawcett, Sally Hepworth, Joanna Nell, Karina May, Anna Downes, Anne Freeman – the list goes on!

To Alice Ierace, Fiona Pogson, Jayne Murphy, Deb Wise, Leonie Lincoln, Pip Prentice, Georgina Blaskey, Michelle Tizzard, Cath Adelbert, Tanya Andrews – you girls are the best. Christina Cole, thank you for supporting school soccer and for giving me your name for a character in this book. Esther St John Gray, thanks for not freaking out when I told you I'd stolen your surname for Luella. I couldn't help it – it's just too perfect. P.S. I miss you!

Joey (love you, sis), Rob and my babies, who are five years older than they were when I first started writing novels: you are the best support crew I could hope for. Kids, I promise categorically that what I *actually* said was not, 'I will send the dog to the sausage factory,' but 'the dog is *like* a sausage factory.' You have it in writing.

This story is for my parents, who wanted only two children but accidentally got me almost a decade after completing their family. They'd got rid of all their baby paraphernalia, which I hear was rather inconvenient in the days before Facebook Marketplace. I'm sorry about that, Mum and Dad, and also for the new piano I made you buy and tune every six months but never used. I understand now, as a parent, what an absolute pain in the arse that must have been. I love you both very much indeed and am truly grateful for everything, including the rows of Agatha Christie books and VHS tapes you allowed me to devour as a child – to say they fed and watered my love of crime fiction is an understatement.

Lastly to the booksellers, bloggers, bookstagrammers and readers who have embraced my books: I don't know where to start, because it always makes me teary, but please know your support and kindness means everything. You have my sincerest thanks.

If you loved *The Private Island*, get your hands on Ali Lowe's other gripping thrillers . . .

Question: How long does it take to tear someone's life apart?

Answer: Sometimes just one night.

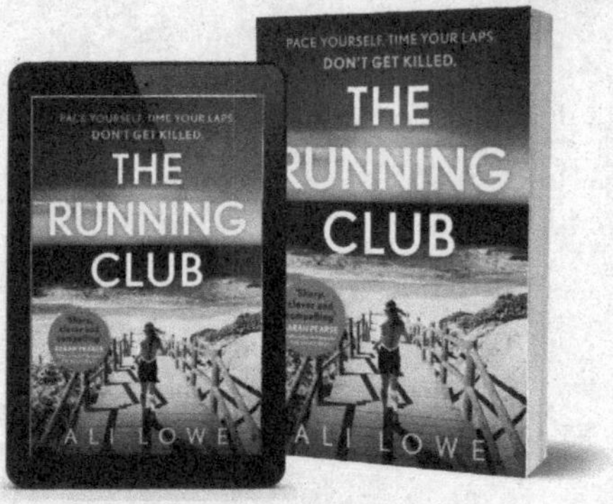

The rules of the running club are the same as they have always been: keep your breath steady, keep your mind sharp, record your laps!

Only now there's a new one: don't get killed.

How far would you go to save your children?